Mystic Mansion

Ocean Street

Mason Cemetery

Vancouver Inn

Mason Fire Hall

Bella's Restaurant

Last Call Tavern

Jo's House

THE COVE

Black Five

a Novel

J. Lynn Bailey

POORHOUSE
PUBLISHING

Published in the United States by Poorhouse Publishing˙
Big Bear City, California
www.poorhousepublishingllc.com

POORHOUSE
PUBLISHING

Poorhouse Publishing and the key logo are
trademarks registered in the US Patent and Trademark Office.
All related characters and elements are trademarks of Poorhouse Publishing.

Library of Congress Control Number: 2015940945
Bailey, J. Lynn
Black Five / J. Lynn Bailey.—1st ed.

ISBN: 978-1-943468-99-7
978-1-943468-97-3
eBook: 978-1-943468-98-0

Jacket, endpapers, and interior illustrations by Lisa Falzon
Jacket and interior format and design by Heather UpChurch

First Edition

For Bella, Maddy,
Teyler & Kate

CONTENTS

Little Bird

The road is narrow
Little bird,
It widens as you go;
Don't be fearful of a change
Or the lessons you will know.

Failure builds you
Little bird,
To form the path you choose,
But the voyage and adventure
Molds the pieces into you.

Don't be scared
Little bird,
You're stronger than you know;
The fright that grips your heart
Is that which makes you grow.

It keeps you grounded
Little bird,
For greatness you'll achieve;
Take the leap and fly away
For it's the world you will see.

PROLOGUE

October 31st 1994

Selacs, rat-like rodents slightly larger than a house cat, scurry with snake-like tails across the cobblestones in search of anything in their path to devour. They are scavengers, preying on anything they can subdue, suck and eat: blood, organs, skin, and carcass. If not careful, the tail, with its mouth and fangs, can devour its own body entirely, like an ouroboros. Selacs eat *anything*, including small children.

On this night, even the selacs run for cover.

The village of Cuore is in ruins.

An explosion sounds in the distance, the decrepit business signs of local merchants tremble in response. The narrow cobblestone road twists through the center of the once vivacious old village, now just a ghost town. Trapped fairies in glass lanterns emit a glow in various shades of green, blue, red and purple. Hanging in midair, they project a haunting glow through the thick, suffocating fog that lurks in every accessible space. The fairies, plagued with sadness and fear, beg for release. The skeletal remains of Nighmerian merchant shops and living quarters, now just crumbling brick, line the road that winds through the eerily still town.

He is coming. Another explosion sounds, this time closer.

Three large figures emerge from the shadows. Their black liveries rub together as they march with force and purpose, mimicking the sound of tortured leather. Their faces are hooded, veiling their malevolent intent as they move closer to their victims with each impetuous step.

Another explosion tears through the fog, unnervingly close.

"Kill every Nighmerian. Find her," the tallest of the three shouts to the others. "Bring the Five to me. She will complete the creed." A deceitful smile spreads across his lips. "Serve your leader, kill the Nighmerians and find her," he commands, his face contorting into a demonic snarl. He points a veiny, translucent finger toward the innocent targets of his rage and, with a soul-crushing roar, the morterros surged forward.

Ten miles away, at Relyett Castle...

"Immortal child, 105-7256012, male, born on the fifth of September, 1994 to Norris and Yetziera Lutz. Bloodline: Vampire. Immortal child, 505-7256013, male, born on the fifth of September, 1994 to Ulysses and Armenta Sochi. Bloodline: Warlock." Lothario yawns as he reads the next birth credence, his voice employing a tone of disgust. "Immortal child, XXX-7256014, female, born on the fifth of September, 1994 to Rolfson and Agatha Krest. Bloodline: Notte. The Demi do not speak of the *nottes,* the classless half-breeds who spread themselves like oozing poison on the lower coast of Nighmerianotte, the Scogliera district.

Lothario's eyes narrow as he pauses to stare at the next birth credence. The rain pounds against the oval-shaped, stained-glass windows of the observatory. Thunder ricochets within the castle walls as several massive torches hanging from the stones illuminate Abram and Lothario causing their shadows to dance upon the stone floor.

"The rain has not ceased in days," Abram says in an agitated voice. He puts his oil pen down and rubs his eyes as he waits for Lothario to read the next birth credence. When he doesn't, Abram turns, annoyed, to see Lothario staring intently at a piece of parchment. "Lothario?" he urges his colleague, "What is it?"

"Bloodline: *undetermined*," Lothario whispers as he looks to Abram. "Could this be it? How is this possible?" Excitement gathers in his voice.

Abram seizes the parchment from his colleague and holds it to the candlelight. He places his reading glasses on his nose and reads, "Immortal child, 005-006. Oh…" his breath catches as he scans the rest of the report. "Born on the thirty-first of October, 1994 to an *unknown* Salvatore DeLuca, mortal, and Annalisa San Angelo, witch. Assigned sentry: JoAnne Gemello. Bloodline…" he gasps, "*undetermined*." His voice lowers to a whisper as he looks to his colleague with pure exhilaration, like a child witnessing magic for the first time. "Call Giuseppe. We must assemble the other members immediately…Finally, our Sanguine has come."

The five members of the *Demi* gather at one end of the long rectangular table in the dining hall of Relyett Castle. Rain relentlessly strikes the tall inset windows, intoning a menacing tune. A colossal fireplace, composing most of the wall at one end of the dining hall, illuminates the surrounding stones with a soft touch of orange. Stone statues of distinguished species sit above its giant mantle: vampire, witch, sentinel, and warlock. Unmoving and sinister they watch, tracking all with their eyes.

On one side of the room, unlit torches line the massive stones walls. Oil paintings of past Demi members dating back to 514 A.D. proudly adorn the opposite wall. Elaborate flags representing the five districts of Nighmerianotte, Pollone, Zanna, Volare, Strega and Scogliera, hang prominently below the paintings. Above the fireplace, is the dogma of Nighmerianotte, written in red script in the language of Italian: *Ordine, Fedeltà, Servizio*—Order, Loyalty, Service.

"We must not arouse the Republic of Nighmerianotte until we know it to be absolute truth," warns Nyah, her velvety and eloquent voice muted, belying her excitement. Her pale green eyes and striking features set her aside from most immortals. Her silky, coffee-colored skin glows in the firelight. Her short, dark hair lay close to her head, exposing her high cheekbones.

"The Five... with black blood." Lothario hands Giuseppe the scroll.

He rolls it open. His eyes dance across the page. "Further tests confirm the blood submitted on the thirty-first of October, 1994 is, indeed, the blood of the Sanguinary, the Sanguineous, the Sanguine. Bloodline: *Black Blood...*"

Excitement spreads as Nyah, Lothario and Abram begin to whisper amongst themselves.

"She is a black blood, a notte. A half-breed. She should be treated as such." Olly's elitist distain resonates off the stone walls of the dining hall. His long, mousy nose twitches from left to right while his shoulder-length, golden locks dance against his back. His beady eyes, too close together, and tall forehead give his face a peculiar look.

"Olly," Nyah says, "She is a black blood yes, but she is our Five. She is our only hope. She is the only one who can kill him and restore our world."

"If he does not locate and kill her first." Olly's words are hushed as he stares hard at the credence. "Besides, who is this *sentry*? This woman they call JoAnne. She is a mortal, a limite, a nobody. She does not know the first thing about *our* world. She is not accustomed to our values, our beliefs or our rules."

"Olly," Giuseppe interrupts, "Just because one is a limite does not make one incapable. Do not be such an elitist."

"Fine, but the *sentry* has always been of Nighmerianotte. This is unheard of," Olly argues rather loudly, a repugnant look on his face. "A limite? It is unacceptable."

Giuseppe looks up from the birth credence. The 494-year-old vampire pushes it across the table. His colleagues gather around it excitedly, with the exception of Olly. Giuseppe leans back in the overstuffed chair. Deep in thought, he places his hands behind his head. His ashen, thin face brightens as he turns toward the fire. His silver hair matches the neatly-shaven goatee that curves around his thick, perfectly-shaped lips, crimson red and moist.

"Highest," says Olly, "she is still a notte. She is not pure-blooded Nighmerian. Even if we can protect her, we cannot rest the fate of our world on a filthy notte. This is simply unacceptable. It is absurd." Olly motions to the credence with pure hatred.

"I assume you have a better idea, Olly?" Lothario's smooth voice cuts through the thunder outside. Standing eight-feet tall, his height is unmatched by any other immortal. His long, lean jaw and defined cheekbones give his face a muscular look. His crystal-brown eyes are hooded with condescension toward Olly. "Highest, the only point upon which I agree with Olly is keeping her with a sentry in the mortal world is troubling. We know the dangers in that."

"We seem to have a difficult time protecting our Five in Nighmerianotte. Now a black blood? This is a first. We have never tried this. It seems to me, this is our only alternative." Abram strokes his beard with the palm of his hand. His bushy eyebrows animate his every expression as his frizzy long, brown, unkempt hair lay messily around his shoulders. His short stature exudes his humble confidence.

Giuseppe removes his reading glasses and says, "It is law. We cannot remove an immortal child from the *sentry* if the biological mother signs the credence. The parents know what is best for the child."

"Highest. With all due respect, I think this is an extremely poor choice. It is simply a matter of time before he finds her. What if history repea—"

Giuseppe ignores Olly's pleas. "Nyah, the protective spell, is it ready?"

"Yes, Highest." Nyah nods.

Olly tries to hold his tongue but speaks anyway, "Highest?"

"I know what she is, Olly," Giuseppe says.

"I apologize for my insolence, Highest, but?" Olly pleads in one final attempt to convince the leader of Nighmerianotte.

Giuseppe's eyes narrow as he slowly looks toward Olly. "Abram. Retrieve the sentry and bring her to us. Olly, let us prepare to take possession of the Five in the customary manner. She will be here soon." His eyes leave a sulking Olly and move to Lothario. "Lothario, contact Church and let him know we will meet the Detail at portal number two with the child. Being a black blood, she should have no issue getting through the portal to the mortal world." He glances back to the credence and announces, "It is time." Giuseppe's brow furrows as he takes the birth credence in his long narrow fingers.

Chimes echo through the castle, indicating the presence of someone at the door. "They are here." A loud ricochet of thunder rattles the chandeliers above as the Demi members glance up in surprise. The rain and thunder relentlessly beat a merciless tune, haunting and sad.

Giuseppe turns and walks to the roaring fire behind them. "This," he whispers to his peers and confidants, "shall remain a secret until she comes of age."

He tosses the birth credence into the fire and watches it burn. "The Black-Blood Sanguine. The Five."

CHAPTER 1

Stability

Tuesday, September 4th 2012
Present day, 6:01 a.m.

"**M**orning, Dottie." I smile, leaning into the small walk-up coffee window.

"Good morning, Sugar. The usual?"

"Please." I tighten the scarf around my neck.

"Beautiful morning, huh?" Dottie says as she goes about preparing my order.

"Hmmmmm," I agree as I glance down Main Street. Its dawning silence welcomes me. My eyes barely make out the lush green belt that borders the little town of Mason. The pre-dawn fog clings to the tree-tops, haunting, yet comforting.

Black lampposts and grandfather maples line Main Street, adding character to the small sleepy town. Charm, even. Timeless Victorian architecture gives Mason a touch of old, a touch of new, and perhaps a dab of mystique. I exhale deeply and watch as my breath hovers in the cool morning air then, like the haunting ghosts of my past, it fades into oblivion.

"How's Jo?" Dottie shouts over the steamer.

"Good." My thoughts quickly fade. "You know Jo, trying to do everything for everybody." That's my go-to line when anyone asks about Aunt Jo. What else can I say about the *saint-of-a-woman?*

Dottie nods and pushes both coffees through the small window. "I'll add it to your tab."

I smile. "Thanks." I replace my ear buds, grab the cups, and start down Main Street toward the cemetery. My mind is elsewhere this morning.

During the summer, Mason serves as a hub for travellers heading north to Oregon and south to San Francisco. Travel guides list it as one of the "must-sees of small town USA." Movie crews pile in every couple of years to film the next blockbuster. It is great for the local economy but film production shuts down Main Street for weeks at time, making it difficult to get around town. Not great when our little piece of heaven has only one straight shot from one end to the other. Talk about detour hell.

Mason is a place where everyone knows everyone and everyone knows everyone's business. Gossip? Yes, but I will take that any day over the problems in other parts of the world. It's like Mayberry but with Wi-Fi. Unlike our counterparts in So Cal, Mason possesses all four seasons and celebrates each one. Fall has always been my favorite. The maples display their brilliant yellows and deep oranges, giving town a homey feeling. The lampposts are decorated with wreaths, made by the senior resource center, of those same leaves. The smell of fresh rainfall and earth drifts through the sleepy little town making everything smell new and clean.

Rain is nothing new to our quiet little town.

It rains.

All the time.

While most kids my age are dying to escape the isolation of Mason, I secretly love it. Sure, I play it cool, like I can't wait to escape with them, but Mason gives me the stability I yearn for. I love the unchanging atmosphere, where everything runs like clockwork. The town's fire station whistle even rings every day at noon and at dusk to signify lunch and sunset. It's a place where I can forget what my broken life was like before I moved here.

At least it is most of the time, not today.

Despite all of the warm and fuzzy stuff, nothing compares to the tranquility and solace I find in Mason Cemetery. It's my place of solitude, the place I go when I need a break from reality. When memories from that dreadful day invade my mind, I need a place to hide, a place to think. I try to push his death out of my mind, try to forget Frankie's screams, but even the Cemetery doesn't allow me escape from that. He was a bad man but he didn't deserve to die. I was eight years old and terrified, for myself and for Nadine.

My past haunts me like murderous grief, eating away at my conscience until I am nothing. The thoughts are a distraction, like a swarm of gnats around me. I can wave them away as much as I want, but until I move beyond them, they will continue to harass me. The thought makes my stomach clench in knots and my chest tighten. I forget how to breathe. I remember what the therapist told me. *Breathe, Penn. Inhale and then exhale.*

I do.

I breathe in, and I breathe out.

In and out.

I follow Main Street to the Vancouver Inn and take a left on Ocean. As my chest begins to loosen once more, music plays softly in my ears.

I pause, thinking I hear footsteps. *Penn pull yourself together, it's probably your imagination.* I wonder if this feeling will ever fade. I've always felt the need to look over my shoulder. Like someone is watching me.

No. I hear footsteps. Fear begins eating away at the last vestiges of rational thought.

Breathe, Penn. Breathe, I tell myself as I keep a steady pace.

Is it the footsteps or my uncontrollable heart beat? Maybe it's the music. It must be the music, right? I refuse to look behind me or turn down the music. Even if I turn it down, the thumping of my heart will fill the silence. I keep walking, hastening my steps.

Total panic sets in as I realize that if no one is awake at this hour, no one will hear my cries for help should I meet my demise on this September morning. Will I be another unsolved murder turned into a movie-of-the-week? *Stop freaking yourself out, Penn. You're so dramatic.* My throat is dry and tastes the way cold smells, metallic and strange. *All you have to do is make it to the top of the cemetery, Penn. Kendra will be waiting for you and whatever it is will be gone. Now run.*

I ditch the coffee and throw my legs into overdrive. Feverishly, I pull open the wrought-iron gates just enough to squeeze through, the chain wrapped around the bars stretched to its limit. I sprint up the hill toward the top of the cemetery, my heart beating so hard it feels as though it will burst from my chest.

The footsteps are close behind me now. It sounds like more than one set of footsteps.

More than one, meaning they, meaning TWO.

They are closing in on me, but I can't seem to move any faster. My lungs burn as I race up the steep hill. Fearful my pursuer is close, I prepare to fight as I wait for a hand to slide across my mouth and drag me to the ground. News headlines play in my head: *17-year-old girl abducted from small town U.S.A….17-year-old Mason girl: Body recovered from atop the Mason Cemetery…Small town mourns for the loss of the Penelope Jackson.*

A low growl causes me to run faster.

I trip, the fall sending me flailing to the ground. My hands hit the damp grass and slip from beneath me. Unable to right myself, I roll onto my back. This isn't the best outcome but I still have fight in me.

I hold my arms out in front of me. "Please. Please. What do you want from me?" I plead, giving up on the fight before it's begun. I cross my hands over my face, too scared to peek through them at my assailant.

The sound of panting rouses me from the horrible drama playing out in my head. *What kind of assailant pants?* I look through my fingers and see a fuzzy, drooling face staring at me in confusion.

"Murphy, what are you doing?" I pull my hands up and protect my face from the licking of an overzealous dog. My heart still pounding, I pull myself to my feet. Murphy sits, confused by my earlier pleas for mercy. "Dang dog," I give him a rub behind the ears as relief spreads through my body, my heart rate slowing. "Where's Bradbury?" I bend down, taking the Lab's face in my hands. He whines and looks away nervously. Normally a playful and outgoing dog, today he seems skittish. I've never seen him this way before. His usual hangout is the Last Call Tavern, the one and only bar in Mason. When you see Murphy, you know Bradbury, his owner, isn't far away. "What is it, Murph?" He whines again. "Alright buddy, come on. I'll drop you off on the way to school." His tail thumps loudly against the wet ground.

We finish our trek up the hill, Murphy following closely behind. I sit in my regular spot, trying to act normally, with Murphy next to me.

No one ever accused me of being normal. During my first year of high school, Ms. Dempsey, the nosy, school psychologist, pursed her lips together, closed my file and said, "You know, Penelope," she paused, "none of this is your fault."

What I wanted to say to her was, *Lady you don't know a damn thing about me. By the way, you have lipstick on your teeth and your breath stinks*. I politely nodded instead.

The social workers and psychologists were baffled because I functioned like a normal child lacking the typical abnormalities of a neglectful upbringing. However, they did note tendencies to react irrationally to persistent fears. At least that's what the social worker surmised after reading my file.

I knew I was different but I was not crazy.

Did they expect I'd be some crazy basket case sitting in the corner sucking my thumb? Sure, I know there's something different, something out of the ordinary about me. Terminally unique, maybe, but far from "grab the straight jacket" loony.

I watch Kendra huff up the steep hill in her big black combat boots, her headlamp dancing like a bobble-head doll, the light bouncing from headstone to headstone.

"Thirty seconds and counting," I yell in my loudest whisper.

"Okay, seriously," she gasps as she places her hands on her knees. "That hill. . ." She pauses again to catch her breath and gasps, "gets steeper and steeper. Every. Single. Morning."

I smile as she plops down on the other side of me.

"What gives? It was your morning for coffee." She looks down at Murphy and doesn't question why he's here.

"I fell," I lie, unable to summon the courage to tell her the truth. "Did you see Bradbury in town?" I stroke Murphy's head as he pants in my face. *Dog breath. Yuck.*

Kendra's electric pink hair creates a pink aura surrounding her head like some sort of helmet.

It's Tuesday. The day of the week dictates Kendra's hair color. I can always count on pink for Tuesday because she hates pink and hates Tuesdays. Her words not mine—*Tuesdays are worthless. A tweener day that does not signify the beginning of week, middle of the week, or end of the week. Just a big old waste of time.*

We sit, side by side, staring at the beautiful valley below. From the coastline on our left to the neighbouring town of Lake Providence, different shades of green are patched together like a quilt by a network of fence lines. Mountains covered with gigantic redwood trees protect our valley. The sunrise silhouettes the outline of Lake Providence and Mason against the dimly lit sky. As the sun makes its debut, the birds stop chirping, the occasional turkey stops calling and the bloodhound stops howling. The sun peeks over the shaded outline of magnificent redwood trees, igniting the valley in pure magnificence.

There's only one word adequate for describing the event: *stunning.*

We sit in stillness, taking in the peaceful sunrise. Our worlds become silent, just for a moment and it's awesome. It's the best part of my day.

Kendra stares blankly ahead, choosing her words carefully. "So, I take it you did not hear about Bradbury?"

"No, why?" I look back to Murphy who is now lying down. His ears perk up and he begins to whine again as he looks at me with another pathetic look. I place my hand on his neck and give him a gentle pat. I notice Kendra is stalling, unwilling to tell me what happened, so I push her. "What? Tell me."

Kendra pauses for a minute.

"They discovered his body this morning in a shallow grave under the Mason Bridge."

"What?" My jaw falls open.

"Yes, his body was discovered by a fisherman about four o'clock this morning. The funeral will be in a couple days. Just as soon as the police determine what happened."

"What?" It was more of a rhetorical question. I think of Kay, Bradbury's wife, and their young daughter, Anna. The dairy was their only income. As far as I know, they live paycheck to paycheck with Bradbury's drinking causing many of their financial problems.

"Poor Kay and Anna…and Murphy," I say. We both sit a minute as the sun slowly rises.

Kendra stirs a bit. "Rumor is it was some sort of animal attack." She gives me her infamous, sideways grin. This tells me two things: she doesn't believe the animal crap for one second and she knows more than she's letting on.

Without basis for my observations, I play into the question-answer dialogue she has established. "What do you think it was?" Now I'm looking down at Murphy, stroking his head. "Poor guy," I whisper as Murphy's ears twitch.

She smiles again as she scans the scenery. "I do not think it was an animal attack. I will leave it at that."

"Fair enough," I say, proving my observation correct.

"Everyone has to go some way, right?"

I gawk. Even for Kendra this comment seems out of place and callous.

"The family will go on, Penn. Just like people do when their loved ones die. They move on. Besides, what can we say or do to make his family feel better? Absolutely nothing." She stares at me. Kendra's reaction catches me off guard. I'd expect her to feel some pity for Murphy at the very least, considering she's such an animal lover.

"Let's drop Murphy off with Sal on our way to school." I get up, Murphy following my lead.

"Are you ready for our first day of senior year?" Kendra slaps me on the back with a grin. "Tell me something," she says as we descend the steep cemetery hill. "If I asked you to cut off my arm rather than subject me to those juvenile degenerates for another nine months, would you do it?"

"Of course I would." I smile, "but you wouldn't ask me to cut off your arm. You talk as much with your hands as you do your mouth. You'd never be able to adequately communicate again."

Kendra laughs. "Touché."

Mason High is a blended school comprised of stoners, jocks, aggies, cheerleaders, geeks and preppies. By blended I mean some jocks are stoners, some aggies are geeks and some preppies are cheerleaders. Then there's Kendra and I. We don't fit anywhere but we fit well together. She's been my best friend since we were eight. Social services moved me to Mason to live with my aunt Jo after Nadine, my foster mother, died. It was a summer day when we met. Jo sent me uptown to get milk and dessert. As I debated between chocolate cookies and snack-cakes, a little voice boomed behind me.

"Do not squeeze the snack-cakes!"

I turned around to find a little blonde girl, no taller than me, wearing big black combat boots. It was the first time I saw that sideways grin of hers. She laughed and said, "Mr. Davenport gets bent when you squeeze the snack-cakes."

"Are we walking to school this morning?" Kendra huffs, pulling me back to the present.

"Yes. We are. It takes just as long to walk to my house and get my car as it does to walk to school. Besides, we have to drop Murphy off." *Does he know what happened to Bradbury? Did he see it happen?*

We squeeze past the locked gate, head down Ocean and stroll down Main Street.

"Morning Mr. Davenport," Kendra yells across the street to the storeowner sweeping the sidewalk. He waves and mumbles something about the snack-cakes. "I cannot believe he still gets worked up about that. I mean, seriously, it was like ten years ago," she says, still watching him.

"Boots, I highly doubt it's about the snack-cakes. He's just cranky."

Boots is Kendra's nickname because every day in the third grade she wore big black combat boots that were almost as big as she was.

We leave Murphy with Sal, the keeper at the Last Call Tavern. I try to express my condolences about Bradbury, but Kendra cuts me off. "See you, Sal."

"What was that all about?" I ask as she pushes me further down Main Street toward the high school.

"We are going to be late," Kendra says.

We slide into first period right after the bell rings.

"Oh, Miss Salvino, Miss Jackson, so glad you could grace us with your presence," Dr. Dover says cynically as he scans the room. "Just because you are seniors does not mean you can cut class or come in late.

Keep in mind, I still have the ability to fail you from this course. This is, after all, the first day of school." His eyes fall on us.

"In our defense, Dov—" Kendra starts.

"You know what they say about excuses, Miss Salvino," he says, not making eye contact, a rhetorical question, of course.

Dr. Dover is funny, in a smart quirky kind of way. I like him well enough, but he always has an uncomfortable look on his face. I'm not sure if he's in constant pain, deep thought, or if he has to use the facilities.

Kendra slides back in her chair and shakes her head. "Well played, Dr. Dover." She nods, "well played."

Travis, a prime member of the jock race, raises his hand. "Hey Dover?"

Dr. Dover grimaces. "*Doctor* Dover. Please, Mr. LaVene," he says, frostily.

Travis continues as if he doesn't hear a word, "Is it true they found Bradbury's body underneath the Mason Bridge?"

Dr. Dover isn't just the AP anatomy teacher at Mason High; he's a forensic anthropologist, the principal at Mason, and the town coroner. Since nothing really happens in Mason, his teaching and principal gig are what keeps him busy and money in his pocket. Yet, everyone refuses to call him Dr. Dover in school. I suspect if he didn't make a big deal about it people probably would. They don't because they know how much it irritates him.

Dr. Dover freezes and looks at Travis as his head tilts ever so slightly, a sweaty sheen forming on his forehead. He takes out his handkerchief and blots his face then looks down at his notes and nervously places his hands on the lab counter in front of him.

Nobody moves a muscle, unwilling to break the dead silence that quickly fills the room.

Finally, he looks up at the class. His face is grey.

The big hand on the clock moves. *CLICK.*

"Please, Mr. LaVene, enlighten me on how you," he motions with his hands, "stumbled across this information, would you?" he says as his lips tighten into a thin straight line.

"Dude," Travis laughs. "Dover, this is Mason. The most excitement we get in this town is when someone is arrested for drunk in public, and it's usually Bradbury."

The class erupts into uneasy snickers.

Dr. Dover pauses and looks out the wall of windows then back to the class. "Yes, Travis," he replies with a sigh as he takes his lecture notes and piles them neatly on the counter while scanning the room again with a heavy expression. "Dale Bradbury's body was discovered early this morning under the Mason Bridge."

A sickening silence hangs over the classroom.

The clock moves again. *CLICK.*

"What did he die from?" I sputter. *Crap, did that just fall out of my mouth?* I have a knack for speaking up when I shouldn't. It's more a nuisance than anything really. Kendra appreciates it as she says *I keep it real.* This isn't one those times I should keep it real. Actually, it's highly inappropriate. I feel my face go flush as I sink lower into my chair, hoping nobody heard me. I look to Kendra, whose stare is burning a hole in the side of my face. She's beaming. *They heard me.*

Dover blasts a glare at me that could drop an elephant in its tracks. *Crap.*

"I heard it was some sort of animal attack?" A voice rings into my ears.

26

I don't look back. I don't have to look back to know who said it.

That dang voice haunts my dreams.

Dr. Dover looks in Jesse's direction. There's a long pause followed by a change in the subject as he begins his lecture on cell communication.

Jesse. His voice alone makes my stomach tie into a big ball of knots. A messy, snarly knot I cannot untie. He doesn't know he has this effect on me, I'm sure of it. I've never said it aloud to anyone, not even Kendra, but I know she sees it on my face every time someone brings up his name.

CHAPTER 2

Cobras & Spiders

The last bell of the day finally rings. I head out the front of the high school to the parking lot and spot Jesse getting into his old white Ford.

Oh stupid girl. You grew up with him. He's your friend first. Tell him, I think to myself. My

strides are long and purposeful.

Maybe it's his cool, clean aftershave. Maybe it's his touch or the way he smirks when he looks at me. Maybe it's just him. I'll be damned if I don't go all schoolgirl every time he looks at me. Thank God hearts can't talk. Mine would have thrown me under the bus many times. *Jeez, breathe, Penn. Think of snakes, think of spiders, think of anything that isn't him.* Something about Jesse always keeps me on my toes. From his perfect skin tone (inherited from his father), to his bluish-grey eyes and muscular build, he is one hundred percent memorable.

My face grows hot. *Stop, Penn.*

I've never quite been able to put my finger on it but he always leaves me wanting more of…him. It's not as if we've ever had a thing, maybe a thing minus the relationship drama but not a *thing* thing. He has a quiet confidence about him. As if he doesn't have to prove anything or be anyone he's not. He's quiet when he needs to be yet speaks up when he feels he should. He has a private arrogance, always so sure of himself, like he can take you, or leave you. Either way, it's not a big deal to him. I feel like there may be more with me, some unspoken connection. Maybe it's just the wild imagination I'm accused of having.

I haven't seen him since the party at the end of junior year, and the desire, the need, to be close to him is undeniable. His family owns a local dairy on the outskirts of town. He took over last year when his dad became sick and his mother, Sydney, passed away from ovarian cancer. It takes up all of his spare time and, apparently, his entire summer.

Lyssa, your typical jock groupie, blows past me on her way to accost Jesse. I've lost any chance of beating her to the objective but her interference will not stand. I must deal with her swiftly and severely. He's mine, even if he's not mine and I just think he's mine.

"Hi Jesse," Lyssa says, leaning into his passenger side window. "Are you coming to the party this weekend?" She giggles, eyeing him up and down.

Seriously? I roll my eyes. *Pathetic.*

"It depends on Jackson." Jesse looks toward me as I approach his truck.

"It does not." I lean into Jesse's side window and give him a dumb look. I take in his scent, his face inches from mine. This isn't unusual, we grew up together. We've swapped spit. Not in *that* sense. Kendra made us all become spit siblings. *Gross, I know.*

24

It's different now. I can't explain why, but everything feels different since he pulled the prom card last year. That and last summer in the back of his truck. My body is fully aware of his presence and his gaze burning a hole through the side of my face right now.

I try to breathe. I look to her. "Hey Lyssa, if you're looking for a one night stand, then Jesse's definitely not your guy. I hear your boyfriend might be interested, though." I give her a plastic smile as I tilt my head to the right and mimic her tone, "Ummm-k?"

Lyssa rolls her eyes, leans back, whispers something, probably derogatory, and walks away. "Later, Jesse. Call me when you don't have the goodie-two-shoes squad hanging around your neck like a noose."

"I am not a goody-two-shoes!" I yell, looking to Lyssa who waves her hand behind her. "Just because I don't make myself available to the entire student body, girls included," I whisper as I look at Jesse. "What are you laughing at?"

Jesse laughs harder, resting his head against his headrest.

I stare at his perfectly-shaped neck, wanting to touch it, kiss it. I ease out of Jesse's window. "Somebody has to protect you. Some of these girls will eat you alive. Literally."

"Come on, Jackson." He goes to reach for my arm but then stops mid reach.

No, please, touch my arm.

He grins as he meets my gaze.

That crooked smile.

That stupid crooked smile has given me butterflies since we were eight.

That stupid crooked smile tells me he's only telling me half-truths with the rest being pink flamingos and flying pigs. You know, happy stuff. He's holding back. As he pulls his arm back, I watch the muscles flex.

Then I notice it—*a tattoo?* On his left arm, barely peeking out the bottom of his short-sleeve shirt there is a thick black band tattoo of some sort.

I look back to Jesse, shock registering on my face. I don't even have to say what I'm thinking because he knows me. "Long time no see, I guess?" I brush a strand of hair out of my face with my finger. I rub my lips together hoping the lip balm still gives my lips enough shine.

He stares at my mouth.

I rub my lips together again.

"Stop doing that," He growls.

"Doing what?" I say with intentions no better than Lyssa's.

He shakes his head. "Anyway, yes, I got this in June." He rubs his hand over the band. "Guess I have not seen you in a while?" He looks back at me, the same look he gave me the last time we saw each other. The same look that makes my knees want to buckle and my heart want to jump into oncoming traffic. The look that leaves me breathless.

I look down at his hands. I like big hands and long fingers. *Penn, get a grip. Stop this nonsense. Say your piece.* This makes me flustered. I don't want to feel these things. "Are you kidding me? Where have you been? I don't hear from you all summer and now you just show up, out of the blue, and act as if everything's back to normal?"

"You missed me, then?" His look is hard, as if he doesn't want me to have missed him.

"Shut up." I cross my arms. "'*You missed me, then?*'" I poorly imitate him. Jesse laughs hard, still staring intently at me.

"What do you want me to say?"

The knot in the stomach tightens. *Stay angry, Penn.* "Oh, I don't know. How about, 'Sorry I didn't call you back for two months. How are you? How was your summer'?"

There's a long pause.

"Are you going to the party tonight?" He says, finally breaking eye contact.

"Jesse, seriously, don't try to change the subject. Look at me." I glare at him. "We haven't even had a chance to talk about what happened."

"Come on, Jackson. What is there to talk about? You had too much to drink and I took you home. End of story." He slips his sunglasses on.

I stare at him, stunned at his faulty remembrance of that night. "That's weird." Sarcasm colors my tone, "my recollection of that night is completely different." I play his game.

The night is still fresh in my mind. It was the last week of school, the last party of the year...

"Penn, I should get you home," he whispered as we sat side by side against the cab of his truck. "It is late."

"Why? Am I not good enough for you?" I said, only half-kidding and terribly tipsy. "We've been friends since we were eight, Jesse. Aren't you in the least bit curious?"

He pulled away to look at me. "Is that what you think?"

His almond-shaped eyes searched mine, hungry for an answer I don't have. He turned and slowly put his arm around me, pulling me close to his side. My drunken head fell and rested on him. I felt the heaviness of his heart pounding in his chest.

"We need to get you home," he whispered, adjusting his Red Sox cap and grabbing my arm to help me out of the back of his truck. He silently walked me to the passenger-side door, as if I was a troubled child. In one swift movement, he thrust me up against the cab of the truck, the sensation of his body against mine sending all of my senses into overload.

I felt the warmth of his breath on my neck as he whispered, "Jackson, not a day goes by I do not think about you." He paused and moved closer to my ear, "I think about the way you push your hair out of your eyes and the way you twirl your ring when you are deep in thought. I think of the way you look at me, the way you watch me." He pulled back, holding me against the truck at arm's length. "But Penn, you and I will never work, you cannot want me. I cannot give you what you want or need. Please understand."

My heart skipped a beat as I tried to catch my breath and open my eyes. With one quick movement, he opened the door and placed me in the seat. As the truck door slammed shut, so too did the door to my heart. The door I opened so willingly for him and him alone. My heart crumbled. *Stupid girl.*

I wanted to act as though nothing had happened and that his assumption was a huge misunderstanding, but I couldn't. I rested my head against the seat, swallowed hard, and tried to comprehend what just happened. One minute I was sandwiched between the truck and his body, the next, I am sitting in his truck, alone, my heart in pieces on the ground. The passenger-side door of Jesse's truck jerks open as I am forcefully drawn back to the present.

"Hey, hotness," Vanessa Reynolds purrs, sliding into the passenger seat next to Jesse. She makes a disgusted sound when she notices me standing on Jesse's side of the truck. "Hi wench," She mumbles, glaring in my direction. I look behind me, pretending not to notice her stink eye. An evil grin spreads across her face as she places her arm around Jesse and intimately kisses the corner of his mouth.

I can't move. I can't breathe. I cannot believe what I am witnessing. I sputter out one of my inappropriate comments, "Seriously? Are you dating the she-devil? What's next, adopting Rosemary's baby? I don't believe you."

"Much has changed, Jackson," Jesse's voice is low. He says it like it's an apology.

My feet won't move. I'm stunned. I want to run to the passenger-side door and pull Vanessa out by her hair. I want to smash her face against the hood of the truck. I want to scour the kiss off Jesse so her evil cannot spread but I can't move.

CHAPTER 3

Murder Under the Bridge

September 7ᵗʰ 5:40pm

The rumors begin to fly in our small town. Some say Bradbury drank himself to death, while others believe it was suicide. I don't know if anyone actually believes it was an animal attack. An animal attack just seems, well, odd. The entire town is edgy. Nothing like this ever happens in Mason. People die of old age or illness, but nothing like this.

It's Friday and a quarter past five. The Mason Fireman's Hall is packed. Aunt Jo and I file in toward the back corner and take two vacant seats right as Chief Watson takes the podium. Next to him stands Dr. Dover, acting as the town's Coroner.

The Chief clears his throat as Dr. Dover whispers in his ear. Chief Watson nods. He looks tired, as if he hasn't slept in days.

"Thank you all for coming," he begins, "it is with great sadness I must report the death of Dale Ernest Bradbury." He pauses. "At 4:13 a.m., on September, 4th, Dale's body was discovered by a fisherman under the Mason Bridge. His body was found in what appeared to be a shallow grave."

A hush falls over the crowd.

"Thanks to Dr. Dover's diligent work, the autopsy results have been filed with the Holcomb County Coroner's office. Pending the outcome of toxicology reports, the cause of death has been tentatively ruled an animal attack."

The crowd explodes with questions, all speaking at once. Some stand and shout while others whisper to their neighbors.

"Please, folks, one at a time." The Chief places his hands on the podium.

Dan Larkspur, an old dairy farmer, stands up. "An animal attack? I've seen animal attacks Chief, and this doesn't sound like any animal in this area, or any area, for that matter. What kind of animal buries their victim in a shallow grave?"

Dr. Dover leans into the microphone, "We cannot answer that at this time."

"Have you found the animal, Gary?" Ginger, the postmaster, calls out from two rows back, crossing her arms.

"No, we have not. Until we catch this thing, we are implementing a few rules to insure your safety."

Silence and fear hang in the room like a low fog. I scan the huge auditorium and find Kendra, and her hair purple because it's Friday, sitting two rows over with her legal guardian, Francis. She is picking at her split ends, seemingly unaffected by all this, like she's sitting through a lecture on cuticle care. I know she knows more than she lets on and this proves it. I continue to scan the room for Jesse and spot him in the far back corner, closest to the bathrooms. Travis, Jesse's best friend, is standing next to him, arms crossed, leaning up against the wall. Then there's Vanessa. *Ah, yes. How can I forget the heartless, poor excuse of a cheerleader?* She glares at me, which tells me one thing; she feels I'm a threat.

Good. I smile and wave.

She leans over and whispers into Jesse's ear. He laughs as his eyes find me.

I hate that I love his laugh.

His smile quickly fades, his eyes full of conflict, awkward almost. Vanessa pulls his face to hers. *Whatever. No biggie,* I lie to myself. It's not like Jesse belonged to me, anyway. Besides, I'm more worried about him and his erratic behavior than I am about anything else. *Seriously, a tattoo? I mean, really? Not that it doesn't work in his favor, because it totally does. Gah! Penn, stop!* Jesse is fair game and free to do whatever he wants, with whomever he wants, whenever he wants. Just because he's never committed himself to anyone doesn't mean anything. It only proves his behavior is, indeed, unpredictable. *Ah! There's my voice of reason.* Maybe we don't belong together. I wouldn't be in this predicament if he hadn't given me such a mixed message last summer.

Who am I kidding? That's a crock.

Why Vanessa? She eats freshmen girls for lunch with her uncanny ability to make them bleed through her unkind words. Vanessa Reynolds is a *mean girl*. She has her head so far up her own butt, she can see out her mouth. For whatever reason, since the day I moved to Mason, that monster has had it in for me, calling me out on any occasion solely to be hateful. One day, sophomore year, I wore white jeans to school prompting Vanessa to ask in front of the entire student body, in the cafeteria, "Uh, Penelope, are you on your period? You might want to go check."

I wasn't on my period, so I quickly countered with, "Does your mom know your dad's sleeping with Mrs. Pembrook?" This was Vanessa's first experience with my scathing wit and my non-existent propriety filter.

The entire cafeteria grew silent.

Very silent.

Awkwardly silent.

Scary silent.

My first thought was, *that was uncalled for, Penn. It was hurtful.* My second thought was *I just woke the beast.* I didn't care.

Immediately, I felt terrible. Although it was true and everyone knew it, I felt awful I'd embarrassed her like that, even if she is a heartless creature.

The Chief's voice echoing in the large auditorium draws me out of my reminiscing.

I fish my phone out of my pocket and text: What r u doing w/ her?

I don't hit send. Instead, I hit the delete button. I type another text: Vanessa Reynolds, really?

I erase it again and type another:

Hope she makes you happy.

I delete it.

I retype it.

I hit *send* even if it is the biggest line of crap I've ever fed anyone.

"...First, the town curfew will be 7:00 p.m. That means no one, absolutely no one, will be out after 7:00 p.m. Second, lock your doors at night. Officers will be coming to each house to make sure doors are locked and everyone is home and safe. Finally, all residents over the age of 18 will be issued a can of mace that should be kept with them at all times."

Rick Hinds, the town pharmacist, chimes in, "These seem like extreme measures for an animal attack, Chief. If these measures are appropriate, do you know what kind of animal it is, Dr. Dover? What aren't you telling us?"

Dr. Dover nervously taps his hand against his slacks to an unheard beat as he leans into the microphone. "I cannot answer your question at this time."

The Chief ignores Rick's question. "You will see an increase in law enforcement as we are collaborating with the Sheriff's department for added protection and assistance in the search for this animal," Chief Watkins continues, trying to change the subject.

I wonder what Bradbury's last moments were like. How did they find his body? Was the body dismembered? Was it bloody? Morbid, I know, but I can't contain my curiosity.

"Folks, we will release more information when it becomes available. Please be patient and please, please be safe," Chief Watkins sighs. "If you see anything out of the ordinary, call Rodney at the department immediately."

Jo and I drive home in silence. It's odd for my aunt to be so quiet.

"Aunt Jo?" I say, staring out the passenger-side window as we drive home.

"Hum?"

"What do you think it is? The animal, I mean."

She stares out the windshield blankly. "I am not sure, baby girl," she whispers as if she is a million miles away. I look out the window as Lenore Mason, the great, great, niece of Seth Mason, the town's founder, makes her way down Main Street. She appears to be carrying on a conversation with her invisible companion. She's dressed in three layers of clothing with dingy-colored socks and mismatched sandals. Though her age is probably mid-forties, she looks to be about sixty. She calls herself a gypsy but most of us know poor Lenore Mason is crazy. Lenore, for many reasons, reminds me of Nadine. It's probably the way she keeps to herself or the way she walks. On the other hand, it could be the way she talks to herself, I'm not sure.

"Jo, pull over, please."

Lenore jumps as I get out of the car. "Lenore, where's your walking stick?" I quietly close the car door behind me.

"Get away from me! You are the devil!"

I look around, people are stopping to watch the show. Lenore is in one of her *everyone-is-the-devil* moods.

"Lenore, I'm not the devil. I'm merely trying to help. Where's your walking stick. You're limping again. See?"

As she retreats from me, she begins limping, badly.

"Please, Lenore. Let me help you. May I take you home?"

She catches her sandal on the grass and falls backwards, landing on her butt. Quickly, I walk to her and try to help her up.

"Get away from me devil child, you're trying to kill me!" She pushes me away as she slowly gets to her feet. "You are the devil. You will rot in hell for your sins." She stares down her long bony finger at me. Enacting some ancient gypsy curse on me, I'm sure.

Raising my hands in surrender, I back away. "Okay, Lenore. Okay." She lowers her hands, still staring at me. She turns and hobbles away like an old hermit, looking back at me every couple of seconds. Probably checking the effectiveness of her curse.

I climb back into the car, defeated.

Jo smiles.

"What?" I ask.

"Nothing." She says, grinning ear to ear.

"What?" I sigh.

"I am proud of you."

"Why is she so mean?" I watch as we drive past Lenore, her lips moving at a rate of speed indicating anger or fear. "I know what you're going to say. *Judgement can be an inaccurate assumption when you haven't lived a day of their life.*'"

I watch Jo's grin as we make our way home. Her old saying and my encounter with Lenore makes me think of my last morning with Nadine. The morning social services came and took me from her.

She'd been dead for at least nine hours. She was on our ratty, old, blue couch still wearing last night's makeup. Our place was located in Santa Maria, California on Bunny Street. Drug dealers, gang bangers, pimps and prostitutes littered the street like slow moving traffic.

I remember I was on the floor in my red Snoopy nightgown watching the turn-knob television that rested on an old milk crate. I was eating stale cereal, and watching an old episode of Tom & Jerry. I spent more time swatting fleas from the filthy brown shag carpet than watching the show.

Nadine? Nadine, my name is Collette and this is Sharon. We are social workers for the state of California. We are taking your daughter with us, she said as she set some paperwork next to a stale plate of mac-n-cheese on the counter. *Nadine?* They said together. Sharon came to my side as Collette went to speak with Nadine. She rolled her over and nearly tripped over her own feet as she quickly backed away from Nadine's dead body.

I will never forget the sight. Her face was bloated and blue. Her lifeless eyes rolled back into her head. Rigor had already set in, making her body look unnatural as she lay there.

I started to cry. "My mommy didn't feel good so I rolled her over."

"Penn? Where did you go?" Aunt Jo grasps my hand, her deep blue eyes full of concern. I can't speak.

Jo takes the keys out of the ignition. "You okay, baby?" I nod as I try to swallow the lump in my throat.

"Come on, let us go inside." She cups her hand on my cheek then pushes the strands of hair from my face, like she used to do when I was little.

She knows where I went.

Our house is located on Jacobsen Way on the outskirts of town. There is a circular driveway and a cluster of tall redwood trees standing in a semi-circle in front of our two-story restored Victorian. It backs up to the green belt that surrounds the backside of Mason and rests just down a slope from the giant redwood forest. Across the way and to the left of the house, an old hay barn and slaughter shed sit side by side, both reflect age and neglect. We use the hay barn for storage and the refrigerator in the slaughter shed when we have company. Other than that, they haven't seen any action since Jo bought the place twenty-five years ago. When you walk into our home, a massive staircase leads up to the second floor with walkways on either side of the second story. Downstairs, and to the left, there is a formal dining room and a gourmet kitchen. To the right and down two steps is the formal living room with a fireplace and bay windows that face the green belt on one side and the front of the house on the other.

Aunt Jo starts dinner, I join her in the kitchen. "I want you to take this casserole to John on your way to the hospital on Saturday morning."

I roll my eyes. "Seriously, Jo? Again? Last week he chased me off the porch and yelled something about calling in an artillery strike if I ever came back."

"Penelope, listen to me. He just came home from the war. We have our freedom because they fight for it. Never forget that."

The chime indicating breaking news plays on the television, halting our conversation. Jo and I turn to the television.

"On the national front, the remains of the John Doe in the grue-some *St. Louis Cemetery #1* murder investigation have been identified as Salvatore DeLuca." The camera pans to the taped-off cemetery where police officers and detectives wander in and out of the crime scene.

Jo gasps, drops the spatula and runs to the television. I follow her. She stands in front of the television, shaking. The view changes to a man in a uniform, standing behind a podium. "We are investigating all leads," he says. "That is all we can say at this time. We will not be taking questions." Reporter in the crowd fruitlessly yell questions to the infor-mation officer on scene. The camera switches back to the news anchor in the studio "Now on to other news this evening…"

"Aunt Jo, are you okay?" I walk over to her and place my hand on her shoulder. "Aunt Jo?" I try to find her behind her empty eyes.

"Yeah, uh, I am okay, honey. Uh, I need to make a phone call. Din-ner is on the stove. Help yourself."

"Don't you want to eat toge—?" She is half way up the stairs and out of earshot before I get the question out.

I wait. I wait thirty more seconds. *I can't just stand here.* I follow her up to her bedroom finding the door closed. I reach for the doorknob but what I hear stops me from opening the door. She's on the phone whispering, but it isn't English. Spanish, Italian? *Italian.* I sat through an entire eight-hour lecture series in Italian during first year only to come away with "Potresti passarmi i piselli," which translates to, *please pass me the peas.* I think.

"Devo dirglielo," she whispers gruffly. "Quando? No. No." She pauses again, getting impatient. "She has to know now, Church." She sighs. "Quando si terrà il funerale di mio fratello? Sì, sì. I'm leaving in the morning, Church. I need to get the journals."

The phone clicks.

Crap.

I tear my ear away from the door, tiptoe downstairs at warp speed, and throw myself on the couch. I have no time to process my aunt speaking in a different language or that she has a secret she's not willing to share. There has to be some explanation. There has to be. My head becomes clouded with every possible "what if" scenario such as: a zombie apocalypse, a radioactive disease, maybe she's not my real aunt, maybe she's a secret agent selling top secret information to the Italian government. *Shut up, Penn. For Real. Enough. Get a grip.* My insides begin to twist and turn like my mind.

The stairs squeak as Jo makes her way downstairs. She reaches the bottom and turns to the great room.

"Is everything okay?" I ask, still pondering different scenarios, as I feign interest in what's on my phone.

She pauses, draws in a deep breath, and walks over to the couch to sit. "Baby girl, I need to take a trip to New Orleans. I am leaving in the morning," she says as if she's telling me she's running uptown to the store for milk.

Still trying to act causal, I ask, "Why?"

"It is personal." She pauses.

There's something she's not telling me. "Can I go with you?" My eyes narrow.

Jo looks at me with her tender eyes. "Not this time. Besides, you have school and I need you to take care of Duke and Heathrow."

My face grows hot. "Why not?" I want her to tell me the real situation. Not so much because I want to know what's going on, but because I want so badly to trust that she will always tell me the truth.

Jo laughs. "Penelope, have I ever given you reason not to trust me? Why all the questions?"

I stare at her. *You're right.* "Who's Salvatore DeLuca?"

CHAPTER 4

Amy

Saturday Morning, September 8th at way-too-early o'clock

I haven't slept well since Jo left four days ago. My head is swimming with random thoughts. Question after question run through my mind. *Why did Jo leave? Why is she still gone? Why can't she explain who the dead guy is, or was? What is she not telling me? When did she learn to speak Italian? Why do I care so much about who Jesse is dating? Why is Vanessa such an evil wench?*

Jo's texts are minimal. She clearly wants me not to worry. I try not to.

My phone vibrates with a text from Kendra: Going to the Cove tonight rite?

I text back: All in. What time?

Kendra responds: 9 sharp.

Me: 9 flat. I will be ready. LOL.

43

After a pause my phone buzzes for the last time: Ur jokes are not funny. C u then.

I jump in the shower and get ready for work. Every Saturday I volunteer as a candy striper at the Holcomb General Hospital. Its located twenty minutes north of Mason. At first, I fought Aunt Jo about volunteering. The last time I was in the hospital was when social services took me from Nadine and I wasn't ready to go back. They poked and prodded at me, whispered words like: extreme neglect, malnourished, abuse. I told Jo I'd rather pull out my molars with a crowbar than spend my day off at the hospital, but she insisted. She said something about giving back to the community. In the beginning, I did it to make her happy. Now, I do it so I can practice my skills on the patients. The patients have grown on me, especially Amy.

I step out of the shower and wrap myself in a towel. The thought of Nadine enters my mind and suddenly I'm eight years old again.

I waited in the patrol car, watching as Collette from social services spoke to a man of great importance. I based this assumption on his professionalism and stature. The way he carried himself and the fancy clothes he wore did not indicate he was with CPS. I thought to myself, *I bet he's a good dad. I bet he has two daughters. I bet he plays dolls with them and tucks them in at night.*

They both shook their heads as they looked back to me.

Pity. I hate pity.

Then, around the corner, from the direction of our apartment, the paramedics wheeled Nadine out on a stretcher covered with a white sheet. I knew it was Nadine because I'd spent the last nine hours with her body, alone. They loaded her into the coroners van and I never saw her again.

I didn't cry. I couldn't cry. I just watched.

I'm staring at my seventeen-year-old self in the mirror again. My long, wet, dark brown hair clings to the middle of my back. I've never cried about Nadine's death after the morning social services came to get me. Maybe because I felt relief the day she died. Nadine was the only thing I had resembling a parent. She gave me a place to live and I guess that was better than living on the streets.

I continue to stare at my reflection. I feel put together despite the whirlwind of emotions swirling through my head. It shows someone who seems a stranger to herself at times: small frame, narrow jaw, long cheekbones, light-colored skin, slightly bigger nose than most, and big, round sage eyes. The girl staring back at me appears strong, a direct contrast to the fragile child I really am. A precious glass doll, spiderwebbed with cracks, waiting for the blow that shatters my facade, leaving me in pieces. It's best to keep these secrets deep within my soul, available to no one. I bury them deep inside, and keep them there.

I pull up to John's house. He lives on Trident Lane behind the fairgrounds in an old Victorian. The shutters on the upper level hang by a single hinge and spooky cobwebs decorate the house like a scene set for a Halloween haunted house. A sheet covers the two front windows and a new black Ford sits in the driveway. Dings, dents and scratches litter its exterior. A small sticker in the lower left-hand side of the back window reads *Semper Fi.*

I slide the casserole off the seat and carefully get out of the car. *Great,* I think. I carefully climb the rickety old stairs and knock.

I stop.

Sobbing. *Someone's crying.*

I knock. *Why, Penn? Why would you knock? Just go. Leave it on the porch and run.* My voice of reason dissipates like breath on a window. I can't help it. I need to know who is crying.

I hear a loud banging sound and, all of a sudden, the door swings open.

"You again?" he yells, slightly swaying in the doorway, his eyes bloodshot and face unshaven and gaunt.

Startled, I speak, "Y-yeah. Um, my aunt made you another casserole. I don't mean to pry but is everything okay?"

His cell phone rings a vaguely familiar tune, *eight-six-seven-five-three-oh-nine*. I know the tune. He holds the phone a mere inch from his face and stares at it, willing it to stop ringing. He's shaking and I see the awfulness in his eyes. His lips and cheeks quiver, his chest heaves in and out. He looks at the phone, unable to answer. His eyes dance from his phone then to me and back again. He grabs the casserole from my hands and slams the door in my face.

I stand, motionless, and stare at the door, unable to process his pain.

I think of what Jo used to say to me about unseen wounds and it hits home.

Rumor has it he blames himself for his brother's death. John joined the military right out of high school and was deployed to a combat zone shortly after basic training. At John's insistence, Andrew joined the military as well. John's tour ended a short time before Andrew's began. Andrew died three days after arriving in Afghanistan when the truck he was driving triggered a roadside bomb. It's hard to imagine what our soldiers endure while in battle. It's hard to imagine what families sacrifice for their loved ones who serve. I see the fear and hurt in his eyes and I want to take it all away.

I walk back to my car in a daze.

It's 9:45 a.m. on the dot when I walk into *Holcomb General*. The buzzing lights and the smell of sterile surrounding knock me out of my daze. If the color *white* had a smell, it would smell like this. It makes my stomach want to purge the gummy worms I ate on the way here. My shift starts at 10:00 a.m. but, like Aunt Jo always says, "Fifteen minutes early *is* on time."

"Well good morning, Penelope Jackson," says Laurie, the charge nurse of the unit, sifting through paperwork over her half-moon glasses.

"Laurie, we have lives to save today," I say, trying to shake off John's sadness. "How's she doing?"

Laurie lets out a sigh as she holds a clipboard in her hand. "Go see for yourself. She's been asking about you all morning." She smiles. I like her smile. It's warm and inviting, kind of like Aunt Jo's peach cobbler. "Oh, and at some point today, be sure to check on Gertrude. She's back again. She's convinced she'll die in forty-eight hours. Blood work came back normal, again." Laurie rolls her eyes.

Crazy old bat. "On it," I say as I wave behind me. The perfection of the white, sterile hallway is stifling.

I peek into room 142.

"PJ!" the little girl hoarsely whispers as her blue eyes focus on me. That's her nickname for me. I hate it but she loves it so I'll let her call me PJ for as long as she can.

Her hospital gown hangs loosely off one shoulder. The hospital, for many reasons, doesn't have gowns her size. This one is at least two sizes too big. Dark circles under her eyes show fatigue from the chemotherapy and radiation but her attitude doesn't show it. Her bald head glimmers in the sun's rays shining through the window.

"This is top secret." I walk over and sit next to her on her bed. Kids this young shouldn't live in hospitals and shouldn't be bald. I look at her, then around the room, pretending I am about to show her the biggest secret ever. "Guard these with your life. Whatever you do, don't show Nurse Elaine. Pinkie swear it."

Amy looks around and sticks out her tiny pinkie. "Pinkie swear," she whispers and looks at me with her big, beautiful baby blues. They tug at my heart and I have to swallow my sadness. "Gummy worms!" she whisper-yells as she claps her hands and takes one. She scoots back making more room for me on the bed. "Thanks, PJ. You're the best!"

Amy spills all the gossip from the previous week: What her sister is doing, how her mom is feeling, and everything in between. She never talks about herself or her experiences. Amy is seven years old and was diagnosed with Alveolar Rhabdomyosarcoma, a rare form of childhood cancer, last year. She handles her disease with grace and strength. She's seven and fighting for her life.

I first met Amy early last year when she came for her first round of treatments. She's incredible, resilient, and beautifully strong. Not a tear shed since her diagnoses, at least none I've seen. Our world knows many heroes, but no hero of mine ever battled cancer the way Amy has. *Grace.*

"Do you think you can bring Duke back to visit me, Penn? He's so cute and soft." She smiles as she looks up at me.

Something about Amy makes me feel small and petty. It could be her attitude toward her cancer, or the way she looks out for her sister and mother. It could be her bravery, or her willingness to see the positive amidst adversity. Whatever it is, it makes my insides scream with madness. "Tell you what, once the treatments are done, you and I will go to Aunt Jo's and I will give you a tour of the farm. We can drag Duke along with us."

"Promise?" she squeals.

"Have you ever known me not to keep my promises?"

She looks down to the gummy worm in her hand. "No, but I know other big people who haven't."

I pause, unsure how to proceed. Amy doesn't talk too much about her past, so when she does, I make sure to pay attention. I notice there doesn't seem to be a father in the picture and I never ask about him. Aunt Jo did the same for me. She never made me talk about my past. I love her for that. I figure Amy will tell me when the time is right, or say nothing at all, and that will be okay.

I know I can't heal Amy, yet. Although I've tried many times, the power doesn't seem to work on cancer the way it does on broken bones and flesh wounds, but I try anyway. I started coming to the hospital on my days off, twice a day, when I knew Amy was receiving treatment. It became a little weird and people were beginning to notice, so I backed off.

"Amy, have you grown since last week?" Nurse Elaine cheerfully dances into the room with Amy's treatment. Jenny, Amy's mom, follows the nurse in and stands in the doorway, leaning against the frame.

"Hide the evidence," I whisper loud enough for both Elaine and Jenny to hear me. Amy shoves the bag of worms under her covers. I wink at her.

I walk over to her. "Thank you," she whispers, her red, tired eyes swimming with tears. "She really enjoys you."

I look at Jenny. The hurt and pain in her voice is so visceral, my entire body feels it. I don't think this has anything to do with my healing ability. I think it has everything to do with who I am. If she knew what I've done in the past, she'd probably take her daughter and run. I want to reach out and touch her arm, to show some act of kindness, instead, I turn back to Amy.

"Hey kid, I'll be back after your treatment okay?"

"PJ?"

I pause, turning back into the room.

"What kind of clothes did the skeleton buy?"

I pause. Amy loves one-liners. I secretly do too. I think for a second. "I have no idea."

"Bat-to-school clothes." She erupts into a fit of hoarse giggles.

Her laughter makes my heart swell. I'm grateful Amy has come into my life.

"Later gator," I say to Amy and turn to leave.

I catch Jenny's eye one last time. Her eyes fill with tears and I have no idea what to say or how to act. I give her a nod and quickly walk by.

Outside, I take a big gulp of sterile air and lean against the wall. The lump is still there and I try my best to get rid of it. I take another deep breath as my insides begin to ache.

For reasons I do not fully understand, a strong urge leads me to the emergency room. This is not the first time I've felt this. I know what the beckoning means.

The little boy is sitting in bay number two in the emergency room with his mother. He's holding his misshapen right arm in his lap, grimacing at the slightest movement. They are waiting for the doctor to read his x-rays and set his obviously broken arm.

"Hi." I pull the curtain back. "I'm Penn. What's your name?" I look at the big brown-eyed little boy.

"Levi," he says, burying his head in his mother's side.

"He's shy. I'm Linda," she says, holding out her hand. "Levi fell out of a tree in the backyard and, I think, broke his arm. They've given him a little pain medication." She looks at her son with adoring eyes. "That seems to have helped. We are going to stay out of trees for a while, aren't we," she says, more of a command than a question, as she looks down at her son.

"You know what always makes me feel better, Levi?" I bend down to make eye contact with him.

He looks up from his mother.

"A cool bandage." I reach into the front pocket of my volunteer uniform and grab a lime green bandage with zebra stripes.

He smiles and looks up at his mom as if to ask, 'can I have one?' She nods and I take it out of the package.

Levi carefully uncovers the arm resting on his lap.

Yep. That's broken. My morning coffee almost makes a second appearance all over the hospital bed. I examine the arm; the bruising is quite extensive already.

"Is it gonna hurt?" He looks at me, tears welling in his eyes.

"Are you kidding? This bandage will give you super powers and, I promise, you are going to feel as good as new." I carefully place the bandage where most of the bruising has already formed, but I keep my hand hovering above his broken arm. I mentally prepare for what comes next.

My hands begin to tingle, and warmth flows through my body. I know what comes next as I look at Levi and his mother, acting casually. "I'm giving you your super powers." I whisper as the feeling overcomes my body. Numbness. Everything grows silent. My hand still hovers over his arm. My hands begin to sweat and my heart races as I focus on his arm.

Here it comes.

The pressure always starts in my head, then moves to my shoulders, arms, stomach, legs, and, finally, feet. Not that I've ever been run over by a snowplow, but, if I had, this is what I would imagine it feels like.

The feeling of hundreds of tiny nails coursing through my veins nearly break me every time.

It takes my breath away.

It a*lways* takes my breath away. A loud hum rings in my ears and I cannot hear.

Everything stops.

"Thanks for the bandage, Penn," Levi says as he looks down at his arm.

I clear my throat, trying to gather my faculties, my condition seemingly unnoticed by Levi and his mother. *I'm getting better at this.* "Now," I recover, "remember, you may have some super powers now." I look to Linda and warn playfully, "Mom, don't be surprised if he can lift cars or run like lightning."

She chuckles as Dr. Lee pulls the curtain back. "I see you've met the best candy striper in Holcomb County." Dr. Lee looks to me then to Linda and Levi. "I'm trying to get this bright young woman to consider medical school. She's great with kids." He turns to Levi and whispers, "Have your super powers kicked in yet?"

Levi giggles and hides his face behind his mom again. His mother mimes the words "thank you" to me.

"We have to get another set of x-rays," Dr. Lee sighs. "It's clear it's broken, but I think you might have moved during the x-ray and I need a better one to determine if you will require pins."

I quietly make my exit with a silent wave and leave the ER to see Gertrude. *He'll be fine, Dr. Lee.* A rush of adrenaline comes over me. *Levi will be absolutely fine.*

I make my way down the sterile hallway toward Gertrude's usual room in the short stay unit. Gertrude is a weekly patient at General and insists on the same room every week. General now keeps that room open for her inevitable arrival. She's always convinced she is dying of something. *Price is Right* blares from the television. Gertrude's husband passed away two years ago after fifty years of marriage. I suspect Gertrude wants the doctors to find something wrong with her so she can die and reunite with her husband. I also think she can't bring herself to take her own life, hence the weekly visits with pages and pages of Internet research about the disease she has that week. Each week the diagnosis is different.

I smile as I set her chart down, and shake my head. I think what Gertrude has is "lonely." I think she misses her husband so desperately the pain outweighs her desire to live. "Good morning, Ms. Lundy."

"Oh, Penn, I'm so glad you're here so I can say all my goodbyes. I'm gonna die within the week! Look at this paperwork I found on the Internet." She thrusts it my direction.

My eyebrows furrow as I take the pile of disheveled paperwork from her hands. I scan through it. *Another self-diagnosis.*

"Gertrude," I look to her, "you aren't dying from a rare blood disorder. You are not going to die in forty-eight hours." I try to take my time with her. "You're healthy, according to all the tests we did last week and the week before, and the week before that."

"No, no. I know I have this. This," she motions toward the papers. "I can't even pronounce the name." She huffs as she crosses her arms.

I sit down next to her and look at the television then down at her bony hands. She has thin skin with patches of brown and purple. The purple spots indicate a recent bruise, most likely an IV. Her hands look soft, like grandmother hands. She still wears her wedding ring.

"Missing Henry?" She's toying with her ring.

"Every day that I breathe." She nods slightly, trying to hold in her emotions. I feel her heartbreak in her words, spoken and unspoken. Sometimes I wish my power to heal worked on emotional pain like Gertrude's, like John's. However, if we didn't hurt, we wouldn't know our pain? Would we ever change? Would we ever know the best life has to offer? Would we know what heartbreak or brokenness feels like? I think emotional hurt is far worse than any flesh wound or broken arm. I think our physical wounds heal much faster than our emotional ones.

I should know.

I look back at Gertrude.

"Gertrude, listen." I pull the chair close to her bedside. I want to touch her hand but don't. "You need to live. You need to enjoy your children and grandchildren. Sadness, death, they aren't easy. You're still grieving and coping with the loss of your best friend. Don't you think Henry wants you to live the life you have left and enjoy it?"

She nods.

"Just because he isn't in the physical world anymore doesn't mean he isn't with you." Gertrude nods again and wipes her eyes.

"I know he's with me."

"Then live, Gertrude. Stop subjecting yourself to this hospital with all your life-threatening ailments. You and I both know you have everything to live for."

"How?" she whispers, barely making eye contact. "I don't know how."

"Well for starters, go wrap your arms around that sweet red-headed grandson you always show me pictures of."

She nods and wipes another tear.

"Go live, Gertrude."

I look at her and wait for her to look at me. I nod and stand up to leave.

"Young lady, you are wise beyond your years."

"Perhaps." I smile through my guilt as Frankie's screams come back into my head.

I head back down to the ER, trying to convince myself for the millionth time Frankie deserved to die for what he did to Nadine night after night but I didn't mean to do it. It all happened so fast. Nadine called Frankie her *friend*. Looking back, now I know Frankie sold Nadine's body for money. Nadine was addicted to anything that made her mind numb and thoughts cloudy, constantly chasing an unattainable bliss to escape her personal hell.

I show up in time to see Levi and his mom talking to Dr. Lee in the waiting room. Hiding around the corner, I'm careful to remain unnoticed. Levi is happily jumping around his mother, moving both arms excitedly as the neon green bandage clings to his arm.

The bruising is gone. I smile, shaking off the feeling Frankie still gives me, even beyond the grave.

Dr. Lee and Linda exchange smiles and baffled glances, both seem extremely relieved. I move closer. I want to hear Dr. Lee's justification. I grab a white surgical mask and a blue hat at the nurse's station to disguise myself. I grab a file and pretend to read it.

"Linda, I can't explain it. Although the first x-ray was blurred because this little rascal moved, it clearly showed two bad breaks and I definitely thought we were going to have to put pins in. The second x-ray showed, well, nothing. A perfectly healthy arm. No breaks, nothing. Zero."

Levi says, "It was the green bandage Penn gave me. She said it would give me super powers!" He squeals with excitement as he pretends to fly around his mom.

CHAPTER 5

Prom in a Barn

Saturday, September 8th 7:52 p.m.

I pull into the driveway and see a candle burning in a mason jar on the ledge of the porch. Every Saturday night he puts one out. This whole candle ritual started because of our junior prom. We were supposed to go together as a group: Kendra, Jesse, Travis and me. I was at the hospital all day and Amy had a rough time with her treatment so I stuck around most of the evening to make sure she was okay. It was hard to watch that sweet little girl struggle to breathe for hours on end, her tired eyes screaming for sleep. Her cancer is aggressive, so is its treatment. Sometimes, I wanted the doctors to stop so she could have a chance to rest, even for a night. It wasn't my call or my place, so I sat there with Amy and held her hand until she fell asleep that night.

I always wanted to go to our junior prom. Silly, I know, but I wanted to get dressed up in a beautiful gown, wear my hair up and put on a little make up for a change.

After leaving the hospital, I drove up the driveway, catching Jesse in my headlights. He was on the porch, fiddling with his pocketknife. A candle in a mason jar sat to his left.

Every part of my heart became his in that moment.

I shut the car door and walked up the steps.

"You missed your prom." He said, standing up and stretching as though he'd been sitting for too long. He tilted his Red Sox cap back and set it lightly on the top of his head.

I tried to smile but the tears won out. I just wanted to curl up in his arms. "I know. I'm sorry, Jess." I leaned into the railing next to him. "Amy had a rough night."

Without another word, he took my hand and massaged my knuckles. I loved how he did that. Most times he did it hard to taunt me but not that night. That night he was soft and gentle.

"Come here." He pulled me to his chest and kissed my hair. "Nothing about that situation is easy, Jackson. I know you would take her place if you could." He kept his lips on my head.

Don't cry, Penn. Don't you dare cry! You don't get to cry. Don't even think about it. Amy. She deserves to cry. If only he knew how true his statement is. Sometimes, I wished I could talk to someone about it all, about my healing powers, and how I tried, many times, to heal Amy. I choked down my emotions and slowly nodded.

He pulled away. *Don't pull away. You always do that.* "What time did you get here?"

Jesse glanced at his watch, "Oh, a little while ago. Everyone deserves a prom."

"Wait, you hate prom. The only reason you were going with us was because you lost a bet with Boots. Oh my, God." I covered my mouth. "You went, didn't you?"

He sighed, stepping off the porch. "I waited for you, but you never showed. In my defense, you know how Boots gets if we do not make good on bets." He shook his head.

I follow his lead across the yard.

He opened the door to the old hay barn and guided me through, his hand on the small of my back. The feeling of his touch sent shock-waves through my body. His breath on my neck almost made my knees give way. I wanted nothing more than to be in this moment, forever.

I looked up.

It was magnificent.

Flameless candles lit the interior of the barn. Every shelf, rail, hay bale and available flat surface was covered with candles. The twinkling lights left me speechless.

"Jesse," I said, my words but a whisper, "it's beautiful."

He took my hand in his and led me to the center of the barn. "Everyone deserves one dance at their prom. Come here." He pulled me under a chandelier of white tulle. Paper lanterns floated effortlessly above us, suspended from the roof. "Dance with me."

I looked into his eyes, hypnotized by candle light. "There's no music."

He pushed my hair out of my eyes. Chills resonated through my body as I wrap my arms around his neck. He gently placed his lips to my ear as his hands slide around my waist. From his lips came the sweetest sound I've ever heard. I nuzzled deeper into his neck as I let the sound of his voice and the touch of his hands guide me in a world where only he and I existed.

And so, here we go.

You go your way,

I'll go mine.

One day, we'll meet again.

Under different circumstances

In a different world, another time.

The strength you have is

In your heart.

Gather your strength and go.

Go.

Go.

Go.

No.

No.

No.

Stupid girl.

Stop.

Truth be told, I wanted to spend forever exactly like this, in this perfect moment.

"Jesse," I said, looking into his eyes.

He pulled my head to his chest again.

Don't cry, Penn.

Love. What a dumb word.

Lust.

Desire.

Want.

These are words I believe in.

Love.

Not so much.

If I did believe in love, this moment might have given me a glimpse of what love could be like.

The flicker of the candle on the porch draws me back to the present.

I barely have time to set my purse down when the doorbell rings. I don't know if I can deal with any more people today. It's mentally draining to heal and I need time to recover. I'm not expecting anyone except Kendra who shouldn't be here for another hour. I look through the peephole as my heart begins to pound. It's Chief Watson.

"Hi Penn," he says as I open the door. He looks to have aged at least five years overnight.

"Chief Watson." My heart rate triples as I assume the worst. "Is Aunt Jo okay?" Panic sets in.

"Oh yes, yes. I'm sure your Aunt Jo is fine," the chief assures me. Relief surges though my body. "That's not why I'm here, Penn." *He knows and he's coming to arrest me. All these years later, they have found out what I did to Frankie.*

"I'll be keeping an extra eye on your house since your aunt is out of town. Please make sure you're in by curfew. Got that?"

I slowly release the breath I didn't realize I was holding and my heart slows a bit. "Of course, Chief." I lie, and lie with enthusiasm.

He turns to leave.

"Uh, Chief?"

He stops and turns.

I try to stop the words before they exit my mouth, but I can't. "Do you know what kind of animal this thing is yet?"

He takes in a long breath and looks at his feet. He rubs his forehead as if trying to form an answer. "Penn, whatever this thing is, please just promise me you'll be safe." *This thing. This animal. I've never seen anything like it.*

Another question sneaks out. "What did Dale's body look like when you found it?"

Shut up, Penn.

Chief Watson has been the chief for as long as I've lived in Mason. Before that, according to Aunt Jo, he'd been a Lieutenant in the homicide division of the LAPD for twenty plus years. Dead bodies are nothing new to the chief.

I catch him off guard. His eyes narrow as he moves closer to the porch. "Penn…" he chooses his words carefully, "I've seen death and dying. I've seen murder. I've seen gruesome murder…but," he pauses as his voice changes pitch, "I have never seen anything like this." He places his hands on his hips. "Be safe, Penn," he says and leaves.

Well that's comforting.

I lock the door and walk to the window, watching until his car disappears. I play it over in my head. *I've never seen anything like this.* Chills race through my body. It's not his statement but an ice-cold blast that makes the hairs on my neck stand up.

Penn, calm down.

I turn back to the window. For a split second, I think I hear something, but I can't tell if it's real or my wild imagination mixed with fear.

Penn, you're freaking yourself out. Calm down. It's probably nothing. Irrational fear.

"Duke," I whisper. His nails click on the hardwood floors as he trots into view. He stops suddenly and sniffs the air. His ears lay back as a low growl escapes his throat. "Come here, boy," I call, but he refuses to move. He sniffs the air again, growling louder. He stops sniffing as another icy blast engulfs me. Fear settles in my heart, constricting my breathing, clouding my judgement. *Penn breathe.* I look around the room, searching the dark corners. Duke is at my side now, pressing protectively against my leg, barking ferociously.

Then there is nothing but a loud silence.

My cell phone rings. I jump as my heart leaps out of my chest. It rings again as my shaking hand reaches for the phone. *"Caller ID UNKNOWN."*

It rings again.

Suddenly, I can't move. I'm paralyzed with fear. I think hard, unable to remember what to do. The Chief is gone and Jo is in New Orleans, what the hell am I supposed to do? *Answer it!*

Slowly, I raise the phone to my ear and hit the talk button.

"Hello?"

Silence.

"H—hello?" I say again.

Dead silence.

Then I hear it: breathing on the other end of the call. It's the kind of breathing born of nightmares. Slow, controlled breaths meant to arrest you with terror. Then silence. A cold sweat forms on my brow. Is the caller in my house? I listen intently, hoping for the silence of an empty house. Panic rings loudly in my ears.

"Who is this?" I say, trying to keep fear out of my voice.

Breathing, again.

"Who. Is. This?"

Again, nothing.

I wait, taking a deep breath to clear my head. Chief Watkins can't be far down the road. I can hang up and call 911 from my cell phone. Can they run a trace on the call to track the number? Is Mason PD that sophisticated? I highly doubt it.

"I am calling the police right now." My voice cracks as I hold back tears.

Crap.

A chilling chuckle travels through the phone line and down my spine.

"Gotcha," the hoarse voice whispers.

CHAPTER 6

The Cove

I breathe in a deep breath and collapse on the couch, my hand barely able to hold the phone.

"Penn? You okay? I was kidding. Are you okay?" Kendra's voice rings out. Her tone changing from joking to serious. "Are you alright?"

"Kendra Salvino," I say, my body still trying to recover from the rush of adrenaline. "If you ever do that to me again! You. Are. Dead!"

It's 9:05 p.m. when we arrive at the Cove. A chant rises from a group of partygoers. "Curfew! Hell No!" The bonfire soars high in the air, sending red-embers into the cold night sky. They dance and twinkle like stars before fading into the darkness. We grab our lawn chairs and follow the sights and sounds of teenage mayhem. Kendra pauses. "Okay, tell me one more time, what happened tonight before I called?" She hands me a flask.

"What's this for?"

"It will calm your nerves." She nudges it my way.

"Kendra, you know how I feel about this." I hand her the flask back. I watched Nadine slowly kill herself with this stuff.

"Come on. Seriously. It will calm your nerves. Trust me. You need it." She pushes it toward me.

I take a sip. The alcohol burns the entire way down my throat, exploding in my stomach and making me feel lightheaded at once.

"Disgusting!" I say, through my gags. "Why would anyone drink that?" I gag again as I push it back to her.

I compose myself and tell Kendra the story once more. She listens silently, analyzing every detail as she mulls it around in her head. "Why do you care so much? There has to be a logical explanation. Besides, it was probably me, overreacting and freaking out. You know how I get." I take the flask and swallow another sip. There was definitely something more to her concern than simple curiosity. It's not like Kendra to worry. It was causing me to panic all over again.

I take Kendra's advice, no matter how disgusting, and take one last pull from the flask. It's for my nerves, I tell myself.

We make it to the bonfire. A guy in a gorilla mask runs around the party trying to scare the partygoers.

" Salvino! Jackson! You're up!" Travis motions to the keg with a funky little shake of his hips.

"Come on, Trav! You know I don't drink the hard stuff." Kendra laughs as she shakes her flask at him. "I will be right back," She whispers to me. "Find us some fresh sand?"

I nod and scan the party. I find him, half way around the massive fire. His white t-shirt stands out against his tan arms. One hand pushed deep in his pocket while the other holds a red plastic cup. His Red Sox cap pulled low on his head. Feeling the liquid courage, I debate marching over to him to ask about the tattoos, and the ridiculous fling with the she-devil. Because that's what it is, a fling. I'm certain of it.

Kendra suddenly appears next to him and begins talking to him.

Jesse is staring at the fire as Kendra streams information to him, trying to remain unnoticed. I notice. Jesse's shoulders tense. I see it. The look on his face changes from stoic to anger, hate even. He nods, turning back to Kendra to whisper something to her. The look on Kendra's face has changed as well. She nods and walks around the fire in my direction.

Jesse's eyes find me. He's biting his lip as he adjusts his cap. He does this when he's nervous. *Jesse's nervous?*

Vanessa comes bounding up behind him like a lost puppy. She grabs his chest. *I feel my hatred for her boil in my gut.* I want to punch her. I want to make her hurt like she makes me hurt. Jesse's focus stays on me only briefly as he slides his arm around her. She whispers something in his ear making him smile.

Well isn't that nice.

"Penn? Hello? Come back to the mortal world," Kendra says, waving her hand in my face.

"What did you tell him?" I ask, looking away from Jesse and the succubus. "You're okay with him dating the biggest soul-leech on the planet?"

"What do you mean?" She sets the chairs in the sand, ignoring my question completely.

"I saw you talking to Jesse. What did you talk to him about?"

"They are not dating," she says, looking at me like I'm crazy. "By the way, do you like me with bangs or no bangs? I'm thinking about getting my hair cut." She holds her bangs away from her forehead.

Baffled, I look back to them and then to Kendra, shaking my head. "What? No. You are deliberately trying to change the subject. Don't do that." I glare at her from my spot in the sand. "Ok, yeah, bangs. What do you mean *not dating*? You're kidding, right? They can't keep their hands off each other."

"I told him to tell Travis if he wants a date, he'd better never, ever shake his hips like that again. Ever." Kendra shakes her head as she plops down in the chair.

I know better than that. "It looked a little more serious than that." She knows I'm onto her.

"Enter total hot stuff. Hey, Lucas!" Kendra waves to LP's star running back.

"You remember Lucas?"

"You can't change the subject and expect me not to notice," I huff as I look to the six-foot-three giant standing in front of me.

"Hey, McHotty, can I get a tall order of hot beef?" Kendra laughs. I'm pretty sure it's the booze talking because Kendra would never say something like that. The odd thing is, I've never seen Kendra drunk.

"What's up, ladies?" He sits down in the sand next to me.

"Hey." I push my hair behind my ears as I watch my friend stand.

"On that note, I'm heading over to the keg to give Travis a ration of crap about the flat beer everyone is complaining about. Cheapskate."

Lucas is the guy every mother warns their daughter about. He's hot. He's tall. He's extremely athletic. He's smooth and he's easy. He's a walking cliché. He has a busy reputation and lacks the understanding of the "keep it in your pants" speech from seventh grade sex education.

He's going to be a dad.

Apparently, he got a girl knocked up from a late night love session while on spring break last year in the Florida Keys. Rumor has it, his parents are going to pay the child support until he's of legal age.

"It's been awhile, Penn."

I laugh again. "Yeah. It has. The last time I saw you was probably eighth grade when we were both stuck in a closet for seven minutes."

"You know I never told a soul you chickened out." He flashes his all-American smile, white and toothy.

"Hmmm. That's how you remember it? " I give him a sideways glance.

"Nope. Truth be told, I was scared out of my mind."

I laugh. *Yeah, right. Liar.*

"You don't think guys get nervous about kissing girls?" Lucas gazes at me like a prison inmate.

I giggle. Not laugh. Giggle. *Okay, lame. Did I just giggle? Vanessa Reynolds sellout.* I should be slapped across the face. It's the booze.

We spend the better part of the party reminiscing about old times. Lucas attended grade school with us, but moved across the river to Lake Providence when his parents divorced.

As Lucas and I talk, I scan the crowd. Across the bonfire, Jesse stares at me. Part of me wants to make him jealous, but part of me doesn't want to see him hurt. Part of me wants to protect him from Vanessa, but an even bigger part tells me he knows what he's doing. Jesse doesn't need protection.

If I said I didn't care for Jesse, it would be the biggest lie I've ever told. If he's going to move on, I will let him. I hate I care so much for him. I'd rather not, actually. With likes and loves comes pain and sorrow, and that sucks. It's not worth it. Not anymore.

I flirt with Lucas as I sip my beer, sensing Jesse's disapproval.

"You want to go for a walk?" I ask Lucas.

He flips nonexistent hair behind his shoulder and, in a shrill, girly voice, says, "I thought you'd never ask." He reaches over and helps me up.

I see Jesse from the corner of my eye. He's fuming as Vanessa clings to his arm, squawking like a parrot. She's always talking.

We follow the sound of the waves. The full moon lights the beach as the waves rise and fall with rhythmic precision.

"Do you know the biggest star in the galaxy?" Lucas whispers, looking up toward the sky.

I let out a huge laugh. "Tell me something, Luke? Do these bull crap lines get you anywhere with the ladies? Do you know what clichés are?"

He smirks. "Actually, they do."

The loud music and screams fade as we walk farther from the party.

"Kill the lines, Romeo." I give him a sideways stare. *Be nice, Penn.* I breathe deep. "Anyway, where are you going to school next year?"

"Ohio State." He pumps his fist in the air. "You?"

"Don't know yet. Probably Redwood College." I nod, already regretting asking the question. The truth is, I don't have a plan. I don't have a college plan or a future plan. I have a *nothing plan*. A plan to do *nothing*. Not that I don't want to do something, I do. I have a *nothing plan* to carry out the non-existent goal I don't have. I don't want to be *that* person, in her mid-20's going to high school parties, with the only thing going for me is a job at Mason Grocery in town. I need more than that.

Lucas grabs my hand. We stop walking as he smoothly maneuvres his hand around my waist and pulls me closer.

Huh. Not bad.

He gently lifts my chin toward his mouth.

I let him.

"Penn, you're mysterious and a little, what's the word, unconventional? That's what I find totally hot about you. Since we were kids, you always seemed to be a million miles away but you get it, you know? You're smart and hot." He smirks and continues, "I know you're trying to make Jesse jealous and I'm fine with that."

Maybe the alcohol decreases my inhibitions. Maybe it's the fact that, secretly, I want it to be Jesse I'm kissing, but either way, I fall into his kiss.

I need this.

I wonder what it would be like to kiss Jesse. His lips are warm and soft. *Are Jesse's the same? Would he kiss me the same way Lucas is kissing me right now? Would Jesse kiss me with more urgency? More passion?*

My arms fall to my sides.

This isn't my first kiss. My first kiss was Jeffery Sanders at Kendra's fifteenth birthday party. We played seven minutes in heaven and, once again, it was disastrous. *Awful, really.* It was wet and messy. I felt the need to towel off when we finished. His tongue went everywhere but in my mouth. I think it was Jeff's first kiss too. When we finished, I felt like I received a facial from a Bassett hound versus a kiss.

Lucas operates on a completely different level. His soft lips glide across mine and he pulls me closer.

He's a dad. I'm kissing a baby daddy.

I keep picturing Jesse. I'm so confused right now and I know it's the booze. I know it feels good, but so wrong because I have absolutely no feelings for Lucas. I'm letting him kiss me and I like it. A lot. My cheeks grow hot as my body responds.

I need to stop this. It's not right.

I pull away. "What about your baby and your baby momma?" I pause and try not to laugh about the way that came out. "I'm sorry, Lucas. I am. Truly, I didn't mean it. Well, not really. Sometimes I blurt out inappropriate comments." I stop talking because I know how stupid I sound. "I talk when it's silent. I don't like awkward silence." *Shut up, Penn.* I want to reach up and smack my own forehead.

He sighs deeply as his hands drop from my waist to his sides. He runs his hand through his short blonde hair. "Who told you?"

My head cocks. "Uh, I don't remember but, Lucas, we live in a tiny, tiny town. I'm pretty sure everyone knew the second you bagged her in Florida."

He laughs silently, rubbing his hands against his face, and looks toward the night sky. "Yeah. Hmmm." He laughs. "It's a boy. She, Amanda, is pregnant with my son. I didn't leave. Just so you know. I just…"

"You don't have to explain anything to me."

"Really? Because you asked." He places his hands on his hips and meets my gaze, clearly annoyed. "I didn't even know she was pregnant until her parents called mine. That's why I'm going to Ohio State. Amanda lives right outside Columbus. I'm going to do right by my son."

"So you and Amanda are…?"

"No. No way. I simply want to be part of Bentley's life. That's the name she, we, chose, I guess. My parents said I can't move until I finish high school."

I nod. We're still standing close. I feel his warm breath on my face when he talks. "That's commendable, Lucas. You know, you'd be quite the catch if you kept it in your pants more. You're kinda notorious. Girls talk."

He pauses and turns to face the ocean. I can see his jaw tighten. "You know why my parents divorced?" He pauses, waiting for a response, "Dad sleeps with his much younger secretary. Dad leaves mom. Mom is absolutely devastated."

"Lucas. You don't have to be the kind of guy your dad is." I say, without any emotional attachment.

"I saw my mom die emotionally. I heard her crying, in her bedroom, for months. If I keep it simple, no one gets hurt." He shrugs.

"Are you going to be *your* dad, or someone Bentley can look up to?"

This strikes a chord with him. He reacts as though I've punched him in the gut.

"Stevens, if you do not back away from her now you will wish you had."

I turn to see Jesse standing ten feet from us on a sand dune. My insides come alive with voracity. I need him.

A sleepy grin spreads across Lucas's face as he turns around.

"Come on man, aren't you here with somebody else?" Lucas says, motioning toward Vanessa, who's just joined the crowd.

Jesse's aqua eyes glow under the moonlight, beneath his cap.

I tilt my head slightly. I've never seen Jesse's eyes shine so brightly.

"What? You gonna kick my ass now, farm boy?" Lucas blurts out.

"Come on, Lucas. Don't do this. Just stop." I pull on his arm. It's stiff, rock hard, and not budging.

A grin appears on Jesse's face. "You want an ass beating, Stevens?"

"What? You want some of me, Jesse? I'm right here," Lucas says.

Vanessa grabs for Jesse's arm but he avoids her with ease. She stares at Lucas and me. I return a condescending, fake smile.

"It would not be fair. I would kill you and then have to tell your parents. I like your parents, so I am going to let you live tonight," Jesse says with satisfaction.

"Boy, you're a cocky son-of-a-," says Lucas, clearly flustered, puffing his chest out and walking toward Jesse. They're like two alpha males fighting over their female. I watched it on the Discovery Channel.

Jesse shoots down the sand dune toward Lucas.

"Grow up, you two!" I yell. Jesse and Lucas are now on each other as I watch the melee.

With one swift movement, Lucas's fist comes hurling toward Jesse's face, smashing his nose.

I scream.

Jesse doesn't budge. He barely moves as a smirk spreads across his face. "Are you finished? Because I am about to rain punches on your face like a bad miracle."

"Jesse. No." A voice comes from the shadows.

Everyone looks into the darkness where the voice originated, everyone except Jesse.

Jesse looks to Lucas. "Punch me again, Stevens. I will drop you so fast your feet will ask where you went."

"Lay it on me, Jesse." Lucas raises his fists.

"No, Jesse," The quiet, calm voice from the shadows sounds again.

Jesse touches his nose where Lucas's fist made contact. "You got lucky, Stevens," Jesse whispers as his jaw tightens and he pops his neck.

Jesse peels his eyes away from Lucas. His eyes, I notice, are back to normal. He looks at me. Just like that, the world disappears. The distant beat of music is gone. The sound of the waves crashing on the shore grows silent.

"I'm out," Lucas throws his hands in the air. "Penn," he pauses, "thank you. For everything." He smiles as he looks at Jesse. *"Real fun,* call me when you don't have this psycho following you around, huh?" He makes his way back to the party.

Jesse's eyes remain fixed on mine.

"What was that all about?" I whisper, "What are you doing? I don't get you." Let's be honest, deep down, every girl wants the boy of her dreams to do two things: chase her and fight for her. Would I ever be caught dead saying this out loud? *Not. Ever.* "Who's the dude in the shadows?" I look over to his silhouette. "Your entourage?"

Vanessa, still on the dune, is watching closely. "Jesse, come on," she pleads.

"Your puppy's calling for you," I say.

"Jesse, we must go," the voice in the shadows repeats. Again, I look in the direction of the voice, but only make out a silhouette of someone extremely tall.

"What gives?" I look from the silhouette back to Jesse. I pause. Jesse is now only inches from me. My heart starts to hammer against my chest. I feel the heat radiating off his body.

I swallow hard. I don't move. I don't breathe. I don't speak. I don't think I *can* speak.

"Jesse. Let us go." The voice in the shadows demands.

Jesse smiles and gently pushes a strand of hair out of my face. I feel his thumb slide across my cheek.

Please, knees, don't fail me now.

He slowly lowers his lips to my ear as if he's going to say something. I feel his breath on my neck. He doesn't say anything. He simply lets go and disappears with the shadow from the darkness.

I'm not sure I can move. I give myself a minute. Once I recover, I look to see what direction they went, but they are gone.

I look above the dune, toward the party and find Vanessa still staring at me. Hate oozes from every pore on her body. She flips me off, turns and walks back to the party.

"Now I'm the bad guy." I plop to the sand, facing the ocean.

"You ready?" I hear Kendra's voice behind me.

"Like two hours ago," I say.

She grabs my hands to pull me up.

Sunday September 9th 7:42 a.m.

As I rehash last night's events, I focus on the conversation Kendra and Jesse had. It went unnoticed by everyone else, but I know them best, and there was something more to the conversation than Kendra let on. The more I think about it, the angrier I become. They are hiding something, I'm sure of it. What it is, I'm not sure, but I will find out.

The anger burns, growing like a sore that won't heal. I feel an urgent need to know what they are hiding. *Why wouldn't Kendra tell me what the heck is going on? It's not like her. What would she talk to Jesse about? They both turned to look at me, I'm not stupid. They saw me and I saw them.*

I pick up my phone and text Kendra: Meet me at the cemetery in 10. Need 2 talk.

I throw my hair in a ponytail, put on some pants and brush my teeth. She dropped me off at home last night, refusing to stay. She never stays. She said she had some bizarre phobia about spending the night in other people's homes. I've never spent the night with her either. She claims Francis gets too weirded out.

I walk to the cemetery. The leaves are beginning to turn their vibrant oranges, yellows, and reds. I squeeze through the wrought-iron gates and hike to the top of the hill. Pacing back and forth, I debate using the butt-chewing method of information extraction or the ever popular tearful-begging approach. When she doesn't arrive five minutes later I plop down in the damp grass. As the morning dew begins to soak through my pants, I realize she's silently standing a few feet away.

I jump to my feet, nearly wetting myself in the process.

How did she get up here without my seeing her, or hearing her? We stare at each other. She's not saying anything.

"What the crap, Kendra?" I yell.

She looks at me, still silent.

Her eyes are filled not with confusion or anger, but concern. She walks quietly to me and hands me a coffee.

"Thanks," I say, sitting down again.

She sits down next to me. "Do you know what that was last night?"

"Yes," I yell, cutting her off, "it's called a secret. Then you feel you have to lie to me about it when I know you and Jesse were talking about me."

She repeats herself. "Do you know what that was last night? That feeling that overcame you in your home, before the party?"

I stare, unable to answer. *How did this so quickly turn back to me? Does she think I'm crazy? Maybe she does. Maybe my irrational fears are becoming too much to handle. Maybe this is where she has an intervention and has me committed.*

Wait. Is she baiting me?

Kendra's face turns white.

She thinks I'm nuts and she's ready to deliver the news that 'they think I might be happier in a lockdown facility someplace out in the woods.

I know it's bad because she's not speaking. She looks scared, she's afraid of me.

I've lost it. The cheese has officially slid off my cracker. "Please say something, Kendra, because your expression is starting to freak me out." I try to stand but she holds me down.

"We need to talk," she says, but she's on the phone?

She is on the phone?!

"Yeah. Now. Meet you in five. Jo's." Kendra puts her phone in her back pocket. "We need to go. There is a lot we need to talk about."

"I'm not crazy, Kendra."

"I know you are not crazy." Her stare is hard but not from pity or anger. *It's fear.* "Look, we need to get back to Jo's, like, two minutes ago." Kendra looks at her phone then to me. "Come on."

CHAPTER 7

Reality in Pieces

Sunday, September 9th 8:02 a.m.

"Kendra. Stop. Tell me some truth. Give me something," I plead, trying my best to hide my fear while keeping pace with her.

"Honestly, Penn, even I am having a hard time telling the truth from the lies." She pauses when she sees the look I'm giving her. The, *I'm not buying it* look.

"You want to know what I know?" I say as we continue toward my house.

I spew.

"I know I thought I could trust you. I thought I could trust Jesse. I know last night changed that. I know I saw the two of you talking, seemingly about me. Now I know neither of you will admit to me what that conversation was about." I grab her, turning her to face me, but she doesn't react. "It's draining, Kendra. It really is. Then, I think about all *this crap*. I think about how weird it is I feel like an outsider after all these years. I think how messed up I am. I'm messed up in so many ways, Kendra. I've done things I'm not proud of." I pause, panicked, scared I've gone too far. I pause because Frankie is the first thing that enters my mind. *His screams, his cries for help. His agony.* I want to tell her about Frankie but I don't. I don't tell her about Frankie because I'm terrified, not of the punishment I might receive, but of what she'll think of me. "Kendra, right now I need you to tell me the truth. Please."

She wants to speak but she doesn't. Her unspoken words tell me even more.

She can't look at me. She's staring at her feet as we walk, her eyes filling with tears. "Kendra," I whisper, wanting to comfort her. "I'm a big girl, tell me." I think about reaching out to her but I know Kendra and she knows me. We're here for each other. There's something to be said for silence. It's comforting, in some small way, to be with another person and not feel the need to speak. That's true comfort. I know Kendra needs this right now. Whatever she is thinking, mixed with the fear I see in her eyes, is reason enough for me and I can accept that.

That is truth.

We push through the front door. The house is quiet and calm.

"In here," The voice of Aunt Jo echoes from the great room.

We turn and head toward the living room.

Jesse stands facing the big bay windows and doesn't acknowledge us. What is he doing here? "Jo?" I call, looking for my aunt. "I thought…"

I see a man I don't know, yet his face seems familiar. He becomes an immediate distraction. I eye his long, lean, six-foot-four frame starting at his black boots. I work my way to his lean waist and his un-tucked black polo. The three buttons at the top lie open, exposing a thick black tattoo line starting at the base of his neck. His facial features separate him from the boys my age. His chiselled jaw, hazel eyes, perfect nose and five o'clock shadow give me reason to breathe deeply. A scar, starting at the top of his right eyelid, traces over and down his cheek. Its prominence makes me wonder how I missed it moments ago. I notice now, though, he is speaking.

Oh crap…he's speaking. To me. *Penn, look into his eyes.*

I meet his gaze and my insides melt.

He hesitates at first, but walks to me like he's trying to be delicate with me.

Holy hell. I hope my hands aren't sweating. I try to be cool. I casually – at least I think it's casual – wipe my hands on my pants.

He holds his hand out. His voice is low, and dark. Something in his eyes is familiar, yet, I can't place him. I honestly don't think I would ever forget his face.

I swallow hard.

Crap. "What?" My face is hot. *Crap.* "Sorry. What?" I look awkwardly into his eyes and lose any chance at regaining my train of thought.

He gives me a cunning smile, one of understanding for my current condition. "Penelope, my name is Church LeBlanc."

He stares at me like I'm some sort of endangered species and it makes me uncomfortable. His crystal-hazel eyes lock on mine. He doesn't move. *I don't even think he's breathing.*

Immediately, his demeanour enchants me. It doesn't help that his ridiculously handsome face is killing off my feminine sensibilities.

As our hands touch, his face softens but his grip stays firm. A sense of relief registers in his eyes as though he is the one struggling with this inner turmoil.

Come on, Penn. You've met attractive men before.

Jo walks over to me and takes my hand from Church saying, "Baby. Come here. There are urgent matters we must discuss with you at once." She pauses as another man steps out from behind Church.

Kendra rolls her eyes. "You had to bring him with you?" She looks to Church.

"I am right here, Kendra. You realize I can hear every word you say? I may not have a beating heart, but I am not deaf," replies the man.

Not have a beating heart?

"Penn, this is Carmine *Le-douche-blanc*," Kendra says, flopping down in a chair.

"Oh, there is no need to be formal, Kendra. We are all friends here," says Carmine, smirking.

"Kendra, please, this is not about you and Carmine," Jo scolds.

"Hello, Penelope. It is good to see you again," Carmine says, ignoring Kendra's comments.

I awkwardly shake his hand, its cold feel takes me by surprise. *Do I have a fever or something? Why is everyone so cold?*

"Have we met before?" I ask.

He looks to Jo, confused by my question. "Have we not told her yet?" Carmine smiles mischievously. "Ah, stupendous. This will be a delight." His eyes grow to the size of saucers. He has the same hazel eyes as Church.

"Penn, come and sit." Jo pats the spot next to her.

Obeying, I sit. "I am going to get straight to the point." Her hand takes mine. I look around the room and find Jesse still staring out the window. Church's hypnotic, hazel eyes made me forget more than Jesse. I started the morning angry with Kendra and Jesse for keeping secrets.

Now I'm afraid they are having me committed. Kendra is still in the chair, popping her knuckles. She does that when she's nervous.

"That icy cold blast you felt?" she asks.

"Yes. What about it?" I look to Kendra.

"Are you kidding me? Is this an intervention? You all think I'm crazy, don't you? Are these guys here to take me away?" I start to panic.

"Heaven's no, baby girl." Jo laughs awkwardly. "We all know you are not crazy. What you felt was real."

"This is not right," Jesse whispers angrily. He chuckles to himself and shakes his head. "Right now? You are going to tell her right now? We do not even know if it was him." He looks at Jo. "Unbelievable." He combs his hands through his hair in frustration.

"Jo, can we please get to the part where Penelope is being hunted by Vacavious? All this back and forth is only prolonging the inevitable." He places his hands on his hips. When he does this, I notice he possesses the same tattoo Church does.

His mouth snaps shut. He wants to speak, he tries to speak, but he can't. It looks as though someone glued his lips together. He glares at Kendra. She smiles as she whispers and her finger dances in the air.

Jesse smiles a devious smile. "Nice, Boots."

I cock my head and look at my friend, my best friend, whom I've known since we were eight. The best friend I thought I knew everything about. The best friend who did something I cannot explain to a man I just met but she apparently knows well enough to despise. I look at Carmine. His lips are sealed but his mouth is still moving.

Kendra grins at Jesse then looks at me. She winces, clearly having done something she should not have, at least not in front of me. "*Crap,*" she whispers. She looks away, guilt in her eyes. She sighs and says, "Carmine, if you so much as breathe another word that is rude, crude or just plain mean, I will do torturous things to you. Got me?" With a swish of her finger, Carmine lets out a huge breath.

"Crazy witch," I hear him mutter.

I must have looked on the verge of losing my sanity as concern replaced the anger in Kendra eyes. Concern replaced the anger in her eyes. I need the truth right now. I need the truth because I feel like my stability is teetering somewhere between going and gone. *I need the truth.*

Kendra rises from the chair and walks to me, kneeling in front of me. She doesn't touch me. She kneels down and looks into my eyes. "Penn, I need you to know that once you have heard us out, once all has been said, please know we are doing everything we can to keep you safe. There are reasons we waited this long to tell you. Please understand." She looks down at my hand. It's shaking. I see it's shaking but I can't feel it.

I try to swallow but my mouth is so dry my lips are sticking to my teeth. My hands begin to sweat. "What is going on?" I look at Jo who's staring straight at me.

Silence.

Silence.

Silence.

Silence.

"Carmine? Who's Vacavious?" I ask him because I know he will tell me the truth, no matter how bad it is. I ask him because he doesn't care about protecting me from the truth. "Everyone, besides this guy," I point to Carmine, "is tiptoeing around this. Stop protecting me."

"Smart girl." He laughs, shaking his long ashen finger in my direction. "Ah, where must I begin? He is murderous. He is dark. He kills without reason. He is the leader of the evil that lurks in the shadows of the worlds. He is a sadistic monster who finds pleasure in taking the lives of innocents for fun. He has been collecting your kind for centuries. Basically, he wants you dead and we are not sure why."

"M-my kind?"

Carmine looks toward Jo. "I take it you did not give her the journal yet?"

Jo pulls her hand back and slaps Carmine upside the head. "You are such a sweet young man, Carmine, but sometimes you speak when you should not." Her stare is cold as she turns back to me.

Jo takes my hands in hers. "You were born with a powerful, powerful gift, Penelope." She positions my hands over hers as I've done so many times at the hospital when I'm healing patients.

"What are you talking about?" *There is no way she knows.*

"Penelope, I know." She looks me straight in the eyes. "I know you can heal people."

"You knew?" My voice a whisper. "All along you knew?" The thought resonates in my brain. *Wait. Wait. Jo knew. She knows.*

Jo nods. *Mind blown, she's always known.*

"You made me go to the hospital." My head spins as I come to the realization Jo sent me there because she wanted me to practice. "It makes sense now."

Jo shakes her head as our eyes connect. "Honey, you are the Five. The last Sanguine Nighmerianotte knows to be alive." She methodically provides the information she knows, always cautious with my feelings. "You are a healer and infinitely sacred to Nighmerianotte. You are rare and unique. You also possess an extremely rare blood type. In Nighmerianotte you are called the "Black Five."

"Stop. What?" I try desperately to understand what she tells me but nothing makes sense. *Maybe I am going crazy.* Nighmerianotte, Black

Five, Sanguine, none of this makes any sense. Who are these men who claim to know me better than I know myself? They know Jo but I've never heard her speak to or of them.

"You were told Nadine adopted you, but we never discussed your birth parents."

"Stop, Jo. Stop all of this." Fear and anger collide, clouding my thoughts even more.

"Penelope, I know this is a lot to take."

"My parents?" I whisper as my eyes fill with tears. "My parents?" My voice cracks as my emotions get the best of me.

Jo stops, looks down, and rubs her hands together awkwardly. Her eyes meet mine.

"You want to know what Nadine had to say about my parents? What she told me?" I swallow hard, trying to control my emotions. *You need to know this Jo. What she put me through.* "Nadine told me they were drug addicts and traded me for a dime bag. She said she took me in because I was the ugliest baby she'd ever seen and she felt sorry for me. Those parents, you mean?" The thought of Nadine takes me back to when I was eight. They need to know what I endured. Anger seethes from every pore. "Her lifeless body lie on the couch. I had to roll her over so I wouldn't have to stare at her face. I still see her face in my nightmares. Her blue face and the small trickle of blood that seeped from her nose still haunt me. I sat with her dead body for hours until social services and the police department stormed the room to 'save' me." I glare at all of them, unable to hold my anger in check any longer. "I guess you're going to say you all had something to do with that, right? Did you all watch as my childhood died with Nadine on that couch? Did you all look on as the doctors dissected my brain to determine the long-term damage caused by Nadine's mental abuse? Did you pat yourselves on the back when they determined my mental state was fair, a job well done?" My anger turns to bitterness. Nadine died the day after Frankie. They never recovered his body and now I have a clue as to why.

Jo's lower lip quivers as I see her eyes well up. I know this has to hurt her. She continues anyway. "Your biological mother was eccentric. She was talented. She was beautiful. She was born a Nighmerian and she loved you."

"Be quiet!" I yell.

She continues, tears now streaming down her cheeks. "Your mother, Annalisa San Angelo, was a powerful witch. Nighmerianotte is a world unlike the one you have grown to know. It is magic and it is powerful, but it is dark. For the past one hundred years, it has been especially dark. It has become a place of death and fear."

"Can't you hear me? I said stop! I don't want to hear any more of your lies." I spent the last seventeen years questioning why my parents did what they did, questioning my own life. Asking why I was put on this damn Earth if no one wanted me.

"If you want to live, Black Blood, then you had better shut up and listen. Jo is trying to save your life," Carmine's states, re-entering the conversation.

"Let her be, Tick. Penn has every right to feel this right now. Unfortunately, it does not mean anything will change." Kendra's voice grows softer as her eyes meet mine, as if she's trying to break the news more gently. Fear and anger fester inside me like an infection, raging through my body.

I hear Jesse sigh and mutter something under his breath. His anger is evident in his stance and his words.

Betrayal.

"Penn, just listen. Please. We had our reasons for withholding this from you." Jo looks to the others, searching for something, anything to say. Church stands, eyes wide, staring at me with concern. Kendra and Jesse look helplessly at each other while Carmine stares at the floor, looking rather bored. "Hear us out."

I sit silently, nothing left to say, waiting for Jo to continue.

"Nighmerianotte is a place where immortals, the Nighmerians, live. It's a world where they can walk the streets as we do in this world."

I am on the verge of shutting down as I try to make sense of all I'm being told.

"They are not living but they are not dead. They exist evermore." Jo pauses, seemingly to gauge my receptiveness of all she is telling me.

I laugh, not knowing how else to respond. I can't accept this, how could I possibly accept this? There are no words to express what I am feeling right now. What I do know is I can't stay here and listen to this crap anymore.

"I've changed my mind," I announce. "I think an intervention is a great idea! You there," I point to Church, "I'm ready to go with you to the funny farm." I go to stand up but Carmine steps forward shoves me back down in the chair. Kendra gives him the stink eye and holds up her finger. He immediately releases me and takes several steps back with his hands in the air. I sigh, looking at Jo as she continues.

"Your father was human, a limite. Which means you have mixed bloodlines. You are half mortal and half immortal, a black blood."

My heart skips as she uses that word, a word I am unfamiliar with. "A limite?"

"Limite is a person from the mortal world, a human. Nighmerians refer to us as limiti. It means we are limited: limited in our abilities, lifespans, basically everything.

94

"I went back to New Orleans to empty out a safe deposit box he kept for you." Aunt Jo walks to the cabinet in the far corner of the room. "This," she says, returning to my side, "is for you, a journal from your father. It will explain everything, Penelope." The brown leather-bound book has a belt holding the two covers together. The massive pile of pages between the two covers looks old and weathered.

I stare at the stack of pages, words from my father, written in his own hand. They are not the words of a crack head. I don't know what to think. I thought I was the result of a one-night stand. All this time I felt unwanted by my biological parents.

"Why didn't my father save me from Nadine? Why didn't he love me?"

"Read this." Jo pushes the journal to me, her lip quivering.

"We had to keep you safe, Penelope," Church says.

I lash out. "You thought Nadine's home would be the safest place for me? Seriously?" I yell. "You put me with a drug addicted alcoholic in the worst part of town and thought it safe?" I stand up.

Church steps forward. "I take full responsibility, Penelope, as the head of your security detail, it was my decision to place you with Nadine. It was the safest place for you at the time. For what it is worth, you were never in harm's way. We kept a close watch on you at all times." His eyes fill with something. *Guilt.* He looks away.

"Security detail? What are you talking about?" I shake my head. "What is he talking about, Jo?"

Church nods and explains, "Yes. Carmine, Kendra, Jesse, and I are a security detail assigned specifically for your protection."

"Wait. What? How can Jesse and Kendra look after me if they are the same age as me? Obviously they weren't wandering the streets in

Santa Maria when we were children." *The jig is up. Gotcha.* I cross my arms.

"This is coming out all wrong. Penn, look, I am a witch and Jesse," she looks across the room, "Jesse is a sentinel." She sighs again and combs her thumb and pinkie across her eyebrows, staring at the ground. "I perform an aging charm to keep us aging at your pace. When you were eight, we were eight. When you were fifteen, we were fifteen." She stares at the floor, searching for a better way to explain what is happening.

This is total crap and I'm done. This stopped being funny about five minutes ago and now it's just sad. Game over," I declare.

Before I can escape the madness, Kendra gently places her hand on my knee. She closes her eyes and chants something under her breath repeating it several times. With a flick of her wrist, crystals fall around her head like snow, sprinkling her entire body with flecks of light.

"See," she says in her eight-year-old voice. "I truly am a witch. Everything we are telling you is true."

I sit in shock, utter disbelief holding me hostage in my chair. My mind tells me to run, escape this madness, but my body refuses to listen. All I can do is stare as the life I once knew to be true disappears before my eyes. Everything and everyone I thought to be fixed in time and memory now lay in question.

"Snack cakes for life!" she says and then lets out a laugh.

I need something real, something tangible. I reach out and touch Kendra's cheek. It feels real so maybe it is. I pinch her cheek.

She swats my hand away and rubs her rosy cheek. "I hate when you do that."

I now know what it is to be utterly lost. I lean back in my chair, absolutely speechless.

"Calm down, Penn, everything is going to be fine. Breathe." She takes several deep breaths, coaching me through my mental break. Every breath brings with it the realization that this is real. The little eight-year-old girl in front of me is Kendra. I can see her before me. I can touch her, talk to her, and even hurt her.

"Are you okay now? Kendra asks, her face full of concern.

I nod, incapable of speech.

With a snap of her fingers, she transforms into seventeen-year-old Kendra.

My breathing quickens and I feel lightheaded. My vision becomes hazy as I begin to sway in the chair. I'm going to pass out.

Jesse turns from the window, "Stop. Enough. Look at her." He bobs his head in my direction. "Do you not see what we are doing to her?"

"Jesse, she must know all of it." Church pauses. "As much as it pains her."

"Look vamp, *I know her*. I know her because I have been with her every day for years. It is more than I can say for you."

Vamp. As in *vampire?* I look at Church. His face appears chiseled and handsome, like a statue of a Greek God. I notice the scar next to his eye again. It's no thicker than a half an inch and about two inches long. Could be anything, though. Maybe a dog bit him or maybe he was in some sort of accident.

Or maybe a werewolf?

"Jessence, do not let your temper get the best of you. Did they not teach you that in the academy?" Church says.

"Leave it to a sentinel to develop feelings for their charge. I thought the academy took care of those feelings?" Carmine cocks his head.

Every muscle in Jesse's body is shaking. "I have the strength to kill you right now and the temptation is growing." Jesse tries to calm himself, his fists clenched at his sides.

"You would not do that, sentinel. It is against the rules to kill a first class Nighmerian." Carmine's tone is drenched with mockery. "Besides, the elixir should be taking effect soon and these feelings you have will no longer exist."

First class Nighmerian? Elixir? "What the hell is going on?" I yell, but they continue as if I'm a soundless voice.

"We are not in Nighmerianotte anymore, Carmine. Nighmerianotte does not exist," he huffs, "not the way we remember it. Vacavious turned our world into a hell where evil reigns. They have all gone mad." His body is wound tight.

I turn my anger toward Jesse. "Since when do you care about my wellbeing? Since when have you had a say in my life?" My words visibly hurt him as he slowly turns to me. He smirks.

"Jackson, just so we are clear, I have always had a say in your life, and," his voice becomes even lower, "I have *always* had your best interest at heart. Believe it or not."

"Jessence, she does not have a choice now, does she?" Church's words are purposeful.

"This is on you, then. We are supposed to protect her. The Demi have entrusted her life to us. You, of all people, should know that." Jesse says, disgust filling his words.

"And you, of all people, should know I have always had Penelope's wellbeing in mind." Church counters.

"Are you sure about that?" Jesse turns back and glares at Church. "Because there was a dark period in your life where you did not."

Church's knuckles turn white but his calm demeanor prevails. "I will let that statement go since, perhaps, this is not you and the elixir has yet to take full effect, but this is the one, and only, time." His eyes narrow as he and Jesse stare at each other, neither backing down.

"I am leaving." Jesse turns and walks to me before going. His stare exposes me, my every vulnerability. There's so much more to the look he's giving me, his eyes penetrating and forceful, wanting even. It's a long moment before he looks away.

"Jo, I will call you later."

With that, he leaves, slamming the door behind him.

I take deep breaths, trying to gather my thoughts.

There is silence for the first time since arriving home. "Are you supernatural, Jo?" I blurt out. "Who else is supernatural?" My voice is calm and monotone. I feel empty, devoid of all emotion. I am spent yet have so many questions.

Like, zombies?

The undead? Not dead but kind of dead.

Ghosts?

I'm freaking myself out. *Stop, Penn.* "So what is it? Are you dead or alive? Do you kill people?" I pause because I know this sounds absolutely bizarre. "Come on, joke's over. Everyone spill," I say, my adrenaline rising once more.

"Actually, the correct term is 'Nighmerian' or 'immortal'. Preferably, Nighmerian. Supernatural includes a whole other lot we do not associate with," Carmine says. "Yes. We kill people, all the time. We feed off warm bodies. You know, the living ones." He licks his lips as his eyes grow brazen.

"You are disgusting and your sense of humor is absolutely terrible." Kendra rolls her eyes, still trying to be empathetic toward me.

"No." Jo places her hands in her lap, breaking eye contact, answering my initial question. "I am your Sentry."

"What's that, exactly?" I huff as I cross my arms and shake my head.

Unbelievable.

"When an immortal child is born in Nighmerianotte, the mother signs the credence, a type of birth certificate, and she always assigns a guardian should something happen to both parents and they cannot care for the child. The Demi were quite surprised when your credence came through and they saw what you were. They were more surprised that I, your Sentry, was of the mortal world. They were hesitant to abide by the Sentry assignment, but it is law. If the credence is signed, it cannot be changed."

I look up.

"Your parents left you with the Demi, knowing fully well they would take care of you."

"Why were they upset you were my sentry?"

Jo lowers her voice. "I am of the mortal world. Never in the existence of Nighmerianotte has a Nighmerian child, especially one of your type, been placed in the mortal world, much less with a mortal sentry."

CHAPTER 8

Insanity

"Are you going to read the journal?" Kendra asks, plopping down on my bed and resting her hands behind her head. I push the journal aside.

"No. I'm going to wait until everyone's gone, dump it in the bath tub, and set it on fire."

Kendra smiles. "You want to talk about it?"

"No." I lie down next to her. "Let's not talk about whatever just happened, and do something normal. Like homework?"

Kendra nods and grabs my anatomy book. I start on my English assignment.

"Wait." I cringe. "You don't have to do homework." There's salt in my pitch. "I mean, right? You're a witch, right? How could I have been so stupid?!" I smack my forehead with my binder.

Kendra shrugs. "I know it is hard to believe. Want to know the truth?"

"Not really." I stare at my notebook, contempt resonating in my voice. I'm still mad at her, at everyone. I'm still not sure if I'm mad because they kept all of this from me or because I have no idea whether any of it is true. I feel like the butt of some massive joke, waiting for the reveal when everyone tells me how foolish I was to even consider all of this possible.

"Well, I am going to give it to you anyway." She takes a deep breath then speaks. "For the record, I am not sorry. We had to do what we had to do to keep you safe, to keep you alive. It hurts to see you in such turmoil. About your parents, I mean." Her voice trails off as she stares at me, willing me to understand this whole mess. Casually, she looks back to her book and then to me again. "This whole homework and going to school thing?" She gives me a sideways glance. "I kind of like it. It gives me a sense of normalcy. It makes me feel like I am a part of something. Do not get me wrong, the students at Mason High are ridiculous, but I did not have this when I went through the Academy. It was strict, and regimented, like military school. There were no dances, no parties, nothing like that."

"Academy?" My heart softens a little.

Kendra points to the journals. "Everything you need to know, Penn, will be in there. Like it or not, believe it or not, this is your reality now. You have a choice, Penelope Jackson. Are you going to accept this reality or sit here, hoping it is not true, and wait for Vacavious to find you. The Penn I know would fight. She would do anything it takes to survive." She pauses. "You cannot tell me after all you have been through, you would not stand for what you believe in. I have always known you to stand up for the underdog, to stand for what you believe in. This fight is not yours alone, it is ours. Together we must stand for who we are and defend our world. So," she shrugs, as she puts her ear buds in her ears, "are you in or out? The choice is yours. It is really that simple."

Her words play repeatedly in my mind. I never saw myself as a fragile person until this exact moment. I replay each word, analyzing them like a poem I am required to explain.

We must stand for who we are. Fight or no fight, this is your reality.

What is reality? Until this morning I thought I knew, thought I had a firm grasp on it. My biggest concern when I woke this morning was finding out the secret my best friends were keeping from me. Now that I know what that secret is, my biggest concern, if I am to believe my friends, is my very survival.

Twenty minutes pass as I stare at the journal on my bed. I contemplate my options, concluding there is but one. I have to read his journal, my father's journal. I dreamed for so many years of having the opportunity to meet my real parents. That opportunity now lay but inches from me. Is it even possible to avoid reading it? Do I even have a choice or has that been taken from me as well? I throw my pen down and gaze out the window. A chill shoots through me from my spine to my feet.

It's him again.

He's standing on a branch in the massive redwood tree outside my bedroom window, leaning against the trunk with impeccable balance.

His pale skin stands out against the dark red bark. He's close enough I can see his face but not his features. I know he can see me as he focuses on my window, on me. I set my laptop aside, careful not to disturb Kendra, lost in her own world, her ear buds barely visible. I walk to the window. Like a scene out of the Matrix, he leaps effortlessly to another branch, twenty feet above. I follow him with my eyes. His grace is undeniable.

With strength and power, he descends the giant tree, branch by branch. He sails through the field that separates us, as if floating above the ground. There's something about him that is both terrifying and desirable. I stand in awe as I watch him cross the field.

He stops abruptly as a pack of dogs break his stride.

Without thinking, I tear out of my room, down the stairs, and through the back door. I don't think, I simply run to him. *Why? I have no idea.*

I jump the porch, skipping the stairs, and run into the open field where I last saw Church.

Kendra is already at Church's side.

To the left, I see the pack of dogs, much larger now that I am on their level from the ground. They no longer appear to be dogs, their size being closer to that of wolves. Who am I kidding, their size is closer to that of a car than a dog. If they are wolves, they are overgrown, seriously overgrown. Still reeling from the revelations of the day, I can form no logical assumption as to what I am running into. Yet I run.

"Pietro and his pack of overgrown mongrels," Kendra whispers in my ear, not breaking eye contact with their leader.

"Who's Pietro?" I whisper back.

Three shadows emerge from the house, quickly moving toward us.

The pack begins to surround us, snarling, circling. It is clear they are wolves, however, what kind I have no idea. There shouldn't even be wolves here, not in this town, not in these woods.

As the three shadow figures move into view, I am able to identify them, at least two of them. Carmine and Jo join our group. The third is the yet unnamed man who drew Jesse away from his beach brawl.

My mind clearing, I make the leap from the world I know to the one I am expected to accept. The newest citizens of our small town must be werewolves. Why shouldn't they be, a vampire shook my hand just hours ago while a witch looked on.

The black werewolf snaps loudly as he lunges forward. As he does, the man in the robe grabs his throat. The werewolf yelps, twisting violently to escape the man's grasp.

"Pietro, you must be lost," he says, releasing his throat and allowing him to regain his footing. Pietro holds his ground, slowly returning to his human form like some sort of film special effect. The werewolves surrounding him do not move. I count them. Eight in number, they outnumber us by two. This isn't good.

"We had to see for ourselves, Lennon." He grins. "The Black Blood, the Five." He leans around shadow man, Lennon, to get a glimpse but Church steps in front of me.

"She smells amazing." He sucks in a huge breath as his pack sniffs the air.

"What do you want, Pietro? Do you not have some dirty work to attend to?"

"Curiosity got the best of me." He laughs, shrugging his shoulders.

I'm in the middle of a circle formed by the others, a human barrier of sorts.

"I ask again, Pietro, what do you want?" Lennon backs slowly away from the pack, tightening our circle.

"Merely a drop, that is all. Then we will be on our way."

Lennon laughs and then abruptly stops. "What is it you know? What have you been told?"

"Enough," Pietro says, tensing as if waiting for an ambush.

Lennon looks to Kendra. "Please, my dear girl, let me know what Pietro is truly doing here?" he asks, clearly agitated Pietro is wasting his time.

Kendra moves to the front of the circle and stands in front of Lennon. She locks eyes with Pietro who looks visibly shaken. I hear Carmine whisper behind me, "He looks Pietro-fied."

I smirk.

Pietro tries to look away but can't. His body is frozen, eyes locked on Kendra who chants something under her breath. Her words grow louder as she continues to chant. It's in Italian and it's beautiful. It's rhythmic, almost hypnotic.

The other werewolves try to move but they can't. They are paralyzed, stuck where their pads rest. They begin to howl as Pietro's head begins to shake vigorously.

Kendra's words grow in intensity and volume. Her body is taut, her shoulders hunched up to her ears.

The howls increase as Kendra's chanting grows louder.

Pietro screams as the howling of his pack reaches an agonizing level.

Then everything stops. It's silent.

It takes Kendra a minute to regain her senses. She turns to Lennon.

"Surprise, surprise, the usually rogue werewolves, up to no good. All he wants is a drop of Penn's blood and he is not leaving until he gets it."

As the words leave Kendra's lips, Pietro lunges at her, only to be met by Carmine's fist. He lands on his back but rights himself quickly. Carmine, Kendra, Jo and Lennon quickly surround me, tightening their protective circle even more, buffering me from Pietro and the pack.

"Pietro, I do not want to kill you. You know how easy it would be for me to do so. So please, take your pack and go." Lennon motions to the trees.

"What a beauty." Pietro licks his lips, exposing a purple tongue, still eyeing me up and down. "I'm not leaving until I get a drop from our Five." He uses the word "our" as though I belong to him, to all of them, like I'm a *thing*.

Church laughs. "Not a chance."

"Perfect, you first." He lunges for Church.

I get to him first. I grab a fistful of fur as he transitions back to a werewolf. I interrupt his leap, but end up flat on my back for my trouble. I try to catch my breath as he jumps on top of me, thrashing his huge canines inches from my throat.

I feel a switch turn on in my head as my mind takes hold of his. I feel my mind fuse with his as I squeeze, trying to make him hurt.

All I see is red.

My instinct to kill becomes stronger than my restraint. I squeeze harder as Pietro slumps over me, howling in agony. He cries louder and louder as I squeeze.

I think of Frankie again...*his screams*. Not even these memories can pull me out of the darkness I have entered. I proceed, unrestricted.

I love the feeling coursing through me, a euphoric feeling of invincibility. He howls for me to stop but his cries only make me want to squeeze tighter. I want to squeeze harder. I desire it, the feeling is addictive. Someone is yelling, someone who is not Pietro.

"Penn, stop. You need to stop!"

Then it's over.

With one last cry, he returns to his human form, dropping into a heap on the ground. Blood trickles from his mouth and nose.

Panic sets in.

Oh no. No. No. No. Not again.

A gentle tug on my arm draws me out of my daze. "Not bad, Five," Carmine says, stepping to my side. Church pulls me to him.

Please, let him live.

After a moment, Pietro moves his head. Lennon helps him to his feet. The werewolf wipes the blood from his mouth.

"I thought that was going to last forever." Pietro looks to Lennon and then to me, and smiles. "Penelope, my name is Pietro Luges. It is an honor to meet you." He extends his hand and bows as I back away from him and his pack. The pack, in wolf form, bow their heads in unison, as if I'm royalty.

This is awkward.

Jo puts both hands on my shoulders. "You just dropped one of the most powerful werewolves Nighmerianotte has ever known."

"She did a stellar job of it. I thought my brain was going to explode." Pietro moves his neck back and forth.

"Thank you, Pietro." Lennon nods.

"Wait. Are you kidding me?" My heart slams against my chest, anger coming on in full force. "You mean to tell me that was a test? I could have killed him!" My spine shivers as my mind drifts back to Frankie. I shake the memory from my head and look to the group as my chest heaves with anger.

"Oh, you could not have squeezed hard enough for that. Not with your lack of training." Carmine stops as he sees the look on my face.

"Shut up, Carmine," I snap. I turn to my detail. "Don't ever, EVER do that again. If you ever want to test me, you will ask me first. Nobody's life is worth that. Are we clear? " I annunciate every word, my tone slicing through the afternoon air.

"We serve the Demi. We have been waiting for you since we heard the rumors you survived." Pietro attempts to break the tension. "It has been a pleasure, Black Five."

Stop calling me that. My fists are in balls at my sides.

Pietro whistles and, just like that, the band of wolves disappears into the fog forming in the trees.

"Come on, let us go inside," says Jo. "Dinner is ready." She looks at Carmine and Church. "There are blood bags in the refrigerator in the barn." My jaw drops upon hearing this. Everyone else is acting like this is a normal occurrence. *Oh, now that the werewolves are gone, let's go eat, huh? Blood bags?*

Jo places her arm around me as we walk back to the house. "You are right, Penelope. We spent the last seventeen years making decisions for you. Now," she shrugs, "it is time we allow you to make your own choices."

I say nothing. It's unnerving discussing life and death in the same manner as the weather. *Try to murder this guy, would you? See how that goes? Don't worry though, we won't let you kill him.*

Is this part of my world now? A new norm where death is common-place and survival of the fittest is the prevailing belief system?

Jo continues, "The first time you use mind fusion, it has to be unintentional. It works in the same way your fight-or-flight response does. Until you learn to trigger it on your own, it must be activated by extreme stress. It has to grow from deep within you. It has to be a genuine reaction to trigger the process. We needed to trigger your gift before we could train you to use it. Only then can you transition to Nighmerianotte."

This isn't my first time. I already have one kill under my belt. It happened when I was eight when I should have been playing Barbie dolls and joining Girls Scouts.

"Penelope?" We're almost to the porch. I stop and turn. The man they called Lennon towers over me. I don't fully comprehend how tall he is until I'm standing next to him. He must be at least eight feet

///

tall. He raises his massive hand, and I take it. "My dear, Penelope, it is a pleasure." He beams. His voice is deep, articulate even. His neck is thick and his ashen face is narrow and weathered. His eyes retain a youthfulness his body has not known for years. "The last time I saw you, you were an infant. Your gifts are quite impressive. However, something tells me this was not your first time?" His eyebrows rise.

I meet his gaze, but neither confirm nor deny the accusation. Right now, I feel like a bomb exploded in the middle of my life.

"Penelope, this is Lennon." Church puts his hand on the small of my back, catching me by surprise. My posture straightens. He removes his hand as if sensing my reaction. He leans toward me and whispers in my ear, "He is a sentinel and Jesse's mentor."

We've met, I think to myself.

Lennon looks to Church and they exchange glances. Church nods as Lennon walks past the house toward town. "Does he know where he's going?" I ask.

Church laughs. "He always knows where he is going." His nearness makes me feel slightly uncomfortable and extremely intimidated.

Kendra's voice breaks Church's trance on me. "Carmine, the only thing I would save you from is yourself." Kendra stops when she gets to the top of the stairs and I can tell, by her reaction, she regrets the words already. *Is she trying to push him away?* She closes her eyes and shakes her head.

"I am merely asking, if I were burning alive, would you breathe life back into me?" Carmine stops.

"Carmine, I would not even pull your body out of the salt water if you were burning alive, so I most certainly would not breathe life back into you as that would require me to extinguish the flames. I would rather watch you burn." Kendra smiles indifferently.

"Where's Jesse? I mean, if you're my security detail, then, surely, he would have popped up, right? Oh wait. That's right. It was a trick to see what I can do."

Church looks into my eyes. "You like him exceedingly, it seems."

Why would I give an answer to that question? Especially to a total stranger? I can't hide the fact I care for Jesse, deeply, but I can hide the fact my attraction to him is only one small piece of the way I feel about him.

My actions this morning were a direct result of my feelings for Jesse. No matter how much I deny it, they are always lingering in the back of my mind.

I watch Church as he watches me. "Are you well, Penelope?"

Then there's this guy—Church.

"What? Who?" Lost in my own thoughts, I blush. All I can think about is the feel of Church's touch. Then I remember he is among the people responsible for shattering my world. My thoughts grow dark and cold, replaced by rage.

"Look, Penelope. I know you are hurt right now." He places his hands on my shoulders. My body goes tense as I feel his freezing hands through my shirt. He quickly removes them.

"What do you know about hurt? You're a vampire, right? I mean, you don't actually feel things." I want to make him hurt like I do.

Church's eyes narrow. "Let us go inside." He puts his arm around me and pulls me toward the door.

I shrug his hand away. "I know the way." *Nice, Penn, real grown up of you.*

Church stops and, as if in slow motion, he pushes me to the wall placing his hands on either side of me. Caught off guard, I cock my head and stare at him. I can't get passed the way his eyes burn into mine. I feel like a rare gem, or oddity, something he's never seen before.

"What are you staring at?" I hide the feelings my body threatens to expose. My heart begins to pound as he holds me captive.

Church laughs. "Let us go sit down. There is more you need to know."

He removes his hands from the wall. Grabbing my hand, he leads me to the dining room. The table is set for five. Our drink cups are preset, two filled with milk and two filled with a thick red substance. My stomach wretches at the thought of blood in a cup waiting to be consumed. The disgust registers on my face.

Carmine, Kendra and Jo are already seated at the table. Church prepares to pull my chair out saying, "Allow me." Instead, our hands touch and I feel myself drawn to him. I look away as he slowly removes his hands and I pull out the chair. "I got it." I refuse to swoon over someone I scarcely know, regardless of the strange magnetism drawing us together.

We sit in silence as three of us scarf down Jo's famous chicken noodle casserole.

Carmine reaches for his glass and slowly takes a sip. The thick substance oozes down the side of the glass, like tomato paste, leaving a ring around the glass as he places it back down on the table. I try not to make a face. I try to imagine it's a raspberry protein shake, not blood. I can't get the thought out of my head.

It's blood. "Where did the blood come from?" I ask, taking a bite of the casserole, adding normalcy to our conversation. I move it around in my mouth, attempting to swallow without throwing up.

Carmine laughs. "Cute, fuzzy, farm animals. We simply snap their necks and drain their blood. We preserve it in the freezer in the barn. You should check it out."

Kendra scoffs. "Liar." She turns to me. "It is from the local blood bank." She takes another bite.

"So you feed on human blood?" I notice Church hasn't touched his glass.

"We have been feeding on human blood since we were assigned to your detail. Feeding on animals is so inhumane. We like to kill because we are malicious creatures of the night and live solely for the thrill of the hunt."

"Lying always was your forte," Kendra says in a caustic tone.

Carmine stops mid drink and turns to Kendra. "That was a low blow, Kendra."

She breaks eye contact and stares down at the tablecloth.

Church leans forward and places his elbows on the table, his eyes on me. "Once the training is complete, we will transition to Nighmerianotte to meet the Demi."

"For years, the Demi have believed there is more to Vacavious's desire for your blood than simply your abilities to defeat him." Church continues, "Black bloods are the only immortals capable of killing another black blood."

"Whoa, what? Training? Who says I even buy into all this crap, let alone want to do whatever it is you have planned for me?!" I push my casserole forward in protest.

Carmine whispers something in Italian. "You do not get to decide, Five. There is no choice." He smiles.

"Everyone has choices, Carmine," Kendra whispers. Grief drips into her words like a sad song. She slowly chases a pea on her plate.

Carmine freezes. His face, although ashen already, turns ghost white. His jaw grates as he stares straight into Kendra. The look he gives her is either heartache or ultimate regret.

The cold silence is deafening.

"What do you mean I don't get a choice? It's my life." I change the subject, allowing Kendra her sadness.

"Okay, try this on for size." Carmine scolds me. "You turn 18 and he kills you. The end. Do you even realize the consequences for the rest of us?"

"No." I try to remain calm but my blood begins to simmer again. I sigh. "I don't because I've only had a few hours to figure out what in the world is going on."

"Stop," Jo says. "Honey, read the journal. Please. I promise it will make more sense." Her pleading voice and the sincerity in her eyes cut straight to my heart.

"The other Fives are presumed dead. Killed by him," Kendra says, putting her fork down and trying to act casual.

"Why are they presumed dead?" I take her bait because I see she's trying to throw me a life raft.

"Their bodies were never recovered and sentinels have never been able to find them."

I shrug. "The bodies were never recovered, right? They disappeared?"

Everyone is silent and all eyes are on me. I reach up and blot my mouth with my napkin, wondering if I have food on my face.

Church nods. He places his thumbs on his chin as he rests his elbows on the table.

When I realize I don't have anything hanging from my mouth I say, "I mean, think about it. Why have the Fives been the only ones to be kidnapped? Why kidnap and kill them? What if they were kidnapped and kept alive?"

"Blood Queen does have a perspective we do not have, a fresh perspective." Carmine taps his finger on his glass. "How would the Five survive? Without human blood, they become vegetables."

I freeze as I make the connection to me. *The Five cannot survive without human blood yet I am a Five. This makes no sense at all.*

Jo smacks Carmine upside the head again. She clears her throat and says, "Penn, there is one more thing." She pauses, looking to Church and back to me. "Once you turn eighteen, to complete the transition of the Five, you must feed on human blood. If you do not, your body will deteriorate into a vegetative state. Although you will live, you will have no quality of life. It will be awful."

Define awful? Awful, like I sit in a chair all day and drool on myself or awful as in painful. Either way, the awful life might be better than a life of feeding on humans. My stomach lurches again as I look at the blood-filled glasses.

Jo touches my hand. "You can feed without killing, Penn."

I stand. As I do, Church stands with me. I place my hands on the table for balance as a wave of vertigo strikes me. *Information overload. Breathe, Penn. Just breathe. Please don't vomit. My eyes dart from the red glasses to a picture in my head of someone feeding on a lifeless body.* I shake my head. *This can't be right. How can this be right?*

Jo tries to calm me. "Penn, this does not mean you cannot eat what you want. It just will not sustain you like blood will."

Carmine pipes in, "Come on. You act like this is a bad thing. You could be sitting in a convalescent home pondering the hours of your meaningless life. Blood is not all that bad."

"It is! Feeding," I grimace as I swallow my saliva, "on blood. It's disgusting. It's not right and I can't believe I'm having this conversation." *I need some time.* I feel bile building in my throat as panic sets in.

"Penn. It is okay. Go." Church puts his hand on mine.

I leave the table and run to my room. *I need to breathe.*

CHAPTER 9

Secrets. Deceit. Lies.

Sunday, September 9ᵗʰ 10:05 p.m.

I lie on my bed and stare at the ceiling, trying to absorb everything that's transpired. *Everyone has steered clear of my room.*
Confused.
Lied to.
Let down.
Saddened.
Angered.
Unsettled.

I feel like I barely survived some kind of natural disaster. I am drained, mentally and physically. I stare at the journal, still on my bed, still unopened. If it had a title, I wonder what it might be: *For My Daughter, Love Dad. Journal of Crap* or *The Regrets I Pass On.*

I swallow, leaning forward to grab the journal. I undo the clasps holding the pile of seemingly unrelated pages together. My heart stops when I see his handwriting.

If I didn't know better, I would think these pages are written in my own hand. It's my handwriting but his thoughts, his experiences. I rub my hand against the black ink. The same place his hand must have rubbed as he wrote. I open it to page one...

From the journal of Salvatore DeLuca:
Please forgive me, my penmanship is atrocious. It's called Nighmerianotte. Its history dates back to 514 A.D. There are no birections..."

Birections? That's weird. Probably something he overlooked. I keep reading.

"...a left here, a right there, merge on to this freeway then take that highway. No. Below the mortal world with its own sun and moon, it exists. There are five districts in Nighmerianotte: Pollone, Strega, Volare, Zanna and Scogliera also called "the cliff." There are four portals, only visidle...

Visidle? Does he mean, *visible?*

"...to the immortal eye. They are located in Palermo, Italy; Sailem Bend, Australia; Mason, California and Tanzania, Africa. Portal locations

are simply doors. Doors that lead to and from this world. Doors that, to a mortal, simply lead to a bathroom, a closet, a toilet, a dining room, or a garage.

The portals have been locked since 1912. The Republic of Nighmerianotte, the Nighmerians, the immortal creatures, the 105's, 205's, 305's, 405's, 505's and, most importantly, the Five (the Sanguine), can enter Nighmerianotte under certain circumstances, but they cannot leave. They're trapped, left to survive with scarce resources for the last one hundred years. When resources required for life become a fantasy, everything becomes real.

It's a place where the Nighmerians used to live peacefully. Where they lived and relied on each other to take care of what was theirs. Now it's a place where fear and evil exist alive and well. It's a place where murder is a common occurrence. It's desolate and silent. With cobblestone roads that swerve through the old cities, only darkness guides the way. Nighmerianotte was not always like this.

It used to Be a place where Nighmerians co-existed and lived well. They passed freely among the worlds. It used to be a place where food wasn't scarce, a place where light brought comfort. There was A difference between night and day. Now the only difference is time with nothing to signify the sun or moon, just darkness.

Darkness? And why the change in capitalization.

It used to be a place where lights shined bright from local storefronts, taverns and living quarters. Where laughter and chatter filled The air like rain in Seattle.

Not anymore.

Now? Now the Nighmerians stay hidden, in their quarters, and only when the urge to eat comes in full force do they venture out, fearing his return.

Each Nighmerian is born with an identifier: 105 for vampires, 205 for witches, 305 for sentinels, 405 for werewolves, 505 for warlocks, and 005 for the very rare occasion a Sanguine or a "Five" is born. Following the identifier, a sequence of numbers specific to the Nighmerian, like a social security number of sorts. The identifier is used to determine bloodlines and distinguish the difference among Nighmerians. This code appears on the inner left thigh and can only be seen by an immortal's eye.

Nighmerianotte keeps track of months in the Italian language, which, by the WAy, used to be the primary language of Nighmerianotte. Although now, it's more of an old world idea.

Calendar months:

January = gennaio
February = Febbraio
March = Marzo
April = Aprile
May = Maggio
June = giugno
July = Luglio
August = Agosto
September = Settembre
October = Ottobre
November = Novembre
December = Dicembre

Time is tracked a little differently:

Matins: late night / midnight
Lauds: at 3 a.m. or at dawn
Prime: around 6 a.m.
Terce: around 9 a.m.
Sext: midday
None: around 3 p.m.
Vespers: around 6 p.m. or after dinner
Compline: around 9 p.m. or before bed

Each specIEs used to begin training at six years old and train year round until the age of eighteen. They trained to feed properly, strictly a no kill approach for those who drink blood. Their training was specific to their bloodline. They learn their craft, the 105's, the 205's, the 305's, the 405's and the 505's. They spend years training to fight their instincts and perfect their natural born skills. It molded them into who they are. Made them think rather than use their instinctive nature. When mistakes were made in training, the entire class paid greatly. If one person failed training, the entire class failed the training. It was perfection at its finest and nothing less would be accepted. No laughing, no smiling, no talking, no mistakes.

Train. Study. Eat. Train.
Train. Study. Eat. Train.
Repeat.

They trained to achieve excellence, to work as a team, Protect their Republic embedded in their brains.

Not in the past one hundred years has an official training taken place.

He made that clear.

He used fear to enforce it. That's what he does. He uses fear to control. An untrained Nighmerian is unpredictable and can be lethal if in the wrong place at the wrong time. They are referred to as the "rogues." That's exactly what he wants. He wants Nighmerianotte in chaos. He wants them to feed off each other, kill each other, which is exactly what they are beginning to do.

Under stealthy direction of the Demi, secret trainings are conducted at Reylett Castle. They train only the best. Handpicked by the Demi, they train extensively. They must prepare to fight in the event the Five lives.

The 105's, the vampires are Regarded as the highest on the species chain. They are first class Nightmerians. Their position in Nightmerianotte, the function that they serve, is to lead. They are extremely fast and unbelievably strong. Strength doesn't begin to cover what they're capable of. Just to give you an idea, once I saw a rogue 105 rip out a six-foot wide Redwood tree stump. They have the gift to erase minds and make people forget about the past. Many times I have considered asking a vampire to do just that, erase the pain and the heartache but it would erase the memory of you, my daughter. This is a price I am not willing to pay, ever.

Are they trained to kill? yes. Is it instinctual for them to kill? yes. Do they learn how to fight? yes, but by all means, they try to avoid it. Once they feel threatened, it's game on. They feed on blood, but they do so sparingly. Vampires try to only take what they need. They will not take a human life or human blood except as a last resort. Even then, they try to take only enough to nutritionally provide for their bodies. However, this must be practiced. Otherwise, it can be deadly. Their eyes change colors depending on their mood. Since they only feed on blood, their bodies are extremely lean.

Next are the 205's, the witches. They, too, are first class Nighmerians. Their function in Nighmerianotte is to inform. They rely on their hyper-senses to be the eyes and ears of Nighmerianotte. Although they cannot see the future, they can piece together their dreams, intuitions and feelings. Anna knew what you were by the reoccurring dream she kept having four months into her pregnancy. The deep pain she felt was a sign. She knew. That's when the tremors started.

Witches are reserved yet almost as powerful as vampires with their magic, spells, elixirs and potions. Some witches might be better with specific elements: one witch with specific spells and another with mixing elixirs. Anna said that while she and Stanna Salvino were in training, no older than twelve years old, they were exchanging shape shifter spells. She turned her best friend into a snake. Anna was terrified of snakes. Stanna, the snake, chased her around the academy trying to get her to reverse the spell while all Anna could do was run from the snake. Needless to say, they got everything worked out but she was no longer allowed to cast spells on Stanna, regardless of the type. Spells weren't her strong suit. I can still see her face in my mind when she told this story. I remember her laugh and the laugh lines when she tried to mimic her twelve-year-old self, running from a snake who was actually her best friend. I have that memory tucked away in my head, only to pull out when the sadness comes dack.

Dack? Back?

Witches have the gift of verity. They can extract the truth from any mind. Witches usually have long lean faces with high cheekbones, extremely long eyelashes and fingers to match. This is a tell-tale sign you're working with a witch. They also fly, but not by broomstick. It's called a widget, a board, no taller or wider than the foot of its rider. Widgets are custom built for their riders taking into account the rider's weight, height, head circumference, likes, dislikes, skill set, and what they eat. Widgets can move as fast as an average car. Part of the training for witches is to learn to operate their widget. Anna said there were many, many novice witches in the infirmary during widget training.

Next are the 305's, the sentinels. They are regarded as the confidential class of Nighmerians and always male. They know all the secrets of Nighmerianotte. After all, their function in Nighmerianotte is to protect. They work directly for the Demi.

Sentinels are assigned to one of the five districts when they get their wings. At eighteen, they are given their wings after completing their training. Since sentinels don't sleep and fly at a high rate of speed, they can cover a lot of territory. Their endurance is unmatched. They used to patrol both worlds, Nighmerianotte and the mortal world. Since Vacavious locked the portals so long ago, those on the mortal world side stay on that side to keep those struck in the mortal world safe. There are laws in Nighmerianotte and they are found in a book called, the Decreti. For a sentinel to gain his wings they must reference every code to every law of Nighmerianotte in the Decreti. Sentinels know the territory of Nighmerianotte and mortal worlds better even than the warlocks. They are extremely resourceful. Sentinels can create anything out of nothing: a candle out of a leaf, fire out of rock, and a knife out of a branch. They can survive in extreme conditions. They neither marry nor feel love because they are stripped of their ability to love during their training. They are left with lust and desire to fulfill their requirement to reproduce to maintain the bloodline. They are owned by the Demi and take their oath to protect Nighmerianotte very seriously. Sentinels can reach heights of seven feet tall and are in extremely good shape for the work they do requires it. They have several indicators. Indicators are like tattoos and serve as badges of honor depicting missions they've been on and lives they've saved. ThEy use their bodies as a canvas.

Next are the 405's, the werewolves. They're regarded as second class Nighmerians. Their function in Nighmerianotte is to serve. They work well with structure and direction. They serve on missions for Nighmerianotte and work closely with the sentinels and warlocks. Werewolves get their directions from the sentinels. Werewolves are brilliant trackers. They have a strong sense of loyalty, specifically to the sentinels. They can be rogue, even edgy but they never forget their code: service. They are incredibly strong, gigantic and can bite through anything. Werewolves can also shift to dogs if need be. They are usually lean from surviving out in the elements where they usually live. They feel more comfortable in the Fall Forest, on the border of the Zanna district.

The 505's, the warlocks. Their function in Nighmerianotte is innovation. Warlocks build, and create. They are second class Nighmerians. They are extremely intelligent, have a photographic memory and are cartographers by trade. They can map and find almost anything. Typically, they are shopkeepers where they sell what they make: weapons, maps, magnifying glasses, widgets, glassware, stemware, candles and medicines. There is said to be a communication device that a powerful warlock built for the Demi back in the 1500's. It's called a PCS (personal communication stratagem) but no one has ever seen it. The warlocks grow no taller than four feet in height and are usually rounder in the middle as their function keeps them sitting at a desk.

Last, the Nottes, the XXX species. Nottes have no cLASS. They are a mixet species: vampire/werewolf, sentinel/warlock, etc...Nottes are looked at with pity. Mixed marriages are also looked down upon, especially in the formative years of Nighmerianotte. At one time, when a Notte was born, the dominant bloodline of the mix determined what was documented on their birth credence, therefore, no half breeds. As time progressed, the Demi wanted to know who were Nottes and who weren't so that when election time came, Nottes would not be included. It's quite sad actually. They do not have a function in Nighmerianotte. Most of them usually fall into the expectations of Nighmerianotte, which is, bottom feeders and freeloaders. Nottes are forced to live in the Scogliera district. As a classless species, they are not allowed to live anywhere else. This district is located on the cliffs looking over the Black Sea. For centuries, Nottes have carved out tunnels in the rocks to build their homes. Sadly, many, including small children, have lost their lives by plunging to their deaths into the Sea of Black. The "cliff" is the term used because the terrain is steep and can be extremely deadly. Nottes must be creative and extremely cautious in getting in and out of the cliff side. The Nottes learn to swim as a means of survival should they survive the fall from the cliffs. They are especially familiar with the Black Sea and teach their children to swim at an early age, as they are not included in the training set forth by the Demi because of their bloodlines. Nottes do not succumb to the perils of ocean water, like other species, because of their mixed blood.

The Demi. The function of the Demi is to govern Nighmerianotte. The Demi consists of five members representing the five main species of Nighmerianotte: vampire, witch, sentinel, werewolf, and warlock. The Demi members are voted on by their species. Nominations are sent to the acting Demi who have the final say about all nominations. Although it isn't common, nominations have been rejected by the Demi and new nominations requested. The only way an election takes place is if a Demi member can no longer make a sound decision, death, or a unanimous vote for banishment by the other members. Typically, once a family has served, the nomination remains with that family. The Demi make the rules, hold court proceedings, create punishments, record and clear all birth credence's and sentry assignments, and assign sentinels to districts.

Currently the Demi is comprised of:
Giuseppe Calì Leader of the Demi (bloodline: Vampire)
Nyah Fall (bloodline: Witch)
Lothario Masi (bloodline: Sentinel)
Olly Ace (bloodline: Werewolf)
Abram Kravec (bloodline: Warlock)

The last, and most important, species is the Sanguine, "The Five". They are called the Five because their bloodline is just that, zero-zero-five. The Five is the most precious to Nighmerianotte because their role is to save. The act of saving life is the purest, most unselfish gift one can possess. It is unclear to what extent they can save because the Fives are taken too quickly.

When I searched for the word Sanguine, I found words like: blood red, murderous, homicidal, and violent. To Nighmerianotte, it means: savior. While the Five may possess some of these traits, above all they are considered healers. When Pia, the first Sanguine was born, The Demi was told by Freya, the oldest and wisest witch at the time, the five will save you from the darkness but be careful not to wake the dark blood. The Demi didn't know what she meant.

Two days later, Freya was found hanging from a rafter in her living quarters, her head below her body. A pureblood Nighmerian can only die in the following two ways: beheading or salt water. The Demi knew, without a doubt, that what Freya said that day was absolute truth. Smeared in blood were the words: the black blood is alive and well.

Black blood is a Nighmerian born with both human and immortal bloodlines. Legends say that the blood mixture is far more powerful than pure immortal blood. When the black blood is awakened, Nighmerianotte is at risk of extinction. When Nighmerianotte began to take form in 514 A.D. Freya saw this coming. She saw the danger and the evil that was to come if a black blood lived. She performed a conception curse to prevent any black bloods from surviving birth. This is why they die at birth. However, two lived through their birth....one is you, who is also the Five and The other, Vacavious.

The only way a black blood can be killed is by another black blood. You are Nighmerianotte's only hope, if you live.

Only Four Sanguines have been born during Nighmerianotte's entire history, and all four have been kidnapped on the day of their birth or soon after:

Pia Lourve (born in 1157 and kidnapped on the day she was born)

Remi Adonia (born in 1414 and kidnapped five days later)

Antoinette and Ophelia Cassano (twins born in 1936 and kidnapped fifteen days later)

All clues point to Vacavious and his regime as the kidnappers yet there are no direct links to them because there are no bodies. He stays hidden most times, only making appearances to kill. The Sanguines simply vanish. Babies, innocent babies, vanished into thin air. If it is Vacavious, what does he want with the San-guines? They're healers and considered precious to Nighmerianotte because of their abilities. Why kidnap them?

The Demi have been creative in trying to keep the last two Sanguines hidden but their efforts have not been successful. The first kidnappings were considered coincidental by the Demi. They weren't. They were hunted. Some believe the Demi know far more than they admit. This caused a great divide among Nighmerianottes. Half of the Nighmerians are angry because they feel they have a right to know, especially the parents of those missing. Other Nighmerians trust the leaders and have faith in the knowledge that "they will see us through".

Vincent "Vacavious" Serpente made his marRK in 1912 when he cursed Nighmerianotte into darkness and shut down the portals. How? Nobody knows but something happened in 1912 to trigger such an eVent. Vacavious was born a black blood but they deemed him a Notte at the time. He was treated as such and lived on the cliffs of the Scogliera district.

On February 5th, 1936, Vacavious and his morterros massacre many of the Nighmerians. In the wake of the destruction, bodies lay like trash, beheaded and heaped in piles. The Demi believe Vacavious was recruiting new members and building his own regime of immortals by killing them and sucking their souls to create a living, breathing, flesh-eating carcass that walks and kills, also called a morterro. While morterros are blind they are as fast as lightning, especially when they smell fear. Dark sockets where their eyes once were, black desiccated veins intertwined beneath their translucent deteriorating skin and razor sharp teeth that can destroy anything in their path are the hallmarks of the morterro. They are hooded creatures that possess no humanity at all.

The stench of a morterro is as distinct as it is awful. I've smelled one and there is only one word to describe it: death. It's a decaying body but alive, moving, and killing. Morterros have made sojourns to the mortal world. Several unsolved murders where dismembered bodies have been found in shallow graves date back to the 1800's. Dismemberment in Nighmerianotte is a sign of hatred, and morterros dismember bodies with their teeth. Many of these killings are attributed to animal attacks. These murders prove two things: morterros can cross over to the mortal world which means Vacavious probably can too, and, they could be converting innocent limiti to killing machines. This is bad, for both worlds.

My breathing becomes shallow and my heart begins to pound in my chest. I know what killed Bradbury.

This, quite possibly, is what Freya saw coming centuries ago.

When the massacre of 1936 occurred, "The screams of those killed that day," said one Nighmerian, "are the screams I hold in my head today. I haven't slept more than three hours at a time since the first massacre." Coincidently, on February 5th, 1936 twin Sanguines were born. They were kidnapped 15 days later.

Nighmerianotte is where your mother, Annalisa San Angelo, was from. It's also where she died. It's where you were born. Those words are hard to speak aloud, they are even more painful to write. Writing creates a forever memory. I didn't write this to expose Nighmerianotte. That's not it at all. I write this so that you may someday understand why we left. It pains me intensely to know we had to give you away. I want you to know that you were loved deeply. Leaving you with the Demi would allow you to have a chance at life. In order to live, you must know everything there is to know about the place that exists between heaven and hell.

I want you to know how much I love you. I want you to know how your mother and I met and fell in love. Every little girl deserves to know that story.

Annalisa (I call her Anna) and I met in New Orleans in July of 1993, at a Walgreen's, of all places. It was storming something fierce. Hurricane Maudlin was making its way toward the Gulf Coast and I was traveling there on assignment to report on the hurricane. It had been a slow couple of weeks for news. I am, was, a photographer for a national news organization out of Tampa, Florida.

I spotted her between the 'As seen on TV' products and the hand held reading lamps. Her impeccably perfect December skin made her bright green eyes stand out like brilliant yellow stars. Her thick, jet-black hair hung down to her lower back. Her lips were full and rose pink. I watched her for several minutes until some water on the slick floor got the best of her. Even her fall was graceful.

Fate.

I didn't believe in it before. I didn't believe in magic or immortal creatures either but I do now. I didn't know I'd fall in love with a witch but I did. When she spoke, it was like soft musical notes that took away my sadness. Sadness that I didn't know I had. Her words brought my soul to life. She had sharp features, high cheekbones, angelic eyes and long eyelashes and fingers. She had a sense of calm about her. In hindsight, maybe she saw me coming. Maybe I created the calm in her. I rushed to her side, trying not to look too eager and helped her to her feet. That was it. We met. We fell in love.

We stayed in New Orleans for a few weeks then moved into a place together in Mason, California. It was that quick. I just knew. There was a portal there and a friend of Anna's lived there, Jo. Six months later, we found out Anna was pregnant.

That's when Anna told me about Freya and the black blood curse. I'm human. She's not. Our baby would die at birth. It must have been so hard for her, knowing our sweet child would die. Feeling your movements, listening to your heartbeat...I cannot imagine the agony she must have gone through carrying you to term. She and I agreed, despite the probable outcome of the pregnancy, to carry you to term.

We transitioned to Nighmerianotte almost immediately. We knew you would likely die at birth so we didn't tell a soul, aside from Anna's best friend, Stanna Salvino. Her belly grew and she adjusted her clothes accordingly so that no one noticed. As you grew, so did our hearts. We wanted so badly for you to live. During the duration of her pregnancy, I did research, met with the Nighmerians, studied the culture of Nighmerianotte, the caste system, traditions, values, Vacavious, everything. There had to be a way for us, the three of us, to be together. The fear gnawed away at my brain like a constant sadness. your mother grew so sad over those nine months. I wanted to make her feel better. I wanted to take her sadness away. She never talked about it. Maybe Nightmerianotte had it all wrong. The more I tried to convince myself of that, the worse her dreams and tremors became. I just wanted her pain and fear to go away.

On October 31st, 1994, you were born. I held your tiny little body in my arms for the first and final time...that is when I understood unconditional love. It ached so badly. I trembled as I held you. I rubbed my thumb against your soft cheek and held your tiny fingers as they curled around mine. I cupped my hand and rubbed it over your full head of dark hair. I watched your chest rise and fall with each tiny breath. I waited for those sweet tiny breaths to stop.

They didn't.

you kept breathing.

I held you close to my face. your scent, the scent of innocence and love, made me cry. I watched as you dreamed. you looked so peaceful. I wanted to curl up in your mind beside you and never let you go. I wanted, from the depths of my soul, to watch you ride your first bicycle, help you learn to tie your shoes, read you stories at night.

I wanted to feel your hands on my face when you said 'I love you daddy' or listen to you giggle as I chased you around the house. I wanted to listen to your worries and tell you that it would be okay. Because everything would be okay, everything would be perfect, if we couLD be a family. I know that's selfish. I know. I wanted to protect your pureness, your innocence from the evil that would haunt you.

It's a horrific place to be, knowing you cannot protect your child. Horrific. Take me. Hunt me. Kill me, I would say to myself.

You were perfect with your mother's full rose-pink lips, my Italian nose, her long fingers and long legs. You looked so much like your mother it caught me off guard. Sunless skin, bright green eyes, and eye lashes that almost required a hair comb. You took my breath away. You made my heart swell and I knew, without a doubt, I would die for you.

You gave us the gift of unconditional love. Love far different from any other. My heart was complete, yet yearned so badly.

Then your mother checked the inside of your upper thigh to see your identifier.

She stifled a breath and couldn't speak or move. As I held you, I asked her what was wrong. I begged her to tell me what she saw.

Then her words pierced my heart, almost killing me. "She's the Five. She's the Sanguine."

It took everything I had, everything I had, to leave you on the doorstep of the Demi that night. If you didn't die, we knew you would be hunted. We didn't know if the Demi could keep you safe but it was the best option we had. We had to deter Vacavious. With help from many Nighmerians, Anna's family, and best friend, Stanna, we were able to get the word out that the newly born Five was somewhere in the Fall Forest. For Nighmerianotte knew you were the Five but only the Demi knew you had the black blood.

Stanna and her coven paid for assisting us... not immediately, but Vacavious came back for them. He massacred the entire coven.

We left you with the Demi. I will never be able to articulate what it felt like to leave you. There are no words to describe the loss and grief I felt for years to come. Thinking your child may die is a feeling I wish upon no one. The way it made me feel, and what it did to my heart, I know Anna felt the same. Her senses told her it was the right decision.

We took off on foot. We didn't have much time to separate from you. You were born exactly four hours prior. We parted ways once we reached the Forest wall knowing the He or

144

the morterros would soon find us. It was only a matter of time. We felt when one of us was caught, they would have to search for the other one and it would buy more time for the Demi to hide you. The last place they would look is with the Demi.

Saying goodbye to you, and your mother, in a matter of hours, I lost myself.

I lost everything, my whole world.

We kissed goodbye. Our chests together, our hearts beat as one. It was the last time I heard her sweet voice or felt the warmth of her lips on mine.

They found her. I know because I heard her cries. I fell back against a tree and wept, listening to her cries, 'kill me. you will never find my child'... Then it fell silent. She would never give them the information they asked for, so they murdered her. I never wanted to forget what they did to her so I waited, I listened. If I kept the memory, and it triggered this rage I felt inside, then I would never forget. It would give me fight. I know, without a doubt, she died protecting you. I pray they didn't turn her into a morterro, that they let her soul go. God, I pray.

For some reason, I lived. I made it through one of the five portals back to the mortal world. I lived under an alias and kept as far away

145

from you as I could. He knew who I was and it was a matter of time before he found me. I know he was waiting for me to make a wrong move and reveal your location, but I wouldn't. I think that's why he's keeping me alive. I'm his only hope, until you turn eighteen of course. Then, the protective spell that hides your location expires and you will be exposed. In some small way, I wanted him to find me. I wanted him to kill me. Some days I wanted to expose myself to the morterros, or him, but I couldn't. I couldn't willingly die knowing you were still alive.

I lived in a hole in the woods, right outside New Orleans. I went back to the Big Easy because I felt closer to Anna that way and to you. I had good memories there. Now, all I felt was emptiness. I couldn't go back to Mason because I was worried I'd attract too much attention, knowing there's a portal there.

Jo sent me pictures. She'd send them to general delivery in New Orleans. I befriended a man named Sam who worked for the post office. He would bring them to a small coffee shop in the French Quarter and stick them behind the outside gutter in the alleyway. Every morning I bribed Louie, one of the homeless men, with coffee, scones and bus fare, to check under the gutter. He'd bring whatever he found and take the street car from St. Charles to St. Louis Cemetery #1 and toss them in the trash can right outside the gates. I would wait fifteen hours exactly (just in case someone was watching) before I disguised myself and picked through the trash to find my pictures. If there weren't any, I'd wait in the shadows, just in case the mail came late. This became my life. I waited for pictures of you.

From ages eight to seventeen, I watched you grow into a beautiful young lady. Every morning, when I look at your pictures from my hole in the ground, I'd stare, breathless, because of how much you resemble your mother. The longing for you never went away. Your smile gave me comfort. It gave my heart a little piece of mind knowing you were happy. I knew Jo didn't tell me where they'd put you after you were born for fear that I would give in and come for you. I'm grateful they didn't, because I would have. The pain was too much to bear. Often I'd sleep with the sweatshirt I wore the night you were born simply for the feeling it gave me that you were once near to me. I wouldn't think about Anna. I couldn't. I needed to keep moving forward...whatever the cost.

Penelope, if you make it, in Nighmerianotte, at Bank of the Nighmerians, in the old cellar, under the stairs that lines the stairwell, there's a brick wall. It's the fifth brick from the corner and the fifth brick from the bottom. You'll need a witch to open it. You'll find what you neEd.

My sweet daughter, be kind to all you meet. Be genuine. Be true to who you are. Love with your whole heart. Stand up for what you believe in. Never let fear silence you or sway your better judgment. Fight for what is right and trust your gut. Most of all, know that we, your mother and I, love you. We have always loved you. We will always exist in your heart. Always.

Love always,
Daddy.

His words, my father's words, have touched my heart, causing a lump in my throat too big to swallow. My heart hurts in a way only my father and mother can mend. My tears beg my eyelids to let them fall, but a dark spot in my soul won't let them, a tainted spot. A spot so deep and buried amidst the raw emotion, I don't know if I will ever recover.

I close the journal and feel the dark spot grow a little more.

CHAPTER 10

Black Blood

I turn off my light stare into nothingness. Darkness.

He loved me. My father. A sweet gentle man who loved his family more than he loved his own life.

My mother loved me. They wanted what was best for me. For so long I've had so much contempt for them. Hate. Yet, they laid down their lives, for me.

For the Five.

The Black Blood.

Then there's my detail and Aunt Jo. What they must have sacrificed to secure my survival astounds me. If I am what they and my father say I am, I see I have three choices:

One, I can move to the farthest reaches of the Amazon Rainforest and live in hiding (and denial) for the rest of my long life.

Two, I can join the witness protection program. *Hi. My name is Penelope Jackson, and I am the only living black blood from Nighmerianotte.*

I need to hide from an immortal that calls himself Vacavious. If you can keep me in hiding for the next 500 years or so, that would be great. Thank you.

Three, I can do what they are asking me to do. I can fight.

My eyes adjust to the darkness and glow of the moon visible from my window as I replay his beautiful words in my mind. I jump. "Jesu-" I see him in the corner of my room, staring at me.

"You are perfect when you are alone with your thoughts, do you know that?" Church's voice is hoarse.

I swallow any emotion I feel. *Push it down, Penn. Further. Don't let anyone see.*

"What?! Are you spying on me? I thought I was clear when I said I needed some time." I quickly glance down and see my skimpy pink tank top and pull the covers up to my neck.

He leans back, resting his head on the wall, still watching me. "You have read it?"

I don't look at him. "Yeah."

"And?"

I shake my head because I'm afraid to speak. *What if the words don't come? What if I speak and I break down?* What my father, mother, my detail and the Nighmerians have sacrificed for me, it's selfless. I swallow. "Vacavious killed my father and that's why Jo left for New Orleans."

Church's stare is hard. I know he's trying to think of the right words to console me. Mend me. Put the pieces back together. I see the longing in his face. I push down any emotions that are welling up in my throat and in my eyes. "Don't give me pity, Church." I don't do a good job at conveying how I feel. I never have. Emptiness is the only way I can describe my feelings about the death of my father. It feels like a gaping hole of emptiness that spreads like cancer. Fear extends the emptiness. I'm different. I have always set myself aside as different. Even in a world filled with immortal creatures, I'm different.

What if I'm not different? What if it's me that makes me different, sets me apart? Before, I was the weird kid with no parents, running from my past. Now I'm the Black Five with dead parents and still running.

Dead parents.

There's a long pause before he speaks. "I used to sit right there when you first moved in with Jo." He points to the massive redwood tree outside my window.

Breathe, Penn. Just breathe.

"Well, if I don't have a choice in the matter of you staying," I turn on the light and grab a hair tie as I scoop up my hair, Church's face changes. He takes in a deep breath as if smelling a rose for the first time. "Leave it down."

I pause, caught off guard by his tone. I don't like that he's telling me what to do, yet, for whatever reason, I obey and I let my long hair spill around my shoulders. "Happy now?"

His mouth turns at the corners, revealing a slight smile. "Yes."

His smile makes me nervous. I'm not sure if I'm nervous because he makes my heart pound and my palms sweat or because I'm not sure of what he's capable of.

"You'd stare at me from the tree? That's a little creepy," I say in a snarky tone.

He laughs. When he does, there's a low growl, an unhumanly low growl, that's both seductive and a little intimidating.

"Is this the part where I ask if you're a 105?" I say.

"Does that scare you?" His whisper is almost inaudible.

I pause. *No,* I want to say. "Don't flatter yourself." I pull my knees up to my chest. "Are you?" I push my father's words further away.

Church cocks his head and asks, "What do you believe?"

This isn't going anywhere. "Did anyone ever tell you it's rude to answer someone's question with a question?"

"If I told you I was, would that change anything? Would you look at me differently? Would it change the situation?" His eyes meet mine.

"That's hardly fair. You know everything about me." I feel my face grow hot again. "Probably everything. Besides, I'm going to find out anyway."

Church laughs, his deep, throaty, growly laugh again. "If I do, then what?" He raises his eyebrows, obviously amused.

A question with a question. "Lame. Stupid, actually. How old are you?"

"Old."

"How old?"

"Really old."

"You're," I pause, looking for the right word, "ambiguous. Has anyone ever told you that?"

"Many times." He moves so quickly by the time my eyes can focus on him, he's next to me on my bed, sitting. I feel the coolness of his skin. "Penelope, I am 302 years old." I love how my name rolls off his tongue. All too quickly, he moves from my bed to the window.

The moon accentuates his pale skin, giving him a ghost-like hue. Almost translucent.

It's stunning.

I stand, and for reasons I can't explain, walk to him. I feel an overwhelming desire to reach out and touch him. I want to feel his skin. I reach out, allowing my fingers to dance down the side of his forearm. Mesmerizing. "You're beautiful," I say breathlessly, unaware of my words and uncontrolled actions.

He takes his finger and pushes my hair behind my ear. "You have no idea, Penelope." I flinch.

"Why do you do that? Every time I touch you. You flinch. As if I would ever hurt you." He's wounded, his words, barely a whisper. In a matter of seconds, he's in my personal space. "If I cannot touch you, can I be close to you," he takes a step forward, "like this?"

Close.

Intimately close.

I don't move. I catch my breath as my heart beat quickens. His stare is firm. "Can you lift your chin for me?"

My eyes dance toward the ceiling as I awkwardly move my chin up and over, exposing my neck.

"Push your hair back, please." I feel the weight of his breath and his statement. Chills overtake my entire body, and not in a bad way. I try to catch my breath again but I can't. His lips are inches from my neck, but I can't seem to pull away.

He whispers in my ear, his lips barely grazing my earlobe, "Does this scare you?"

I have no idea what to say. *Yes. And no. The last time I felt like this was with Jesse.* Guilt turns in my gut.

I don't answer because I don't know if I can put two words together, much less a sentence. *Yes, because I don't like the way you make me feel and no because I like the way I feel.*

Without a single touch he whispers, "Let it be known, Penelope, I have spent the last seventeen years fighting for you, keeping you safe. Not because of *what* you are, but because of *who* you are. Not a minute goes by that you are not in the forefront of my mind." He pauses. "I need you."

His voice is now angelic. It's soft. It's caring. It's familiar, as if I've heard it a million times. Yet, as those last three last word exit his mouth, it becomes brash and almost panicked.

Usually I can think of something articulate or sarcastic to say but right now I can't. It's scaring the crap out of me. I swallow hard again. My nerve endings are beginning to tingle. *I hope he doesn't pull away and look at me because I know my face is seven shades of red right now.*

"I...I...I don't," I sputter, trying to compose myself.

Church brings his finger up between our mouths, which are inches away from touching, and hushes me in the melodic way one shushes a crying baby. "No, Penelope. You need not respond, I simply needed you to know."

I pause, letting all the emotions, words and feelings soak in. After regaining my composure I say, "Tell me about you. I mean, you know so much about me. It's only fair." I push my hair behind my ear. I take a deep breath, praying I don't look totally awkward, but I don't back up.

He falls back on the bed and kicks his boots up on the footboard, hands behind his head. His sudden shift pulls his polo up, exposing his perfection in a way that makes my face hot. "I would rather see how you are doing with all this, Penelope."

Jeez, Penn. Pull it together. It's just a little skin. I move to the window, feeling I might die of heatstroke. "What?" I ask because I have no idea what he just said.

"I said I would rather focus on you right now." He gives me that look again, the one which stares straight through me, exposing everything.

"Please, Church. Give me some normalcy right now." I plead, because that's the last thing I want him doing, *focusing on me.*

"I would rather not." He looks up at me as he turns on his side, his hand holding his head.

"It's hardly fair. I know virtually nothing about you. You who has been protecting me my entire life." I comb my hand through my hair, trying not to make eye contact, attempting to act casual.

"You do that when you are nervous."

I stop. "I do not."

He smiles and the glint of the moon catches his scar.

"What happened?" I walk to him and carefully bring my hand to his face.

Church shakes me off, "Ask me *thee* question." He sighs, rolling onto his back, his polo stays low, covering his mid-section. *Thank you, Jesus.*

"What? What do you mean? What question?"

"Who turned you? That is what you want to ask me?"

I look back to him. "Yeah."

He smirks. "Yes, I am sure that is what you meant." He turns back to his side, facing me once again. I try to tame the butterflies in my belly with my hand. "I was not turned. I was born to Nighmerianotte as were my brother and two sisters. We were born into the Cali Family."

Cali Family…the name rings a bell. Wait. "Giuseppe is your uncle?"

"Correct. My father and Giuseppe are brothers. I grew up a normal vampire in a two-vampire household. Black castle, training at the academy, you know." He gives me a smirk.

I laugh out loud. "I'd take your childhood over mine any day." I try to laugh again but his look wraps around my heart. I didn't mean that how it sounded.

Immediately he looks away. "You know, Penelope, I do not want to bore you with my family and the production that goes along with it because, truth be told, every family has drama." He pauses and says, "I would like to spend some time with you." He's still. Eerily still. "Can I tell you what I know about you?"

"Fire away." I shake my head. "I'm complicated."

"I know you are scared of snakes. *Terrified*, really."

Gulp.

"I know you hate oat cereal and processed cheese."

Gulp.

"I know you have the biggest heart of anyone, anyone, I have ever met in my *entire* life and I love that about you." I try to breathe once more. "I know you put up a tough front, but I can see right through it."

Stop.

"I love that you love to read romance books and hide them between your mattresses like smut."

I quickly turn my head to him and blush. "I do not."

"Yeah? Let us have a look, then?" He reaches over the side of the bed and begins fishing under the mattress.

"STOP!" I yell, my face growing even redder. "What else have you got?" I attempt to divert his attention. *Busted.*

He doesn't say anything for several seconds. "Penelope, I know you long for your parents because I can see it in your eyes. I know you are hurt because I feel it. So it is all right to be sad. It is okay to be human. It is okay to feel."

I'm paralyzed.

He takes me into his arms, without making eye contact and presses my heart against his.

I feel like he just broke through one of my walls of defense, exposing a painful memory.

I let him hold me. As he slowly lets go he lays down on the bed and scoots to the far side to make room for me. I lay down beside him.

"Penn, promise me something?" He leans away to look into my eyes.

"Your job is to stay ordinary with extraordinary gifts until your eighteenth birthday so we can finish your training. Stay ordinary and embrace the time you have."

Training? Right.

"Once we transition, the portals are locked. We can cross over to Nighmerianotte, but there's no way out. We may not return to the mortal world. You must understand that."

I know what he means. He means I have to say goodbye to Amy and Jo, in case we don't make it back.

"It is obvious Vacavious is well invested in bringing down our world. The Demi will give us more information once we can cross over."

I shake my head. "This is crazy, right? I went from a seventeen-year-old high school senior to a unique Nighmerian with black blood who supposedly is the only immortal capable of killing some super villain. Seriously, tell me this isn't crazy?"

Church laughs. "You are right in all cases but one, Penn. You have always been a unique Nighmerian with black blood. It is that uniqueness that forced us to keep you, the Penelope everyone has known for seventeen years, safe and hidden away. It does sound crazy, though. I think we have waited so long for you to get to this point that we are unloading everything a bit too fast."

"You think?"

There's a long silence because I don't know what to say. Surely, I am the underdog in this battle. I don't know how to kill a ruthless murderer and I'm not sure if the internet will be helpful in this situation. "Church, seriously. I don't possess any magic. I'm just a teenager. I don't have superhuman strength, nor am I athletic. I have two left feet and

I'm a terrible dancer. Not that dancing has anything to do with this." Clearly I'm flustered. "I mean, my biggest worry in the last three days has been AP Anatomy homework and whether or not it's my night to cook dinner," *oh, and don't forget about the murder you committed when you were eight.* "I don't know the first thing about hunting a black-blooded killer before he kills me."

"How quickly you doubt your abilities, Black Five." He gives me a snide look.

Black Five. Okay, yes, I can heal but it's just something I've learned to do more as a hobby.

"You realize you are his match? You are the only one who can kill him because you share his strengths and abilities. Your training will help foster the special skills and abilities you come by naturally. If you want to win, you must first believe you can win. I'm afraid I cannot help you with that. You must believe in yourself first."

I look to him again. "Has anyone ever told you, you are way too philosophical?" This position, with him, on my bed, is way too comfortable. Way too easy. Magnetism. So I stand up.

His hand hovers over where my body was.

"When do we start? The training, I mean?" I pick at my thumb, trying to look cool and unafraid, but my nervousness is evident.

I have irrevocably given Church consent. I will fight.

"This Wednesday night. I need to make sure everything is arranged with the Demi and the portal transition when we are ready. We only have seven weeks until your birthday. We will give you weekends, in the beginning, to regain your sleep. You will need it."

I nod, not because I agree I need sleep, but because there's nothing left to say. The sacrifices everyone has made decides for me. It leaves me with no other choice.

He continues in a more professional tone as he stands and walks toward the door, "The training is broken up into five categories: physical, mental, weapons, senses, and gifts. From 10 p.m. to 11 p.m. you will have physical endurance training with Jesse." Church pauses. His stare meets mine. I think he's waiting for a reaction. I don't give him one. I don't even blink. Instead I ask, "Why at night?"

Church explains, "You must train in the dark because you will fight in the dark." His voice is lower now. "From 11 p.m. to 12 a.m. you will have mental endurance training with Carmine. From 12 a.m. to 1 a.m. you will have weapons training with me. From 1 a.m. to 2 a.m. you will have senses training with Kendra. Last, from 2 a.m. to 3 a.m. you will have gifts training with Jo."

I nod again. I feel stupid asking this question but I ask it anyway. "Do I need to prepare for anything? What should I wear?"

A low, deep chuckle escapes Church as he shakes his head. His voice cracks, "Something that will allow you to move freely." He moves his stare from the floor to my eyes.

I feel my face grow hot as I smirk. The way he looks with his sly grin, I can't help but like it. He moves to rest his forearm on the doorframe and rubs his hand through his disheveled black hair. I trace the definition of his bicep with my eyes and, suddenly, I'm aware he's looking at me.

Busted. Again.

"This is awkward for you, Penn. I make this awkward for you. My deepest apologies. That is the last thing I want this to be." I see the muscles in his arms contract once more as he puts his arms over his head, resting his fingers on the top of the doorframe.

I deflect. "No," I answer defensively. "It isn't awkward." I try to laugh it off. "It's fine." I sigh and look around my room as if I'm seeing the Smithsonian for the first time.

"I have been waiting for you your entire life."

Can't speak. I cannot utter a single word.

My entire life?

No. Yes, it is. It is awkward. I toy with the sterling silver ring on my finger. *Say something, Penn. Say something.* "Okay, so I'll wear workout clothes and a sports bra."

Oh no! Did I seriously say that out loud? Crap. Crap. Crap. I quickly look up to Church. "I'll um, okay, well, I'm going to go to bed now. Yeah." I quickly turn my back toward him, facing my room. I smack my forehead and silently curse myself. "I'm sorry, Church. Sometimes I don't think before I say things."

"You forget, Penelope, I have known you your entire life." My back is to him but I know he's smiling as he says this.

He already knows.

"Right." I nod slowly. "So, uh, I guess I will see you soon? With clothes on."

Dear God, make me shut up or rip off my lips, please. "I'm going to shut up now." I shake my head slowly, my face on fire.

"Penelope?" I hear his voice, barely a whisper.

"Yeah?" I turn from the dresser.

There's no one there.

CHAPTER 11

Shenanigans

Monday, September 10th 6:52 a.m.

"Black Five? Rise and shine, immortal. Time for the mind-numbing job of staying ordinary with extraordinary skills." I hear Carmine's words swirl together.

"I'm awake. Don't you know how to knock?" I ask hastily as I throw my covers back.

"I will be walking you to school this morning." Carmine stands in the doorway, ignoring my obvious hint.

I laugh. "No, you aren't."

Carmine mimics my laugh. "It is sincerely cute how you still pretend to have choices for your life. See you downstairs."

"Whatever." As I shut the door to my bathroom, I hear the door to my bedroom close quietly.

I'm on my way downstairs when my phone chimes.

Kendra: Meet you at the cemetery in 15?

Me: Yes. I may have company.

Kendra: Who?

I don't answer, knowing she wants to rip Carmine's face off with a rake. Probably…most likely.

Carmine meets me in the kitchen as I grab an apple and a bottled water.

"I'm going to meet Kendra," I say, hoping it'll discourage him from stalking me. Or as he put it, "walking me to school."

"I know." Carmine gives a lasting look at his phone before shoving it into his pocket. "Ready?" He looks at me.

I groan in disapproval. "Whatever. You have a cell phone?"

"Does not everyone?"

"Yeah but isn't it kind of weird for you? I mean, you're from a different world."

"So are you."

I laugh. He has a point. "Okay, how long have you been here in the mortal world?"

"Since the portals have been locked, just over a hundred years, but who is counting?" He closes the front door behind us.

I fall behind, lost in thought as I watch him walk toward the cemetery.

"But wait," I say, catching up to him. "If the portals are closed, how am I going to transition over when my training is complete?"

"There are ways to get through the portals, but it is not easy. One can get stuck on the other side, which is why I have never tried."

We walk in silence as we near the cemetery. Usually the birds chirp when I walk to the cemetery but it's eerily silent and there's only one possible reason.

"Did you make the birds stop chirping?" I look around for birds but see none.

"Animals are instinctive and they can sense predators in their environment."

"Right."

We come to the gate of the cemetery. I push through the small space while Carmine jumps over it, clearing its top by five feet. The fence stands at least fifteen feet tall.

I stand and watch. "Seriously? Let me guess? A 105?" He lands next to me.

"What gave it away?" he beams.

As we walk up the hill, I notice his eyes and facial features are softer than Church's. He has a younger look than his older brother and his features are not as hard and ridged.

"How old are you?"

"298 years young." He sees Kendra and his expression softens.

I look up to see Kendra facing away from us. "What did you do to make her so mad?"

He sighs and says, "Long story. Let me know when you have a couple of years and I will bend your ear."

My eyebrows raise. "It must have been bad because I have never seen Kendra treat anyone the way she treats you. No offense."

He doesn't answer, but instead, clicks his tongue as we make it to the top.

"Why is the tick here?" she says in a flat voice, her back still to us.

"Kendra, look, we have to work together, so you have to deal with the fact I am going to be in your life, whether you want me here or not."

She gets up and turns around. Her eyes narrow as she gives Carmine the death stare.

Carmine's lips form a thin line out of frustration, or guilt, perhaps. Or hurt? Empathy? He doesn't say anything.

Kendra's eyes don't move. They remain fixed on Carmine's. "It was far better when you stayed out of my way," she replies, fuming. Carmine stares back. She wheels around, grabs her backpack, and marches down the hill.

"Kendra, wait up." I try to catch up to her.

We are down the hill, through the gate, and on Main Street before I catch my breath. I struggle to keep up with her. I wonder if her witch abilities allow her to walk at the pace she's walking.

"Do you want to talk abou—"

"No." Kendra cuts me off as she marches toward the high school.

I don't say anything, still trying to keep up with her. Kendra mutters something under her breath, but I can't understand what she's saying aside from "protect…Carmine…bloodthirsty…"

We make it to the high school in record time. I follow Kendra to the football field and see the banner for the Milk Can game. *Crap. That's coming up.* I've been so wrapped up in myself, I haven't paid at-tention to the biggest football game of the year. Lake Providence High plays Mason High every year in the battle for the milk can. The symbolic prize is a milk can but there is more to it than that. Yep, a regular ol' milk can, plus victory engravings dating back to the 1960's. With the win comes puffed up chests, and bragging rights for the next 365 days. Not to mention, home field advantage for next year's game. It's like an all-out war between the two towns. Well, not really a war, but we mentally prepare for the game all year. For two weeks leading up to the bout, the town's high school kids pull pranks. One year, LP turned loose a Holstein in the enclosed hallway of Mason High. As the prin-cipal quietly worked in his office one morning, he looked up from his computer to find the Holstein staring at him, chewing her cud. Another year, we stole the prized husky, Jack, from LP's principal's house. Lake Providence students also stole the Milk Can from inside Mason High. They must have tired of losing every year. Both towns seem to step up their shenanigans a little more each year.

The pranks have become a tradition.

The one Kendra pulled this year was epic. She listed Lake Providence High School and its students, staff and faculty for sale on Craig's List for $2,012. I hear they are still doing damage control. Kendra promises after the big game, she'll make it right.

I watch her march into the middle of the football field. She screams, her chest heaving in and out. She screams once more as the sky grows dark with ominous clouds. The clouds rolling in are black and dense. She yells as she bends over and places her head in her hands. Lightning tears open the sky as thunder shakes me to my core. The clouds billow in so quickly it looks as though a tornado is forming.

I walk to her. I think twice about putting my hand on her shoulder but I do. "Kendra?"

She's crying. *She's crying.* I've never, in the entire time I've known her, seen Kendra cry. I feel the need to put my arms around her so, with hesitation, I pull her whimpering body to mine. She rests her head on my shoulder. We stand there for several minutes, me holding her. As her tears subside, the clouds retreat behind the redwood hills of Mason and the thunder ceases.

"You okay?" I ask as she pulls away and covers her eyes. I push her hair behind her shoulder.

She wipes her eyes with her palms.

"Do you want to talk about it?"

"Not yet. Someday, but not now."

I nod as she picks up her backpack.

"Was that you?" I look toward the sky.

She barely smiles as she wipes her smudged makeup from under her eyes. "Yeah."

"Kick ass." I look up at the sky as I follow in line with her back to the high school.

"When I get mad or sad enough that tends to happen. With Carmine coming back, I am reliving memories I would rather not."

"You need some silence?" She nods as she puts herself back together again. I don't feel so weird with my own odd gifts. My only regret is we couldn't have done this sooner.

We make our way to first period through the back entrance to the hallway. Hardly anyone ever uses the back door early in the morning.

Kendra walks through as I follow. She stops and I bump into her back. "You know what? Let us go through the front door." She tries to push me back through the doors we've just come through.

"Kendra, don't be silly. We can just—"

Then I see them. I freeze. I try to catch my breath but I can't. I bite down on my lower lip.

I can't think. I can't feel. All I hear is the sound of my heartbeat slamming against my chest. Finally, my breath comes but it isn't enough. I'm trying to wrap my brain around what I see but I can't. Someone touches my arm but I can't tear my eyes away from what I'm witnessing.

Jesse has Vanessa slammed against the locker. He's holding her face in his hands. His eyes are closed. His lips are interlocked around hers in what can only be described as desire. Their bodies are pressed tightly against each other, oblivious to all else in the world.

He's kissing her. He's kissing her in a way I've imagined he would kiss me. I don't want this to hurt my heart in the way it does.

I watch as he pushes closer to her, as if that's possible. He pulls away, still lingering on her lips, his eyes hooded with wanton desire. He looks away only to open his eyes in my direction.

He stops.

I watch as the blood drains from his face.

He doesn't move.

It's only him and me in this moment. We're staring at each other and I can't catch my breath. It's gone. My heart begins to pound in my head and I can't move. Again, I feel a tug on my arm. This time, I follow. Kendra takes my arm and leads me outside, behind the school. She takes my shoulders in her hands. "Penn, are you okay?" she's concerned. Her voice is full of empathy. "Penn, are you okay? Talk to me. Say a word. Any word. *Fart. Burp.* An obscene word. Just say something."

I stare at her, momentarily, unable to speak. Then I find my voice, "Does—" I say in shock. I do not know the words that are about to come out of my mouth, "Does he love her?"

He's just a boy.

He's a boy who has had my heart since we were eight.

Kendra winces as she mutters something under her breath. She doesn't hug me, but instead, just stands there, staring at me. Eye contact is her thing.

"Jackson?" I hear his voice.

His voice.

Kendra turns to Jesse. "You actually think now is the right time, Jesse? After the slam fest we just witnessed? Seriously?" Kendra places her hands on her hips. "You have got to tell her. She does not get it. You are breaking her damn heart."

"Boots, can you give us a minute?" he sighs.

Kendra looks at Jesse for a long moment. "You had better be more discreet next time," she hisses through a clenched jaw. She turns and stalks toward the back doors of the school.

Next time.

The doors slam behind her.

I slowly turn around.

The silence between us makes me feel like we're more than just a few feet apart. I feel his eyes on me but I'm afraid to look up. I feel absolutely stupid I reacted the way I did. Jesse doesn't belong to me. He doesn't owe me an explanation. He isn't my boyfriend nor has he ever been my boyfriend, but those words don't come to my mouth.

"Jackson," he whispers again as he moves closer.

"You don't owe me anything, Jesse. Nothing. Not a damn thing." I try my best to keep an unemotional voice. I'm so mad at myself right now, mad for caring so much, and mad for the feeling that's causing my heart to hurt.

I look up, finally, and I look into his eyes. Guilt and anguish seep from his being. Jesse places a hand on his hip and rubs his forehead with the other.

"Jesse, I don't do pity. So don't feel sorry for me." *Ugh, Penn, how did you let it get this far? How did you not see this coming?*

Jesse jerks his head back. "Pity? You think I feel sorry for you?"

"It's fine, Jesse." I break eye contact and push past him toward the double doors.

"No." He grabs my hand as I walk past. "Please do not go. Look—"

Our backs are to each other but he grabs my hand and our fingers intertwine. "Please, do not go."

I sigh.

He takes my hand in his. He hesitantly begins to massage my knuckles.

I hate I can't get past him and move on. I hate the fact I love the way his hand feels in mine.

"I am trying my hardest to fight every single feeling I have for you. I cannot love you. I am not capable of love. I cannot be in love with you. You have to accept that because of what I am. You and I cannot work." His grip tightens but he doesn't move. "That is why I need you to walk away from me. You and I will never happen. Do you understand?" His voice is direct yet full of emotion. His words say no but everything else screams heartache.

All the air is sucked out of me, like I was punched in the gut. *Penn, don't think. Don't feel. Don't pay attention to what your body is trying to tell you right now.* "Jesse, I'm fine." I pull my hand away because I can't bear another second basking in the feeling he gives me.

Raw.

Untainted.

Innocent.

Pure.

Love.

I leave him and the door slams behind me.

I pour into the desk next to Kendra in class. She gives me the, *'you good?'* look.

"I'm good." I lie. Good would be a feeling that everything is right with the world. Good would mean I have peace of mind. Good would mean my heart doesn't ache, that it's not broken. Good would mean I don't have some sort of weird immortal power. Good would mean I have a mom and dad that aren't dead. Everything is not good. Everything sucks and I feel my world crumbling around me. I look back to Kendra.

"Liar."

Kendra and I somehow manage to make it through our classes, despite our crazy morning. I don't see Jesse the rest of the day, and I'm thankful. I don't see Vanessa either, which is probably for the best because if I had, I may have been tempted to punch her in the throat.

CHAPTER 12

Tradition

Wednesday, September 12ᵗʰ 6:05 a.m.

Kendra is already waiting for me at the top of the hill. I see her vibrant orange hair. It's a new color for her. I need to tell her it doesn't work. She reminds me of some sort of road worker, or better yet, deer hunter.

As I approach, Kendra raises her eyebrows. "They are trying to reschedule the Milk Can game because of the curfew crap." She hands me my coffee.

"What? They can't reschedule the Milk Can game. It's tradition. Every year, same time."

"Do not blame the messenger." She laughs and says, "Besides, our job is to protect your life, in case you have forgotten. With all the commotion, especially at a football game this big, that will be difficult to do. It is a recipe for D & D. So it might be a blessing in disguise."

I raise my eyebrows. "D & D?"

"Distraction and Disaster. Add a little bit of commotion, a miscalculation, and a little pinch of evil and it is game over. You are dead." Kendra shrugs. "We cannot have that now, can we?"

I ask her the question that's been in the back of my mind, the one I keep forgetting to ask. "Was it a morterro who killed Bradbury?"

She nods. "Yep. Clean kill, but it was not looking for you. He was rogue. Church took care of that."

"Can't Church notify Chief Watson so the curfew can be lifted?"

Kendra's eyebrows rise as she slowly turns toward me. "And say what? Hey, we will take care of the animal attacker. It was a morterro, but a couple vampires are taking care of the problem. All is well, friends." She holds her hands out in the air like some sort of politician.

I laugh. *She's right.*

"It will run its course. The fear will subside. Plus, we have extra sentinels patrolling Mason. It should not happen again."

"Can I ask another question?

"Shoot."

"What should I expect? In the training?"

Her grin turns into a smirk. "Expect to be pushed to your limits. Expect to want to die rather than live another day in training. Expect to be pushed like you have never, ever, been pushed before." She puts on her glasses and sips her coffee.

Super. Looking forward to it.

"Can I ask you another question?"

Kendra doesn't say anything because she knows what is coming. "You want to talk about the incident on the football field the other morning?" I whisper.

Kendra doesn't answer. Her tragedy. Her own deep soul hurt. There's a long silence but it isn't awkward. "Not really."

I wait and stare at the horizon.

She sighs deeply. "Yeah, maybe." She takes in a long breath and sets her coffee down. She crosses her arms around her legs and rests her chin on her knee. "My brother, Leo, and I were toying with a shape shifter spell. My coven transitioned to the mortal world long before Vacavious locked the portals because I was doing special training for the Demi. We heard he was looking for us because we helped your parents try to escape."

Questions flutter through my mind I want to ask. *How old is Kendra, really? Did she meet my mother and father? What were they like?*

I don't ask.

"My brother..." her voices goes quiet as if she is remembering this for the first time, "had turned me into a rat." she smiles. "Vacavious and his pack of filth appeared out of nowhere, calling us traitors. My father told them to leave, that they were not welcome in our area of the mortal world, that it did not belong to him. My father would not back down..." her voice remains stoic and her eyes tearless, as though she's giving a testimony or police report. "He killed everyone. My father, my mother..." Kendra pauses, "my brother. Our whole coven was murdered that night. Once he finished, he set fire to their bodies so the limiti would not see the absolute evilness of his crime." She pauses again, her voice full of agony. "I listened to their screams until I could not hear them anymore." Her lips are barely moving. "It is a little weird. I do not remember much from that night, but I remember the days that followed. The world kept moving, Penn. People went to work, to school, made phone calls, even laughed. I remember one day walking in the rain, unsure of where I was going. I was walking to nowhere." Her shoulders slumped and I felt her sadness like a dense, wet fog. "I did not notice the rain until a man asked me if I was all right. He was wearing a raincoat, carrying an umbrella. I remember hearing the rain on his umbrella, like rapid gunfire. The world kept moving. My parents and my coven were dead but the world kept moving."

I don't say anything, because I can't. I can't find the words. I can't put into words the feeling in my heart because I know her heart is breaking all over again. I see it in her eyes, in her lack of expression.

Kendra nudges me. "You got me through that. When the Demi assigned me to your detail, even during my darkest days, being part of your detail, having a job to do every single minute, allowed me to get out of my head." She tries to divert my attention from the sad story she just told me. "This is all weird, right?"

"I'm more concerned about you." Still staring up at the sky, I feel her eyes on me. "Yeah, it's a little weird. Okay, it's a lot weird, but the part about you protecting me, it's kind of beautiful." I grab her hand refusing to let my friend hurt without me. I want her to know I'm here. "I'm so sorry about your family, Boots."

She gives my hand a squeeze. "Me too."

Wednesday, September 12th 11:07 a.m.
Fourth period means Psych, and Psych means I have to endure the sight of Vanessa and Jesse together. That is if they can manage to make it to all their classes today. Besides, I have my own life to focus on: My impending fate, my training, my transition to Nighmerianotte.

The tardy bell rings as I quickly make my way to my seat and scan the room for Jesse and the She-devil. Nothing. I don't see them. I silently slip into my seat as a tiny sense of relief comes over me. I set my backpack down next to my desk and grab my pencil and paper. I glance at my phone sitting in my backpack. There's a text message from Kendra but I can't check it now. If I'm caught with my phone it will be taken away for the day. I look to the front of the classroom. Ms. Stanton, with her frumpy, teakettle-shaped body, begins her lecture on social cognition. It's just me and Ms. Stanton and the rest of the class. Minus Jesse and Vanessa.

Awesome.

A giggle sounds from the door. *Dang it. Dang it. Dang it!* I sigh. I know that stupid giggle. I didn't even have to look. My body tightens as they make their way to their seats in front of me. Ms. Stanton doesn't look up from her notes. Half the time I think Ms. Stanton is sleeping anyway.

"Sup, Jackson." Jesse flicks my desk with his index finger.

Sup? Who is this dude becoming? What is Vanessa turning him into?

My insides turn outward and my stomach tightens. "Don't do that." I growl. His eyes are red, almost sleepy looking. "What the heck is wrong with you? Are you on something?" I look directly into his eyes as he sits down in front of me.

Jesse smiles flirtatiously and holds his index finger and thumb about a half inch apart. "A little bit." He bites his bottom lip.

"Are you crazy? You're going to get into deep shi—"

"Miss Jackson, Mr. Falco? Something you need to share with the class?" Ms. Stanton's places her hands on her fluffy hips.

Jesse smiles and is about to say something but I interject. "No, Ms. Stanton. We were just discussing the topic. Sorry for the interruption."

I glare at Jesse as if to say, *'I will kill you if you speak again.'* Vanessa is turned around, facing me. She, too, has a glazed look about her. She glares at me before turning around and laying her head down on her desk.

Jesse turns to face me, and I warn, "Jesse turn around. You are going to get caught. Just shut up and we'll talk later."

"Listen, Jackson." He takes my hand and strokes it as if he's petting a dog. My face is red. I'm not sure if I'm more scared we're going to get caught or what is about to come out of Jesse's mouth. I genuinely don't want to hear anything he has to say.

Ms. Stanton doesn't seem to notice this time. Vanessa's head hasn't moved and is still resting on outstretched arms on her desk. I'm almost positive she's sleeping by the way her body is oddly still.

He sighs as his eyes meet mine. His eyes have never been able to lie to me because they reveal so much more than words can say. "I am drunk on a potion and you…you! You are the reason I have to take this magic potion." He laughs as he smacks my hand.

My heart sinks. *Deflect the comment,* I say to myself. *Close your heart. Think with your head.*

"Jesse, just face forward." My heart hammers in my chest.

"You are right. I am drunk." His faces changes. "I know what I want and I cannot have you. I am supposed to fight these feelings. I am not supposed to care. Because that is who I am!" Jesse's voice rises. He's angry. I've never seen him like this before.

"Penelope and Jesse!" Ms. Stanton waddles a little closer to us. "This must be far more important than cognitive dissonance?"

"Yes, actually, Ms. Stanton, it is," he says, still staring at me. "What is it called when someone cares enough to walk away from the only thing he has ever cared about?" Then he turns to face Ms. Stanton.

"Well?" he yells, assuming there's some sort of psych terminology for it, but I don't think there is. He's toasted.

Ms. Stanton looks confused. "Uh," she thumbs through the textbook. "I don't think there's a diagnosis…" Her voice trails off.

Now I'm mad. "What the hell are you talking about? What about sleeping beauty here?" I motion to Vanessa who is clearly passed out on her desk, mouth breathing. "I don't feel like I know you at all anymore!" I yell back.

Now we're both yelling and it's ugly.

Jesse flips around again. "What part of 'I cannot be with you,' do you not understand?" His eyes are full of fire. "Stop getting angry at me! I cannot love you! Stop loving me!"

The entire class is silent.

Words have left me but it hurts. His words burn a hole right through me. "I wish I'd never met you, Jesse Falco, because if I hadn't, I wouldn't feel so damn messed up right now. Plus," I yell, "I have bigger crap to deal with right now than your stupid love affair with the stupid mean girl passed out on her desk!" This I yell at the top of my lungs.

I grab my backpack and walk out.

Before I even make it seven paces down the hallway his hands are on my shoulders. He turns me around and pulls me to his chest. "I am sorry." He rests his chin on my head and kisses my hair. "I am so sorry, Jackson. I do not want to make you hurt. I am so sorry. It is not you. It is everything. I am sorry." His voice cracks and his arms are around me. He holds the back of my head with one hand while the other circles my waist. I feel him kiss my hair again and again. "I am so sorry."

"Jessence." It's Lennon. Jesse doesn't budge. He holds me tighter. He needs this and so do I. Somehow, my arms are already around his waist. His body is against mine. His heat. His heart. His entirety. I feel his heart thumping but it's beating so fast, I can't count the beats. This makes me hold him tighter. He's stroking my hair. "Jessence, we must go," Lennon says.

I'm thinking Jesse will let go soon, but he doesn't. I try to pull away but his grip tightens around me. I hate that I like the way this makes me feel.

"Jess—" he begins again.

"Lennon, give us a minute. I just need a freaking minute with her, okay?" his muscles quiver.

This time, I pull away and look at Jesse. I search his wanting eyes as his stare burns a hole right through my heart. I can't speak. It's the same look he gave me the day of his mother's funeral service.

I flash back to a year ago when Sydney died. After the service, Jo had a get-together at our house. I found Jesse in my room when I ran upstairs to change my top after spilling punch on it.

He said to me, "Sorry, I just needed to be alone." He looked up at me with his huge almond-shaped blue eyes. He was spread out across my bed on his back, hands behind his head, staring at the ceiling.

I said, "Oh, okay, I'll go."

Before I could turn to go, he reached and grabbed my hand. "Alone with you, if that is all right? Lie here with me?"

Without another word, I climbed up on the bed with him. We lie there, in silence, listening to the sad awkward chatter downstairs. "It's okay to be sad," I whispered as I turned on my side to face him.

He turned toward me, lying on his side to look at me. He chose his words carefully before they fell from his lips. "I have never been able to show emotion, Jackson. Ever. No tears. Nothing. I feel it in my body. The sadness. Here," he takes my hand and places it on his chest. "Do you feel that?"

Of course, it's a heartbeat. Yet, it's inconsistent and the beats are way too far apart.

Bump...*Bump*

Bump...*Bump*

Bump...*Bump*

"Your heartbeat? It's not right," I whispered in awe.

He placed his hand on mine that rested on his chest. "That is the sound of sadness."

"Let us go." Lennon's voice is a whisper but his tone slices through the air. The sudden interruption of silence drives me back to the present.

I look to Lennon. His gaze is heavy on me and I know what he wants me to do, but I can't bring myself to do it.

I can let go but I can't walk away.

I wait for Jesse to turn and walk away because I simply can't.

"Jesse!" A shrill voice sounds from down the hallway. "Where are you going?" Vanessa, obviously still paying the price for what she consumed at lunch, walks feebly toward the three of us. Jesse doesn't acknowledge her. He's still staring down at me.

"Let us go," he tells Lennon, no longer buzzed. He takes one last look at me and then quickly turns, and walks with purpose down the hallway and out the double doors.

Vanessa turns from them to me and stares me down. "What did he say to you?" she seethes.

I laugh. "You're a hot mess, Vanessa. Go home and sober up or whatever evil succubi do to cleanse their souls."

I turn and walk back down the hallway. A small part of me feels sorry for her. Damn empathy.

Wednesday, September 12th 2:01 p.m.

Mr. Sullivan's English class inches slowly by. It's dreadful, really. I'm not sure if it's because of what happened earlier or that I've watched Melvin Pinkerton, the smartest kid in the school, and chess champion, pick his nose twice, and eat it.

Both situations make me want to hurl.

My phone vibrates and I glance down to see a text from Kendra. I smile at her timing. I glance up to see Mr. Sullivan turned around, writing some sort of punctuation rule on the board that makes no sense at all. I open the text: Want 2 see something funny?

I nod immediately.

From his pencil holder on his desk, a pencil shoots up a flame. Not a huge flame but enough to get everyone's attention.

Mr. Sullivan pauses, sniffs the air and slowly turns around. He jumps toward the flame, confused as to why one of his pencils is on fire. The flame disappears.

"That was odd." Mr. Sullivan hesitantly turns around to finish writing his sentence.

The flame, this time, shoots higher than before. I turn my head and glance in Kendra's direction.

The flame disappears.

The whole class is staring in silence, looks of amazement spread across their stunned faces.

Mr. Sullivan is now plastered against the chalkboard, a befuddled look on his face.

Then a loud scream fills the classroom. I look at Kendra as if to say 'you've got this, right?' She's focused.

A whoosh blows past me as thousands of butterflies pour out of the pencil and swarm the classroom.

The class erupts into a collective *ahhh* sound. The screaming from the pencil continues as I stare at purple, orange, red, blue, yellow and green butterflies. *Beautiful.* I look to Kendra who is now grinning from ear to ear.

Totally baffled, Mr. Sullivan yells, "Everyone out!"

Someone opens the door and everyone spills into the hallway. A billowing trail of butterflies flows from the classroom and down the hallway.

Just like that, each door to each classroom flies open as students, teachers and butterflies pour out in confused wonder.

"Fist bump," Kendra whispers as she puts her fist out. I bump her fist as we slowly make our way out of Mr. Sullivan's English class while students run amuck.

I look at my best friend in wonder as the swarm of butterflies float up and down the hallway like a rolling wave somewhere in a magical world where things like this do exist.

"Someone open up the front doors!" a teacher yells.

A stream of thousands of butterflies flows out of the school like a fast moving river current.

"Nice, Boots," I whisper as I lean closer to Kendra.

"Yeah. Not too bad." She places her hands on her hips as she leans back, admiring her work, watching them fly overhead and out the front door.

CHAPTER 13

Training Day

Wednesday, September 12ᵗʰ 9:59 p.m.

The sound of the air horn blows me out of my bed.

Literally.

I stand in my bed and dance around in a circle trying to wrap my thoughts around the awful noise that tore me from my sleep. Reality begins to seep back into my mind, slowly.

Crap. I must have fallen asleep.

A chuckle sounds behind me. A familiar chuckle.

"Jackson!" Jesse blows the air horn again. "Let us go! We have training."

His words are cut short as I leap toward him with evil thoughts. I grasp at the air horn but he holds it out of reach.

"An air horn? Really, Jesse?" I jump off him, pushing the loose strands of hair behind my ears, breathing heavily. I look down.

Oh-no. My face reddens as I slowly look up to meet Jesse's stare. He looks away, probably for my benefit.

Where are my pants? I tug on my t-shirt, stretching it as far is it will go to cover anything unhidden. I sidestep to my dresser.

"Meet you down stairs in one minute." He gives a smirk.

Stupid smirk. Sometimes I want to slap it off his face and watch it hit the wall and slide down to its death. "Whatever. Get out and take your stupid air horn with you." I find my black yoga pants as the door shuts behind him. He sounds the air horn again.

I jump out of my skin and curse him under my breath.

My phone chirps. I lunge to the bed as if I'm expecting someone. I'm not.

It's an unknown number.

Unkown Number: Hello, Penelope.

Me: Who is this?

Unknown number: This is Church LeBlanc. The texting concept is quite new to me. After seventeen years, Carmine finally talked me into getting a smart phone. I apologize if my texts are lengthy and far too detailed.

He spells everything out. Huh. That's cute.

Me: UR funny.

Church: Smile face.

I laugh out loud this time.

Me: (;

Church: Right. Anyway, see you tonight.

"Jackson, let us g-o-o-o-o-!" Jesse's voice echoes in the foyer. I roll my eyes but I have to admit, I'm looking forward to our time together. I grab my phone and head downstairs. Jesse's seen me at my worst so there's no point to lip gloss. I'll probably sweat it off in no time anyway.

I don't need to care anymore. He made it quite clear at school today. Wow, did that really happen only today? I file the emotions it brings away and focus on the task at hand.

I run down the stairs, tying my hair into a ponytail. "Get rid of that stupid horn."

I stop at the bottom of the stairs. Mesmerized.

Whoa. Whoa. Whoa.

I swallow hard and act like my attraction to him is not a distraction in the least. I sure as hell don't let him know I'm checking him out.

I can't do this, not with him. I can't.

I hear the tension in his voice, "You ready?" He swings his arms in front of him, stretching.

"Yeah. Uh, no." I turn on the small lamp next to the sofa. I sigh. "Jesse, I don't think I can do this with you. It's too close, too personal. I can't."

"You do not have a say in the matter, Jackson. You first," he whispers as he motions toward the door. I sigh, but do as he says. I walk in front of him as he places his hand on the small of my back and pushes in the softest way possible. *Please don't do that, Jesse. Please.* I don't have it in me to ask him to stop. My stomach nearly explodes with butterflies.

We walk down to the circular driveway. "Go ahead and stretch so you do not pull anything. Here, you are going to need this." He pulls two headlamps from his shorts pocket and tosses me one.

"What? No. I hate headlamps." I don't know if I have a misshapen head but they're always too tight or too loose to be even remotely comfortable.

Without answering me, he waits patiently for me to comply. Begrudgingly, I put mine on.

It's foggy tonight. No surprise in Mason. We rarely ever see the stars at night here. Mason is under constant threat of rain or fog. Located right off the coast, fog seems to be a permanent fixture.

We don't say much as we stretch, our lights dancing around each other. It's hard to have awkward small talk when we've been friends for so long. *We were friends first.* Now it's uncomfortable and I don't like how awkward it is. He made his choice and, whether I'm okay with it or not, I will try to remain his friend. After all, look what he's sacrificed for me.

I finish my last stretch and get to my feet.

"Come on, Ethel, I only have an hour with you."

I stop breathing. If hearts could cry, I think mine just whimpered.

Just one hour, sixty minutes…3,600 seconds.

One hour a night for five weeks. 25 hours…1,500 minutes…90,000 seconds.

I breathe deeply as my heart clears a larger space for him without my consent. *Make every second count.* "Let's hit it," I try to say casually.

We take off side by side. This isn't so bad, training with Jesse, I thought it would be worse. Granted, we are only four minutes in but this will be good. Quality time with one of my oldest friends. A friend who also happens to be dating the biggest cheer-wench in the world. It can't be that bad, right? Nah, this will be good for us, for our friendship. Doubt begins to fester in my head. I push it out with another thought.

The weather.

The fog swallows us whole as we jog. Several minutes pass. The smell of the seaweed and high tide fills my nose.

We run in the eerie silence of the late night. Trust me, 10:15 p.m. is late for Mason. Come five o'clock in the evening, the whole town begins to shut down, aside from the Last Call Tavern and Bella's, one of the best Italian steak houses in Holcomb County.

I can't see ahead of us and it makes me a bit nervous. "The fog is getting thick," I say to Jesse, hoping he will agree and turn around. I don't know where we are. I look behind us, but all I can see is thick white fog reflecting the light from the headlamp.

"Yep. Keep moving," his voice is paced, like his breathing. I try to catch a glimpse of his face to gauge his reaction but he remains stoic and focused. By this time, I am starting to feel the effects of our run. My breathing becomes labored and more difficult to regulate. My lungs burn as I gasp for air. As some point, the ground changed from pavement to sand, we are on the beach.

"Stop," he says abruptly and tilts his headlamp so it isn't shining directly in my eyes. "Give me twenty good push-ups."

"What?" I say as I draw in a couple of deep breaths.

"Give me twenty. You heard me."

"Here? Right now?" I counter.

"Now," His tone is more commanding.

I pause at first, still hoping he's kidding. "Seriously? In the sand? Twenty push-ups?" He nods and I sigh loudly. I get down on all fours, my hands disappearing into the sand.

I can hear the quiet waves making their way up on the shore.

I straighten my legs, holding myself up by my tiptoes, my arms extended in front.

I push one out.

"Count them out loud," Jesse commands.

"One."

"Two." I push out.

"Three…" I hold my body up.

"Four," I say. My arms begin to warm.

"Seriously, Jackson? After four you are already wobbling? Come on. Dig deep."

"Ffffive," I call out. This is embarrassing. I make a mental note to head back to the gym, stat.

"Dig deeper, Jackson. This is not your grandma's weight training class. Come on, let us go. Do not waste my time." Jesse claps his hands together several times like some sort of crazed coach.

I huff. "Shut up, Jesse. I bet my grandma could kick your ass." I pause, immediately sorry for trying to be funny, wishing I knew my grandparents.

"Your push up form sucks. Here," he says as he crouches next to me and firmly places his hand on my stomach. He pushes causing my entire body to straighten.

Oh my. My whole body grows hot. "Don't touch me, Jesse," is all I manage to sputter as I push out another. Seven.

Jesse leans to my ear. "Any excuse to touch you, Penn, will be used. Every single time."

I don't know if it's the push-ups or my throbbing heart that makes my face burn. A tiny smile forms at the corners of my mouth. *Don't smile, Penn. Don't listen to what he is saying. Fight through it. He made it clear what can and cannot happen between us. Even if he likes to play all angles it will only hurt in the end.*

"Come on. Dig deep. You are only at eight. Not even half way there."

My arms wobble horribly and my legs cramp, but I don't dare say a word. I push up to number nine. "Nine," I say, my voice seemingly unaffected.

"I said twenty. Push, Jackson."

"I am, you big jerk face!" The least I can do is twenty measly push-ups, right? If this is the extent of my physical training this should be a piece of cake. *Think of...the kiss between Vanessa and Jesse. Dig Penn.*

I push out six more, my muscles feeding on the adrenaline rush caused by that memory. I stop at the top of sixteen.

"Four more, Jackson." His hand is still on my stomach. *Please move your hand. No, don't. Don't move your hand. Wait. Yes, please, please move your hand.*

I feel the sweat dripping from my face. "Don't...talk...to...me," I huff as I lower myself once more. My arms are now shaking so badly it's making my shoulders shake. *Don't give Jesse the satisfaction. Now, go.*

"Eighteeeeeeeeeeen!" I yell as I push up one more time. I inhale and exhale loudly. *Two more, Penn. Only two more.* I exhale once more. "Niiiiiiinteeen."

I can't. I can't. I can't do it.

My arms and shoulders are burning so badly. Burning like they're on fire.

"One more," he whispers in my ear.

I would roll my eyes if I could, but I lack the strength. *One more, Penn. Just one more.* "This one's for you, jerk face." *Vanessa.*

"Twenty!" I collapse in the sand on top of his hand.

"Shake it off. Move, Jackson." He manages to get his hand free.

I shake my head as I lie in the sand. My arms and shoulders feel numb. If we are at the beach that means we have run at least three miles.

"Get up, Jackson. Run!" he calls behind him.

"Okay, okay." I get to my knees. Jesse jogs back and reaches for my arm. Before he can grab it, I jump to my feet, avoiding his touch. *Don't feel sorry for me. Don't help me, Jesse.* "I have this." I stand, looking into his shadowed face. Our eyes connect and I see regret and sadness in his eyes before it quickly fades behind a weary smile.

"Run." He takes off back in the direction we came. I'm behind him. "The body can handle far more than the mind says it can. Shut out what your mind tells you and find a rhythm." Jesse's voice lulls me.

It's hard to quiet my mind running next to you, Slick. Maybe if you stopped touching me, I might be able to focus. I deflect fear with sarcasm. Kendra calls it avoidance. I call it creative expression.

We run for what seems like forever. Again.

Sand.

Water.

Pavement.

Sand.

Water.

Pavement.

I begin falling behind but keep running. Jesse remains two strides ahead of me and my eyes stay fixed on his toned body. It takes my mind off my burning lungs and leg cramps. My legs are moving and I have no idea how. He doesn't look behind so he must hear my breathing. He knows I'm following.

The fog is thinning and my nostrils are no longer overwhelmed by the stench of seaweed. This tells me we are close to home. We are back on the pavement and my legs appreciate it immensely.

"Home stretch, kick it into gear," I hear Jesse say.

I put my head down sprint as fast and hard as I can, my body lunges forward.

Three strides into my sprint, I crash into his back and stagger backwards.

"Jackson?" He laughs.

196

It takes me a minute to get my bearings. My breathing is ragged. "You told me…" I try to catch my breath again. "You told me to kick it into high gear!" I take in a mouthful of air, and gasp, "I feel like I head butted a brick building!" I pinch my nose checking for blood.

"Come here, let me look at it." He walks toward me.

"No. Don't. Don't. I'm fine." I shrug him off and the tension between the two of us grows.

"Hold still." He places a firm grip on both shoulders, and examines my forehead.

His scent, a scent I've always been able to find comfort in, has become my greatest enemy. It invades my nose and lungs like unwanted feelings. He hesitates before he meets my gaze, as though he expected it. He looks from my eyes to my mouth and back to my eyes again. *Look away, Penn. Look away. This will only end badly for you.*

"I'm fine, Jesse. Really." He doesn't release my shoulders. His eyes are heavy, and it breaks my heart. "Stop…"

"Time is up," Carmine's voice rings out behind Jesse. He pulls away quickly, taking a piece of my heart with him.

"Tomorrow night, Jackson. You are mine." Jesse disappears into the fog.

Carmine looks at me, sweaty and drenched from the heavy mist. "You look like death." Carmine's face scrunches.

"Awe, you're just saying that." My cheesy grin widens as sarcasm festers in my words. I look back toward the direction Jesse went, but he's gone, vanished into thin air.

"No, really, when is the last time you ate?"

"Not sure. Why do you care?" I say, still breathing hard, stretching my legs so they don't cramp.

"Come." He grabs my hand and leads me toward the shed next to our house.

"I'm fine, Carmine," I insist.

"No, you are not. Look," he turns me in his direction, "you have to take care of your body. There is no way, *no way*, your mind and your body will be able to perform at the level we need it to if you are not giving it proper nutrition." He pulls me into the old slaughter shed and closes the door. A tin light hangs overhead with a small table beneath it. Carmine reaches into the old refrigerator in the back and pulls out two blood bags.

"I don't want it." I cross my arms and sit down on one of the stools like an indignant little girl.

Carmine throws his head back in a loud howl, tossing the blood bags on the table. His face is serious as he leans forward, placing his elbows on the table. "Drink."

I sigh. "I'm fi—"

Carmine's vibrant eyes have become a lifeless gray. His faces distorts slightly as his canines appear. In a blur, he is behind me, holding my head back by my forehead with his hand.

Panic freezes my heart. My strength is no match for his as I try to free myself from his grasp. *What on earth is he doing?*

With the same hand that holds my forehead, he plugs my nose.

Unable to breathe, I gasp as I open my mouth and swallow air. I stare into his eyes as I pull at his hand. His gray eyes are haunting, his mood dark, almost scary.

What are you doing? I want to say, but the words don't come out. He grabs the blood bag and tears the tab with his mouth, starting the flow of blood. I want to scream but close my mouth to keep him from emptying the bag into it. I plead with my eyes but he only stares back, a cold black stare. He patiently waits, smiling, for me to open my mouth for another breath. When I do, he squeezes the blood into my mouth. I can't taste it but I feel its thickness fill my mouth. I blow, forcing the blood out of my mouth and into Carmine's watching eyes. He smiles, licking his lips before he wipes his face on his sleeve.

"I appreciate your thoughtfulness, but in my world, it is impolite for a gentleman to drink before his guest." Carmine's smile grows as he reaches for the second bag, again ripping the tab with his teeth. He once again fills my mouth with blood, cups his hand over my mouth, and waits. I won't swallow, I refuse. I will show him. My lungs burn, begging for oxygen. A small trickle of blood seeps from the corner of my mouth and drips down my cheek. I don't want to drink someone's blood, human blood. I don't want it. *Please,* I plead with my eyes, *don't make me do this.*

"Swallow!" he demands. "Swallow or pass out. It is of little consequence to me."

I have no choice. I claw at his hands in a final attempt to free myself, to no avail.

I'm out of air and I cannot breathe. So, I swallow. And swallow. And swallow. Almost immediately, I feel my body floating. The high is euphoric. I drain the bag, forgetting about breathing. No longer concerned about what I am drinking or where it came from, I want more.

I feel powerful, restored. Moments ago, I couldn't imagine ever drinking blood, let alone human blood. Now, I can't imagine living without it. It tastes how *amazing* feels. Pure euphoria. I feel safe, warm and content.

Untouchable.

At some point during my hemoglobin induced euphoria, Carmine released my head and collected another bag from the refrigerator. Now he sits across from me draining his own bag. He stares at me as though he knows what I just experienced, his canines still in full view. I feel as though I'm staring into a kaleidoscope. His head is in four different quadrants, twisting to the right, distorting as it turns. My ears are hot and my ears are ringing. I feel like my body is floating. Weightless. Limitless.

"Can you stop the ringing?" I shout, trying to pick one of the four heads to look at.

He laughs. "Enjoy it while it lasts, Black Five."

"You mean this ends? Please don't let it end." The feeling slips from my grasp with each second that passes. Can I come to terms with what I've just done? Hell, if I came to terms with taking someone's life, I can come to terms with drinking blood from a bag.

Everything is becoming clearer by the second. The ringing has ceased, and Carmine has only two heads now, though they are still floating. Finally two fade into one as my thoughts become clearer.

Silence.

"How? How could you do that to me, Carmine?"

"Let me paint you a picture, Penn, of what will happen if you do not drink human blood." His eyebrows rise as he leans back in his chair, his tone curt, rude and sarcastic. "First, your hands and feet will go numb and turn black. They will stop working. Your legs and arms are next as they, too, will go numb and turn black. You will neither be able to blink on your own nor move your head nor speak. You will enter a vegetative state in which you will live, forever. You will be aware of all that occurs around you as your brain will continue to function normally," his tone goes higher. "The only thing you will have control over is what you choose to think about during your endless hours of stillness," he pauses, a devious grin spreading across his pale face. "You will not even be able to go to the bathroom on your own or wipe your own a—"

"Carmine. I get it." I stare at him then to the empty blood bags that lie grotesquely on the table, sucked dry. "But seriously, how could you?"

He doesn't answer. His lips are firmly pressed together. "You think I did this to hurt you?" He asks, voice full of resentment.

I slam my fist down on the table. "It's someone else's blood, Carmine. I can't take someone else's blood. That's stealing. You're stealing someone else's lifeline."

Carmine shakes his head. "It's not your choice anymore, Penelope. This is what you are. You can choose to hate me for it, but if not me, it would have been someone else. Would you prefer it had been Kendra, Jesse, your Aunt Jo, maybe? Everything else aside, you would not be able to survive without it. You speak of the lifeline you stole, but what of the millions of lives you will save when we return home. It is your service to our world. You save but, in order to save, you must drink blood." He stops speaking and stares at me. I glare back. "Besides, it was donated, by a person, to the blood bank. It was given of free will." He picks at the table with his fingernail.

Do I hold my tongue? Of course not. I whisper, "Not to us. Not to you. It was donated with the hope someone could use it to help the sick." The words flow out of me quicker than I can catch them.

He clicks his tongue at me. The eerie silence gnaws at my conscience. He speaks slowly, enunciating every word, "Is that not what you do, Penn? Help others who are sick?"

I feel the blow deep in my gut. I bite my lower lip as my eyes dance from his face to the empty blood bags and back again. I don't answer him because I know he is absolutely correct.

Carmine leans forward, his complexion gray under the dim light. "I will break you, Penelope Jackson. Now, let us begin the hour, shall we?"

I know he means to push me beyond my limits and, for the first time in this entire process, I am truly scared. I try to hide the fear pushing its way up my spine. I swallow and stare into his eyes, too afraid to look away. *Don't show fear, Penn.*

"Who are you?" Carmine leans back in his chair, a little too casual.

I smirk like he's kidding. "Penelope."

"No." His voice is slightly louder now. "Who are you, Penelope?" He cocks his head this time.

Jerk. He's baiting me.

"Penelope Jackson," I counter.

"No!" Carmine shoots up and kicks his chair back. He places his knuckles on the wooden table and leans under the light. His pale skin shines brightly. "Who are you?" He asks again, his canines bared. I wonder if he keeps them out for some sort of intimidation.

For unknown reasons, I stand. "Pen-el-o-pe Jack-son." I pronounce every single syllable so he hears my words clearly.

His face is stoic. "What? You think since you were raised by trailer trash I am going to play into your stupidity?" he asks in a low tone. "Are you stupid, Penelope?"

A flash of anger bursts through me. "I answered your question," I seethe through my clenched jaw. *Don't back down, Penn.* I feel my heart thud against my chest cavity.

"I did not ask for your name, stupid girl."

My blood begins to run hot. I cock my head to one side. "Who am I, Carmine?" I call his bluff.

"Do not toy with me, Five. Answer the question!"

I stare hard. *Is he bluffing? He wants to know who I am? Why? He knows.* I'll play his game. "I'm a daughter and a niece. A friend."

"Come on! Cut the nonsense!" Carmine yells in my face. "Who are you?

"What do you want me to say?" I scream back in his face, my chest full of angst as my breathing quickens.

"Think, Penn. Use your brain. Why am I asking you this? For my health? Everyone knows vampires are dead. They do not care about their health. They do not have health. They have no working hearts, remember? Vampire's hearts do not work."

I know what he's asking. "The Sanguine. I'm the Five." I stop breathing, waiting for his response.

"Precisely!" he yells toward the roof of the shed. "What is the Five? Please? Hmm? Enlighten me?"

"I can heal. I—" I stutter because I don't want to believe the words that are about to drip from my mouth but I say them anyway, "I drink blood to stay strong. I can kill people with my mind." The truth spews from my mouth in torrents. I place my hand over my mouth in an attempt to stop the flow. I feel dried blood around my mouth and my hands begin to quiver. I suddenly feel nauseous and faint.

I'm not human anymore.

Now, I'm going to ask you once more." His voice is dark now. "Who are you?"

I turn to Carmine and reply with confidence, "I am the Five."

"Good." His eyes are slits now, his voice barely a whisper. He sounds vulnerable. It makes me wonder what happened to make Kendra hate him so much. "I will always give you truth, no matter how badly it may hurt. No matter how scary it may be. I am happy to be the bad guy if that is what the situation requires." His face is sad. His heart may not beat but it aches. I know it because I see the depth of his sadness in his face. "Now, leave me. I do not want to see you until tomorrow night."

I stand, unclear of where I am to go next.

Carmine doesn't look up. He stares down at the blood bags on the table. I wonder how he feels about what he had to do to me. Does it hurt him? Who is he hurting for?

I walk out of the slaughter shed in a daze. Everything happened so quickly. My body feels rejuvenated and brand new. I feel stronger. I feel weightless.

CHAPTER 14

Fireballs and Labyrinths

"You had better be careful. I hear the creatures come out about this time of night."

Church is standing directly behind me. His words cause me to blush. His tone picks away at a feeling deep inside me that makes my thinking go a little haywire.

I reply, "I'll keep an eye out."

He towers over me, leaning on a tree. "You are with me for the next hour. Weapons training. Follow me, if you will."

Church has a way with his eyes. Sometimes he looks at me as though he holds the weight of my world on his unbeating heart, while other times he looks at me with remorse. Sometimes he looks at me with complete admiration and sometimes as though seeing me is painful.

Tonight, he's looking at me with admiration. His eyes are wide and he wears a smile.

Church is beautiful. He is beautiful physically and in his humbleness and empathy. When I am with him I feel his dedication to me.

It takes me back to that night in my bedroom when I saw the glow of his beautiful translucent skin. His skin doesn't have that radiance tonight but it is still so beautiful.

I sense mental scars in his being. Maybe he's killed someone, maybe many? Behind the radiant skin there exist fresh wounds. He's broken, like me, yet in different ways; ways I don't understand yet.

He's searching my eyes now, trying to read my thoughts. "I cannot tell what you are feeling right now, Penelope." He maintains his distance.

"I can't either."

There's a long silence between us.

"Follow me."

It's dark in the old hay barn. A single candle lights the old picnic table that sits in the middle of the open floor. Church is careful not to touch me as he motions me through the door and shuts it behind us.

"Please, Penelope, join me, will you?" he guides me to the picnic table.

A soft hum emits from one of the items lying on the table. It looks like some sort of magnifying glass with a red-orange fireball orbiting around it. It looks old, as if the rust has eaten the handle alive. A thick piece of glass sits in the middle. I assume it's a Nighmerian weapon. I carefully sit down at the table as Church sits across from me.

"These are some of the weapons used in Nighmerianotte. Some are far more dangerous than others. They are designed to incapacitate but are capable of killing. It is imperative you know we train with a no-kill approach. Nighmerians believe killing another is a last resort. Always. Do you understand this?"

"So the mortal world has it all wrong?" I remember my father's words.

"No, not in the least. We are trained impeccably well. So well, in fact, ninety percent of the time, we do not have to kill. Part of our training is learning to control our kill or be killed instinct."

The humming of the fireball grabs my attention. "This is called a nuck." Church catches the fireball orbiting around the magnifying glass. The humming stops. He opens his hand, and the fireball hovers around his hand for a second before it reattaches itself and begins to orbit around the magnifying glass again. The humming resumes.

I'm mesmerized.

I hear a smile in his voice when he says, "This weapon was created by the warlocks. By trade, warlocks are cartographers and inventors."

"Yes. My father mentioned that."

"They use magnifying glasses in their work. The warlocks wanted protection so, with some help from the 205's."

"The witches."

"Yes. The nuck came to fruition." Church pauses. He seems a little uncomfortable. "Penelope, this might sound a little personal, but have you seen your identifier yet? The reason I ask is, it was a defining moment for me. It gave me some sort of identity. Yes, I was born into the immortal world but crossed over a lot. It was confusing for a nine-year-old little boy. The moment I saw my identifier, I gained ownership of who and what I was." He reaches out and carefully places his cold hand on mine. I stare at it. He tries to move his hand, but I catch it between mine. Sometimes silence is all that needs to be said.

I swallow the feelings starting to creep up.

Identity. What is that, anyway? Have I ever had an identity? Now everything is unclear and muddy. I can't answer his question because guilt is blocking my thoughts. His hand is on mine. They're big but not long and boney like I'd pictured a vampire's hands. Jesse's hands are big too. Jesse. I think about the run I was just on. Guilt digs at my heart like a dull knife. Why feel guilty? I don't belong to anyone.

Am I betraying my heart?

I'm nobody's possession or property. "I want to see my identifier... just not yet." My eyes slowly make their way to his.

His staid stare pierces my heart.

"Any time you are ready." His voice is steady.

The tension between us is too much.

The barn door opens.

"Sorry, I am late." The barn door slams behind Kendra. She whispers something under her breath and with one swoop of her finger, a chair appears. She plops down in it as though it's nothing. She winks at me and waves like an anxious cheerleader, one thing Kendra is definitely not.

"Right on time. I was telling Penelope some history." Church stands, placing his hands on his hips. His blue jeans hang from his hips showing the leanness of his physique. "Anyway," he continues, looking down at me as if we are in class, "The 205's and the 505's, the warlocks, with some trading of services, worked a deal. This took place back in the 1930's. It is a relatively new weapon to Nighmerianotte being that nearly all weapons were created around 900 A.D. At least that is what we have documented thus far. Anyhow, the nuck shoots fireballs far more powerful than a bomb will ever be. In the wrong hands, the nuck can cause serious destruction. Truly, it should only be handled by witches and warlocks as they are the ones qualified to handle them.

You must know how to use one in case it is the only weapon at your disposal."

"Join me." Church stands up, walks around the table, and stands behind me. A chill surges through my body.

"You never want to point the nuck at anyone, or be in front of someone handling one. There have been misfires." He reaches his arms around me and takes my hands in his. I feel the strength and coolness of his chest on my back. This time, I don't shiver. I welcome the feeling it gives me.

Can he hear my heart? Can he feel the butterflies in my stomach?

His cool voice interrupts my thoughts. "Take the nuck in your hands, Penn. Carefully." His fingers intertwine in mine. They look like puzzle pieces that fit perfectly.

Pale and pink.

He's close. I feel his breath on my neck. It sends a chill down my spine as his breath lingers, bringing the hairs on my neck to attention.

The weapon has a low vibration that hums louder as the tiny fireball orbits around the glass. "Without touching it, do you see that tiny button to the right?"

"Yes," I whisper.

I feel his head turn, looking toward Kendra. "I'm ready." I hear Kendra walk toward us.

"Now," his voice is throaty, "carefully move the nuck toward your face, and peer through the glass."

I do what I'm told.

"Focus on that wine barrel straight ahead. Do you see it?"

I'm terrified to laugh. It's awfully hard to miss it being it's the only object at that end of the barn. "Yes."

"Once the wine barrel fills the frame of the glass, I want you to carefully push the button. Do you see the barrel, Penn?"

"Yes." I'm holding my breath.

"Push it."

I do.

The fireball orbiting around the magnifying glass stops. It wails so loudly I want to cover my ears. I feel like my eardrums are going to explode, yet I don't dare move.

A gigantic flame erupts from the glass into the form of a ball as big and tall as the barn wall. It wails once more.

Then, it blows out the back of the barn, disintegrating the barn wall instantly. The fireball shoots up toward the sky so fast I almost miss its departure.

"Palla di fuoco, torna da me! Sono la tua Regina della magia!" Kendra walks ahead of us as her hands point toward the sky where the fireball disappeared. She repeats herself, this time louder and with more force. "Palla di fuoco, torna da me! Sono la tua Regina della magia!"

Then silence.

Church steps in front of me.

No. Not anymore. I step next to him and we are equals. He looks down at me and our eyes meet. He doesn't move.

A loud squeal sounds as the gigantic fireball hurdles toward us with fierceness, where the wall used to be.

Kendra holds her hand in the air as she chants the same line she's said out loud several times. Then the fireball, right in front of my eyes, shrinks to the size of a pea and disappears into her hand.

The noise stops.

She carefully pulls her arms down and slowly opens her hands. The fireball hovers over her hand as it did in Church's.

2/2

"Whoa! That was bomb," I whisper.

"I know, right? Kendra turns around, wearing a huge grin. "Finally, someone who appreciates my magic!" she bumps Church's arm. She lets the tiny pea-like fireball gravitate back to the magnifying glass once more.

"My work is done here. You coming?" She stops and looks at me.

I'm staring at where the barn wall used to be, trying to come up with a way to tell Aunt Jo I nucked her barn.

"Oh. I forgot." She turns to where the barn wall once stood in its massiveness. "Fissare."

The barn wall slowly appears as if a mirage.

"I will wait outside."

Kendra's gone and the candle is once again the only light in the barn. Church remains standing next to me. *Ask him. Ask him all of these questions that have been on your mind, Penn.*

No, don't. Ask him. No, no, perhaps you need a little more time before you ask him such personal questions.

Ask him.

Don't.

"Do you breathe? I mean, do you need oxygen to live?" I ask still staring at the barn wall. *Great. Awesome, Penn. You probably sound like a complete idiot.*

"Do I need oxygen to live? No. Do I breathe? Yes."

I laugh. I laugh because this seems all too unbelievable. The more I know about Church, the more it scares me.

"You are scared, Penelope. I feel it. It is not terror but pain." He doesn't move a muscle. "There is emotion attached to it." He sighs. "I need to walk away. I need to walk away and let you focus on your training, but I cannot bring myself to do it."

I look up at him. His jaw flexes. He's clenching his teeth. "No." I try to stop but the stupid words fall out of my mouth. "I don't want that." I turn toward him. "I mean, yeah, it's a little distracting but it isn't anything I can't get used to." *Stop, Penn. Shut up.* "Don't leave, please." *Oh, stupid girl.*

He's still staring straight ahead, chewing on his lip. I find this to be something he does when deep in thought. "Your hour is up. Kendra is waiting for you outside." He doesn't look at me. "You should go." Just like that, he says it to me.

I look down, and then back to him. "Yeah, you're right." *Stupid. Stupid. Stupid girl.*

"Hey lady killer, you done with Penn yet?" Kendra's voice sounds at the door. "Oh sorry. That wasn't how I meant it. My bad." She laughs.

"Be here. Tomorrow night. Be here, Church." I want, so badly, to reach out and touch his arm. My fingertips barely graze his arm. "Please." He doesn't budge. His face is hard.

I turn and follow Kendra to my next session. We're outside when I ask her, "Why do you call him lady killer?"

Kendra laughs. "Have you seen him? Every woman practically throws herself at him, mortal and immortal alike. Plus, there is that whole vampire killer thing." She sighs. "Penn, look, you have got to get over Jesse. His people, the 305, are destined to serve. Their ties are strong. He will never dishonor his code, the sentinels, The Republic of Nighmerianotte or the Nighmerians." She doesn't say anything else. She knows. Sometimes she knows me better than I know myself. I hate that about her but I love it. Silence speaks for us when there are no words.

"We are headed to the backfield," she says as we make our way toward the back of the house.

We stand before a wall of massive brick covered in jasmine and ivy. She has obviously been working her magic because this wasn't here before. "This, my friend, is a labyrinth." She pulls back some greenery to expose a wooden door. "I want to see how you do. The jasmine will keep your scent hidden."

"My scent?"

"It depends on the direction of the wind, but morterros have an impeccable sense of smell. We are wondering if your scent is what brought the rogue morterros to Mason. They are dumb as rocks and cannot see worth a crap but they can smell. Even though a spell protects you, you are out in the open and more exposed than we are comfortable with. The labyrinth is excellent for training you in utilizing your senses. Do not worry, Penn, I highly doubt you will run into a morterro. Besides, the moon and the temperature have to be right. Many things have to be in order for us to see a morterro in the mortal world."

"So, good luck. Oh, your headlamp?" she turns back to me.

"Yeah, got it." I hold it up. I turn to the door and back to her. "Are you sure about this?"

"Good luck. You have one hour to get to the other side." She holds up a single finger as her voice trails behind her.

"That's it?" I call back to her. "That's all you're giving me? A headlamp?"

She looks over her shoulder. "I will see you on the other side, Five."

"Great," I whisper. "This is a hell of a first night of training, more like a crash course to death." I look up to the top of the door. It must be twenty feet tall. I push back a leaf covered branch to search for a handle.

"Hey! Watch out!" I hear a voice. "Leaf me alone!" A loud cackle sounds from the direction of the door.

I jump back. "Who, who's there?"

"You coming in or not?"

I dance around in a circle. "Who's there?"

"Just your garden variety ivy. We are here to help you. Now pass through the door and step into the abyss, if you dare." A totally fake sinister laugh sounds from the direction of the ivy leaves.

"Levion, give the kid a break. She is new." A high pitch voice sounds now, from the same direction.

"How is this possible? You're leaves." *I'm talking to leaves.*

"Five, you have fifty two minutes to complete the labyrinth. We suggest you start now. Or else," the high pitch voice continues.

Is this a trick? Do I continue? I look back to see if Kendra is anywhere to be seen, but she isn't. I look the gigantic door up and down. Careful not to touch the leaves, I push it open with a crrrrrrreak and enter. I jump as it slams behind me.

It's dark. The only light I have is my headlamp. I begin to wonder if the batteries will give out. The ivy and jasmine cover the brick that towers fifteen feet above my head. I can see the sky above, which is somewhat of a comfort. The temperature is slightly warmer in the labyrinth and there's a soft breeze pushing through the three paths in front of me.

Straight ahead looks pretty dark. I'll go left. I will go left because I'm left handed.

"Forty-four minutes and counting," I hear. I know it is the leaves. A thought crosses my mind. *Are they just here to mess with my head?* Then she gives what she obviously feels is sage advice. "You must rely on your senses to get you through."

That's it! The five senses: touch, taste, sight, smell and hearing. Instinctively, I touch a leaf. The leaves seem to have an opinion on everything.

"Ouch!" one of them says.

"I'm sorry." The leaf is ice cold. I take a few steps deeper into the labyrinth. I touch another leaf.

"Do you mind?" an accented voice says.

I don't apologize this time. The leaf is ice cold.

I back track to the beginning of the labyrinth and decide to take the path all the way to the right. Something doesn't feel right about the middle path.

I swallow and feel the tightness in my throat as I adjust my head-lamp. The right path, but is it the correct path? I take two big steps in. I reach out and touch another leaf.

Ice cold.

I take a couple steps further down the dark path. I feel the warmth of the wind kiss my face, like the Santa Ana winds. I remember them as a child living in Santa Maria. Not that I went outside much. How-ever, on the occasions I did, they always seemed to intensify. Something about the wind was, and still is, calming.

I touch another leaf. Ice cold.

I turn around and head to the middle path. An uneasy feeling grows in my stomach. *Penn, Kendra would not set you up to get seriously hurt, right?* I stare down the third and final dark path.

"Thirty four minutes." I hear.

This has to be it, right? I turn to the labyrinth wall and touch a leaf. It's cold as well. This can't be.

I take two steps further and swallow my frustration. I switch sides to the other wall. I reach out and touch a leaf.

Not as cold. *Not as cold.* Okay. I take three steps further. I hear rustling of branches and leaves, twisting and turning.

I look back to the opening.

No. No. No. No. I try to run but instead I run straight into the wall of ivy. The opening is gone. The ivy and jasmine have grown over the opening of the path. Panic begins to set it. *Focus. Pay attention to your senses. Go deeper.*

As I walk, I hold out my hand and graze the leaves. Some leaves make snide comments while others are highly offended.

I keep walking, a tinge of excitement building inside me, until a fork in the road comes into view. *Crap. This is great. This is just fantastic. Which way? If it were lighter in here, I could see a whole lot better.* It's dark and it seems to be getting darker the further I walk. Colder too, yet the leaves keep getting warmer.

I look behind me. The path I once followed is now nothing but a wall made of ivy and jasmine.

Wait. I smell something. I cover my nose because the smell is getting more rank by the second.

There's only one thing that smells like this. *The smell of death.*

No. This cannot be. Kendra said there are parameters that must be met. Is it the labyrinth? Is the labyrinth playing tricks on my mind? I try to hold my breath but gasp for air. *Morterros smell fear.*

Penn, you're *The Five*. You can kill with your mind. You're powerful. Believe that. You're powerful. Senses. Rely on your senses. "I can't," I whisper to myself.

"Twenty-seven minutes." I hear, this time more of a whisper.

I turn to the right side of the fork and brush my hands against the leaves. They're cold. Damn. I turn to the left side and do the same thing. Cold. My heart starts to pound.

A hissing sound. My queue to follow? Yes, that's it.

Follow the sound. Use my senses.

I'm in the middle of the fork. I listen. It's coming from the left. I go left with caution. The hissing sound is hushed at first. The deathly smell is still with me. It's getting stronger the further I walk into the blackness. All I can see is the narrow stream of light from the headlamp that splashes along the path I walk. The hissing sound is getting louder and the pathway is getting narrower the further I walk into the labyrinth. Dread fills my thoughts.

Penn, shake it. Fake it. Don't show fear.

My heart is beating so hard I can feel it in my ears.

I trip on something. My hands hit the ground, thankfully, before my face does. My hand closes on something scaly and moving. The hissing sound is directly in front of my face. It grows louder and I feel something at my ear, like a tongue. I follow the light cast by my headlamp.

OH CRAP.

Snakes.

I cry out, scrambling to lift myself from the ground, scared to look down. My body is trembling. I stand and try to run backwards, falling yet again onto the nasty reptiles.

Dear Lord, please help me. They're everywhere. I swallow nothing because my throat is so dry I think it will crack open.

I feel a snake wrap around my arm. I cry out. I'm terrified to touch it so I shake my arm to dislodge it.

Epic fail.

I shine the light on the serpent clinging to my arm.

I have to touch it. *Fight through your fear. Fight through it, Penn. Touch it. Touch it.* I feel its scaly skin encircle my arm.

I want to vomit. I want to pass out. I want to pass out because this is too much. Kendra, of all people, knows I'm terrified of snakes. *Note to self, kick her butt when I see her again. What if I don't see her again? What if the snakes eat me alive?*

My entire body begins to shake. *Penn, it isn't an anaconda, right? Wait, what if it is?* My mind flashes to a picture that circulated on the internet months ago about the anaconda who swallowed a drunk guy in India. My insides go numb. *I can't touch it. I can't touch it.* What if it is?

Amy. Think of Amy. Amy. Oh my sweet little Amy.

Fight, Penn.

I grab part of the snake, I'm not sure which end, peel it off my arm and throw it. I stumble backwards toward the fork in the path.

The snakes are slithering my way, hissing. It feels like I have skin lice, crawling under my skin. *I probably do. Snakes probably carry skin lice.* I keep my headlamp pointed in their direction. I unsteadily walk backwards. "Think rationally, Penn," I say.

The smell of death is back and it's stronger than ever. I can't move my head because I don't want to take my light off the awful snakes slithering my way now.

My back hits something hard. It knocks the air from me for a moment. The stench is so potent I have to choke back the vomit making its way into my throat. I whine out of fear. It's cold, whatever it is, and it utters an unearthly sound.

I turn to look at what I've hit.

I run. *Don't show fear. Don't show fear. Don't show fear. Don't show fear.* I'm totally freaking out.

Think of Amy, Penn. Think of her. She's fighting a battle. You are fighting a battle.

Though I can't feel them, my legs maneuver in the dark as though they know where they're going. I look ahead, shining the headlamp but...it's a dead end.

Wow. This is bad.

I hear the moaning behind me. *Don't show fear, Penn!* I hit my head with my fists and turn to face my fight. I will not go down without a fight. I will not.

The morterro floats toward me. The snakes, once forgotten, slither around my ankles making backward movement impossible. The morterro is moving way too fast.

Think of Amy. You're fighting for Amy. Push the fear out. Amy. Amy. Amy.

CHAPTER 15

Saving Lives

Black holes, where eyes once rolled, stare blankly toward me. Collapsed black veins under translucent layers of skin cover the entirety of its flesh. The smell is unbearable. It makes me want to rip off my nose and feed it to the snakes.

I try to hold the fear at bay with thoughts of Amy. She's a fighter. I have to live to save her life and in order to live I have to kill this hellacious thing that wants to rip off my face and eat my flesh.

Though it cannot see me, it's inches from my face. It sniffs at the air with two holes serving as nostrils. Its jaw hangs open and I know where the death smell is coming from. A low moan from its mouth makes my chest rattle. I feel its saliva drip from its mouth, onto my bangs before sliding down my cheek. I cringe.

I gag at the stench. I try not to wretch but fail. I choke it back as my eyes begin to water. The taste of bile lingering in my mouth.

It can't see me, but it smells me. *Focus, Penn.* I close my eyes. "Focus," I whisper.

Then everything falls silent.

It's all gone.

In a flash, something wraps around my throat. The hands of the morterro, I grasp at its hands but the grip is so tight no air can pass through.

It opens its mouth to expose its razor like teeth.

Its grip tightens and I'm gasping for air. I cannot breathe.

Quiet your mind, Penn. Quiet your mind. Take hold of what brains it has left.

I open my eyes and stare into its black seeping holes. Its transparent complexion makes my mouth go dry. I barely manage a gasp.

With that, I close my eyes again and pull my head back. I let the energy take hold of its brain. I squeeze. A frightening sound escapes it, a loud, blood-curdling moan. Its hands immediately release my throat. Its horrid black face smashes against mine as it wheezes and drops to its knees. I stumble backwards trying to keep my focus. This time, I feel my body grow quiet, tranquil. The harder I squeeze, the more I crave. I squeeze again. And again. And again. *Bliss.* I squeeze until I no longer hear the wheezing.

The thud of its head against the ground awakens me, bringing me out of my hypnotic state. "Nice work."

I spin around. "Holy, Carmine!" I gasp rubbing my neck, breathing heavily.

Kendra and Church stand beside him. "I do not get it. The labyrinth was woven with jasmine. How did a morterro get in?" Kendra puts her hands on her head.

"Come on, Boots." Carmine starts.

"You do not get to call me that, Cold Blood." Kendra says, turning to Carmine.

Church bends over and examines the morterro. "Nice work." He pauses, and with one swift movement, removes the morterro's head. It spins around on the ground like a top. "This one will not kill anymore. It is some sort of hybrid." He inspects the neck where the head once was, like some sort of science experiment.

"I knew it!" Kendra yells. "Vacavious is stepping up his game. He is growing in sophistication. Dang it." She looks at me. "You all right?"

I give her a cocky sideways glance. "Am I all right? Kendra! You had snakes chase me!"

"Yes, but you handled it so well. Besides, how else was I going to get you to use your sense of touch?"

"I touched the leaves!" My eyes bulge from my head.

"Right, but you needed to work through the *fear*. You have to use all five senses, especially when fear is a barrier. I thought when you heard the hissing you would run away from the sound, not toward it!" Kendra examines my neck. "That is going to bruise."

"I'm under the protection spell. They shouldn't be able to find me, or choke me out."

"Correction, Vacavious cannot find you, yet. Not all morterros operate under him. It looks like a rogue who simply got lost. Maybe picked up your scent somewhere along the way. It is the same one that killed Bradbury. I have been watching it. Keeping an eye out. Making sure it did not do too much damage." Carmine picks up its head. Half of its ear is missing. "Yep, same one. Fox took a chunk out of it the other night. Looked like it made him mad too." He laughs a dorky snort.

"What happened to 'the mood, temperature and crap have to be in place for a Morterro to make a showing in the mortal world'?" I mime in my best Kendra voice.

Kendra ignores me. "What?! I thought you and Church were taking care of the morterro who killed Bradbury! You mean to tell me, you have been tracking it in the mortal world? In Mason? Next to our Five for a couple of days now and you did not even think to say anything to the Detail?" Kendra moves toward Carmine with force. Church catches her arm.

"He said something to me. We took care of it, Kendra."

Her eyes fall on Church. I've seen that look before. It's the look when Kendra wants to rip your face off and feed it to wolves. I've seen enough paranormal programming on television to know pissing off a witch is never a good idea. "You of all people, Church, our leader and the one we trust, needs to be honest and tell us everything we need to do to carry out our mission," she pauses, allowing her scathing words to penetrate his unruffled confidence. "I hope you are not letting your feelings get in the way of our duty to protect our Five." She turns but, before she leaves, she waves her index finger in the air. "Vattene. Vattene. Labyrinth scomparire. Vattene!" Kendra yells, directing her disdain toward Church.

Much like the barn wall, the labyrinth walls move upward and slowly disappear, like a mirage.

Church doesn't reply, but Kendra's words have dealt a visible blow. The unsettling words are truth and Church knows it. He knows it because I see the expression on his face.

"Labirinto, scompari!" Kendra mutters under her breath as she walks away, "Yeah, obviously the jasmine does not work. Note to self."

We all gag as Church lifts the morterro's body on his shoulder. "Brother," Carmine covers his nose, "what are you doing?"

"Research. I want to know what makes the hybrids different. Penelope, meet Jo inside the small milking barn. She is waiting."

To my surprise, I'm not tired. Despite the evening's events, my body feels rejuvenated and not at all like it's two in the morning. "Wonderful." I mutter under my breath. To my amazement, I've managed to hang on to the headlamp Jesse gave me.

The outdoor lighting on the barn creates an eerie orange glow. I slide the barn door open. "Jo?"

"Hey, Sweets." She comes into view holding a bunny rabbit.

Then several bunny rabbits jump out of the shadows. Their white tails thumping against the hardwood floor as they hop.

"What's with all the rabbits?" I pick one up and hold it up to my face as I stroke its head.

"We are going to play a game." Jo wipes the sweat from her brow. There's a makeshift platform underneath the orange-hued light. She grabs a rabbit and places it on its back on the platform. It tries to use its back legs to fight off her grip but fails. With her other hand, she reaches below the platform and grabs a long blade.

My heart stops.

My grip tightens on the rabbit in my arms. I try to dispel the premonition that creeps into my mind. "Jo, what are you doing?" I stop petting the rabbit as I eye the blade closely.

"The game is called *life or death.*" Aunt Jo's stare is hard. She takes the blade. "Are you going to give this animal life or let it die?" She slides the blade against the rabbit's small neck.

I can't breathe and my chest begins to ache.

No. No. No.

"Jo! What are you doing?" I run to the rabbit's aide as thick blood oozes from the fresh wound. "What are you doing?" I yell. The rabbit is no longer fighting. In fact, it isn't moving at all. Suddenly, I forget what to do. *Focus, Penn. Clear your mind.*

My instincts take hold as I raise my hand over the lifeless body. I focus all my attention on this little life. My hands begin to tingle, and warmth fills my body.

Numbness.

Everything grows silent. My hand is still hovering over the rabbit. My hands begin to sweat and my heart begins to race. *Here it comes.* The pressure begins in my head then travels through my body to my feet and back to my hands. Then, the feeling of nails slicing through my veins takes my breath away. It always takes my breath away. A loud hum rings in my ears, resonating through my skull.

I hear a mumbling, "Focus, Penn." It's Jo's voice but, by this time, my eyes are shut and I can't open them. The pain becomes too excruciating to bear. I cry out, sure the pain will be the end of me.

I feel a kick.

The rabbit. Please let it be the rabbit.

I open one eye and then the other. My eyes flutter open as it jumps, its little nose twitching. It jumps to its feet and off the platform. I breathe in a huge sigh of relief and look at Jo. She's cutting into another rabbit. "No! Jo! Stop!" I yell as I run to aide yet another rabbit.

"Again." Her voice is monotone and her stare is ice cold.

The whole process starts over again.

The whole process starts over again until each rabbit has been saved—twice.

My body is depleted of any energy I might have had earlier. I place my hands on my knees as I lean forward and take in a big gulp of air. I feel like I'm going to throw up, again.

"Taste it." She looks down to my fingers covered in blood.

My head snaps up to Jo. *Not you too,* I think to myself.

"Taste it." Her stare is still cold. "Put your finger in your mouth and taste the blood. Now."

I shake my head, confused. "No. That's disgusting. This is too much. It's crazy, actually."

She walks to me. "Do you trust me?"

"Of course, but what you're asking me to do right now, it's repulsive. It's one thing to eat from a bag, but it's another to feed from a live animal."

She's inches away from my face, "Do you trust me?" Jo takes my hand.

I don't say anything because I'm still trying to comprehend what she's asking me to do. I nod slowly.

She takes my index finger and puts it to my lips. Begrudgingly, I open my mouth, grimacing. At first, I hold my breath so I don't taste it. My conscience is eating away at me.

I breathe in, taste, and smell. Suddenly, my senses are once again heightened. It's not like drinking human blood, not even close. I try to take it all in, every last drop. I put another finger in my mouth. Then all four.

"Easy," Jo says, pulling my fingers from my mouth.

There aren't words to describe what's happening. "What happened?"

Jo walks to the platform and wipes off the blade.

"Now you will know the difference between human blood and animal blood because there is a difference. It keeps your cravings at bay but it is not the same. It will not provide your body with the proper nutrition it needs."

"Why has this never happened before? I mean, I've had steak before."

She gives me a peculiar look. "That is not blood. It is simply water and protein from the meat. The blood is removed when they prepare the animal for sale. You have never fed straight from a live animal before so you have never experienced these effects."

I gawk in disgust. "Oh my goodness. What did I do? What is happening?"

"Follow me." Jo grabs my hand forcefully. "There is more. Turn your headlamp on."

We walk outside. Jo walks to a piece of plywood and uncovers a hole. It's a big hole, big enough to fit a person. I hear a hissing sound as I walk to it. I don't want to look but I do.

Not again.

No. Nope. What is with these people? I can't do this. I raise my hands. I press my fists against my head as my chin starts to quiver. No. I cannot even speak because all I can focus on is running. Again. I look down into the hole. Full of hundreds of slithering snakes, sliding around each other, coiled into a big mess of knots. Their heads lifting and hissing.

I cringe. I realize my skin is crawling and I grow clammy. "No. No. No. I can't do this." My jaw tightens. "I can't," I whisper as I turn and walk away. My stomach grows queasy with each step. What does she want me to do with a hundred snakes? Save them?

I'm hit in the back of the head. I stumble forward but I catch myself as a snake falls onto the gravel in front of me, blood oozes out of the open pink belly of the serpent. If there's ever an opportune moment to throw up, now is that time. So, I do. Once, twice, and a third for good measure.

Another thud against my back as another snake hits me. I wipe my mouth with the side of my hand. I turn around to look at Jo. "You threw a freaking snake at my head?!" I scream. I'm breathing heavily. My mouth tastes of vomit. She's got the blade in one hand and another snake that's trying to coil around her other hand.

I want to throw up again, but I can't because there's nothing left.

"Are you going to spend your whole life running, Penn? Running from your fears, your feelings, yourself?" Her tone is sharp and crisp. She enunciates every single word clearly. "Be who you are."

I hear her, loud and clear. I grow angry. I feel a vein pulse in my neck as I look at the two snakes in a pool of blood. Like the bunnies, I can't let them die. Can I? I can't let them get the best of me. I can't live in fear. I can't continue to run from my feelings. I can't continue to run from myself. The anger is compounding and I feel like I'm about to explode.

Fear collides with blind faith as I begin healing the snakes. I watch as Jo throws more snakes my way.

I heal each of them.

I fall backward on my butt as I watch hundreds of snakes slither back into the hole.

My body has nothing left.

I can't lift my arms, so I lie down on the gravel, staring up at the night sky. Fatigue takes hold of every muscle in my body. I can barely move my eyes as Jo comes into view. "Come on. Let us go inside." She helps me up and places my arm around her neck.

She sits me down at the dining room table. "Drink this." It's a glass full of blood. At least Jo puts it in a glass. My stomach grows queasy. I try to refuse until she says, "Penn, just drink it." Her voice is much gentler now, more relaxed, like *my* Jo. She is no longer the hardcore rabbit killer I witnessed outside.

So I do. I drink the entire thing. "What is happening to me, Jo?" My body feels brand new.

The feeling starts again, this time, at my toes. The euphoria sets in. *Human blood.*

I feel like I'm on top of the world.

Untouchable. Unstoppable. Nighmerian Avenger….wicked good.

It's short lived. Jo sits down next to me with her travel mug. She takes a sip from it.

"Stop fighting, Penn. Stop fighting your feelings. Stop fighting who you are."

"Jo." I put my forehead on the table. "I don't know who I am anymore. Maybe I never knew who I was to begin with. And now," I laugh, lifting my head, "I definitely don't know who I am."

"You are just beginning your life. Do not put that expectation on yourself. You are still growing, and changing. If there is one constant in life, it is change. Running from your feelings and not facing life head on hinders your growth. You are not allowing yourself the opportunity to become the person you are. The power is in you, Penn. All you have to do is open up to it. Welcome it. Embrace it." She kisses my head. "Now, go get some shut eye before school."

I don't argue because I'm tired. Exhausted.

My alarm sounds. Church's words play in my head. *It takes a while for the blood to get into your system. Once it does, you won't require much sleep.*

I'm freaking exhausted. I contemplate missing Dover's AP Anatomy class. After all, is college even in the cards for me now?

Wakey, wakey eggs and bakey!" Kendra sings in an utterly disturbing tone.

"Shut up. Go away." I pull the covers over my head.

"Nope. Come on, Chicken Butt."

"I'm not going. Tell him my cat ate my homework. Or, better yet," I pull the covers from my head, "tell them a man-eating snake my best friend conjured up ate my homework!" I glare at Kendra who doesn't acknowledge anything I said.

"Nope. We have to play this out as if everything, and I mean everything, is normal. Remember: we have to stay under the radar. You missing class? Totally not normal,

Miss I-haven't-missed-a-single-day-of-school-since-the-fifth-grade." She throws back my covers, and barks, "It is go time."

"Hell."

CHAPTER 16

A Meeting with the Chief

Thursday, September 13ᵗʰ 2012

It's hard to get my head back in the game after what I experienced last night. How am I supposed to live in a world where evil and magic don't exist? How am I supposed to live in a world where I am not a fighter? I am not a survivor? How am I supposed to live an ordinary life with extraordinary gifts?

Identity? What identity?

Jo fills my stainless steel water bottle with blood, thinking I will need it, but I won't. Everything that happened last night, it doesn't seem real. It's like I'm stuck in some sort of bizarre sitcom or something. I mean, I drank human blood last night. Human blood. I know this sounds crazy, but my body feels weightless. Like, I'm rejuvenated. I feel more comfortable now drinking blood once I turn eighteen to make my transition final.

"I still can't believe you put snakes into the labyrinth last night." Kendra throws her backpack in the backseat as she gets in the car.

Kendra laughs.

"I still don't find it funny." I pull out of my driveway.

"Did you learn something?" She peers at me through the corner of her eye.

"Yeah, don't trust your best friend." I smile.

Kendra laughs harder. "You got the point, and you did well."

"Still mad at Carmine and Church about the morterros?"

"I cannot stay mad at Church. Carmine on the other hand…" her voice trails off.

"Look, Kendra, I don't know what happened with you two, but it looks as though he truly cares for you."

"Subject change. Oh wait. We have reached our destination." She jumps out and grabs her backpack.

"Thirty seconds to spare, Miss Jackson," Dr. Dover says over his shoulder as he writes on the whiteboard at the front of the class. "Miss Jackson, I need to speak with you after school today." He doesn't turn around to make eye contact.

"Why Dover? I wasn't late," I plead.

"Not about that." He turns around, eyeing me closely. "And it's *Doctor* Dover, Miss Jackson.

Kendra and I exchange glances. Kendra shrugs. *Whatever.*

I look to Jesse's chair, not caring if he and the she-devil are making out in a corner somewhere. I healed bunnies and snakes last night. Their fling, or whatever is happening between them seems trivial right now. Then I remember the taste of the rabbit's blood.

I feel the urge and the craving for blood. I left the stainless steel water bottle in the car. *You don't need it, Penn. Go without. You're fine. Stop thinking about it.*

Dover's voice pulls me out of my bloodlust. "By the way, if anyone has information pertaining to the butterfly stunt yesterday, there will be a reward for whoever comes forward," Dr. Dover announces to the class.

Kendra and I glance at Dover as he stares down the class.

"It was magic, *Dr.* Dover." Kendra gleams, proud of her work. I'm totally floored by her forwardness.

"Yes, Miss Salvino, I'm sure it was magic." His voice is full of sarcasm. He straightens his notes and begins the lecture.

I look at Kendra with my permanent grin.

The day drags on like no other. The fact my entire body desires the one thing that makes my skin want to peel away from my flesh and walk away is making my insides turn with anxiety. What is happening to me? Holding all this in isn't doing me any favors either. Maybe, just maybe, I could tell Kendra. Maybe. I push the thoughts aside, the cravings consume me like a dirty conscience.

Finally the lunch bell rings. I grab my backpack and file out of Ms. Stanton's psych class. "It's a bummer about the Milk Can game. Hey, speaking of the Milk Can game, did you hear about Lucas?" She gawks at me.

"No. Why?"

"He moved. He up and moved to Ohio."

"Huh. Good for him." I smile as we head outside for lunch. Even though the fog and rain eat away at our days most of the time, we usually sit outside. Like a hawk scoping its prey, I see my car as we head out to lunch. I immediately picture the stainless steel water bottle in the cup holder. My mouth waters. The blood cravings have been festering in my head since this morning. I want so badly to march over to my car, rip open the water bottle and drain it into my mouth.

I try to fight it as Carmine's words play in my head in a sing-song voice. *If you do not feed on human blood, you will turn into a vegetable.* "I'll take my chances."

"What?" Kendra asks as we plant ourselves on the front lawn of the school.

"Oh, nothing," I say as I set my backpack down and perch myself against the zillion-year-old oak tree.

"How are the cravings?" she smiles coyly as she sets her backpack down and leans against the tree next to me.

Crap. She knows. "Fine," I lie as I pick at the grass. "I don't even crave it." All I picture in my head is the water bottle. The blood spilling out the sides of my mouth and me in utter bliss.

"Yeah. Okay, whatever you have to tell yourself."

Thursday, September 13th 3:49pm, Mr. Dover's Classroom

"Kendra?" Dr. Dover looks at her as if she doesn't belong.

"Yeah," she says as she leans in, ready to indulge the conversation.

"May I speak to Penn? Alone, please?"

"No can do, Dovester. She must be in my line of sight at all times." She leans back, crosses her arms and gives Dr. Dover the stare down. Then she lets out a laugh and smacks him on the back. "Just kidding, Dovie, she is my ride home." She pops her tongue as she takes her two fingers and points them to her eyes then mine.

I smirk.

He groans. "It's Doctor...oh never mind." He knows she's not going to leave us alone. "Miss Jackson, Chief Watkins would like to speak to you immediately."

"What is this about?" Kendra interrupts.

"A missing person's case, if you must know, Miss Salvino," he says, through clenched teeth.

"Who is missing?" we ask together.

"I can't say at this time. Just meet the Chief at the station?" He looks between the two of us.

"Whatevs." Kendra brushes it off. "Off to meet dear Chief Watkins."

I need blood.

I need blood.

I need blood.

I want to ravage the water bottle in my car, take it into my mouth and swallow every last bit. *It's getting worse.*

Penn! Stop. Focus. A missing person's case?

They finally caught up to me.

I'm hot. It's hot in here. Where's the air? I need an open window because I can't breathe.

"Miss Jackson, are you well?"

"Oh, she is fine. We will head over there now." Kendra nods at Dover as she peels me off the chair.

Dr. Dover looks at the two of us. I'm visibly shaken and he sees this, but he doesn't say anything else.

Kendra drags me out of the classroom, down the hallway and down the steps to the front of the school.

Everything from that night comes back and it's shoved in my face again. *He was going to kill her first if I didn't intervene. Oh my goodness.*

Maybe they recovered the body and they found my fingerprints? That's how they somehow tracked me down. Panic sets in as a mirage of thoughts bombard my conscience.

"Penelope, speak to me." Kendra's got me by my wrists and we're in my car, except she's in the driver's seat. I don't know how I'm sitting in the car because I don't remember getting in. How did she get my keys? "Penn." She grabs the sides of my face. "Talk to me."

I swallow hard. "Kendra." My voice is less than a whisper as I try to search for the right words. At this point, nothing is going to come out right so I just say it,

"I killed someone."

Kendra stops.

She still holds my face in her hands, except this time, she's squeezing so my lips and cheeks are scrunched together in a fish face. She doesn't let go but stares at me. My heart is beating so hard I feel like I might rupture an artery as I foresee the headline in the national newspapers, *Eight-Year-Old Murder Mystery Solved, Killer Finally Caught.* Orange jumpsuits, high electrical fences, a judge and jury flood my mind like a 1980's crime drama.

"Stop. You need to stop. Listen, pull yourself together." Kendra tightens her grip on my cheeks. I try to look away. Kendra holds tighter. "We need to go talk to the Chief so you do not look guilty. Whatever this is, we will handle it. Okay, Penn?" Her eyes are full of empathy and concern.

"I just told you I killed someone, Kendra." I stare at her with a befuddled look.

She sighs deeply. "Look. I have a pretty good idea what happened. We can chat about the person you killed after we meet with the Chief. Come on."

"Please be honest with me right now because I'm trying not to freak out," I whisper.

"You are an amazing person, Penn. You are kind. You are genuine. You have compassion for others. Whatever happened, we will get to the bottom of it, okay?"

I slowly nod my head, trying to believe every word she says. This is not the reaction I expected. I'm half relieved, but half paranoid she's lost it.

The bell above the door chimes as we walk into the police station. The scent of old, musty paperwork fills the air.

"Well, good afternoon, girls," Dorothy, the dispatcher/receptionist says from behind the counter. "Chief," Dorothy calls to the open office door behind her, "Penn and Kendra are here."

My stomach turns. *I'm going to prison. I know it.*

"Perfect. Come on in girls," the chief yells from behind his desk in his office. He's upbeat. If I were going to prison, why would he be so upbeat?

Dorothy gives me a wink as we walk past her. *Crap. She knows too,* I think to myself. All of the sudden, I feel like I have to pee. Really badly. Like I'm going to pee myself right here, right now. *Penn, now is not the time to ask an inappropriate question like,* "Where's the bathroom?" Crap.

"She can hold it." Kendra gives me the evil eye.

"Have a seat, ladies," Chief Watkins motions to the two chairs in front of his desk.

Stacks of newspapers are piled on the floor while strewn papers scatters his desk. Coffee stains amidst the paperwork show signs of hurriedness and disarray. A bookshelf behind the pine desk fills the wall behind him, decorated with old pictures, mostly cop photos. One picture catches my eye, a graduation picture of sorts: the chief, his wife and two daughters. I bet he's a good dad. I look up to the chief and his eyes catch mine. Guilt plagues my insides.

Good daughters don't kill people.

The chief's eyes turn to me. "We've recovered another body in a shallow grave. An eye witness said you were the last one to see the victim."

I try to conceal the sheer terror my body is experiencing right now but I don't know how much longer I can do it. I try to give a peculiar look, but I'm pretty sure I look constipated.

The chief leans in. "Do you know anything about this, Penn?"

I should lie. No. I should tell the truth. Even if I go to prison, the monkey, the guilt will finally be off my back.

Lie.

Truth.

Lie.

Truth.

"It's been disclosed to us you were one of the last people to see Lenore Mason." He says again, biting his upper lip and leaning back in his leather chair, placing his hands behind his head, studying me.

Wait. What? Who? I don't speak because I'm pretty sure he said Lenore Mason. Not Frankie. Oh *Snap.*

Lenore Mason. Shallow Grave.

Morterro.

Obviously, by my expression, he knows I am completely floored by this information. I look to Kendra, who is staring at me.

"I believe I can give you the information you need, Chief," a low, deep voice proclaims from behind us. I know this voice. "May I talk to you alone, please?"

The chief's eyes meet mine, and then he looks to the voice standing behind me. He nods.

"Thank you for coming in, girls." Chief Watkins stands, still speaking to us, yet staring at Church. "I have your numbers if I think of any more questions. I want the two of you to go straight home. This thing is still out there and the bodies are beginning to pile up. Please be safe, both of you."

"Guess we will let you two get to it, then." Kendra grabs my arm and practically drags me up out of my chair.

Church nods and exchanges glances with Kendra as we walk by. Speechless, I try not to look obvious by staring at him. My shoulder brushes his chest; the beginnings of a smile form on his lips.

He closes the door quietly behind us.

"Well that was fast," Dorothy says, not looking up from her computer as her hot pink nails click in rapid succession across the keyboard. A troll with hot-pink hair that says 'I love Bingo' sits on the top of her computer monitor. "Bu-bye girls," she waves, so vigorously her bright pink nails form neon arcs in the air.

The door squeaks behind us as the bell jingles.

"What was that?" I turn my head toward Kendra.

"Keep walking until we are out of earshot," Kendra whispers back as she practically drags me down the walkway to the sidewalk.

We walk a block at a fast pace, down past the Mystic Mansion, an elegant bed and breakfast recently renovated and modernized. The old mansion still has a timeless look about it. Built in the early 1800's, some say the house is haunted. It was featured on a national television show famous for interviewing real people telling their own ghost encounters. The person telling their story on the show wasn't from Mason, he was a traveler who stayed in the mansion. At first it irritated the owners, Mr.

and Mrs. Gunderson, but then visitors from all over the world flocked to the mansion to see the *Widow in Waiting in the Rose Room*. The Gunderson's have been exploiting the popularity of the ghost ever since. For ten dollars, you can pose as the deceased spouse, in a casket, and receive the print as a personalized postcard. The widow in the picture is a cardboard cutout because her visits are random, if not sporadic.

We duck into an alleyway next to the old mansion and rest our backs against the brick wall. Kendra sighs. "I know you killed Frankie, Penn."

A slow moan escapes my throat as I remember watching Frankie's body twitch on the floor. "He was going to kill her, Kendra."

Kendra nods her head. "I know."

"He used to beat her to a bloody pulp and, one night, I'd had enough. My rage blindly took over and I used my powers to kill him. I swear on my life, I didn't mean to do it." My chest heaves in and out as fear builds, making it harder to breath.

Kendra pulls herself up from the wall and stands directly in front of me, crossing her arms. "Now you listen to me. He deserved to die for what he did. He deserved it. Got it?"

I move a small pebble with my foot. "I don't kno—"

"Penn! Yes, Frankie was a low life piece of crap. He deserved what he got."

I nod slowly, not quite sure what to believe.

"Lenore was definitely offed by a morterro. Maybe Church was right about the hybrids." She says as if carrying on a one-sided conversation. "Maybe they are functioning at a level that makes them smarter and far more dangerous." Kendra ponders this as if I'm not standing in front of her.

"Kendra?" I wait for her to look at me but she's still lost in her own thoughts. "Kendra!" I stamp my foot down.

"Whaaaaat?" She looks to me.

"We," I put my palm on my forehead, "we're talking about lives here. You act like this is normal." My eyes meet hers.

Kendra sighs. "Get used to it, Penelope. Death is common in our world."

The color drains from my face. I'm having trouble differentiating the true from the false, the mortal world from the immortal. Somehow, the line between worlds got dark and blurry. Like a mirage, I'm unsure where reality meets illusion. Nothing is what it seems anymore.

Kendra sighs again as she looks at me with her big green eyes. "Is this where I have to get all lovey-dovey and tell you everything is going to be all right again, because I swear, we just did that."

I look up at the sky. The fog is beginning to roll in.

"Look, Penn." She stands beside me. "I know this is a lot to take in. Trust me, the first time my mother turned my brother into a dog for eating from the dog bowl was a little freaky."

I smile. I smile because Kendra can always make me smile. I smile because she knows me so well. I smile because she knows I killed someone and she's still here. I should feel relief, right? Guilt I've carried around for years, assuming nobody knew, and all the while I wasn't carrying this burden alone. Kendra has always known and stayed by my side nonetheless.

"The thing is, I have grown into myself, learned about my abilities and embraced them. Yeah, sometimes it is tough and yeah, I wish I could have lived a normal life, like a normal teenage girl, but that is not my reality. This is my reality." With a swish of her finger, the wall in front of us magically displays a gigantic snow globe, complete with falling crystals.

It's beautiful, magical. It's as if I'm in a winter wonderland and should be wearing a pretty ball gown with crystal shoes. If I was into pretty dresses, that is.

In the middle, images flash by. Her mother, I assume, is the first image, then her father and her brother. Then me. Next, an image inside a huge castle of a group of five exquisite looking individuals. All this image says is power.

"The Demi?"

Kendra nods as she stares up at the snow global she created. "This is my reality." Other images flash through the scene: Jesse, Church, Lennon, Nighmerianotte, and Carmine. A silhouette of a village appears. It somehow looks familiar but, because it's dark, I can't place it. The buildings are relative in size with burning torches. A ring of fire illuminates a tall clock tower. In a strange, eerie way, it reminds me of Mason.

"Penn, we have been protecting you from all of this." She swishes her finger again. As the cityscape scene falls, another scene comes into view, trees, tall and thick. Two people emerge. A man and a woman are running through a heavily wooded forest. The woman is carrying something in her arms. A blanket.

No, a baby. *It's me.*

My mother cradles my body in her arms. She cannot stop crying. My father reaches down to the blanket and uncovers the baby's face, my face. He kisses my forehead and nose. His tears consume him. He wipes them as they fall, looks to my mother, and gently wipes the tears off her cheek as well. They are running through the trees again. It's dark but a man is holding some sort of light to guide their path. The next scene shows the man, woman and infant at the steps of a gigantic door.

An extremely beautiful woman, with looks of sophistication and class, rushes the couple in.

The snow globe changes and Kendra's arm encircles me. "Please, keep watching." The next scene shows an extremely tall, hooded man. His hood falls back against his neck as he and two others make their way down a cobblestone road. He has some sort of handheld light he's holding to his...face?

I catch my breath.

His dark eyes bore into me. Purple veins interweave across his pale face, his nose long and thin. His head and neck are laced with the same purple veins that cover his face. I watch as he turns to a large crowd.

"Kill every Nighmerian. Find her," the tallest of the three shouts to the others. "Bring the Five to me. She will complete the creed and I will be King."

The snow globe disappears. Now, I'm staring at the brick wall in front of me. I'm trying to think but I can't.

She affirms with a downward tilt of her head. "You are the only one who can kill Vacavious. You and he are one, you are both black blood. He simply has no humanity and that's the difference. You have the gift of empathy, compassion, love and humanity. You are not like him."

I can't feel my legs. I know they're there. I'm standing, so they're under me and they're working, yet I can't feel them.

Kendra waves her finger around, a trail of sparkles appearing in its. I'm not sure what she's doing but watch in awe. I squint, trying to make sense of the seemingly random movements. Slowly, something begins to materialize as the sparkles condense into a ball. It dances around, springing to life, and I realize what I'm staring at.

A fairy.

Holy crap. A fairy. Is there anything she can't do? I stare as the fairy flutters around Kendra and stops to stare at me.

She looks to Kendra, then to me again. I gawk at her tiny, beautiful face in awe. She looks like a human, only very, very small. With wings and a wand, of course, because she's a fairy. *Yep, there are fairies too, apparently.*

This is weird. I smile and nod. "Five," She says in a surprisingly raspy voice. Immediately she bows, a look of admiration spreads across her tiny fairy face. She whispers as she flies to my shoulder. She holds up a strand of my hair and peers into my ear.

I look at Kendra. She laughs.

After she examines my ear, she flutters to the front of my face and plucks a hair from my head.

"Ouch." I pull back, rubbing my head. "What was that for?"

"A single hair of the Five gives warning to those who dwell in the sunlight of the Demi of the evils that lurk in the shadows waiting to pounce." A raspy laugh escapes her delicate lips. "May I keep this?"

"Do I have a choice?" I ask, still rubbing my head. I blink hard once, twice, and am quite surprised to find the fairy still there. *She's real. A real fairy.* I'm carrying on a conversation with a fairy.

She flutters over to Kendra's shoulder and lands.

"Penn, meet Lucky. Lucky, this is Penn."

"Now that we have all the bowing crap out of the way, let us get down to business, eh?" Lucky perches herself on Kendra's shoulder. She carefully ties my hair around her neck like a scarf. "Well, how do I look?"

I smile, raising my eyebrows to Kendra. *Is she for real?*

She crosses her tiny arms. I notice she's wearing black, canvas high-tops; they are tiny, black and unlaced. Looking closer, she's wearing black and white striped leggings and a black baby doll dress. Her black hair is pulled back in a tight ponytail. Her black lipstick makes her eyelashes stand out.

"Lucky helped transport you from Nighmerianotte to the mortal world when you were an infant. Fairies have the ability to slip by the portal locks set by Vacavious. We are not sure why."

I nod, like I remember. I nod like its normal to talk to fairies. "Thanks, I guess?"

It comes out sounding more like a *question* than a sincere *thank you*.

"Whatevs. Got your back, Black." She sticks out her tiny fist and laughs.

A fist bump?

I hold up my fist. We bump.

"Beware, though, Penn. Fairies are little misers, just like Leprechauns," Kendra says. Lucky busts up laughing, obviously not offended.

"No way?! There are Leprechauns in Nighmerianotte too?"

"Yep, and unicorns," Lucky says.

"That is awesome," I say, enthusiasm bleeding from me.

Lucky and Kendra both burst into hysterical laughter and fist bump.

"Tots messing with you, Blood," Lucky says in between laughter.

"Bummer. I've always wanted a pet unicorn," I say under my breath. They hear me and laugh harder.

When they finally pull themselves together, Kendra asks Lucky, "Word on the street?"

"Dude...it is really bad, KB. Immortals are feeding on immortals. It is a blood bath everywhere you turn. Nighmerians act as though they have lost all humanity. I have not transitioned in quite some time. We are scared we will get stuck over there." Lucky shakes her head. "I prefer to live a free life and not in one of those stupid jars, displayed to Nigh-merianotte like some sort of freak show. I have seen too many friends captured." Lucky tries to act unaffected.

"What do you know about the morterros that have been lurking in the shadows?"

"Hybrids. Lethal. Not like anything Nighmerianotte has seen be-fore." Lucky shakes her head. "V brought evil to a whole new level with those abominations." Lucky slowly looks to me. "Okay then, see you Sunday?" Lucky stretches and flutters off Kendra's shoulder, my hair still wrapped around her neck. They do some sort of handshake. It ends with the word, "boom."

"Black?" Lucky turns to me. "It has been an honor. Listen," she says as she flies in closer to my ear. I keep a watchful eye on her as I'm sure she's going to steal another hair. "Keep an eye on our girl. She has been a little down lately, eh?" She eyes Kendra.

"On it," I say. I like how Lucky cares for Kendra.

"Nice." She holds up her fist and I hold up mine. "Blow it up. Word." Then, just like a sparkler, she disappears into colorful sparks with a loud pop.

CHAPTER 17

Baggage and the Ruy Lopez

Thursday, September 13th 8:52 p.m.

"Hey Jo, I'm Running out to the car real quick," I yell from the front door. I keep looking behind me. All I need is a little blood. *Just a sip.* Just a sip and I'll feel better. I get into my car and shut the door. The dome light quickly fades and I grab the stainless steel water bottle. "Just a sip." I twist the lid and slowly, almost hesitantly, put the bottle to my lips.

I drink the entire thing down like I'm dying of thirst.

The same thing happens, euphoria and utter bliss. I'm limitless. The numbness takes hold of my body, like I'm floating. Every inch of my body feels untouchable.

I breathe deeply, forgetting every need, every want, I've ever had.

I slowly come out of my dreamy state and put the lid back on the bottle. I rest my head against the seat and scan the darkness in front of me. I'm facing the slaughter shed. I see the light on, which is odd because we never use the slaughter shed, unless I'm being tortured by Carmine or Kendra. Through the window, I see movement. I raise my head from the headrest for a better look.

It's Jo. What's she doing in the slaughter shed?

Then I see it.

I watch her fill her travel mug with a blood bag.

All the air leaves me. She's human. She isn't supposed to drink blood, right? It can't be her.

What the—? I watch her quietly shut the door, mug in hand.

I want to duck. I want to un-see what I just saw. Maybe it's the blood? I look to the water bottle on the floorboard. *Is it bad blood? What if it's making me hallucinate? Maybe I'm blood drunk? Can I overdose? I've lost it for sure.*

I watch as Jo makes her way back to the house.

It's Jo, right?

Okay, Penn, get your head together. She has to have a logical explanation. Maybe she's getting the blood for Carmine? Or Church? Or me?

That's it.

Because she's human and she doesn't feed on blood. Yes. The panic subsides, but only momentarily. I watch as she stops on the porch, and puts the travel mug to her lips and drinks.

Yep, no un-seeing that.

All logic has flown out the window.

Rationalization?

Gone.

Excuses?

Nope.

I try to regain my thoughts. I watch again as she quietly shuts the door behind her.

Maybe I can live in denial? *Why did I have to see that?* Now I'm mad at myself for even walking out to the car for the blood I so desperately craved.

I search around and grab a half-eaten bag of candy and shove them in my pocket, just in case it might curb my cravings. Probably not. I slam the car door and give it a good kick. I don't care if anyone hears me.

I kick it again, and again. The throbbing sensation in my foot makes me stop. I huff and trudge toward the back of the house, trying to remain unnoticed, wanting to be alone. I mutter to myself.

I see a silhouette of a tall figure sitting on the back deck facing the redwood trees.

My anger starts to slowly subside. For whatever reason, he does this to me.

Church. He represents everything I'm not. He's methodical. He's calm. He responds well in all situations. I don't. Simply being in his presence makes me want to be a better person.

I approach him. I want to be near him. He moves his head silently to the left as he hears me. I make my way up the stairs to the deck and sit down next to him.

I feel his eyes staring through me. I feel his smile though I can't see it. I feel his warmth, though he doesn't have any. I feel his heartbeat, even if it doesn't exist. We sit in silence for a long moment because all I want is to be in this moment with him.

"You know," I start, still looking straight ahead, "the first time I saw you, I felt something. Something I cannot describe. Something deep within me." I take in a deep breath, and say, "The first time you spent the night in my bedroom I didn't want you to go. I share this because I'm not sure if it's a true feeling, but I felt something. The other night when you rested your hand on my chest, I thought my body was going to explode, because I liked your hand there. I liked it and I feel guilty because I liked it and because of Jesse. I have always had feelings for him, I guess. You give me something different. You awaken something in me. Since I met you, I can feel. Like really feel things. I don't know what's happening to me right now. I don't know if I'm going to live or die, and it scares the hell out of me, but when I'm with you, it's different. I've got baggage, Church. So much baggage. I know you feel guilty for that. I know you feel responsible for leaving me with Nadine." I pause, trying to halt the treasonous activities of my mouth as information flows out of me like a tsunami. I sigh because I know the wave is too big to stop.

Liquid courage. I'm blood drunk.

"You kept me safe. I believe with all my heart you kept me safe from Vacavious. You kept me safe and I lived." I stop. "He killed my parents but you saved me." The lump in my throat is growing, so I stop again. I can't look into his eyes because I'm scared of the pity. I don't do pity. "I owe you my life."

He doesn't move. He doesn't speak. I can still feel his eyes burning into me. I slowly turn my head to face him. By his look I can tell he wants to take every single hurt and every single fear away from me, but he can't. He knows he can't. The porch light gives his face a soft pale glow. Part of his face is in the shadow, while the other is in the light. A gentle smile spreads across the vampire's face. A sweet, longing, *words-I-have-waited-to-hear* smile.

At this moment, I want to tear away the walls around me and my heart. I want to be done with hiding, running, and lying.

He slowly reaches for the side of my face. His hands are cold to the touch but all I can think about is how I want more of him. My cheek falls into his hand. His eyes dance from my mouth to my eyes and back again.

His lips part and I close my eyes, ready. "I hid the body," he says with his hand still on my face. My eyes snap open. "I was there that night. I tried to stop it but even then, you were far too powerful for me. Your gift for mind fusion is unlike anything I have ever seen."

I stifle a breath. "Frankie?"

"I wanted to trade my life for yours every single day since that night, Penn. Every single day. It is my fault. If only I would have prevented the situation you would not have to live with this awful guilt. Then I watched you. I watched you clean Nadine's face. Bandage her face with gauze. Damn Penn..." He's combing his hair with his hands. "You were eight! Eight, Penelope!" His eyes are full of fury now.

Mine are full of awe.

"Eight-year-olds should be worrying about what to wear to school and what dolls to play with." His voice quivers. "You were worried about where to hide a body and whether or not Nadine was going to live or die. Her face was so badly injured." He's infuriated. His eyes are full of rage. I take his face in my hands but he yanks them away and rubs his hands through his hair. He stands up. I stand too.

My heart breaks for him.

He wants to fix me. Heal my hurts. Redeem my soul. Make me whole. Justify my actions. I took a human life when I was eight.

"Frankie deserved what he got, Penn. He deserved it. You must know that." He paces in front of me.

"I know," I lie. Trying to believe it. Truth be told, he didn't deserve death. Deep down inside me, I know he didn't deserve death. "Come here," I command.

Church cautiously walks toward me as I stand, arms outstretched.

I grab around his neck and hold tight. "Don't let go this time," I whisper.

My heart is pounding against his chest. He groans as his arms tighten around me.

"When I get home from training tonight, will you be here? Stay with me tonight?" I say with intention.

"Yes," he answers. I feel his lips against my neck.

Thursday, September 13th 10:02 p.m., Second night of training

We hit our stride, shoulder to shoulder, Jesse and I.

Stomp, stomp, stomp, breathe.

Stomp, stomp, stomp, breathe.

I can't help but wonder what's going through his head right now.

Stomp, stomp, stomp, breathe.

The fog isn't as thick as last night, but it's a bit colder. My headlamp dances across the pavement and the familiar smell of seaweed and salt fills my airway.

He brushes against my shoulder and I look up, breaking my stride. I feel the ache in my legs. I look at him and he's smiling.

"Wipe that smirk off your face, Falco," I pant, smiling.

A darkness envelops his face taking me back to when we were nine. Kendra, Jesse and I were on the monkey bars after school. Scott Wesley dared me to do a dead-man's drop off the bars. "Bet you can't, because you're a girl," he said with a nasty look on his face.

I never back down from a dare, especially when he used my sex as some sort of handicap. I took his dare but missed the landing completely, and broke my arm. It was a terrible break, and I knew it was broken because the bruising and swelling began almost instantly. Jesse scooped me up in his arms while Kendra grabbed my scooter. I heard Scott say, "I told you so. Stupid girl."

I jumped out of Jesse's arms in a fit of rage and slugged him across the face with my broken arm. By the time we got home, my arm was healed. Nothing. No bruising or anything to show for the accident. Kendra and Jesse played it off like it was nothing. It was the first time I learned of my healing power.

"Remember when," I breathe, lungs burning for air, "we were nine and I broke my arm?"

Jesse smiles. "I do. I also remember you punching Scott Wesley so hard he fell backwards and cried like a baby," he says clearly as if on a leisurely stroll versus running a half marathon.

"No. Remember when my arm healed," I breathe, "and you and Kendra played it off like it was nothing."

"What did you expect, Jackson?" Jesse's face grows stiff, his voice speckled with angst. Not toward me, but the situation. I know this is a sensitive topic for Jesse. I know he was only protecting me, letting me live a normal life, so I let it go.

"How old are you?" I ask, finally catching my breath.

"I was born in 1803." He stares forward, making our run look effortless.

I stop, my muscles tightening almost immediately. He stops several yards ahead but doesn't turn around.

"1803? So that makes you...200 years old?" I bend at my waist and place my hands on my knees.

"Something like that," he says turning back to me.

"Jesse, I feel like I don't even know you anymore. I feel like I'm losing you. The tattoo, your standoffishness, and the fact you're dating the biggest *you-know-what in the world* makes me feel like our friendship is dying." I stand up, looking him dead in the eyes. "I miss the guy who walked me to school every morning in the fourth grade because I was scared to pass old man Henry's house by myself." I sigh. "I miss that guy." I take a few steps toward Jesse. "Where is he?"

Jesse looks down at the ground and shakes his head.

The silence between us turns awkward.

Jesse whispers, "Jackson, I told you, you need to forget about our past. Trust me, it will make things easier on you," he pauses. "You need to move forward and focus on the task at hand. I know how you feel about me." He rubs his forehead with his fingertips and sighs. "I simply do not feel the same. It is my job to protect you. It is my job to be there for you, to pick up the pieces when you fall. That is it. I am here for you because I have to be. It is my job and nothing more."

Swallow, Penn. Just swallow. Swallow your sadness. Swallow your fear. Swallow your heartache and deal with it.

I nod as if the words don't tear at my heart. I act as if they roll off me like the rain.

Jesse and I don't speak the rest of my training session. He keeps his distance.

I go.

I push.

I run.

On Centerville Road, on our way back, we hear the faint cries of a man in pain. They sound close. Riggin's Ranch is only fifty yards behind us. Jesse stops and turns to look at me. I nod, acknowledging I hear it too. We run toward the cries. A homemade light pole casts a dull glow over the pen, barely illuminating the man and bull within. The man stands in a pool of his own blood as the bull withdraws its horn, releasing a torrent of blood.

Wings spread from Jesse's back making a loud whooshing sound. I stand in awe of their beauty: black, beautiful, and shiny. They unfold before my eyes spanning at least seven feet to each side of his body. His feet leave the ground, his wings carrying him over the grizzly scene.

In this moment, I forget my broken heart and how he took my love and threw it away.

The magnificence of who he is, of what he is, fills every thought. The pure beauty of his being makes every negative and sorrowful thought obsolete. He is, in every way, love. Love of self, love of duty, love of life and love of me.

Spectacular. Exquisite. Flawless excellence.

He hovers over the pen, drawing the bull's attention. He lures the bull toward the far end of the enclosure, away from the injured man.

Enraged, the beast follows Jesse. The man, finally free of the bull's attention, slides down the fencepost landing in a heap as more blood pours from his wound.

Oh no.

No. No. No.

It's Travis.

I leap the fence and sprint to him, covering his wound with my hand. Blood continues to pour through my fingers as I try to apply pressure.

The smell of the blood is intoxicating.

Think, Penn. Use your head. This is Travis. Your friend. Jesse's best friend. A human life you must save. "Stop. Please. You're killing me."

"Why, Penn? Why are you killing me?" Memories of Frankie flood back into my mind as Travis's cries of pain remind me of that horrible night. "I'm saving your life, Travis. I'm sorry if this hurts but hold still and be quiet."

There is no way I can fix this without revealing who I am, who we are. If Travis missed Jesse's wing display, he would be sure to notice the hole in his stomach suddenly healing.

Mortal or immortal, it doesn't matter. This life matters more than protecting who and what we are. Any life matters more.

This whole gift, I wonder if somehow I'm tempting fate, I think to myself as I wait for the pain that will soon explode in my veins. *What if Travis is meant to die tonight? What if it was fate that brought Jesse and me here to do what we did? What if we are to witness this event versus change it? What if it is his time to die? What if I'm playing God?*

Life must always prevail.

I find the source of the bleeding and shove my hand deep into the wound to slow it. It takes every ounce of willpower I have not to taste his blood. My hands begin to shake, though I'm uncertain if it is from the fear of losing him or the desire for his blood.

"Oh God," Travis calls out. "Please. Stop." He screams, as his eyes meet mine, begging me to stop, to end the pain.

"Shhh." I break eye contact.

Travis slips from consciousness as I begin the process of healing his wounds. Everything becomes silent. Breathing deeply, my mind quiets. The tingling starts in my head, moving through my body to my feet. The nails dig at my veins and the pain follows like clockwork. I want to curl up and die; I'd do anything to take this pain away. My head begins to pound as if someone is using a sledgehammer on my skull. The entire process feels as though it takes hours when, in actuality, only minutes pass.

I feel the blood slow then stop. I step back and look at Travis, pale and slumped against the fence. Quickly, I remove my hands from his abdomen and see the fresh blood. I stare at the blood on my hands as my body screams for nourishment.

Travis moans as he slowly regains consciousness.

I quickly wipe my hands on my pants and take his face in my hands. "Travis? Travis? I pat his cheek. "Wake up."

He moans again as his eyes begin to flutter open.

I hear Jesse behind me. "He has lost a lot of blood," he says with concern in his voice.

"Travis. Wake up, Travis." my voice more urgent now, "He's too pale, Jess."

"I know." Jesse crouches next to me and forces one of Travis's eyelids open. "He needs blood." Before I can take in what is happening, Jesse takes a knife from his pocket and cuts his own wrist. He forces Travis's mouth open and allows the now flowing blood to drip in.

Travis immediately grabs Jesse's wrist and holds it to his mouth, swallowing. His eyes, now wide and glassy, possess the look of an over-medicated junky.

Jesse forcefully pulls his wrist back as his blood trickles down Travis's chin. Travis stares at us in a trance-like state. "Call Carmine. Get him here now."

As we wait for Carmine, Travis remains slumped against the fence, weak but alive. Jesse takes my blood soaked hands in his and leads me to the water trough. He places my hands in the cool water and begins to gently rub them clean. He stares into my eyes as though looking into my soul, understanding the uncertainty I'm feeling. In this moment, all I want is his love. I know now, without a doubt, if my heart ever broke, he would be the only one able to piece it back together.

Jesse looks away, his jaw tightening. "What do you want from me, Jackson," he whispers breathlessly as if it's too painful to speak.

"Your heart," I whisper.

"Seriously, Black Blood, you sounded as if someone died." I hear Carmine's voice behind us. Jesse quickly pulls our hands out of the water.

"Where is he?"

Jesse and I turn to look at Travis, still slouched against the fence.

"Oh wow, he looks like death. Are you sure you did him a favor? Did you give him blood?" Carmine's eyes dart to Jesse.

He nods without expression, placing his still dripping hands at his sides.

Carmine crouches next to Travis, inspecting the now faded wound.

"Grandma?" Travis's eyes meet Carmine's.

Carmine turns back to Jesse, smiling. "How much blood did you give him?"

"Not enough to make him blood drunk."

Carmine turns back to Travis taking his face into his hands. "Dimenticate tutto quello che è successo stanotte." I lean to Jesse, "What did he say?"

He leans down and translates the words clearly into my ear. My heart stops. "Forget everything that happened tonight."

His words slice through my hardening heart.

Jesse and I finish our run in silence. Although we washed most of the blood off, the remnants make me feel like a killer. I know I saved him but the blood on my hands, the blood that came from his body, I want it.

Every.

Last.

Drop.

I breathe in, comforted knowing the dried blood is there yet hesitant to taste it. I try to wipe my hands on my pants, but it does no good. I shake my head and regain my running pace.

As we finish the last stretch, I think about Jesse. He's deep in thought as our eyes meet. His eyes show panic as he focuses his attention back into the night.

I can't, for the life of me, believe he doesn't care about me.

We hit the driveway and Jesse stops a few feet ahead of me. He sighs and looks up toward the night sky, then walks away.

I let him.

Leave. Walk away. Please, don't take my heart. Give it back. Give it back so I can give it to someone who will handle it delicately.

"Ah, do not worry, Blood Princess. You would just be another notch on his belt anyway," Carmine points out as he steps up beside me. "Give him another month and he will not even remember your name."

"Not worried about it." I lie. I glare at the back of Jesse and turn to Carmine. "Do you think Travis will forget everything he saw tonight?"

"Are you doubting my natural born skills? The gift bestowed upon vampires like an appendage?" Carmine's eyes narrow as he cocks his head.

"I guess that means yes in vampire," I say in a patronizing tone. "What are we doing tonight?"

"Chess."

"Chess?" I say. "You start the first night of training with forcing me to drink blood and now you want to play chess?"

"Come on, let us go inside. I am going to teach you how to master your game." The chessboard is set at the dining room table. I see Aunt Jo's travel mug sitting on the counter.

I cringe.

I don't dare ask anybody. I'm still holding out hope that what I saw wasn't what I think I saw. I want to believe it was someone else dressed in my aunt's clothes or, perhaps, it wasn't a blood bag she filled her travel mug with. Maybe it was cranberry juice.

Don't lie to yourself, Penn.

"You sit here. You are white." He takes his seat across from me. "Chess is a game of patience. It is a game of strategy." He cracks his knuckles then moves his pawn. "If you piecemeal your attacks, your opponent can predict your moves and then hand you your butt on a platter. You are dead."

I move my pawn. He moves his pawn. "You must have a solid team so you can work together. All moving parts must be on the same page."

I move my knight.

He moves his knight.

I must say, this is a welcome change from healing snakes and firing weapons I have no experience using. I smile as I make my last move to complete the Ruy Lopez.

Carmine looks at the board and holds his hands up. "I thought you said you did not know how to play chess?"

"Just a couple moves, I guess." I laugh. "Freshman year it rained so much we moved P.E. indoors. I'm no athlete, so I had Melvin Pinkerton teach me how to play." I shrug. "Not like I'm a pro or anything."

Carmine stares at the board and announces, "Game on." He cracks his neck back and forth as he takes in the entire board. He's anticipating. He's strategizing. He's planning, not only this move, but the ten moves after, both his and mine. He's considering my skill level.

"Never, ever, doubt your opponent. Well played, PJ." Carmine nods in my direction, still studying the board.

I glare at him. "Don't ever call me that again," I say in a serious tone. "Only Amy gets to call me that."

Carmine raises his hands, accepting my overreaction.

"I'm sorry, it's just that..."

"I know," he says with a kindness in his eyes that I only glimpse when Kendra is around. "Now, let us play some chess."

"Which move will it be? The Berlin Wall? The Morphy." I smile. I'm not sure I actually remember how to do those moves, but I remember Melvin droning on and on about them, like some sort of encyclopedia.

He doesn't make eye contact as he mutters something under his breath.

He takes his turn.

I go to move my knight.

"No. Penelope, look at the entire board. You need to anticipate. What will I do next?"

"If I move this piece here, I can take your pawn," I say.

He laughs. "The point of chess is to defeat my entire army, most importantly my King. Take your time. Listen, with chess, there are always second chances, future games." He pauses, "but not in life. Think. Every time your opponent makes a move, you must question why the move is made. There is always a motive. Who is in danger? Only by defending against your opponent's threats will you be successful in battle. Only when you figure out your opponent's plan of attack, can you kill."

He tells me I need to think, and think quickly. Always have a plan A, B and C. He teaches me to see the entire board at all times, know where the players are, and anticipate my opponents every move. I must know what Vacavious is going to do before he does it and have a plan to defend. Always have a clear plan. "Play on his weaknesses," he says.

"What if I don't know his weaknesses?"

"Find them." His eyes slowly move to mine. "Check mate."

CHAPTER 18

Taste Tests

"Reggerio, good to see you, old friend." Carmine stands up.

Reggerio bows to him. "First class."

Carmine shakes his head. "I told you, Reggerio, we no longer have to abide by the rules of Nighmerianotte. We are equals."

Reggerio gives an awkward laugh. "Old habit, I guess."

First class? Equals? I don't ask because Reggerio is here.

"Reggerio, meet our Black Five." Carmine motions to me.

Reggerio turns to me.

"It is an honor, Black Five." He bows. He's no taller than four feet, I'd say. His impeccably kept brown robe loosely circles his round figure. His hair is like hay, long, and more salt than pepper. His beard follows suit, long and salty.

I'm not sure whether to bow back or shake his hand. So, awkwardly, I do both to cover my bases.

I look like an idiot.

"It is nice to meet you, Reggerio."

"Where's Church?" My eyes dance between the two men.

"Reggerio, our most knowledgeable and trustworthy 505, will be filling in for weapons training until it is complete. He is an excellent marksman." Carmine clasps his hands behind his back and looks down to Reggerio.

I know why Church stepped away from training but, in my heart, I wasn't ready. I nod and try to hide my disappointment.

"Lead the way," Reggerio says. "We are going to the hay barn."

Carmine leans in and whispers, "Rules of Nighmerianotte: First class always lead when in a group. Just go with it."

Yeah, I gathered that. I nod and lead us out of the house to the barn.

The hum of the light above the old picnic table fills the empty silence. I see the blade bone on the table. Church explained what it was last night but we never got to test it out.

Reggerio gets down to business. "This," he says, placing the blade bone in my hand. "Should only be handled by the Five." As soon as the weapon touches my skin the handle illuminates in a purple hue. "The purple color is a sign the blade bone is in the right hands." A weathered burgundy stain on the table catches my attention. Immediately my mouth begins to water again. I swallow and try to focus on what Reggerio is saying.

He continues, "The blade bone is used to kill so you can see why it needs to be in the hands of the good at all times." He clears his throat. "The way to kill a Nighmerian with a blade bo—"

"Beheading," I say quickly.

"Correct. So, when you use the blade bone, you must be sure you are ready to kill. It can slice through just about anything: wood, metal, and flesh."

The purple hue is gone. The rust-colored handle feels smooth in my hand. The grip fits my palm and fingers as if custom made for me. The sullied blade looks more like bone than metal. I switch hands and examine the handle. A diamond, similar to the one my father drew in his journal, is outlined with a star at each point of the diamond including one in the middle. I can't help but think there's some sort of link between my father's drawing and the handle. *Coincidence? I think not.* The two bronze hilt guards stretch from either side, etched with what looks to be hand carved designs.

"I want you to feel comfortable with the blade bone. Get a feel for it. It is yours now, Five." He steps closer and turns toward the end of the barn. "See the mannequin at the other end of the barn?"

"Yes."

"When you are ready, I want you to throw the blade bone and hit the mannequin in the heart."

"Reggerio," I pause. "Wait. You're serious? My aim is terrible. I cannot."

"You will never use the term 'I cannot' because you, my dear, can do anything you put your mind to."

I swallow. "Well, you might want to back up, then."

Reggerio, resigning to my request, moves into the shadows somewhere behind me.

"Take your time, Five," he hoarsely whispers.

I lick my lips. "Do I use the handle to throw it?" I zero in on the mannequin.

"What feels heavier?"

"The handle."

"Then throw it from there."

"What? Reggerio, I've never thrown a knife before. This could get ugly, I'm forewarning you."

He laughs. "I will take my chances. Trust your instincts."

Great. Fine. Wonderful. My instincts? Those seem to really work out in my favor, I think, as I remember being chased by snakes in the labyrinth last night. I shake my head and carefully place the handle in my palm and wrap my four fingers around it, then slide my thumb across the top of my fingers.

"Like this?"

Reggerio emerges from the shadows. "Hammer grip is a fine choice."

My eyes fall to the blood spot on the table again. I swallow. *Force it out of your mind, Penn.* I tighten my grip. I take a small step forward with my right foot and try to get into a comfortable stance.

"Good. How does that feel?"

"Okay, I guess." I shrug. *I have no idea, Reggerio. They don't teach knife throwing as a P.E. option in high school. Chess, yes. Knife throwing, no.*

"Now, picture someone or something you loathe. Look at your target. Create a clear path in your mind between the blade and the target."

That's easy. *Vanessa.* I picture her face on the mannequin.

"This is a long distance throw, so you will not want to bend your wrist. This will keep the knife from turning too much in the air. Bend your elbow so the knife is raised alongside your head. As you throw, shift your weight forward to your front foot and keep your momentum. At the same time you shift your weight, swing your forearm forward from the elbow so your arm is straight out in front of you." Reggerio demonstrates the maneuver. "At this point, you will release the knife. Got it?"

"Yes." *No.*

"Good. Throw." He moves back into the shadows and crosses his arms.

"All right, let's get this over with." I square my stance and focus on the mannequin's chest. *Vanessa. Vanessa. Vanessa. Vanessa.*

I bring back the knife and shift my weight forward letting go as my arm fully extends. As it leaves my hand, it shoots forward and slams against the wall to the right of the mannequin.

Wow. Not even close. I thought for sure I would shank that she-beast.

"Again." Reggerio's voice is stern.

I retrieve my knife and start the process again.

And again.

And again.

And again.

And again.

Finally I throw the blade bone so hard it makes a thud sound as it protrudes out of the mannequin's forearm. "Yes!" I call out. "Nailed it!"

Reggerio chuckles. "Not quite, Five, but close. Again."

After twenty-nine tries, finally, I hit her, or the mannequin, in the heart. "YES!" I jump up and down. I go to high-five Reggerio but pause. "Sorry. I got ahead of myself." I pause. "Fist bump?"

He holds out his fist, a little confused. I put my fist to his.

"You remind me of my daughter," he says.

"Yeah? You have a family?"

"I transitioned to the mortal world just hours before the portals were locked. The deal was I would serve as an advisor to the Detail and to be the impartial vote if they cannot agree. The agreement was I could go home every evening at dusk. We were all training for the arrival of the next Five, for the arrival of you, my Sanguine." He clears his throat because the silence between the two of us is awkward.

"So, you haven't seen your family in a hundred years?" I stop.

"My wife and daughter. Because of Kendra, I have been able to only see them. They are still alive but I have not been able to speak to them in an extraordinarily long time."

The snow globe, I think to myself.

"When was the last time she showed you?" I set the blade bone down on the table.

"Fifteen years ago, on my daughter's birthday." He fidgets with the sleeve from his robe trying to act unaffected by the memories.

"Have you asked Kendra? To show you what they are doing now?"

"Oh, no. We never ask a first class for anything."

"A first class?" I say. "Tell me about this first class nonsense."

Reggerio eyebrows rise. "They did not tell you?"

I shrug. "No."

He cocks his head. "Church? Carmine? They did not mention anything about the caste system of our world? Nighmerianotte, I mean." Shaking his head, his obvious disgust is evident.

"Please, Reggerio, I'm all ears. There isn't anything you can say that will surprise me. Trust me."

He shrugs and leans back against the wall. "Well before my departure, first class Nighmerians were held in high regard. Not as high as the Demi or the Five but right below. If a first class was ever behind a second class, the second class must always step aside and let the first class pass. The same is true with the second class and third class, the third class must always step aside.

First class Nighmerians usually live in the Pollone, Strega and Volare districts while the second class and third class usually live in the Zanna district. The nottes live in the Scogliera district, also referred to as "the cliff." He sighs. "Nobody told you?"

Enthralled by his lesson, I shake my head, motioning him to continue.

"Nottes are completely ignored and treated as if they do not exist. It is prohibited for a notte to marry a first class or second class Nighmerian. If this happens, it is unlawful and not recognized by Nighmerianotte. Nottes do not have a voice or a vote during elections for the Demi." His bushy eyebrows rise as his eyes remain on the ground, shifting from foot to foot. "In my opinion, diversity should be appreciated. One should be allowed to marry regardless of the bloodline, beliefs, species, or class and the like. Everyone should have a say in our leader's selection. Everyone should get a vote. No one should be treated the way the nottes are treated." His eyes meet mine. "I never agreed with any of it, yet I know better than to speak my mind."

I pause at first, not wanting to disrespect his upbringing, but say what I am thinking anyway. "But we aren't in Nighmerianotte anymore."

He takes a deep breath and says, "It is hard when you have been trained to do things a certain way for hundreds of years," He lets out a long breath. "Then again, maybe I do not know anything anymore about our world. I mean, much has changed. My family…"

"Black Blood, you ready?" I hear Kendra's voice call out from behind me. "Hi, Reggerio."

"Kendra, can you do me a favor?" I call back to her, my eyes still on Reggerio.

She walks to my side and I give her my patented *I need a favor* look. Reggerio bows to her.

I turn to Kendra. "Will you allow Reggerio to see his family again, please? In Nighmerianotte, I mean?"

She smiles. "Reggerio, you are killing my reputation. I am not supposed to have a compassionate side." She smiles to the 505 as her eyes light up. She swirls her finger, creating a snow globe. Blues and blacks fill the globe she's created. A trail of sparkles dance around the gigantic circle.

In the picture, it's dark. A voice sounds, "Slovi, where did you put father's matches?"

"In the drawer," a voice replies in the darkness.

The mother grabs a candle and it illuminates her bright skin and troubled eyes. She's thin. Frail almost.

A smile of awe spreads across Reggerio's face as he watches his wife dig in a drawer for his matches. *I can't help but wonder what he's thinking.*

"Here they are." She hands them to her daughter.

Slovi strikes the match against the box. The flicker of the match drives the darkness away, illuminating Slovi's face. She's beautiful, but also extremely thin and gaunt. She looks identical to her mother, yet years younger.

I look to Reggerio again. Tears run down his cheeks.

Slovi leans down and puts the match to a small pit, lighting a tiny fire. The light from the flames allows us to see through the darkness. It's some sort of shop.

"It is my old shop," Reggerio whispers to me. The place looks ravaged. It's desolate and dark with shelves leaning every which way, like dominos caught mid fall. The windows are boarded from the inside, and there's no light to speak of other than the fire and candlelight. To the right of the fire sits a cauldron. The daughter moves the cauldron and places it on a hook above the fire.

"The soup should last us for the next two weeks."

A loud, blood-curdling scream sounds from a distance.

Both Solvi and her mother jump.

"Put the fire out, quickly!" The mother hisses. "They are coming!"

The whole room goes dark. "I wish Father was here." Terror resides in her tone.

Kendra stops and turns to Reggerio. The snow globe dissipates.

Nobody speaks.

I hear Reggerio swallow and watch as he slowly nods. A deep sadness washes over his face, a sadness that can only be seen, not described in words. He sighs. "Thank you, First Class."

Kendra nods. "Five, are you ready?"

No. no, I'm not. I'm not ready for any of this. Solvi's words. Her tone. So instead, I mask my fear. "Yeah. Reggerio? Are you going to be okay? Do you need me to sit with you…or something?" I ask.

He smiles. "I will be. Go train. You are our only hope, Penelope Jackson. Here," He hands me the blade bone. "This is yours now, Black Five. Oh," he reaches underneath the table, "and this." He hands me a small sheath. "It goes on your leg." I take the blade bone into my hands and feel the emblem of Nighmerianotte against my palm. The purple hue appears and quickly fades.

I nod in Reggerio's direction.

Reggerio and Kendra help me get the holster on and the blade bone in its rightful place. "That should do it," he says. "Good luck tonight."

Kendra and I make our way outside. The fog has nestled itself in all the open space around the house. She leads me back toward the house.

We walk in silence. I follow Kendra's lead. My head swarms with thoughts of Reggerio and how he must feel.

"Taste testing." Kendra gets her infamous sideways grin.

"What?"

"Taste testing tonight. You will be taste testing different liquids tonight."

Great. "This seems to be a little more lax than last night." I welcome the change.

Kendra shakes her head.

"What?" I jerk my head back in her direction. We walk up the porch steps.

"Don't worry, Jo has something special in mind for you tonight." She gives me a shove with her shoulder.

"Here." She hands me a blindfold. "Tonight we are going to test your sense of taste and smell."

Oh joy. I take it from her. "Have you talked to Church tonight?" I ask, trying to act casual. "He wasn't at our training session."

"Sit here." She motions to the chair across the table. She takes a seat across from me. "Yeah. Why?" She smirks as she grabs a diet Pepsi from the refrigerator. *She wants me to ask. She wants me to be curious about where he's at and why he didn't show up for training tonight.* Our eyes meet.

"What's the game?" I look to the shot glasses.

"Put the blind fold on and I will tell you."

"Why should I trust you?" I play.

"Why not? Have I ever steered you wrong?" She shrugs as if she didn't send snakes to kill me.

I cock my head and raise my eyebrows.

"You have not died, right? Do you seriously think I would feed you poison or something?"

I put the blindfold on. "Do you seriously want me to answer?" The blindfold makes me feel confined and a little uncomfortable. "Now what?" I rest my hands in my lap.

I hear her set a glass down in front of me. "Drink and tell me what you think it is."

I bite my lip. *I trust Kendra. I know I do. Maybe it's the anticipation of what the outcome will be. It can't kill me, right?* I carefully place my hands on the table in front of me and feel for the glass. I put my hand around it and carefully pick it up.

"Drink."

I slowly lift it to my lips. There's no scent, which may be a plus, or not. I smell it again. Nothing. I put it to my lips and drink. The liquid is room temperature and thick, like syrup, but there's virtually no taste. I swallow.

"Well?" She says.

I set the glass down. "It doesn't have much of a...HOLY HELL. My mouth. My mouth is on fire." I yell. "Water. Please. Water."

Kendra goes to the kitchen and grabs the glass of water on the counter.

I gulp and gulp. My lips burn so badly they feel like they are going to burn off. They feel blistered and swollen. "What was that?!" I set the glass down and pat my lips with my fingers. "That was hot. It feels like you gave me straight habanero sauce."

"That, my friend, is the blood of a 202, a witch. Actually, it's my blood. It will burn the insides of your mouth if you drink too much. Remember that." She clicks her tongue.

"Gross, Kendra," I say, still patting my lips. "We are definitely not those kind of friends!" I pause. "Wait. Will that trigger or curb my cravings?" *Crap. I just said that out loud. I openly admitted to have cravings for blood. Stupid.*

Kendra doesn't miss a beat. "No. Not like human blood. Plus, Nighmerian blood does not do anything for you in terms of nutritional value." I hear her set down another glass in front of me. "Next."

She won't kill me, I remind myself. I put the next glass to my lips and open my mouth. The liquid tastes like candy. It's thick and sweet. I take it all in my mouth and savor the taste, swishing it around and then I swallow. Part of me waits for a burning sensation, but nothing happens. The after taste becomes bitter, sour even.

"And that?"

"What do you think it is?"

"Sweet and sour," I say. "Kendra, I have no idea. I think its blood because of the consistency. Other than that, I'm clueless."

"The steadfast 105's blood. Masculine but their bitterness always gets you in the end," she growls.

Great. "Hopefully it wasn't Church's or Carmine's blood," I mutter under my breath. I try to look through the blindfold but all I see is black.

"Next." Kendra sets down another glass.

I reach for the glass and put it to my lips. "Eww, this stinks."

"Drink." I hear her say.

Gross. I want to cover my nose but I know Kendra won't have it. So, I put the third glass to my lips. It has a thin consistency. The smell fills my nostrils and I gag, spitting it back in the glass.

I gag.

I gag again.

Kendra laughs.

"Kendra Brighton. What is that? Disgusting," I seethe as I gag once more.

"Cat pee."

My face grows hot as the stench fills my nose and the taste makes me want to vomit. "You gave me cat pee?" I'm livid.

"Listen, now you know the difference."

"Everything is so wrong about this picture. Why the heck would I have to know the difference between cat pee and blood? Couldn't you have given me, oh, I dunno, water?" I scrunch my face because of its terrible aftertaste and look in the direction of her voice.

"I use it like coffee beans. You know, when you are sampling perfume at Daliah's uptown and they give you coffee beans to 'cleanse your palate.'" She does rabbit ears with her fingers when she says 'cleanse your palate.'

I give her my best stare down, my face of displeasure. "Shut up. I'm so mad at you right now. Besides, how are you allowed to be out all hours of the night for my training? Shouldn't you be at home so Francis doesn't freak out?"

Kendra gives me a what-are-you-talking-about look. "Huh?"

"Francis, your guardian?"

"Penn, she is Nighmerian. Trust me, there are more watching over you than just our detail."

"Oh. Ohhhh. In my defense, you never told me," I say under my breath. "What's next?"

"See, now you are getting into it." She slides another glass my way.

I drink it down. I don't even care. I just want the cat pee taste out of my mouth. Its consistency is thin, like the urine. I'm afraid to breathe because I don't want to know what it tastes like.

I take a breath and wait for my taste buds to kick in.

Pepper and armpit.

Not that I know what armpit tastes like but, if it did have a taste, I assume it would taste like this. I push my tongue against the roof of my mouth, anything to get the urine taste out.

"Well? What do you think?" I hear Kendra say.

"Pepper and armpit."

Kendra breaks into laughter. "Perfect! See, I knew you would catch on quickly."

"What is it?" I wipe my mouth with the back of my hand. I sneeze.

Kendra squeals, "Just that. Pepper and armpit. It is a repellent elixir I am working on to ward off morterros and selacs. It neutralizes any pheromones the body gives off so the good guys cannot be detected. I just wanted to know what it tasted like."

"Kendra, how long have you been conjuring spells and elixirs?"

"Since 1807." She pauses, as if waiting for my reaction. "Well, technically, I started spell casting in the academy when I was 14 in…1821." She slides something over the table, which sounds much bigger than the other glasses. "Here, you will like this one." I put my hands out and feel the cold of the steel beneath my fingers. It takes everything I have not to tear off the lid and swallow every last bit.

My water bottle.

I put the steel to my lips and drink. The blood slides down my throat and explodes when it hits my stomach.

As the warm feeling returns, I lean back and let the euphoria take me away to my paradise.

Ecstasy. Rapture. Jubilation. Bliss. Trance. Daze. Reverie. My body is weightless and I feel invincible. Again.

"All right, Penn. Come back and join the land of the living." Kendra leans over the table and peeks under the blindfold.

I open my eyes and pull my head up. "Does this feeling ever go away when I drink? I mean will it happen every time I drink?"

"No. It will fade with time. Once your body becomes accustomed to the blood."

I try to gather myself.

"Next." Kendra slides yet another glass in front of me.

"Seriously?"

"Drink."

Hesitantly, I put it to my lips. It's blood. I can tell its blood not only by the consistency and thickness, but by the way it feels in my mouth. Each type of blood seems to feel a little differently. Vampire blood is velvety and has a richer taste. The blood in my mouth is thinner and gives off a sultry taste, like pine. It reminds me of Jesse. "Sentinel's blood, the 305."

I feel her smile. I don't have to see Kendra smile to know she's grinning from ear to ear. We've been friends too long for that.

She gives me every single type of blood known to our world, Nighmerianotte: 105, 205, 305, 405, and the 505. Even blood from selacs. *It was disgusting,* almost worse than the cat pee. She gives me selac poison and tells me not to swallow it because a cup full, if swallowed, will make me severely ill. She tells me I need to know what it tastes like because it's a popular method of murdering someone in Nighmerianotte when one does not have access to a real weapon. I think she just wants to see me cringe.

"You did well." She takes the blindfold off. "If you start to feel ill, take this." She hands me a small bottle with a black label. The label reads: Drink only if absolutely necessary.

I look to Kendra. "How will I know when it's necessary?"

She laughs. "Oh, you will know. Jo will meet you at the end of the tree line." She motions toward the door with her head. "Go."

I stand up and start to walk toward the door.

"Penn?"

"Yeah?" I turn to face Kendra whose back is to me, still sitting in the chair.

"You know I would never do anything to harm you, right?"

"I know, Boots."

"And Penn?"

"Yeah?"

"Sometimes in life *not knowing* is the safest option." She turns so I can see her profile. "Sometimes, it is the only option."

I know what she's talking about. I let her words settle in my heart. I want to believe them, so I choose to believe them.

I put my headlamp on as I head down the porch steps and toward the back. There's an eerie silence tonight that consumes me as soon as the fog pulls me in. The blade bone is safe against my leg. The mist brushes my face. I keep my headlamp pointed toward the ground, knowing I have roughly fifty more steps to the tree line. Darkness eats me alive as I trudge forward. I stop and look back toward the house, but all I see is heavy, thick, dark fog.

A branch breaks next to me.

CHAPTER 19

Flying Lessons

My insides jolt, like a thousand needles puncturing my skin simultaneously.

I pick up the pace. My headlamp changes its pattern of movement as my steps become quicker.

Another branch breaks.

My heart fills with dread. I look up and see the tree line ahead. Jo should be there, waiting for me. I feel the blade bone against my thigh with each step. I know how to defend myself, well, kind of.

Irrational fears, Penn. Remember, irrational fears. It's 2:00 a.m. and I'm tromping through a pitch-black meadow. That's not an irrational fear. It's a valid one.

The fog has cleared somewhat so I'm able to see a little further ahead. I look up and notice the gigantic redwood trees of the tree line. Jo's supposed to meet me here, but I don't see her.

"Penn," I hear someone whisper.

This time, I stop. *No. I'm not going to run.* I think of Jo's words to me the first night of training. *No more.*

In one quick motion I reach down and pull out the blade bone. I turn around to face the fog. "Who's there?" I say.

A shadow emerges from the fog, a black silhouette. *I could throw the blade now and I may, or may not, hit my intended target, but two things come to mind: I don't know who this person is, and, what if I miss?* I take my chances and hold the blade in front of me. "Who's there?" I call again.

"Penelope, it is me."

Jo comes into the light of my headlamp.

"Jo. You," I pause. I don't want to tell her she scared me. I quickly lean down and put the blade bone back in its holster.

Jo walks past me and starts the climb up the hill. "How is the training with the blade bone going?"

I shrug. I want to ask her about the blood I saw her drinking, but I don't. I think of what Kendra told me before I left the house. *Sometimes, in life, not knowing, is the safest option.*

A small part of me wants her to come clean, but the other part tells me it's not my place to know, for now. "I'm struggling with the aim part."

"That will come." Jo catches my eye.

We push up the hill, meandering around the redwood trees, ferns and logs. As we climb closer to the top, the fog clears. I don't feel tired. My legs don't burn and my breathing is paced and slow. I'm quite surprised my sixty-something aunt isn't tired either.

"What are we doing tonight?" We are now shoulder to shoulder, bobbing around the trees.

"You will see."

Jo's quiet. "You're quiet tonight. Everything okay?" I step over a fallen log as Jo glides over it, smooth and graceful.

Her answer is mechanical, I know this because there's a long pause before she speaks. "I have a lot on my mind is all, Honey." She grabs my hand as we stand on the edge of the meadow, surrounded by trees. The fog is gone and the moon illuminates the field.

Jo puts her fingers in her mouth like she's going to whistle. Instead, a loud screech passes through her lips. I cover my ears as the sound makes me cringe.

She stops. I carefully uncover my ears and look to Jo who is staring up toward the sky, waiting.

I look toward the night sky.

The stars. The moon.

She makes the terrible screeching sound again. My hands fly to my ears as this screech is far louder and far more ear-piercing than the last.

A screech comes from the night sky.

Then nothing.

Another screech sounds, this time, closer. A mass of black circles toward us, its wings gracefully spread like sheets, blanketing the night sky.

I hold my breath.

Another loud screech sounds from the creature. The wind from its wings blows my hair off my shoulders. It circles several times before coming closer to the ground.

It lands, the ground shuttering.

This thing makes the giant trees look small, even from far away.

It screeches once more. It sniffs the air and stomps in our direction.

I back up a few steps.

"What is it?" I ask in a breathless voice.

"A draghi."

It stands at least twenty feet tall, its black scaly body mostly hidden behind its wings. A long thick tail with three rings at the end, curls around to its front. Its long nostrils protrude from its snout. Horns sit on top of either side of its head and ears stick out like satellites. Its face is ominous, a little sinister and dark for my taste. I don't trust it.

It leans in and sticks its nose out.

I stop breathing.

It takes in a long breath and exhales, blowing me back a few steps. The stench of its breath eats at my nose. It's awful, a cross between dirty cat litter and soiled socks.

"Vai a giocare!" Jo shoos the draghi away with her hand.

I glare at it as I try to size it up.

Jo looks back to me, "Are you ready?"

"I have a feeling this night creature has something to do with my training tonight." A feeling of dread consumes my insides.

"You must kill the draghi. Then save its life."

"I've never saved anything this big, Jo. Or killed anything this big."

"First rule, never, ever doubt your abilities, Penelope. If you believe you will not succeed, you will not."

The draghi sniffs the air one more time. "Play on its weaknesses, Penn."

Jo steps back. "The rules: you cannot leave the confines of the meadow. You must kill with your blade bone, not your mind. You have fifty minutes. When I say begin, the clock starts." She waves her hand in the air and says to the draghi, "Vai dall'altro lato del prato." The draghi screeches one more time then runs to the opposite side of the meadow like an eager dog, shaking the ground below us.

"To kill a draghi, you must pierce its heart," she explains. "Begin."

It screeches again and hurdles itself toward me, shaking me in more ways than one.

As it runs toward me, I think of my training with Carmine: *two steps ahead of the enemy, have a backup plan, your enemy is making a move and you must know why, think like your enemy.*

Animals are instinctual. They use their sense of smell more than any other.

A blast of fire shoots from its mouth.

"Holy sh—" I jump out of the line of fire as another ball of flame leaves its mouth.

This time, I run. I don't look back, but feel it stomping behind me. Fire erupts all around me. I leap behind a tree on the edge of the meadow praying it's wide enough to block the flames.

Tongues of flame reach around the tree like claws, singeing my hair.

Seriously? Now I'm mad. *Now what? Think.* There's no thought into how it will kill. *First, give it a gender. Familiarize yourself with your opponent.* I peek around the tree as the fire ceases. How should I know if it is male or female? Okay, I go with what I know. Attitude? Check. Control issues? Check. Serious case of PMS? Double check. It's a girl. Now that I have that sorted I can worry about how to survive this night. She's pacing and sniffing the air, her muscles working like a machine. She stops and sniffs the air again. She turns suddenly and blasts fire as I fall back behind the tree.

Whoa. Now what? Think. Okay, her neck doesn't look long enough to look beneath her. If I can hide underneath there, she won't be able to see me. I can climb up her body and get to the heart. Good, plan A.

I peek around the tree again. This time, she's facing me, her body centered on mine. She inhales as if trying to find my scent. *Wait a minute.* I peek around the tree and flail my arm.

Nothing.

This time, I carefully stand, hoping she doesn't decide to shoot fire at me again, and step out from behind the tree.

I flail my arms again like a crazed traffic cop. Like a statue, she stands, her massive head pointing upward. She lowers it slightly and I wave my arms once more for good measure. *Nothing.* She's blind, at least nearly blind. I'm sure her sense of smell is what she relies on.

I jump back behind the tree and hear the crunch of a bag in my pocket.

The candy.

I have to get behind the draghi and distract it. I pull the bag from my pocket and count the remaining candies: only five left. I lean out and look behind me, hands shaking.

Standing twenty feet in the air, her rancid breath fills the air around her. She now stands directly on the other side of the tree I am hiding behind. *How did I not hear her move?*

There goes plan A. On to plan B—surprise attack.

I climb the lower branches of the tree, hoping none of them snap. If they don't hold my weight it's on to plan C—I die. Once I'm certain I'm high enough, I circle to the opposite side of the tree and prepare to jump on the draghi's back.

One. Two. Three. I leap from the branches, aiming for the narrow of her neck, right behind her head. Time seems to freeze as all my senses peak simultaneously. I notice the moon is so bright it makes the field look mystical. The smell of the redwoods so pungent it nears nauseating levels. The cool, damp air feels like thousands of tiny needles against my skin. I can hear the heartbeat of the draghi and every twitch her muscles make as she waits, ready to pounce. I grab the candy from my pocket as I leap. Her ears twitch at the sound of the rustling package as I grip it in my hand. The ground shakes as she turns suddenly and screeches a loud, angry shriek.

I toss two candies directly in front of her as a last ditch effort to bring her back into position before I land. I land slightly askew on her back. Her sudden shift after hearing the candy package altered her position just enough that I miss my target by at least two feet. As she lunges forward, ignoring the distraction created by the candy I tossed, I grab for any handhold I can find. Falling now means certain death.

I throw another candy in front of her in an attempt to slow her enough to right my position. She alters her pace slightly, but not nearly enough to reposition myself. I will have to make do.

This isn't good. Two candies left in the bag. She stomps her way up toward the tree line. She leaps into the air while twisting back and forth to dislodge her unwanted passenger, me.

"Not on your life, big girl."

She shrieks as her massive wings spread like a gigantic fan.

She twists again as I grab tightly around her neck. *Crap.*

We're flying.

We're flying. We skim the tree line like a seagull in search of its next meal, dropping down the big hill toward the house. The night is clear, not only in the meadow, but everywhere. I feel like I'm swimming with the stars, and dancing with the moon; they shine like pearl earrings.

Breathtaking. I look out onto the beautiful landscape.

We swoop down through the cemetery, like a fast moving train, the gray headstones moving rapidly underneath. We are high enough not to be noticed against the night sky but low enough to see every building streak past at a heart-stopping speed. Past the church, and down through Main Street, the lampposts glimmer like fireflies. We lace Main Street like a shoestring and skim the roadways leading in and out of the town. We loop back and soar to an elevation that makes my stomach drop. I grip her sides and tighten my legs around her thick neck as she makes multiple maneuvers trying to shake me. The smell of seaweed and salt fills my airways. *I hope her sense of direction is far better than her eyesight.*

She increases her speed and height, forcing me to squeeze even tighter, my muscles beginning to ache. I barely notice my heart racing or the fact the wind on my face grows colder.

We drop back down and skim the ocean's surface like a speedboat. I hold on for dear life, terrified of ocean water. Not the water itself, but what lurks in the darkest spots, hiding, just waiting to grab an arm or a leg. I would probably die. Heck, I'd rather die than swim to shore because the terror of making that trek would likely kill me outright.

The moon reflecting off the ripples for miles and miles answers any questions I may have had about our proximity to land or the absolute vastness of this terror inducing body of water.

Please, don't dump me. Not here.

She shrieks once again as she pulls upwards, nearly vertical.

"She's going to dump me." I hang on so tightly, my arms crush against her shingle-like scales. My legs cling to her neck as best they can. I can't hang on like this forever.

We're vertical and I don't dare look down because the fear will swallow me alive.

"Hang on tight. Don't look down," I whisper to myself over and over.

We fly higher and higher. My arms and legs now exhibiting the first signs of fatigue.

A cramp in my leg gives my body a jolt. It's the leg with the blade bone.

"Oh nooooo!" I scream as my hands begin to slip and I try to grip tighter. The cramp intensifies, moving up my leg. I want to scream in pain but the pain takes my breath away.

I have two candies left. I open the sweaty candy bag, pinched between my hand and the beast, with my mouth.

"Smell the stupid candy, Jerk Face," I seethe through my ache. "Smell it!" I yell, the bag dangling from my clenched teeth.

She shrieks again, as she cranes her neck back, appearing to grin. "Do you smell that? You can drop me but I'm taking the candy with me."

My hands and arms begin to slip as my legs contort in pain, losing their grip. My arms burn so badly all I can do is let go because falling would be better than the searing pain growing in every muscle of my body.

With one final effort, I try to hike my legs closer to my hands, but it's no use.

I can't hang on.

CHAPTER 20

Killing the Draghi

In one fluid motion, her wings turn with a loud swoosh and her body is horizontal again. I slide along her body, catching myself at the base of her tail, the abrupt stop knocking the wind out of me.

Clinging for life, I pull myself forward along her tail until I reach the place it meets her body.

She looks back again and grins.

Jerk. I shake my head and growl, "You want the candy, you smelly beast? Take me back to the meadow. Now!"

She dives toward the ocean. I instinctively grab tighter to keep from sliding back down her tail. I feel her scales shred my thighs like a knife.

My fingernails dig into her scales as I drag myself forward, toward her neck. I mentally prepare for the worst as she continues her dive.

Down.

Down.

Down.

The surface of the ocean grows closer as I stare defiantly back.

As we are about to breach the dark sea, she pulls up. I grab her neck with all the strength I have left, refusing to slide back toward her tail.

Thank you. I gasp.

She flies down the coastline and east over the trees.

We soar around the backside of the cemetery and circle over the meadow. I slowly reach for the blade bone, knowing my task is not yet finished. I feel the handle in my hand as I slide it out of its sheath.

"Easy," I say to her.

She lets out a sigh as she pulls back and her legs reach for the ground.

Two feet.

Then four.

She comes to a running stop, her lungs expand and contract, gasping for breath.

Finally, we stop.

"For you, I whisper as I drop the candy on the ground in front of her. As she leans down to eat it, I slide to her front with the Blade in my hand. "Nothing personal, girl."

I shove the blade through her tough scales, into her still heaving chest and into her beating heart. I leap to the ground, leaving the blade bone in her chest.

Blood oozes from the wound, making my insides quiver. *Desire and regret battle in my mind.*

What does it taste like? I can't help but wonder. The puddle of blood oozes toward me, teasing me.

With a long sigh, she collapses, the ground shaking.

As the final vestiges of life drain through the wound I created, her mouth opens, the candy she so eagerly accepted drops in the now bloody dirt.

I try to focus but the blood invades every thought. I crouch and drag my finger through the congealing pool of blood. "Just a taste. It won't hurt me."

Wait, stop it, screams the voice of reason, but I can't resist. My finger trembles as I put it to my lips.

"Stop."

Jo.

"You must focus on the task you were given, Penelope."

I stare at my blood-covered fingers. "Jo, surely YOU can understand." The words spew from my mouth in a sarcastic tone.

"No. I cannot. Focus, Penn. Save the draghi."

I watch the blood slowly drip from my fingers and wonder what swallowing it will feel like. My mouth begins to water, desire forcing my lips open.

"Penelope, the draghi is dying. If you do not save her now, she will not live."

"Good, she was nasty anyway." I stand up. The blood is now a small pond and thirst fills my mind.

"Penelope, this draghi has a family back in Nighmerianotte. You know what that feels like, do you not?"

"No Jo, I don't. My parents died when I was born. I lived with a drug addicted alcoholic until I was eight. She died, forcing them to send me to live with you." My voice is lower, unable to hide my anger any longer. "I trusted you, Jo. I needed you just like that eight-year-old girl needed you. Then you lie to me?" Sadness fills me. "Remember all that?"

"Save the draghi, Penelope." Her hands are at her sides, balled into fists.

"No." I stand my ground.

She stares at me, cold and detached. I bend down and touch my finger to the cooling pool of blood.

I touch the blood to my tongue, yearning for the feeling of ecstasy I hope will come.

"Do not swallow it. It will not end well." Jo crosses her arms and watches me.

I swallow, or try to, unable to get it down. I gag, unable to swallow the blood or spit it out. I gag again. "It tastes like black tar." I gag once more.

Jo is clearly frustrated.

"Why don't you save the draghi, Jo?"

Our eyes meet.

"This is not my training, Penelope." She sighs. "Save the draghi."

"No. Tell me the truth. What are you? What's in your travel mug?" I yell, hurt that the person I trust more than anyone in this world is now lying to me like everyone else.

A hint of panic in her eyes betrays her otherwise stoic face. "Sometimes, Penelope, the truth is better left unsaid." Her eyes narrow as she turns away, angry and hurt. "Go home, you are no longer needed here."

"Perfect. Good luck with that." I say, placing the last candy in my mouth to remove the taste of the draghi's blood. Anger explodes inside me. I thrash through the ferns and weave around the redwood trees, racing down the hill and away from the mess I know I was partially responsible for.

CHAPTER 21

Forty-Six Days of Torture

Monday, October 29th, 2012

I t has been forty-seven days since my first run with Jesse. I wrestled snakes for the first time, killed a morterro, and flew a draghi. That night seems like a distant memory now.

I've changed.

Those two nights were nothing compared to the nights that followed. Some nights, I begged Father Time to give me a break and hit the fast forward button. *Pleaded, even.*

I've noticed lately my recovery time is much faster, and I'm neither sore nor sleep deprived. I can survive with half the sleep limiti require, three to four hours is a comfortable amount. My body now rejuvenates itself within minutes.

Did I mention the training has been hell?

I would never say that out loud, but for the record, whoever is keeping score—H-e-l-l.

Jesse and I don't speak, unless it pertains to the training specifically. I know it's for the best.

We train.

He pushes.

I push back. Harder.

Jesse has increased my endurance tenfold. He taught me sleeper holds, pressure point moves and how to survive in the elements. He taught me speed and agility are key when power is not an option. No matter how hard he pushed, I pushed back. *The body can handle far more than the mind thinks it can,* he would say. He'd repeat it over and over and over. I tried to tell him where he could put that saying, but he didn't agree.

I saw a side of Jesse I've never seen before. I saw the love of what he does.

It's in him.

Instinctively, it is in him to rescue and protect, to keep me safe. I've also seen the longing when he looks in my eyes. I see his heart through his eyes.

Kendra put me through the ringer too. Thanks to her, I use my senses far more and am keenly aware of my surroundings at all times. I understand how my body reacts to different stimuli. Werewolves make my body break out in goose bumps. Before my training, I didn't know the difference between blood types by their smell, consistency or taste, now I know them all: human, animal, and immortal. I can smell the different species coming from hundreds of yards away. I am so keenly aware of my surroundings, I know what is happening simply by listening.

Listening and reacting was vitally important in my early training. During the second week of training, we were in the slaughter barn and Kendra had an ijet, a sentinel weapon used in Nighmerianotte. It is thrown while flying through the air when patrolling the districts. When thrown, it flies through the air with a faint whisper, nearly inaudible to the human ear. Lothario, inventor and member of the Demi, worked hard to perfect this weapon. They wanted to be able to immobilize an immortal without killing them.

It has two ten-pound weights on either side of a five-foot chain. The chain has thick curved spikes so when thrown the ijet will wrap itself around its victim, the spikes curling into the flesh. When used in battle, the spikes are laced with poison creating boils that ooze pus. It won't kill an immortal but it will incapacitate them.

This one, thankfully, wasn't laced with poison. The shed was dark. I couldn't see and the only instruction she gave me was to listen. When you hear it, jump.

It was only a matter of seconds before the chain wrapped around my leg. It felt like needles pushing into my flesh.

I dropped. The pain was instantaneous. It felt as though my flesh was ripped open and I was swimming in a bottle of rubbing alcohol. I couldn't speak because the pain was so severe.

"Vattene!" I heard Kendra say as she unwrapped the ijet from my legs and shined her headlamp to look at the damage. *Nothing*. I healed that quickly.

"Listen, Penelope. Listen. When you hear it, jump. Now, stand up. Do it again."

I thought it would be painful to put pressure on my legs, but it wasn't.

This time, I was dead set on not letting this thing kick my butt.

"Listen," she whispered from somewhere in the darkness.

I did. Still, I didn't hear anything. Another crashing blow dropped me to my knees again. The pain seemed to grow consecutively worse each of the twelve times it took before, finally, I heard it. It sounded like a high pitched whistle with some sort of melody to it. Once I heard it, I jumped, but it was too soon. The dang thing dropped me to my knees again. Excruciating didn't do it justice. I missed it seventeen more times. I thought I would die from the pain each time. It took me three nights of training to master the ijet, my nemesis.

Reggerio finished my training. Church never came back but I'm not bitter. At least I try to convince myself I'm not.

Jo and I never spoke of the night in the meadow. My training with her was probably the most demanding of all. She made me let every animal bleed out until they were on the brink of Evernotte before allowing me to save them. I think it was some sort of payback. Not payback in a vindictive way, but payback in a tough love kind of way.

I never questioned her again. I did everything she asked of me.

I healed cats, chickens, rabbits, snakes and any number of other species. When emotions are involved, emotions like love, things can get ugly. Jo taught me my timing has to be perfect. When saving a life, not just healing, a small window of time exists to save immediately before the heart stops. I can heal Nighmerians from wounds and some illnesses but not from death. Jo taught me to respect my gift as the Five. I've asked her how she knows so much about the Five if she isn't immortal, but all she ever says is the Demi required her to train like a Five in order to be my sentry.

I don't believe for a second she is a limite, not one second.

She said she spent the first eight years of my life in training in the severe conditions of Nighmerianotte. Of course, she said she couldn't do everything a Five can do, they had to alter the training a bit.

She's lying but I'll cross that bridge when the time is right.

Then there's Carmine. He brought me to submission on that first night because he knew, by submitting, I was teachable. He broke me several more times after that night but, when it was all over, he helped me pick up the pieces. Somehow, I knew he respected my submission, my strength and my determination. He did this for my own good. He did it to save my life. He had to break me. That's his job. Since then, he's pushed me past my breaking point, mentally. I've become enraged and almost killed him. He's taught me to respond, not react. He taught me to think like my enemy, to know his weaknesses and use them.

On one occasion, we started in a pitch black room. The only tools given to me: a headlamp and a rope. He directed me to stand in the middle of the room saying, *"When the rattling begins, don't move. Don't flinch. Think three steps ahead of your enemy."* When the rattling began, I knew what it was. The rattling was constant as the snakes sensed danger. I wouldn't die from a snake bite but the idea of being bitten made me want to jump out of my skin.

If I moved my legs I would be bitten by rattlesnakes. As if snakes were not enough, spiders fell into my hair, and over my face, as if someone had dumped them over my head. I felt the snakes glide over my shoes.

I did not flinch.

I know snakes like heat. I know they like to be warm. Carefully, without making any sudden movements, I removed my Mason High sweatshirt. Spiders fell from my hood as the hissing grew louder. Sweat beads formed on my forehead and my throat became too dry to swallow. My tongue was stuck to the roof of my mouth. I ever-so-slowly glanced up to see what was above my head.

I tossed my sweatshirt among the snakes.

Once the striking began, I knew they were attacking the sweatshirt. I jumped and clung to the rafter with both hands.

I failed the lesson. I did not think like my enemy. My enemy would have killed every snake and spider. *I tried to escape instead.* So what did he tell me to do? *Do it again. Kill every last snake.* So I did. I snapped the neck of each snake and smashed each spider. Then, when the training was complete, I brought them all back to life because that's what I do, for I am The Five.

Two nights ago, he brought a man to our training session, a limite. He asked me if I was willing to drink from the vein. My answer, "Yes." It's not that my morals have changed, only my perspective.

I am a Nighmerian. I must fight for my people. If my duty calls for me to drink from the vein, or take a life, or fight until the death, I will. Without a second thought, I will.

It's my last night of training and Jesse doesn't show up.

"Blood Queen, you ready?" Carmine says, his lips pressing against the door. He peeks in with one eye, trying to be funny. I laugh. Carmine and I have grown close since the training. We have a brother and sister relationship. I put my pencil down. "Please tick, enter."

Carmine throws himself on the bed. "You are still doing homework?" He scans at the pages of my Anatomy book. "You know you cannot go to college, right? You know you will be busy for the next 200 years fighting evil immortals, right? Namely, Vacavious and his slew of morterros," he says in a horrible English accent.

"Yeah. I know." His statement eats at my human side. College had always been in the picture. Being raised in the mortal world, I had expectations of living in the dorms and going out on Friday nights. I may not have a plan, but I have a dream, and it always included college.

"Have you talked to Church?" Carmine bites at his thumb, trying to be casual.

"No. Not in forty-six days."

"You have to know he is watching. He is always watching over you."

I don't say I miss him even though I do. It's how I cope. When Church is with me something whole forms inside. I don't have to be anyone I'm not because he knows me. He knows about Frankie. He knows the issues that have come from Nadine's neglect, although the psychologist and social workers surmised differently. Loneliness can be a scary place to live. When I think about it, I haven't felt the deep ache of loneliness since Church, Kendra, Carmine and Jesse exposed themselves as Nighmerians. They understand me. They get me. We all have baggage be it loss, addiction, guilt, pain, or sadness. Raw untainted emotions that live with us our entire lives. Even as immortals, we carry with us things that haunt us, they simply haunt us forever. The question is whether or not we can free ourselves from the bondage of those emotions and let them go? Or do we choose to live there? There is a strange comfort in unity, even when you are unsure what side you are fighting for. Despite all my uncertainties, at least I knew I was Nighmerian and I wasn't alone.

He was supposed to be there when I got home that night from training. He was supposed to stay with me.

He didn't and I miss him more than I care to admit.

"Enough with the warm and fuzzy crap. Let us go! Oh and grab something you can swim in."

"Swim? I don't swim. I hate to swim."

"You are swimming tonight, Sweetheart!" he says in a remarkably good Jack Nicholson impersonation and way better than his cheesy British accent.

"Seriously?" I sigh.

"Would I lie to you?"

"Great. Well it better not be deep."

"Pack your belongings and put this on."

"A blindfold?" I grab it from him.

"Oh and these."

"Ear plugs?" I draw my head back in question.

"Do not ask questions you know I will not answer." He smiles a big toothy grin.

CHAPTER 22

Fear, a Total Drag

"N.w ta.. my ..nd a.d I w.ll l..d you…"

"What? I can't hear you!" I yell, looking from side to side, listening for the low tone of his voice again.

"Carmine. Please. Let me take off the blindfold. I can handle it, whatever it is. I can handle it. At least let me take out these damn earplugs."

Carmine takes out the earplugs. "Keep the blindfold on. Just a little further, please."

I hear a creak and the hollowness underneath whatever we are walking on. "Holy hell. Are we on a dock? No. Seriously. I don't do deep water." I go to take my blindfold off.

"Absolutely not." Carmine slaps my hand.

My heart starts to pound. "I'm terrified of deep water, Carmine. Please."

"You have killed a morterro, Penn. Come on. Deep water is nothing." Carmine pushes me and my body plunges into the icy cold water. I go under and open my eyes. I rip off my blindfold.

Darkness.

The murky black water of the lake remains shrouded in mystery and horror. Fear sets in my bones as I push myself to the surface with one big kick. I gasp for breath as I breathe in air.

Salt.

The ocean, not Lake Cocytus. Not that the ocean is any better.

Immediately I know my feet cannot touch the bottom and the panic sets in.

Terror.

Imagining all the sharks and other creatures that lurk below the ocean's surface, unbelievable anxiety causes my chest to tighten. The water is freezing. "Please, Carmine. Not this. Please let me out," I whine in almost a whisper.

My hands begin to shake, not from the cold, but fear. I feel something brush past my leg.

"Carmine!" I scream at the top of my lungs. "Get me out of here!" I tread water because I'm too terrified to swim anywhere. "Something just brushed past my leg."

"Hope it was not a shark. I know sharks feed at night."

"Carmine, please, don't do this. If you aren't going to get me out, get in. Please Carmine. For real. I can't see anything below the surface!" I groan as I scan my surroundings, my headlamp still on my head. Beyond close proximity, I see nothing but darkness.

"No can do, Blood. Ocean water is the Achilles heel to the pure bloods. Beside, this is one fear that will hinder you in Nighmerianotte, if you do not overcome it. It's called the Mare de Notte, the Sea of

Night. If the battle for our world takes you to the Mare de Notte you better be quite sure you will be able to fight, even under water. Now, tread water." He casually paces the dock.

"Are you kidding me?" I scream as something brushes up against my leg again, this time harder. I cry out. I want to roll myself into a ball and play dead. I want to disappear because I don't think I can handle the pounding in my chest.

"You want to run, Penelope? You want to get out and dry off? Get warm?"

It's a trick question. I know it. I slowly scan my surroundings again, waiting for the shark fin I know is coming.

"Do you not know one of our districts is partly ocean? District Scogliera is where Vacavious is from. It is quite possible this battle will take place in the ocean. He knows your fears, Penn. He will play on them in evil ways you never dreamed possible. He will not merely kill you. He will torture you with fear, then kill you. So, if you are ready to die, get out. Get warm." He pauses, turns and stares straight into my eyes with confidence. "If you want to live and fight for your Republic, then I suggest you figure out a way to get to shore." He points east. "A mile." Then he walks away from me.

He walks away.

I can't.

I can't.

I heave in and out, near hyperventilation.

You made a choice, Penn. You made a choice to fight for your people. I think of Amy. I think of sweet Amy in her gigantic hospital gown, her bald head and her beautifully sick smile with deep dark circles under her eyes.

You don't have another choice, Amy, and neither do I.

"Seriously?!" I yell toward the heavens.

Okay. Regain control, Penn.

Amy.

I breathe in Amy's face. *You fight your battle, and I will try to fight mine. Whether I meet you on the other side, in Evernotte or here on Earth, I will continue to fight. You're the only thing I can hang on to. You're the only sadness I have in my heart. It isn't pity or judgment. It's your beautiful heart. It's your unselfish ways. It's your innocence. Your purity. It's the love and compassion you have for others. If I can be half the hero you are, you better believe I'll swim. I will swim for you. I will swim for my Republic, for my parents, Jo, Jesse, Church, Kendra and Carmine.*

"Come get me!" I call to whatever keeps brushing at my legs and arms. "Come get me," I call as I take off east in a feverish pace.

One stroke. Then two. Three. Four. Five. Six. Seven. Eight. Nine. Ten. Keep your mind busy, Penn. Pay no mind to the fear. Let go of it. Let go of it.

Eleven. Twelve. Thirteen. Fourteen. Another brush, this time against my stomach. It feels like a large body mass has passed underneath me.

Fifteen. Sixteen. Seventeen. Eighteen. Nineteen. "Twenty!" *I yell, my voice growing hoarse.*

I don't stop swimming. I don't look for shark fins, I focus and keep moving east.

Running on pure adrenaline, I keep going.

I'm getting cold, really cold, so cold my teeth begin to chatter. My arms keep moving and my feet keep kicking.

I see a light not far in the distance. It's moving. The light is moving! This makes my arms and legs work even harder.

This time, whatever is following me, brushes the entire length of my body.

"Not today, water dachshund. Not today." I push hard until the light is shining in my eyes.

"Come on, Penn!" I hear the voice call out. It's close now, within thirty feet. "Put your feet down."

Put my feet down? *Put my feet down?*

I keep swimming. I can't walk as fast as I can swim.

The light is now fifteen feet away.

A few feet from the light I can see it's Carmine with his headlamp. I put my feet down and I walk on to shore. Something's holding me back. It's heavy and it has me by the waist.

I don't look. I focus on Carmine. I'm shaking and I can't feel my arms and legs.

Carmine wraps a towel around me.

"S-s-s-s-something has me around the waist. Get it." I say, my teeth still chattering like an idling motor. "Wh— what's th—th—that?" I say breathlessly as I look down at a long sheet linked to my bathing suit.

"That is your fear, Penn. You dragged your fear with you as far as you could. Then," he unclips it from my bathing suit, "you let it go." He drops it next to me with a loud splat.

"YOU!" My teeth chatter. "That wasn't magical. That was lame. I expected more from you, Carmine LeBlanc." I seethe through my chatter.

"Yeah? Were you scared?"

"Shut up." I reply as I dry off.

"Penn, it is not about the magic. You have to overcome yourself to be who you are. Magic, your powers, will not fix anything." He walks to me. He takes his hand and points to my head, "You have to overcome your own demons so your heart will give you courage to be who you were meant to be. That was a manifestation of your fears. You created that," He points to the waterlogged sheet. "Not me. So technically, you are the lame one."

I can't move. If I could, I would kick Carmine's butt. I would kick his butt so hard I would make him pee out his nose for the rest of his life.

On the ride back to Jo's, Carmine drives. Once my teeth finally stop chattering and I regain some of my faculties, I think about Carmine's words. The mind is a powerful thing, it can dictate our entire life. Do the decisions we make, the fears we cling to and the fears we face, allow us to be the people we become? What we see and what we don't see? How we choose to live our lives? Sometimes, when fear is present, differentiating the truth from reality becomes a difficult task.

What if my life isn't about my past? What if, instead, it's about unbecoming everything I thought I was so I can be who I was meant to be?

CHAPTER 23

Killing Jo

We pull up to the house and I glance at the time. It is 12:01 a.m. and Jo's on the porch with Kendra and Reggerio.

Carmine comes over to open my door but I beat him to the punch. My body is restored.

"How did it go? Do you feel at one with the biggest mammals of the world now?" Kendra jokes.

Jo hands me a mug.

I chug it down like its coffee. I feel the warm, thick ooze slide down my throat. I look to Carmine. His eyes are on Kendra.

"Ready?" Jo looks to Carmine.

"Always the bad guy..." Carmine throws his hands in the air. "Let us get this over with then."

Jo nods her head toward the slaughter shed.

I hate the slaughter shed. I set the mug down on the porch railing.

"Penelope, before you go, a word if I may?" Reggerio says in a warm whisper.

"Of course." He takes me by my elbow as Kendra, Jo and Carmine head for the shed…of dread.

He looks into my eyes like some sort of proud father. He's quiet for a long moment. "You are the Five. I have given you all I can. Make the Republic proud. Fight for us. Fight for what is inside of you. Beat this monster with your black blood. Eh?"

He gives my cheek a light touch with his palm. "I will see you in Nighmerianotte." Reggerio turns to go.

"Wait. You're crossing over now?" Then it hit me. His duty is complete. He did what he was tasked to do. Now, he gets to be with his family.

He smiles like I've never seen him smile before, a smile of pure hope. He nods and turns back to face me. "My dear, I have all the faith in the world you can, and will, bring our world back from devastation."

With that, he waves and walks down the paved road toward town.

I watch Reggerio until he disappears into the fog.

I walk into the shed of dread to find them sitting around the table. Aunt Jo is sipping from her mug, Carmine has a blood bag, and Kendra a diet Coke.

"I hate this shed." I stand next to Jo.

"Oh, come on, Honey. You have saved lives in here; many, many lives." She takes my hand into hers and looks at me with a longing smile. "I love you, Penelope. Remember that. I love you no matter what. I love you for the person you are, and no less." She pulls me into her arms, placing her hand on the back of my head.

Then why are you lying to me, Jo?

"Let us get this over with." Carmine finishes the blood bag he grabbed from the fridge, throws it on the table, and moves into the next room.

Kendra and Jo follow Carmine. I follow too.

Jo walks over to me and takes my face in her hands. "Remember when I said you had to face your fears? Be the person you were meant to be, Penn. Save lives. Have faith you are the person you were meant to be."

Dread reaps my inside like the plague.

Jo nods and takes several steps back. Carmine is behind her. Kendra is several steps behind me.

"You will know what to do." Jo nods and looks up toward the tin roof of the shed.

Carmine pulls Jo back, unsheathes a blade, and slits her throat. It happens so fast I don't have enough time to think, let alone stop it.

Terror fills me, incapacitating those parts of me more mortal than immortal. It swings from my heart strings, taunting me, 'you can't catch me.'

My aunt falls to the ground in slow motion landing on the floor with an absurd thud. A sound reserved for pumpkins smashing on the ground or a baseball bat hitting a watermelon. I'm frozen in place. All I can do is watch her bleed out.

Memories come to me in rapid succession. I see Jo rocking me to sleep during my first nights in her house and her teaching me how to ride a bike. I remember her standing up for me when the school counselor suggested I be on medication for PTSD and her giving me the birds and the bees talk. Flashes of her waiting up for me at night when I was out late bring tears to my eyes. I love the way she loves me enough to tell me what I need to hear and not what I want to hear. She's taken this damaged little girl and made her whole again by loving her for who she is. Suddenly, I don't care that she's lied to me about drinking blood. It doesn't matter anymore.

Unconditional love.

"Save her," I scream to my hands. "Save her." I hysterically scream again. Still, my limbs don't move.

"Penelope, you know what to do," A low familiar tone sounds from behind me.

I turn to see who it is. "You're here," I whisper.

I hear my aunt gag. I turn back to her and watch helplessly as the blood oozes from her throat. Sweat begins to gather on my forehead as a cold chill sweeps through my entire body.

It's quiet.

"I don't know what to do," I say as I lace my fingers in my hair like a crazed lunatic, feeling the panic constrict in my throat. Dread consumes me and my mind goes blank. Jo's eyes are wide as she tries to breathe but can't.

I want so badly to save her but my mind keeps telling me *I can't*. I don't remember what to do. If I could just remember, I could save her.

"Penn. Listen. You know how to do this. Place your hands around her neck." Church's voice is confident. He meets my gaze.

"I can't. I don't remember how," I whisper. A ringing begins in my ears.

"Yes, you do." Church leans over me.

Jo gags again. She uses her hand to cover her gash. Her face is covered with blood.

My breathing stops again. "Please, Jo, don't die," I plead as my body begins to shake uncontrollably. I rock back and forth covering my mouth because the smell of her blood has reached my nose and it doesn't smell good. It smells like rancid meat.

Jo reaches out to me with her hand. Her silent cry and the fear on her face screams at me to do something.

You aren't allowing yourself the opportunity to grow and become who you are, Aunt Jo's words play in my head. *Stop running from fear, Penn. Face it. Be who you are meant to be.*

As if in slow motion, Jo's body goes eerily still, her eyes still focused on me.

Be who you are.

Be who you are.

Be. Who. You. Are.

I place my hands, shaking, around her neck.

Nothing happens.

"Jo, please," I whine as I tighten my grip around her throat.

The pressure in my body doesn't come. The blood pulses out of her neck like air out of a balloon.

Something deep inside tells me to hang on.

Can panic and patience exist at the same exact time? Fate. Is Jo supposed to live? Is she supposed to die?

Am I supposed to save her?

Her body lies limp, her eyes open and staring at me. Her blood is pooled around us. The smell makes me nauseous.

Keeping my hands on her neck, I lean in closer and say, "I am the Black Five. This is who I am. I am a healer. I'm meant to protect my people and save our world. Help me, Jo."

Then I close my eyes and clear my mind.

The world go still and silent.

The pressure starts…from my head to my feet, then back up and through my hands.

The pain is unbearable but I will not give up. I will fight.

I am the Black Five.

For what seems like forever, I keep my hands where they are. The pressure continues longer than usual.

Then it stops.

I carefully open my eyes but she lay motionless, lifeless. Her once lively eyes, now dead.

"Jo. No." My chest begins to ache as the lump in my throat returns, making it hard to breathe. I remove my hands from her neck. My bottom lip quivers. "You can't die on me, Jo. Please." I lean down and kiss her forehead, my lips linger. I'm not sure if the moistness between my lips and her forehead is blood or sweat, but I don't care. "Please don't leave me," I beg. Tears stream down my face.

I hear a whimper and I'm not sure if it's Jo or me. I slowly stroke Jo's bloody face. Horror and heartache consume me.

I lean down and kiss her forehead again. Her blood is everywhere.

The bleeding has subsided and I slide my fingers across the gash as the thick ooze now trickles down both sides of her neck. The wound is healed.

I waited too long. I put my head on her chest and lie down next to her, immersed in her blood. "Jo, I waited too long. You believed in me and I couldn't do it."

"Sapevo che ci saresti riuscita," I hear someone whisper.

Grief makes you mad. It makes you think and hear things that don't exist.

"I knew you had it in you," Jo coughs.

In shock, I look up and into my aunt's eyes, now alert and alive. "Jo!" My entire body is numb. I bury myself in her side just as I did as a child. There are no words that can fill this moment right now. I pull back to look at Jo who is staring at me with the same look she gave me when I was eight. A look of pure love.

Kendra comes up behind us and whispers, "Sangue, vattene!"

All of the blood vanishes from the floor.

Carmine starts to clap, first slowly, then faster. "Not bad, Black Five."

"Was that a compliment from Carmine LeBlanc?" Kendra looks up to Carmine.

Their eyes meet.

Then I see it. How could I have missed it?

They've always been in love.

"Is that a smile from Kendra Salvino?" Carmine wraps his arms around her.

"Blood sucker, do not patronize me." She holds him by his waist.

"Now that is the witch I know and love." He looks to Jo. "Come Jo, we will get you inside. Where is your mug?"

Jo's mug. If she's immortal, then how did that happen? The thought scratches my forehead but I push it back, filing it for later.

Kendra and Carmine lean over to help Jo. "No," I say. "Just give me a minute alone with her."

Church, Carmine and Kendra exit the shed as I help Jo up. I take her shoulders in my hands and I give them a squeeze as I look back at the only mother I've ever had. "Because of you," I pause, trying to gather my words, "I know what unconditional love feels like. You taught me to love. You made me feel love," I pause once more, pushing the lump of fear further down my throat. "You showed me what love and ultimate sacrifice means. I love you, Jo. Just so you know. If anything happens, I love you." I pull her to me and give her my love. I give her limitless love, the kind that only exists between a child and a mother. I touch the back of her head with my hand and stroke her hair. "Mom," I whisper as a barrier in my heart crumbles, allowing my love to flow a bit more freely.

"Oh my sweet girl." Her voice teeters between tears and reluctance to shed them. She pauses for a long moment, as if trying to regain her composure. "I know you have it in you to save Nighmerianotte. I am willing to bet my life on it."

What I hear is, 'I am always willing pay the price to save your life'.

Jo takes her finger and softly caresses my cheek.

"I know." I nod as I pull her to me again. I take in her scent as I bury my head in her hair. "I know."

Carmine and Kendra reappear at the door and take Jo's arm as we exit the shed. "I am not helpless, you two." Jo's shrugs them away. "It is nice to see you playing nicely together." Jo stops, turns, and gives me a wink as she looks to Church who's leaning against the outside of the barn wall. "Take your time." she looks at me. The three of them make their way inside as I watch.

Church. Church. Church. Church.

"You left." I look blazingly into the night sky before I turn around to look at him. "You left forty-six days ago."

"I know."

I turn around. His body rests against the wall in a way that tells me he's tense, deep in thought, or *wrecked.*

"You didn't have to leave." My words are as delicate as my tone.

"I was never far from you, Penelope, I watched, from a distance. Because your welfare, as it always has been, is my number one priority."

His head casually moves in my direction as his eyes fix themselves on mine.

I was naked the day I met Church LeBlanc. Exposed. Bare. Vulnerable. He saw through my demons, the ghosts that linger in the quietness of my mind and my sins. The look he gives me right now is full of pain, longing and regret. It is a look only my heart can fix.

"It...It killed me to not be near you and only watch from a safe distance. It put me over the edge not to be able to touch you, to hear your words and the beating of your heart. To be part of your existence." His look makes my heart want to mend every single thing he feels.

I can no longer deny the attraction I feel toward Church. It's there. His tenderness. His brokenness. I can't ignore it anymore.

I walk to him with purpose and rest my body on his.

He groans from the deepest part of his heart. He pulls my head back brusquely and grips my face with his hands.

"I," he pauses. "I am terrified, Penelope." He pulls my face to his as he stares trying to fight whatever he's feeling. I take his face in my hands.

"Tell me."

"I am terrified of losing you." His head falls to my shoulder. "I am terrified to be with you and terrified to be without you. I cannot live like this." He takes his hand and moves it to my heart. It beats faster in response to his touch. His eyes meet mine. I feel the coolness of his hand and the heat of my chest. Together we are warm.

He cups my cheek with his hand. "I want to look into your eyes when I say this to you, Penelope." He pauses. "I need you to hear this from me." His hand still on my chest, the other still on my face, "I need you in the worst way possible. *I need you.*" His voice cracks. "I have been waiting your entire life for you, but there are secrets I have that you need to know."

His words take my breath away.

I want to pull his face to mine. I want my lips on his. I want to feel the coolness of his skin, and the warmth of his passion. I want to feel his desire for me through his kiss. I want to know what his body feels like, what it looks like, what true love looks like.

His eyes linger on my mouth then move back to my eyes. Determination and fear show in his eyes. He leans in as if to kiss me, my body screaming for him to do it. *As if it is a need, not a want.* A need so innate, my body begins to wither like a dying flower. He leans into the nape of my neck and gently presses his lips to my skin. He groans again, but in a helpless way, as if his heart is dictating his actions.

I close my eyes, trying not to make a sound. I feel my breath quicken but my heart stands still. I give into him, all of him.

He slowly pulls his lips from my neck. With hooded eyes he says, "Walk with me. I need to tell you something before we go further."

I follow, trying to recover from the abrupt mood change. I catch a glimpse of him, his eyes still hidden behind his pain.

Deftly, I try to change the subject, hoping to ease his troubled look. I don't know how much more of it my heart can take. "What happened between Kendra and Carmine?"

"She did not tell you?" He looks down at me, trying to mend.

I shake my head.

He sighs. "When Vacavious found out how the Salvino's coven helped you and your parents escape by diverting the trail from you in the mortal world, Vacavious came back and killed her coven. Carmine arrived minutes after it happened." Church stops and looks down at our hands. Taking his thumb, he gently rubs the side of my hand. "He found Kendra cradling her mother, Stanna, in her arms, rocking uncontrollably. Carmine said he has never seen anything like it. Monstrous." His voice is less than a whisper, but his words unbroken. "They had been dating for almost five years, yet things ended shortly after. Kendra blames Carmine for what happened. She needed someone to blame. Carmine takes it. He takes it because she needs that. She needs someone to take the burden from her. He wants her to blame him so she does not have to live with the thought that she might have done something to prevent their murders."

I look up to Church, my heart giving way. "Like you did for me," I whisper.

He looks down at our hands again, still rubbing my fingers. "I thought if I hid the body you would think it did not happen. I did it hoping you would not carry around the guilt with you. If there was no body to prove anything, I hoped you would think he got up and walked away, or left or disappeared out of fear. Or something. I should have known you would be too smart for such a ploy." There's a long silence. I try to take all of this information in. "Your mother was the same way."

"Thank you," is all I manage. His actions deserving so much more than words.

He cups my cheek in his hand and I hold it there with my shoulder. He looks through me. The intensity of his stare is fierce. "I am so sorry, Penn. I am sorry I put you through what I did. If I would have…"

"Stop. You don't get to say sorry. I said thank you because you have spent nearly eighteen years risking everything to protect me. You're sorry because I had to go through some life moments?"

"I know how hard it was for you Penn. I was with you. I watched you endure the hunger, the loneliness, the fighting, and the murder. I watched you feel unloved. When, in reality, you are so deeply loved." The tinge of pain comes back to his eyes.

I shake my head. "If I hadn't lived with Nadine, I wouldn't be who I am today. Don't you get it? I am who I am because of what I went through."

"Murder at eight years old is not normal." I see the guilt wash over his ashen face once again.

"Well, most eight year olds don't have the kind of power I have, do they?" I smile, trying to catch his eye again. "Many, many Nighmerians fought for me to live. Fought for me to stand here tonight in front of you. There is a reason I am still here." I smile. "Church, I know I have a huge battle ahead of me, but I wouldn't change a thing. Know that if I had the chance to do it all over again, I wouldn't change a thing. You made the right choice, Church."

Forcefully, he pulls me into his arms. He holds me and I feel his hands cup the back of my head. I wrap my arms around his long lean waist. His grip is strong but gentle. He kisses my hair.

Once.

Twice.

Three times.

"Your heart is the purest thing I have ever known. In any world, your heart is a gift, Penn. It is love." He kisses my right cheek. "It is strength," he kisses my left cheek, "and it is courage." He kisses my forehead.

All too quickly, his face becomes shadowed in grief as he takes my hand and leads me upstairs to my room.

"You need to know what I have done before you love me." He sits down on the bed.

I think it might be a little too late for that.

"Lie with me on the bed?" he whispers in my ear.

CHAPTER 24

Punishable by Death

Church scoops me up and gently lays me on my bed. He slides in next to me.

I continue to stare at the ceiling and listen as his words take me to another time.

"It has been about seventeen years since I told this story." he sighs. I got drunk and met a beautiful young witch, Levia, at Warlock's Grog Shop, a bar in Nighmerianotte." He pauses again as if choosing his words carefully for fear of hurting me. "We went back to my place. Things went horribly, horribly wrong. Between the alcohol and the blood I fed on earlier, I had gone mad. Things happened back then, Penn, which I am not proud of. I was a killer. I lived by my own rules and I answered to no one. She and I had gotten into a compromising predicament.

"Her scent was intoxicating. The sound of blood coursing through her veins beckoned me closer. It was rhythmic and the desire for her

337

blood was too much to bear. I placed my lips on her neck and bit into her flesh.

"I drank. Again and again I took from her. I moved closer, cradling her in my arms. The blood flowed into my mouth," He pauses.

"But witch's blood tastes like fire."

"Only to you. Blood tastes differently to other species."

He begins again, but I interrupt him before he gets two words out.

"Church, you don't have to."

He holds up his hand as he grimaces. "Yes, I do. The high was euphoric. I pulled away enraptured, without a care in the world. Her blood transported me to a new world, a world where I was king. I was all powerful, all knowing and untouchable. I drank again. With every drink I felt more indestructible, superior and unparalleled. I could do anything, be anything. I had no boundaries. The high was so hypnotic I could not stop. Like an alcoholic's first drink, I was hooked. Then the hallucinations started. I thought at one point Vacavious was there and I used a blade to separate his head from his body. It was neither his body nor his head." His teeth grind together as he stares at the ceiling. "To this day, I do not remember doing this to Levia.

"Several hours later, I came to on the floor in a pool of blood. I looked around the room. Carmine sat on a stool, head in his hands. Every bone and every muscle in my body was tranquil. It was as if my body had been revitalized and restored to one much younger and more powerful. The world was at my fingertips.

"Then my eyes fell on Levia's lifeless body next to me. Dried blood crusted her neck. It was everywhere. Frantic, I jumped up and grabbed her cold cheeks and cradled her head in my hands placing my ear to her mouth. I screamed at Carmine to help me, but all I heard him say was, 'she is dead, Church. She is dead...' I became hysterical. I bit my wrist and placed it next to her mouth, begging her to drink. *Drink!* I yelled. Her lips were lifeless and blue. I pushed my wrist deeper into her mouth. I tried to revive her for hours, to no avail." He paused again, as if reliving it. "Despair, grief and guilt consumed me. The emotional turmoil was almost unbearable. I wanted to die…"

The whites of his eyes blaze red. His eyes meet mine.

I don't know what to say. The story is both beautiful and heart wrenching.

"Say something, Penn." He kisses my hand.

"I can't," I whisper.

There's a long pause. He's still holding my hand. "Killing another immortal is punishable by death. The Demi decided, because of my abilities, and my bloodline, I would not be sentenced to death but that my life be devoted to protecting you instead. I deserved to die for what I did to Levia but the Demi would not have it. So, Giuseppe retrained me night and day how to protect." His eyes move to mine. "So when I ask if you are scared, you should be. Because I have done it before, Penelope. I have killed before in the most gruesome way possible."

There's a long silence between us and all I can think about is the field right off the highway on the way to Mason. The mustard plants make a bold display of yellow for miles. They are resilient when they bloom, yet only showcase their bold colors in the spring. All summer, fall and winter, they're dormant until spring returns once more. Just as the mustard plants die off in the other seasons, sometimes murdered by the long cold rainy seasons of Mason, they come back every single spring to start anew, full of determination. "*We* can come back from this."

He sighs and turns on his side to face me.

I feel the cold radiating from his body. It's comforting. I don't turn to him. I continue to stare up at the ceiling.

"What are you thinking about?" he asks as he strokes my hair.

"What? You can't read my mind?" I smile.

"Fiction. Do not believe everything you read or see, Miss Jackson." He laughs as he crosses his arms across his chest and tucks his hands under his armpits. "No, I cannot read your mind, nor anyone else's but I sense your feelings. I feel them exactly as you feel them, sometimes more. A vampire's feelings are magnified a hundred times over. So," he pauses and pushes a strand of my hair out of my face, barely brushing my skin with the tip of his finger. "When I look at you, when you talk about Nadine, your mother and father…I feel all of that. I feel you with Jesse."

My insides turn inside out and I'm not sure what to say. I have trouble feeling my own feelings and making sense of them. "And?" I say, not knowing if I can manage anything else.

"You care for him. Deeply. I cannot control that. I wish I could." His voice is barely a whisper.

Not knowing what else to say, I tell him what I feel. "Jesse has no interest in me beyond my protection. Whatever feelings I had for him cannot be returned. For both our sakes, I need to move on."

Change the subject, Penn.

"I hope our talk will not focus solely on who I do and do not have feelings for. I have another matter I need to discuss with you. I wanted to talk to you about the night I invited you back to my room, but we both know how that worked out, don't we?" I try to restrain the disappointment building inside me.

"I am sorry. My intent was not to hurt you." Regret now flooding his face.

"That was then and this is now. I wanted to know if you can make sense of this note. It fell out of the journal my father wrote." I open my bedside table and pull it out. He reads it, his expression unchanged.

This isn't just a war on Nighmerianotte. It's bigger. Much bigger. It's about revenge. Penn is in the middle.

Below the words my father drew a diamond. He marked each point, placing the letters P1 on the right point, P2 on the bottom point, P3 on the left point, P4 on the top point, and in the middle a dot with the letters PP.

I stare at the diamond. I turn the napkin clockwise, then counter clockwise, trying to make sense. Nothing comes. I turn it upside down.

"We know there are five portals to Nighmerianotte." Church's voice was more direct than soft as he turns it right side up.

"The diamond shape is Nighmerianotte. It covers the mortal world territory of three continents: North America, Europe, and Africa." He traces the lines on the napkin with his index finger. "The 'P' stands for Portal, I assume but am not certain." He stares at it. "Can I take this with me? Do some research?"

"That's fine." I pause. "Have you looked through the journal my father wrote?" I look toward the box.

"I would never invade your privacy like that, Penn."

"I don't mean to offend you. I just assume it might have been another security measure." I shrug. "Nothing personal."

He's still. His mind is in perpetual thought. Always contemplating his next move, next word. He's quiet for a minute or so. He clicks off the light.

341

I click my light back on. "I have questions for you."

He clicks it off again. "Ask me in the dark."

"Fine." I get up and walk over to the window sill, and cross my arms. In the dark with him, not a good idea right now.

Church rests on my bed, staring up at the ceiling.

"The Black Blood," I start.

"Yes?"

"So," I whisper, "I shouldn't have lived. I mean, the curse Freya cast, I shouldn't have lived, right?"

"Correct."

"I did live. Vacavious is a black blood and he lived."

"Yes."

"So what if the black blood is linking something bigger than we think? What if my blood links the portals?"

"Why? The portals have been locked for the past one hundred years. It does not make sense that all the other Fives have gone missing and are presumably dead."

"I have a feeling they aren't dead, Church. What if Vacavious is keeping them in a catatonic state? Not allowing them to eat, hiding them, or collecting them, maybe?"

He shoots me a sharp look. "You think he needs them?"

"Maybe." I shrug.

"Why? They are healers."

"There's a healer for each portal. Think about the diamond shape, right? There are five portals." I grab my father's note and turn on the light. "Pia," I point to portal one, "Remi," I move my finger clockwise to portal two, "Antoinette," I point to portal three, "Ophelia," number four, and then I slide my finger to the middle, the "PP."

"That's not a portal." Church leans in. "What does "PP" stand for?"

I turn the paper upside down.

"dd?" He looks at me in question.

"My father was dyslexic." I slowly trace my fingers over the letters "bb...black blood."

Church grabs the paper and stares at it. He slowly meets my gaze. "He is trying to awaken the Black Blood," Church barely whispers. "Devastation to Nighmerianotte. Extinction. This is what Freya predicted, if this map is accurate." He bails out of bed and paces the room, staring at my father's hand-drawn map. "If that is, indeed, what he was trying to do, link the portals with the healers, and the Black Blood in the middle." he pauses.

"Why wouldn't he use his own blood?"

"This makes sense now. You're the Black Five, the last Sanguine. Your father is right. He is not just trying to take down Nighmerianotte but the mortal world too."

We stand there speechless, unable to move.

"I need to make a couple of phone calls first thing tomorrow. Your birthday is in two days, Penn. You probably need to say your goodbyes soon." His voice trails off.

I turn toward him.

He stares at me. In the stillness of the night, he undresses me with his eyes. Exposing my vulnerabilities, my insecurities, my imperfections, and yet, he's still here. He sighs. "You are my kind of perfect," he tells me. This time, he grabs both sides of my face, "I want to kiss you, Penn. So badly, I want to kiss you. Everywhere." He rests his hands on my chest and feels my heart. It's racing. I can't help but think if he moves his hands any lower, where they'd be. "This," he looks toward his hands resting on my chest, "Tells me you like my company and you like our bodies where they are. This also tells me you are scared."

My breath catches.

He removes his hands.

A long time ago, I built a force field around my heart. A gigantic force field that's bullet proof and fool proof. I tried to keep everyone at arm's length for fear my heart would become too emotionally involved and then everything would get ugly.

Church brought it crumbling down.

That's the thing about love. It can get ugly but it can also be perfection.

"As much as I want to kiss you right now, I cannot. You need to feel one hundred percent confident in that decision. I want you to be sure in here." He returns one hand to my chest.

"I'm sure you're a terrible kisser anyway." I shy away, trying to break the heavy stillness.

"Lie with me on the bed. I am going to stay here next to you, right beside you. I will remain by your side until I can feel you love me the way I love you."

I don't say anything.

I don't move.

I just breathe.

Or at least I think I'm breathing. Maybe hyperventilating?

Church places his hand on my stomach this time. My whole body becomes aware of his hand.

"Calm down," He gives me direction. His hand is still on my stomach. I roll over, my back facing him. He tries to move his hand but I grab it and hold it in place. He doesn't resist. He moves closer to me, fitting like a puzzle piece. I grip his hand with mine.

"Stay with me tonight," I whisper.

CHAPTER 25

The Milk Can

"It's not a good idea."

"What do you expect, Church? Aren't you the ones that told me to live an ordinary life with extraordinary talents?"

"That one backfired," I hear Kendra whisper to Church.

"Your birthday is tomorrow, Penn."

"Please, Church. Give me this. This is my last real thing in the mortal world that I will ever enjoy. Besides, you aren't my dad."

"Thank the Demi. That would be awkward," Kendra says not realizing she's speaking out loud. Everyone stares. "Oh, I guess I did say that out loud, then. My bad."

"I can take care of myself, Church. You know that. Plus, I need to say my goodbyes." I stare up into his eyes. "I've made it this far. Please! I'm not going to be trapped inside this house on my last night."

Church's stare is sharp as his cool hand slowly releases my arm. I knew the guilt alone would make him release.

Kendra chimes in. "Come on, Church. I will be with her. It is not like we are going on a cross country road trip, although that would be totally wicked." Her mind wanders as she looks down, "You guys can follow behind for extra protection, just in case."

Church shakes his head. "If anything happens to her, Kendra, so help me, do not make me regret this."

She salutes and clicks her heels. "Roger that, Captain. On guard." She smiles. "Like you and the Tick will not be nipping at our heels." She gives Carmine a flirtatious grin.

Tuesday, October 30th 8:00p.m.

"Ladies and gentlemen, welcome to the rescheduled Milk Can game! Lake Providence Huskies versus the Mason Wildcats. It's been a long standing tradition…" the announcer drones on and on over the low hum of the loud speaker.

Once the hype died down about Bradbury and Lenore, things seemed to return to normal, or as close to normal as possible.

Kendra and I huddle in the bleachers under a red and white Wildcats blanket. "You look ridiculous, you know that, right?" Kendra's face is painted white with red lines under her eyes. Her hair, sporting a festive red for the game, is teased up into a ponytail. "Just for the record, I'm totally embarrassed right now."

Kendra doesn't budge. She's staring at something so I follow her line of sight.

Church and Carmine. I must say, he and Carmine stick out among Mason's population. Kendra waves them up. "So, let us see what this game is really all about," Carmine says, taking a seat next to Kendra. Church makes his way over to me.

I whisper in Church's ear, "Looks like they might be okay after all?"

"Sometimes the heart knows what it wants." He looks down at me and rests his arm on my leg.

"Hey look, its Jesse," Kendra says and whistles.

There *she* is. I spot Vanessa leading the cheer team, next to the field. A stupid smile is spread across her face from ear to ear. I want to slap the smile off her face but instead, I keep the irrational thoughts in my head.

Jesse walks up to her.

It still stings.

His helmet in hand, ready to take the field, she pulls him aside, but they're fighting. I can tell they're fighting because of their expressions. It's heated too. Now they're using their hands.

Uh-oh.

She looks around to see if anyone is looking. Quickly, she takes something from inside her top, grabs Jesse's hand, places it in his hand and closes it.

Jesus! He's doing drugs. I knew it. That explains his erratic behavior, and his outbursts. It explains everything. He's been through a lot in the past year with the death of his mother and his father falling ill. While my mind drifts to rehab facilities for immortals, I watch Vanessa storm off to the bathroom as one of her cheerleader groupies falls in line behind her. Jesse turns around and faces the game. He shoves something in his mouth, and takes the field.

I knew it. There had to be an explanation for all of this. He is going to get an ear full after the game.

I scan the crowd as locals place their bets on the win. It's a sea of red on our side and blue on the opposing side. Even if you don't live in Lake Providence or Mason, you come to the Milk Can game. The place is packed and, if you're brave enough, you wear the color of the team you support. If you do, you get free admission.

The kickoff is made. "We're off!" yells the announcer over the loud speaker, as the blue team kicks the ball down the field. I know Jesse is number eight and he's a quarterback, which I think means, he throws the ball on offense. That's all I know or care to know about football. The game itself is quite uninteresting to me but I absorb the experience.

I watch while my best friend screams beside me as a sea of blue players rush toward the red. Number fifty-four, for our team, Chet Hatfield has the ball and he's running. I have no idea if this is good or bad so I follow Kendra's lead and scream too. She's much more educated in the workings of sports. I have two left feet and my hand/eye coordination has never been my strong suit. "Is this good?" I lean in to her.

"Yes!" she squeals. "Run you banana slug!"

"Run!" I yell, just to appease her.

I love the Milk Can game and not because I enjoy football; I enjoy the story behind it. I enjoy the small town feel. I enjoy the chatter leading up to the game and the chatter for weeks after.

Most of all, I look to Carmine and Church, Kendra and Jesse. I'm with my friends. Friends who have risked their lives so I can enjoy this moment.

The game goes on.

After an hour and fifteen minutes, we are in overtime with twenty-five seconds left on the clock. We're up by three. Kendra is nearly hoarse from screaming and Church and Carmine claim to be disgusted by the barbaric display on the field.

"Now, if the Huskies decide to kick a field goal, and make it, we are in double overtime," Kendra informs me. "Pull your head out, Travis!" she yells as if he can hear her.

He does. He looks up toward us. "Yeah, that is right. You heard me!" He shakes his head. She sits down, and stands back up again but leans down to commentate, "If they miss it, then we keep the Milk Can."

I look at Kendra as she sits down again. "You're nervous."

"No, I am not. I could not care less. I just want the game over."

"No. No." I shake my head. "You're nervous."

By this time, the entire crowd on both sides is on its feet. The Huskies stand on the line as the kicker steps back. Silence blankets the stadium.

My eyes fall on a man in a grey suit standing at the end of the bleachers. He's thin and, even from this angle, he's tall. His face, ashen and gaunt, is unfamiliar; he doesn't look like he fits the bill as a Holcomb County kind of guy. His suit looks stuck somewhere between 1972 and 1985. A strange smile spreads across his face as he tips his hat at me and mimes the words, "Time is up."

My stomach drops. I look to my friends. They didn't see it. I look back to the man.

He's gone.

I frantically search the crowd.

The crowd is screaming. I see a red dog pile in the middle of the field, blood red.

"Final score, twenty-eight to twenty-five. Wildcats," Kendra yells with a smile, "another 365 with bragging rights. Take that mutts!"

Church looks at me and puts his hand on my shoulder. His thumb rubs across my collarbone through my sweatshirt. "Thank you," he whispers in my ear.

"For what?" I'm still searching for the pale man. He pulls me to his chest and says, "Your heart is pounding. I can see your carotid artery pulsating in your neck. What is wrong?"

Nothing. Maybe everything.

"Nothing. I'm just excited about the win," I lie. I want to say goodbye to Amy and I know if I share this tidbit, Church will not allow it.

He looks beyond me. I feel his body tense beneath my hands.

Jesse.

We make our way down the bleachers and onto the field.

I feel eyes burning into my back. I turn around. Jesse is holding his helmet in his hand. His hair is drenched in sweat, his eyes are glued to mine.

Church is trying to let me be, but I see his regret before the words leave his lips, "I may regret this, but Jesse will not be making the transition with us. So," he sighs, "you may want to say goodbye." It takes everything he has to say this to me.

"Thank you." I kiss Church on the cheek.

It's me who's causing this reaction from him.

Why can't I stop? Why can't I say, 'I don't need to say goodbye?'

I want to scream at Jesse, *you asked me to do this! You asked me to walk away!* All I'm able to see is the hurt in Jesse's eyes and in his heart. The regret.

My insides go numb. My jaw goes tight. *Geez, Jesse. Help me. Help me to understand you. I want to understand you.* I wish he could read my mind right now because I can't speak. I can't speak because he does this to me and I'm watching his heart break right in front of me.

"Come on, Penn. Let us get you somewhere safe." Kendra links arms with me.

I turn away from Jesse and allow Kendra to lead me away because I cannot look at his heartbreak anymore. I know what Jesse is feeling because I get the same feeling when I see him with Vanessa. I hate myself for making Jesse feel this way.

Kendra shoves Carmine so hard he almost falls. "Keep your hands to yourself, Carmine, or I will rip out your jugular with my bare hands." She squeals in delight as he grabs her around the waist and kisses her cheek.

Fifteen minutes later, Carmine, Church, Kendra and I walk through the front door of my house.

"Hey, let's talk for a minute? Outside?" I look to Church as I motion toward the porch.

He follows closely behind me. I sit down on the porch swing that overlooks the yard and take in a deep breath. My insides ache and nothing but chaos runs through my head. I don't know what to say but I need to say something.

Church sits next to me, leans back, and puts his arm on the back of the swing. He pauses, removes his arm and places his elbows on his thighs and leans forward. "I do not want to be part of the confusion, Penn. I do not want to cloud your head right now because what you need is clarity. You need clarity and you need focus." He pauses for a long while, then stands up and walks to the banister. "I am so sorry I put my needs before yours because the truth is, Penn, I need you." He lets his head drop. "I cannot focus. That is not okay. You should always be first and I let this get away from me." He walks over to the railing and rests his hands on the overhang.

I'm surprised by his words because if anything, I owe him an apology.

"Listen." I walk over to him and place my hands around his middle and stare into his hazel eyes. "I need to say goodbye to him."

"I know. As much as it pains me to say it, I know."

CHAPTER 26

Beaten Hearts

Tuesday, October 30th 9:52 p.m.

His ranch-style home is on Waddington Road. An inviting porch wraps around the entire house. I haven't been to his house in almost a year, not since Sydney passed away. Two brown milking barns sit behind the house on a few acres of pasture. During the day, you can see the pasture speckled with black and white Holsteins.

I knock.

Nothing.

I knock again.

I hear footsteps but the door doesn't open. I knock again. The footsteps come to the door, but still, the door doesn't open.

I knock again. "Jesse, please answer the door."

There's a long silence, his silence to mine.

357

Matched.

I raise my hand to knock again but the door swings open, he's standing there. I blush as his piercing eyes burn a hole through my heart.

"Hey," I manage.

"What are you doing here, Jackson?" His voice is full of emotion. "Now is not a good time."

I swallow. "It's never a good time for you. It's never a good time to sit down and talk to you. I'm here and you're here, now is a perfect time to talk. Move." I push past him, taking in his scent. The scent that has haunted me and sparked so many different emotions. The scent that makes my heart pound, my senses go haywire and my emotions turn into a big ball of messy goo.

I stop because I see a man lying on the couch. He's frail and obviously deathly sick. It's Luca, Jesse's father. I didn't expect this. Luca was sick, but I didn't know he was this sick. I turn around to look at Jesse and find his back to me. A beautiful diamond-shaped tattoo across his shoulder blades and down the middle of his back. I'm speechless. I want to trace my hands along the intricate design of lines and swirls leading to the center of the diamond and out again. "What is it?"

"The sentinel's seal." He cocks his head up toward the ceiling but doesn't turn around.

The strong, tall man I remembered as a child calls out, "Penn. Please, come sit." I'm still staring at Jesse's back. The sound of Luca's voice causes Jesse's muscles to tense. I turn and walk toward the couch.

His face is thin and frail, and extremely pale. I look back to Jesse who's still facing the door. His fists are tight. Luca's covers are pulled up to his chest. His flannel shirt barely visible above their top. Why didn't he tell me? I could have helped. I could have helped him if he'd told me what was going on.

"Penelope," Luca says in a voice barely above a whisper. He closes his eyes as if it's painful to speak. He pushes himself up and bows his head. "Our Five. It is an honor."

"Luca, please." I cover my face. "How do you know?"

When he smiles, his whole face smiles. It reminds me of Jesse. "I have always known. We have waited a long time for you, my Sanguine." He pauses. "You are still alive. This is a good sign. You are still alive." He pats my hand. His hands are hot to the touch.

"Your hands, Luca, they're burning up. Here let me find something."

He shakes his head. "It is part of the dying process, Penn." I look to Jesse, who still hasn't turned around. "I am glad you are here. There is much I need to discuss with you as I understand my son has not," he says through a coughing fit.

"Luca, please, if it's too much."

"No, no. I am all right." The coughing subsides. He begins to slowly unbutton his shirt. His fingers are frail and they fumble. He wheezes as he fiddles with the buttons.

This makes me feel awkward so I look to Jesse again, thinking maybe his father isn't as lucid as I thought. I help him with his shirt. He also removes his white undershirt. As he leans forward, I see the same diamond-shaped tattoo on his back.

I'm not prepared for what I see when he leans back on the couch. Through his gray chest hair, a red glow comes from within him.

His heart is glowing.

I stifle a breath as I touch my fingers to my lips. My eyes are wide with confusion.

"I am dying, Penn. I am dying of a broken heart."

Sentinels. My mind begins to play the tape all the way through. Sentinels are incapable of love. This shouldn't be happening, right? They can't love. They can't love…

"I don't understand," I say.

Luca leans back on the couch. "When I met Sydney I fell hard, just as my son has fallen for you. She was the most beautiful thing I had ever seen in my life." He pauses. "In Nighmerianotte, when sentinels are called to duty, it is an honor; especially the service my son was called to do. As sentinels, we are trained to serve. During training, a sentinel is trained to think like a soldier, a robot of sorts. We are trained to fight. Our commitment to our world is to protect. Our code is ancient and sacred. When I went through training over 300 years ago, they trained us to think and act according to that code. The Demi found that love was a shortcoming to the sentinels. Needless to say, we could not protect our world in the way it needed if we loved another. The temptation to place one above all others was too high. The Demi created the process of 'Awakening'. The sentinels are stripped of their ability to love. They are physically incapable of loving once they complete the Awakening. They permit them emotions such as lust and desire for reproduction purposes because they need more sentinels. Sometimes it takes a while for our bodies to adjust."

"Why are you telling me all this, Luca?" My heart is sinking with every word.

He ignores me and continues, "Although we are born with this, my heart had already been spoken for and my body never completed the "Awakening". I had already given my heart away. When the Demi asked Jesse to serve the Five, it was an esteemed honor. One only given to a chosen few and one even fewer, once trained, ever get to fulfill. None who enter the training ever think they will live to see the day they will protect the Five. Without a second thought, he trained for your detail with the Demi. Your detail is a lifetime commitment, not just until you turn eighteen. As a Nighmerian, forever is an awfully long time. Sentinels are duty driven, Penelope. During the past seventeen years, spending all that time with you, something happened to him. I know what happened as the same thing happened to me. Some may say fate. He cares deeply for you."

His wheezing grows heavier but he takes my hand is his. "If he were capable of love, Penn, he would love you but it is our duty to protect. We are trained that way. It is embedded in our being, in our minds." He pauses, as his breathing grows heavy.

I hold my breath because what he's telling me is ugly yet beautiful.

"You see, it is my son's duty to walk away from you because he would rather protect your life than love you and risk it." He coughs again. He coughs so hard there is blood in his hand when he pulls it away. I grab a tissue from the box on the coffee table and help him cover his mouth. He wipes the blood from his hand and dabs his chin.

"My son would rather protect your life than be with the one person he has come to love more than any other. If he did not, it would jeopardize your safety. He is not willing to take that risk. He is completing the "awakening" with some help from a special elixir made by a witch. It is dark magic, but it seems to be helping.

Vanessa. I always knew she was an evil witch. If it wasn't against the Nighmerianotte code, I would insist Kendra dispose of that beast.

"Once the elixir settles into his blood stream, there is no turning back. The cycle will be complete and he will do what he is destined to do." His voice is less than a whisper as his eyes drift from mine.

Jesse has turned around now. His face is hard and emotionless, his eyes, almost disturbing. Like looking into the eyes of death. I turn back to Luca.

"Thank you," I whisper and kiss Luca's forehead. "Thank you for having such an amazing son." A single tear falls from his eye. He nods. "Penelope, fight." He raises his eyebrows. "Save Nighmerianotte."

I nod as I turn back to Jesse and slowly walk to him. He doesn't look at me; he stares over my head. He tries to look unaffected, but I know this is killing him; this beautiful being with a beautiful heart that will turn black and bitter. His heart will wither, never to be used again, yet, I understand his decision. Our call to duty supersedes anything we may want as individuals. If it serves our world, it serves the individual. I hesitate at first, and then carefully place my hands on his chest. His body is blanketed with indicators he keeps hidden under his shirt. Indicators of battles, names, scripts, like a beautifully broken mosaic. My hands reach his shoulders and slide to his heart.

Bump..Bump

Bump..Bump

Bump..Bump

"My sound of sadness," he whispers without looking at me.

There's an urge inside me to be next to him. Be in his skin. I reach on my tiptoes and slowly make my way to his face and touch my mouth to his cheek. I keep my lips there because I can't seem to tear myself away. I am not sure if I will ever feel this way again, kissing someone like this. I kiss his neck and his chest then I whisper, "I don't know whether you feel this or not, but I love you. You had my heart first. I know this will not change your decision, Jesse, but please know that while I walk away, you were always the first to have my whole heart."

I slowly come down off my tiptoes. He's still staring straight ahead. He can't seem to keep his mouth still and I'm not sure if it's because he is struggling to keep quiet or keep from crying. I place my hand on his heart once more. I feel the heaviness with each beat. I don't want to take my hand away. I don't want to walk away, but I know I have to.

I search his eyes for something, anything, and come up with only sadness. I remove my hand from his chest, open the door, and quietly shut it behind me.

With each step back to my car, and each step I take away from Jesse, a piece of my heart dies.

Follow me.

Love me.

Follow me.

Love me.

He doesn't.

CHAPTER 27

Fate, a Cruel Tyrant

Wednesday, October 31ˢᵗ 7:27 a.m., My Birthday

I've had a bad feeling in the pit of my stomach since I woke this morning. Maybe it's the impending doom of what my birthday now indicates. I can't shake it. I brought the water bottle with me, just in case. I push the door open.

"Morning." I peer into Amy's room.

She's sleeping. Her thoughts are quiet and her mind is at rest. I smile at the peaceful look on her face. I know this feeling is temporary because I know she's going to wake up to her reality. The dark circles under her eyes are darker than last week. I don't want to wake her but I want to say goodbye.

I have to say goodbye. I pray the right words will come to me.

Goodbye. It's so definite. So concrete. So final.

I watch her sleep. Her sweet little face, her ears, her nose, her bald head. She's eight and she has cancer. It sucks. It more than sucks. I take a deep breath, the sound causing her to stir.

Her eyes flutter as she focuses and turns to me. Her eyes light up and I feel like I've been smacked by a two by four. "Morning, sleepy head," I whisper.

She smiles. "Morning, PJ."

"Hey kiddo." I hand her a gummy worm.

She grimaces. "Not in the mood. I don't feel well today." She stretches. "I'm glad you're here." She's not much for words today and it's concerning.

"You okay?" I scoot back as she sits up.

"I'm tired." Her eyes fill with tears.

I put my hand on hers. "Wanna talk about it?"

"I'm just scared. I'm scared I'm gonna die." Amy looks up to me with her big blue eyes. "Am I gonna die, PJ?"

All the air leaves my lungs. I can't answer her because my words have left me.

I smile. I try to speak but I can't. So I just hold her gaze for a moment as I push the wave of emotion back down.

"Do you believe in miracles?" I take her frail cheek in my hand. She tries to wipe her tears. "Don't catch the tears. Let them fall. You have every right to cry."

Please, Penn, for the love all good things, please don't cry. For Amy's sake.

She nods. Her eyes fill with tears again as she leans into me. Her head rests on my chest.

I close my eyes and wrap my arms around her.

One tear falls.

Then two.

Then three.

My tears fall. There is no stopping them.

"I do. I believe in miracles." My voice quivers. "I believe you and I were put together for a reason. I believe we are meant to be." I pause and try to regain my thoughts and my composure as her soft whimpers burn through my soul.

I pull her to me. *Do it, Penn. Go be who you are.* Church's words dance through my head.

My hands begin to tingle and warmth flushes over me. Numbness. Then the pressure in my head makes its way through my entire body. My heart begins to race. The pain, this time, is fierce. It's like nothing I've ever felt.

Excruciating. *Be strong, Penn. Don't show your pain.*

I want to scream as the pain builds. I keep thinking it will stop at some point, but it doesn't.

It just keeps building. The longer I hold on, the worse the pain in my veins becomes. I groan.

My heart begins to throb and I begin to sweat.

"PJ?" Amy looks up. "What's wrong? Why are you sweating?"

I stop. Everything goes silent. I try to recover. I can't speak. I release her as she pulls back and rests her hand on mine. "I'm okay." Her eyes tell me she doesn't believe, for one minute, what I'm telling her. I wipe my forehead with my hand. I look into this little girl's face and all I see is strength. I see courage. I see love and I see compassion and empathy. She wants to live and she deserves to live.

She deserves every single good thing life has to offer.

"Listen. I need to leave for a little while."

"Leave? Where are you going?"

"You know, I'm not exactly sure. It's magical, from what I understand." Her eyes light up.

"Magical?" Her voice is hoarse. My heart sinks a little more knowing her tiny little body must endure all this. "Like with princes and princesses and unicorns?"

"Yeah, something like that." My heart falls in love with her all over. Her innocence. "It's called 'Nighmerianotte.'"

"How do you get there?" She sits up, interested.

"Through a portal." I smile.

"Wow. Can I go with you?"

"Oh, I wish you could, Amy. I wish you could." My voice trails off. "You need to stay here. You need to beat this, Amy. You need to keep fighting. No matter what, I will always be with you. No matter where I'm at, whether you can see me or not, I will always be with you."

My chest begins to ache. I see Amy's mortality and I can't help but think how my life is paralleled with hers. I think a piece of me died when I was eight. Perhaps I wasn't dead physically, but a piece of me died with Frankie. It died with Nadine and my parents.

The fact is, Amy's still fighting.

I gave up. I walked away. I walked away from my feelings.

I walked away from me. It's easier that way.

There are no take-backs in life. You can't take back what you say, because it's said. Feelings have already been felt. The memory is there and memories never go away. They fade, but they never completely go away.

I stare into Amy's eyes once more as I stand. She looks back and I know she wants to say goodbye, but goodbye for her, too, seems so final.

Jenny walks in with the nurse. "Hey Penn," She says weakly. She's tired and shaking. She's talking to the nurse. Her cell phone rings. "Yeah? Hey." She turns around. "Again?" she whispers. Amy can't hear her and I'm glad for that. "He hasn't come to see his daughter once since she's been sick. Yeah? Well, tell him he can drink until he kills himself for all I care. Our daughter is terminal, she's dying. Tell him that. Tell him to man up. Tell him he may be a Marine but he's the biggest coward I've ever known. His daughter has more courage in her small withering body than he has in his entire being. He never got to say goodbye to his brother before he died in combat, does he want the same thing to happen with his daughter?" She hits the 'end' button.

John. Jenny. Casserole. 8675309. Drunk. Dead brother. Marine. Blame.

I know why I can't save Amy.

Fate: That which is inevitably predetermined; destiny.

My world comes to a crashing halt. I want my reality to leave. I don't want to feel this. Stop, Penn. Fear clenches my throat and I collapse against the wall. Anger eats at my soul. It eats away at my hope. It fills my heart, waiting to kill it with desperation.

No.

No.

No.

No.

No.

God. Please. No. I try to reason with him. *Leave her with me. I will take care of her.* I grasp at my heart. Mine is so full of pain I want a new one, a bigger one, one capable of withstanding all this hurt, all this sorrow. *Bitter. Distrustful. Angry.* I fall to my knees and curl into a

367

ball outside of Amy's room. I bury my head in my arms. My entire body feels like it has turned inside out.

All I can do is cry.

I can't save where I'm not supposed to intervene.

Wednesday, October 31st 6:45 p.m.

I slam my car door and throw back the already broken gate. *You're a lazy piece of crap. You can't even fix a gate, let alone see your daughter.* I think to myself. I catch movement in the corner of my eye, behind the utility pole, but I don't care, even if it's a morterro, or Vacavious himself. I hope so. No, I pray he shows his cowardly face because right now, all I want to do is rip someone's head off.

His big black Ford is sitting in the driveway so I know he's home. I run up the stairs and pound on the door.

"I know you're in there, John. Open the door!" I yell. I don't care who can hear me.

I pace. I look back to the utility pole.

Nothing.

I know going into this situation, in this frame of mind, is not good. Not with my history of mind fusion, but I can't help it. I'm numb with anger. I think of Amy's sweet face. For Amy's sake, I can't kill her father.

I want to.

I slam my fist against the door again. "Get out here, John! Get out here right now!" I pound again.

I hear heavy feet pounding against the floor. The door flies open. He doesn't say anything.

His somber face catches me by surprise. He's sober? "You a-hole! You need to get your sorry ass down to that hospital and see your daughter!" I yell and point in the direction I came. "You know, Amy, your little girl, your daughter, the one dying of cancer!" I clench my fists into balls next to my face. "She's terminal, John." I'm breathing heavy now. I'm light-headed and I know I need to walk away right now. If I don't, I'm afraid of what will happen. I can't kill Amy's father. *Chill, Penn, chill.* "She's terminal." I heave in and out. My tone is breathless. I look down at the bag of gummy worms in my hand. My eyes begin to sting again. I throw the bag at him. "Go be a dad, John. Go be a damn father." By this time, I'm staring at him from the bottom of the steps. "She likes the red ones best, John. Just go be a dad to her. You don't have to be a good dad, just be there. She needs you." I repeat. My voice cracks with the emotion I feel and cannot contain any longer.

John stands there like an eighty-year-old man. I see his brokenness through his eyes. He wears the same face I saw the day I dropped off the casserole.

I turn and throw the broken gate back. "And fix the gate!" I don't look behind me. I throw myself into my car and slam my fists against the steering wheel. I punch it one more time and then rest my head against the wheel. Anger subsides and sadness plagues my heart.

I turn the key and drive home.

He's alive. He gets to live. He gets to live each day not thinking about dying. Maybe that's it. Maybe he wants to die. Maybe dying, to him, is far easier than watching his daughter slip right through his hands. I can't help but think the anger I hold is not anger toward John, but hope for Amy. Hope teetering on the brink of reality. Hope is just a thought, not an action word; you can hope all you want, but does it actually change the outcome of any situation? The reality for Amy I can't even think about.

Hope won't cure Amy's cancer.

Hope can't save Amy.

Hope is just a word someone created to give the forlorn world something to smile about. It's dumb.

No matter how hard I try to heal her, I can't.

Amy is going to die, whether I like it or not. Amy will die and nothing can save her.

I pass children and their families out celebrating Halloween. They are dressed in all the wickedness of the world while asking for candy from strangers. "It just happens to land on my birthday," I feel compelled to yell out my window because of the vile mood I'm in.

I pull into the circular driveway. The lights are on and Jo's car is parked next to the house.

Great. All I want is to be alone. I lightly tap my forehead on the steering wheel while the crickets outside sing an unfamiliar tune. I look down at the floorboard and grab the water bottle I drained earlier. A tinge of guilt braids through my insides.

I quietly shut the door, not wanting to draw more attention to myself. The darkness surrounds me and I get the feeling I'm not alone out here. The fog has settled creating an eerie haze that screams danger. I quickly look from side to side and once behind me, just in case.

I hit the steps and take two at a time, running from an unseen adversary.

I hurry inside and shut the door behind me. I turn around to see Church, Carmine, and Kendra staring back at me. Kendra has already changed her hair color; it matches my mood.

Church gives me a look. He knows and walks to me. "What is wrong?" His arms reach my shoulders and I crumble.

"I can't save Amy." My voice is monotone but what these words do to my insides is nothing I can put into words.

I feel Church. I feel his arms and lips on my head and the heaviness of a sigh. Church is hesitant. I pull back and look to Carmine and Kendra who are avoiding eye contact.

"Where's Jo?" My stomach turns inside out. Carmine hands me a note. "Did she leave again?" I look to each set of eyes staring back at me. I look down at the piece of paper. The handwriting is perfect. Calligraphy. *Who uses calligraphy anymore*, I think to myself.

CHAPTER 28

Sincerely, Vacavious

Dearest Penelope,

It is a sad thing, being left all alone, is it not? Of course, you know a thing or two about that. First Nadine and now Jo. I can assure you Jo will not be coming back unless, of course, you would like to take her spot. Please, come find me and we can discuss the matter. I live in a place where humanity is no longer a way of life. Where fear is alive and well and darkness prowls the land in search of malevolence. Please, come home to Nighmerianotte.

It will be good to finally meet the Black Five. You and I, Penelope, we are so much alike. We share the same deep, dark blood that Nighmerianotte attempted to defend itself against.

Visit me, will you? Think of this as a command, not a request. We have much to discuss. Your aunt's life depends on it.

Sincerely,
Vacavious

Fear makes us do funny things. It makes our minds think dark thoughts. It makes all rational thought disappear. It makes us run and hide instead of facing the situation at hand. It makes our bodies shake and our hands sweat. I try to focus, but all I keep thinking about is why my hands won't stop trembling. I play his words over and over in my head like some sort of song stuck on repeat, an earworm.

'You and I, we are so much alike.'

We are nothing alike.

'We share the same dark blood.'

We don't share the same dark blood. I have empathy. I have compassion. I have love.

You're a coward. How dare you take my aunt—my mother—from me? My insides feel nothing except the pounding of my heart.

How could I let this happen?

The piece of paper slips from my hands and slowly falls to the ground.

Everything is silent. I forget I am among friends until I feel his hands on my shoulders. His head rests on the back of mine. I feel his lips kiss the back of my head. I need his hands. I need his arms. I need him this way. I fall back into his chest as my eyes begin to burn.

In a tiny voice that sounds like mine, I say, "I should have been here to save Jo."

"Listen to me," Church says, his voice controlled as he flips me around and firmly holds my face in his hands. "This is not your fault. You cannot own this. This is on me, Penelope. You hear me?" I feel him nuzzle his nose against my cheek and graze my ear with his cool lips. His breath smells like mint. "Penn, we are being watched and followed, all of us. I need you to be casual and unaffected. Do you understand?" His grip tightens around me and he stares into my eyes.

You're a fighter, Penn. Don't fall apart now. Jo wouldn't want that. She's trained you to be a survivor. She trained you to be the Five. I swallow hard and nod. "Who's following us?" I ask, but really I want to scream, *Come get me! Take me! Not her. I'm the one you want.*

"We do not know," he says.

"What side do they work for? Demi or," I take a step back and try to compose myself.

"If it was the Demi, we would have known about it." Church rubs his chin. "His name is Lax. He is Vacavious's right-hand man. He has been lurking around since the football game."

"How did anyone know where we are at, Church?" Kendra's eyes dance between Church, Carmine and me.

I miss Jo. Jo is my voice of reason. Fear makes my stomach grow into a ball of knots.

Carmine taps his long finger on his temple, deep in thought. "It had to have been leaked. Nobody knew. The Demi and us. That is it."

"Are you saying it might be the Demi, or one of us?" Kendra's tone is curt as she stares down her boyfriend.

He gives her a disgruntled glance, *I know it was not one of us.* He pauses before he proceeds, choosing his words carefully. "What if it was leaked by the Demi?"

Church stops dead. He lifts his head so his eyes meet his brother's. His jaw grinds together as he mulls this over. "Who?"

"Come on, Church, you know as well as I do Olly has had it in for Penn since the moment she was born."

"He does have a point." Kendra says, leaning into Carmine. "Dirty werewolf. There has always been something about him I never trusted."

Carmine's eyes don't leave his brother's. "Lax works for Vacacvious. He leads the morterros like idiots. The blind leading the blind."

The man in the gray suit.

"Church, I saw a man in a gray suit. At the football game. He caught my eye and pointed to his watch. He seemed far too pale to be a limite."

"What?! Why did you not say something sooner?" Church says in an irritated tone.

Kendra's eyes bulge. "Same guy I saw today following me downtown." Carmine exchanges glances with Kendra. Carmine's knuckles grow white as his hands ball into fists. "How did I not recognize him?"

"Lax," Church and Carmine say in unison. Kendra is visibly shocked and angered by this name.

"I was afraid you wouldn't let me say goodbye to everyone."

Church scoffs at my comment. "Why would you think that, Penelope?"

"I don't know. I just …" I meet his gaze. He's hurt. *Why would I think that? Selfishness, I guess?* "I'm sorry." Church searches my eyes for something more. I stare back at him.

"What is one guy going to do to four of us? Two vampires, a witch and the Five against an old witch named Lax." Kendra stops and thinks. "We will head to the portal and lose him once we cross over."

Carmine grimaces. "Have I taught you nothing, Kendra?" He shakes his head.

"If it looks too easy, it is." Kendra recites Carmine's words with an eye roll.

"Oh, good, you do pay attention." Carmine turns to Church and me. "Church and I will take the cemetery side to Main Street." He nods to Church. "You and Kendra will take Washington Street to Main. Stay hidden and keep your eyes open for Lax. We will meet at the back entrance to Last Call Tavern. I have a feeling he will be waiting for us, so stay focused. No mistakes, got it?"

Carmine rubs his two-day stubble with his thumb. Kendra looks at him hesitantly, but then quickly walks to him, grabs his hand and leads him outside.

They are one, united in their own world. Left in the moment, I feel Church's hand against my back.

I look up into his deep, ageless hazel eyes. I take his hand and put it over my heart. My heart beats like an angry Cheetah running at a pace that makes my mind spin. "This is my fear, Church. Do you feel it?"

I can't look away from him. His hand, still gripped in mine, rests on my chest.

I want to give you my heart, Church. I want to give you all of it but a small piece still belongs to Jesse and until I can give all of it to you, it will remain no ones.

I drop his hand from my heart.

His eyes, full of intense longing, dart back to my heart. "I can't," I say sadly, "I just can't...yet."

All he says is, "I know." I want so badly for him to claim my heart but I know what he told me. *He wants me to be sure it's him.* The last thing I want to do is hurt him. One day, my heart will belong to him, without reservation, without barriers. I know this to the very core of my being.

I nod toward the door. "Let's go kill the bastard." I look back to the keeper of my destiny. "Come on, we have a battle to win." I reach my hand out.

We follow the plan. Kendra and I creep down Washington Street in the shadows.

"He loves you, Penelope. He always has. If his heart could beat, it would fall in rhythm with yours," She pauses. "I'm sorry about Amy. Fate can be a cruel tyrant."

Her words cut like razor blades. Her words eat at my faith. Her words make me want to sit with my sweet Amy and watch as her fate takes her to a place I've never been.

A twig cracks behind us. We pause and spin around. Her body in a defensive stance, she pushes me behind her.

Nothing. Nothing but darkness and eerie stillness. "Come on." She tugs me down Washington toward Main Street as she walks backwards. We hit the corner of Main and hide behind the old brick Scarbrough building. Kendra looks back down Washington as our backs rest against the brick.

"Peek down Main and see if you see Carmine or Church."

I edge toward the corner and lean forward.

"Do not lean too far!" she whispers as loud as she can. "I said peek."

I try to defend myself but she puts her finger to my lips and gives me a look. I ease toward the corner and move my head enough to see down Main Street. Flickers from the lampposts are the only lights that line the street.

Nothing.

I ease back and look at Kendra and shake my head.

She nods. "Okay. First," she pulls a vial out of her pocket, "drink this."

I give Kendra the look, remembering the last time I fell for this.

"Would I give you cat urine right now? Really?"

I take the vial from her hand and down it. It burns the entire way down my throat and explodes when it reaches my stomach. "Whoa." I place a closed hand in front of my face, trying not to cough.

"It is concentrated blood, more potent. Now," she puts the empty vial back in her pocket. "Stay close to the brick and ease yourself onto Main. Try not to breathe, okay?"

I give her a bizarre look.

"Whatever, but hold it if you can. You are a ninja tonight, Five."

We slide around the corner of the building onto Main, keeping our backs against the brick wall. We move quietly, passing storefront after storefront, ever mindful of our surroundings and what may be lurking in the dark.

A movement in the darkness down by the Vancouver Inn draws our attention. We stop. I look to Kendra as her eyes narrow, trying to identify the threat.

More movement.

Kendra shakes her head as the corners of her mouth turn up. "It's Carmine and Church."

We make our way toward Hind's Pharmacy. "Step in here." She motions to the alleyway right next the Pharmacy.

"You ready?" A man's voice sounds, nearly bringing Kendra and me to our knees in fear.

Carmine and Church are standing behind us.

"Cheese and freaking rice, Carmine!" Kendra gives him a careful shove. I see Church's eyes swallowing me whole.

"I will lead." Church grabs my hand and leads us out of the alleyway. Kendra and Carmine follow.

The four of us stand there, facing the tavern that protects the portal to Nighmerianotte.

An evil laugh echoes like a voice in a tunnel. The man in the gray suit appears out of the darkness and walks slowly toward the center of the street. His black hair is tied back into a neatly fixed ponytail. His ashen complexion is the same as the night of the game.

Kendra, Carmine, and Church stand in front of me.

"It has been a long time, LeBlanc brothers. Ah, and Kendra. How is the family? Oh, wait. My apologies." He smiles coyly.

I watch as Carmine places a hand on her wrist. "Do not. You know his game."

Church steps forward. "Not long enough, Lax. What can we help you with tonight?"

"Uncle, what do you want?" Kendra moves forward. "You have already killed our coven. What else could you possibly want?"

Uncle. My eyes dance from Kendra to Lax.

Lax lets out a cackle. "You know what I want, Kendra. Come now." He picks at his nails as if trying to distract himself.

I lean to Kendra. "Can't you suck it out of his mind? The truth, I mean?"

Kendra leans back, not taking her eyes off Lax. "It does not work that way. Immortals with matching bloodlines cannot use their gifts on one another."

"We want our Five." As Lax says this, morterros spill out of the darkness like pooling blood. Their stench fills the air as Church looks from left to right. Kendra moves to my right, Carmine to my left. Church takes position in front of me. Fifty morterros assemble in front of us. Dressed in suits, their faces are devoid of any human characteristics; black holes where eyes once looked upon the world and deteriorating skin reeking of death.

"Hybrid morterros," Church whispers.

"How can you tell?" I edge closer to Church.

"Their quality of movement. It is far better than a normal morterro," Church says.

"Great. How do we kill the new breed?" I ask, trying not to let fear get the best of me.

Carmine rolls up his sleeves in an *'ask questions later'* stance.

CHAPTER 29

Battle for Life

"Decapitate, then take their heads. If we do not, they will reattach them and live. Hybrid morterros are a little smarter than the morterros we typically meet. Their brains function on a higher level, leaving their bodies to move more freely. Not much, but definitely harder to kill." Church stares at Lax as he and his army size us up.

"I assume we will battle for the Five?" Lax's words slither from his mouth like a snake.

"Wonderful. This is going to be fun." Carmine tilts his neck from left to right.

"Penelope, stay behind us." Church puts his hand out, motioning behind him.

"No. This is my war. I will not allow you to risk your lives again. You've trained me well. Now it's time to fight together."

Church stares long and hard. "Penn, I cannot."

"You don't have a choice in the matter," I say, rolling up my sleeves, watching Lax revel in our confusion.

Lax motions to one of the morterros to come forward.

Carmine leans in. "You remember what to do, Blood Queen?"

I nod as I watch the hybrid morterros spread into a line on either side of Lax.

"Huh, I would say we are a little outnumbered. Nothing we cannot handle, right? Everyone ready?"

"You bet." Kendra moves to the right of Church.

"I want the one next to Lax. I want to rip the smirk off his face." Carmine smiles.

Lax turns to his morterros. "Prendete il Cinque e conducetelo dal nostro capo!"

"What did he say?" Why not have the nerve to say it in English. Anger builds in me as I think about Jo.

"Get our Five and take it to our leader," The three whisper in unison.

"Fat chance, Lax," I call back to him as he turns around. "I will kill you and serve you to your morterros." *Wow, did I actually just say that?*

I push through my friends and march toward Lax. I fuse with his mind before he knows what to do.

He drops to the ground and calls out in agony. I suck his brain into mine like air into my lungs.

The harder I suck, the more I need.

A blow hits the left side of my body, bringing me crashing to the ground. My head smacks the asphalt before my hands have time to break my fall.

The stench assaults my nose as I feel the morterro land on top of me. I flip around to face its sadistic skeletal face as I did in the labyrinth, but this time with all the confidence of a Five.

The morterro's ooze drips from its mouth to my face. My face grows hot and I want to gag.

I quickly slide the blade bone from my leg and smile as I shove it into its throat. A high-pitched scream sounds from deep inside the monster.

I slice through its neck as its head falls to the street and rolls to the curb. The body crumbles into a motionless heap.

I jump up and drag my hand across my forehead. The gash is already healing but there's blood. I wipe my blade against my jeans and grab the head. My eyes scan the street. Church decapitates two morterros and tosses their heads to Reggerio.

Reggerio? I cock my head.

He gives a half wave as I toss him the head. I look around for Kendra and find her pinned up against a storefront; a morterro holds a bar across her throat. She's gasping for breath as an ijet falls from her grasp. I run up behind the morterro, placing both hands on the handle of the blade bone and swing from left to right, slicing through the neck with a swish. The head falls like loose gravel.

Kendra falls, gasping for air. She picks up her ijet. "Nice."

Two morterros come at us at once. Instinctively, Kendra swings the ijet in circles above her head, getting a good rhythm. As the morterros steps into the line of fire, the ijet slices through their necks.

"Still dumb as rocks, hybrids or not." Kendra shakes her head.

Immediately, I collect their heads and toss them to Reggerio, as if we've done this a million times before. I survey the scene. About thirty morterros are left, but I cannot find Lax. Carmine and Church tag team four morterros and Kendra grabs another head and tosses it to Reggerio.

Kendra runs to my side. "Where's Lax?" I ask breathlessly.

"Probably camping next to the portal." She keeps the ijet at her side.

Another powerful blow knocks me off balance. I fall forward, face down. A morterro jumps on top of me, wraps its disgusting, slimy hands around my neck and squeezes.

My air supply is cut off as my arms collapse. My head slams against the pavement. I feel no pain. Cold sweat trickles into my eyes.

Blood.

Instantly, panic comes over me. I try to breathe but I can't. The morterro's hands squeeze tighter around my neck.

I hear Kendra's screams.

Why isn't she saving me?

I hear yelling.

The morterro pulls back, forcing my back to bend in a way it isn't supposed to. It thrusts me forward, slamming my head into the asphalt several more times turning the trickle of blood into a stream.

The blood is making it difficult for me to see, clouding my vision. The hands around my neck loosen.

Kendra's screams become faint whispers and all I want to do is sleep.

Penn, you must open your eyes. You must not fall asleep. Jo needs you.

At the mention of Jo's name, my eyes flutter as someone grabs my hair and pulls me to my feet.

I try to pry my eyes open but it's blurry. I try to blink. Kendra's cries sound again. I call out, "Kendra!" I realize my eyes are swelling. I blink once more, straining to see anything.

I see Kendra's blue hair and her body's silhouette. It's blurry but there. Someone is speaking, but it sounds as if the voice is under water. "Kendra!" I call out again. "I can hear you!"

An eerie laugh echoes right next to me.

The hand that holds my hair pulls tighter and I feel a blade at my throat.

I swallow.

My vision becomes a little clearer. I can make out Kendra, Carmine, and Church, who are surrounding us. Headless morterros sprinkle Main Street like confetti. *Nice.*

"Please," I hear Church beg. "I will kill you, Lax. Know that. You hurt her and I will torture and kill everyone you love before I kill you. Mark my words."

"Church," I swallow my own blood that has seeped into my mouth. "Don't. Save Jo and yourselves."

My head forcefully jerks back and his face comes into view from behind. His mouth only inches from mine, the blade pushes into my neck. Being this close to him, I'm able to make out the blue veins running through his translucent skin. His green eyes are full of rage. "Now, let us get you home. What do you say, Penelope? It has been a long time coming." I feel the awfulness of his tongue as he licks the side of my face. "Delicious."

Church lunges toward us as Lax yells something in Italian. Almost immediately, he falls to the ground holding his head. Church calls out in terror, cradling his head, he tries to get up only to be knocked down again. "Stupid vampire. Have you forgotten the strength of my magic?

My eyes begin to clear as does my mind. Lax removes the blade from my neck and pulls me like a dog toward the Last Call Tavern. "Penelope, I think it is time you meet Vacavious." He motions with his head to a woman above, standing on the rooftop of the tavern. "Marchesa, come down and take care of our *friends.*" he pulls me by my hair again as Kendra and Carmine stand helplessly over Church.

Marchesa jumps down from the rooftop, like a cat, sneaky and soundless. Kendra and Carmine help Church to his feet as Marchesa saunters up to him. "Long time no see, Church." She eyes him up and down like a brand new toy.

A surge of jealousy starts at my toes. I feel my forehead as Lax pulls me by my hair. I brush my fingers over the gash that's already beginning to heal.

I shove my fingers inside the wound, silently whimpering. Coating them with blood, I quickly put them into my mouth.

I need more blood. I don't know if my blood will rejuvenate my body or my strength but I have to try.

Focus, Penn, I tell myself.

I stick my fingers back into my wound. The feeling of my fingers moving in my forehead, makes my stomach turn. Once again, I put my fingers in my mouth.

The door swings open to the tavern. The smell of stale beer, burnt popcorn and cigarettes consumes me.

He drags me inside.

"Wait," I whisper because my strength hasn't return yet. "Lax, wait." He growls and stops, but doesn't let go of my hair.

"What do you want?"

"My head, it's bleeding. I can't get it to stop. Do…do you want me to bleed out?" I keep my head down, staring at the ground, knowing he won't kill me, at least until I meet Vacavious face to face. I know I'm too weak to use mind fusion.

He turns around.

"Can you at least look at it? I don't think I'm healing fast enough."

Irritated by the delay, he sighs and goes to lean over, but as he does, I throw my head up with such force that Lax's face smashes against the back of my head. He stumbles backwards covering his face with his hands.

I stand up. The gash tries to heal again, but I dig my fingers into my flesh, tearing open the wound, hoping that my own blood might build some strength. I put my hand in my mouth, trying to suck every drop of blood I can before Lax regains his footing. The blood and swollen eyes make it difficult, but I can see well enough to know there's blood spilling from Lax's nose and mouth.

"Wench." His eyes grow dangerously angry as he pulls his hands away from his mouth, revealing missing teeth. He runs at me full force.

I can't move. I close my eyes and wait for the assault.

He slams me against the wall, emptying my lungs of air. My body feels like road kill hit by a fast moving vehicle.

His furious eyes bore into mine.

I manage to smile with the left side of my mouth.

His lips move back and forth and he spits his missing teeth in my face. Blood, teeth and saliva sprays me in the face.

I cough and grin as his fury grows, making his cheeks wobble in agitation.

"You will never, ever get the best of me, Lax." I groan at the same time he presses his arm harder into my throat. He grabs a blade from underneath his suit jacket.

"Watch me," he said, seething as he raises the blade to my throat. "All we need is your blood and the creed will be complete."

The creed. *What creed?*

"What creed?"

Lax laughs. "You think I am stupid, girl?"

He pushes the blade into my throat, allowing a trickle of blood to escape.

Don't let him see your fear, Penn. My smile grows. My eye lids feel as though they weigh a million pounds each. My forehead throbs as a dull ache grows behind my eyes. I know I cannot reason with this lunatic and I know I won't get any information out of him.

He pulls the blade away and puts the tip in his mouth. His eyes roll back in his head with ecstasy. "Oh, mio Dio, much too addicting." He puts the blade back to my neck and pushes on the open wound. I feel the tip of the blade inside my neck.

I whine, because this time, the pain makes me want to die.

He leans into my ear and whispers, "Vacavious cannot wait to meet you, Penelope. Come, we must go at once." He pulls the blade back from my neck and pulls me by my hair, letting my head fall toward the ground like a dog. I stare at the floor as we walk toward the back of the bar.

"Leaving so soon, Lax? I thought the party was just getting started." A familiar voice rings out in the empty bar.

Jesse.

Lax stops, completely caught off guard as a metal bar slams into him so hard he releases my hair and stumbles backward.

"Come on, Lax, stay. Let us have some fun." Jesse smiles. Another blow sends him flying backward. This time a table breaks his fall.

I'm too weak. I cannot calculate the blood loss but I know it's substantial.

I fall backwards in a heap beneath the bar. My head throbs and I cannot seem to stand on my own. The blood runs from my forehead. I put my hand over it but it doesn't help. "Heal, please!" My voice is weak.

I lift my head in time to see Jesse strike Lax's face with a section of pipe. It's a sound I will never forget.

I close my eyes and lean my head against the bar.

The blood runs down my face, over the bridge of my nose and down my cheeks like tears. All I can do is wait. For what, I don't know.

"Jackson."

My eyes flutter open. *How long have my eyes been closed? Did I fall asleep?* I see Jesse. I try to move my head, but the pain creates a shock wave that starts at the top of my head and forcefully exits my ears. "Ah-hhhhhhhh," I scream in pain.

"Uccellino," he says breathlessly, "what did he do to you?" He kneels down next to me, concern fills his eyes. He carefully pushes the matted hair from my bloodstained face. He wraps his hands around my cheeks and cradles my face in his hands.

I try to keep my eyes open but I can't. "That bad, huh?" I try to smile.

Jesse moves closer to me, putting his arms underneath my badly beaten body and lifts me off the ground. My face falls to his chest. I feel his cheek rest against my head. "Jackson, I love you. There is too much I need to say to you. You hear me?" Jesse carries me to the back of the bar.

"Wait," a weak voice calls out.

Jesse turns around and, once again, I try to open my eyes.

Lax. He's standing, unsteady but still standing. His face is badly mutilated. His nose is misplaced and his eyes, smashed in, almost face each other where the pipe met his face. Blood runs from his eyes as bruises begin to take shape.

It's an image that will forever be etched into my memory.

"Your mother and father, Five. They are here."

CHAPTER 30

Power Plays

My insides feel like my outsides, broken and bloody. Jesse stops breathing and lets out a low moan. I look up to his face. All the color has drained. I follow his line of sight toward the front door.

No! It cannot be!

A mother and father. *My mother and father.* My mother looks identical to me. And my father, the words from his journal dance through my head.

I shake my head and close my eyes. Jesse lowers me, allowing me to stand. "Your parents are dead, Jackson. This is Lax's sick game. This is not real. It is just a mirage. An evil witch's spell."

I look to Jesse and back to my parents in disbelief. "Mom? Dad?" I say in a little girl's voice.

They stand there, calling me to them. Their faces are full of sadness, a sadness only seen by a little girl who thought her parents dead.

I look back to Jesse. "Do not do it, Jackson. Please." His voice cracks. He attempts to hold me back by wrapping his arm around my shoulder.

Confusion fills my head. I look back to my parents as they begin to cry.

My heart falls to the ground and shatters. If my body ached before, it now lives in agony. Weakly, I take a step in their direction. Jesse's body goes rigid. "Please, Jackson. No!" He carefully turns me to him. "Stay with me." He takes my chin and turns it up toward him and slowly leans down, delicately placing his lips on mine. A soft moan escapes from beneath his kiss. His lips linger on mine, and all I can feel is his presence. I feel his heart against mine, his hands against my shoulders, and the love in his kiss. His lips quiver as he gently pulls away from me. "Please, Penn. Stay with me." His eyes are clear, yet full of raw emotion he can no longer restrain. "I cannot lose you, Jackson. I cannot allow you to walk away from me again." His eyes move from mine and look toward my parents and Lax. His breathing becomes labored. "Come with me." His hand catches mine and he leads me toward the back of the bar.

"I can't," I whisper through my tears. "I need to talk to them, Jesse. I want to know who my mom and dad are. I can't walk out on them." I look back to them. My father consoles my mother as she calls to me.

Jesse takes my face in his hands once more. He stares into my soul. "These people are not your parents. They died, Penelope. The man who killed them is waiting for you. He is doing this to you, trying to confuse you. He's preying on your fears and weaknesses Jackson."

"Don't say that!" I pull away from Jesse, taking a couple unsteady steps back. I look again at my parents as they lovingly open their arms to me. "Jesse, don't you see? They love me. We can be a family again." I take a few more steps in their direction. "I'm sorry," I whisper as Jesse's eyes fill with fear.

I turn toward my mother and father and wait for their embrace. Their arms wrap around me and I melt into them.

I sob. I feel their lips on my cheeks and their words in my heart, words my soul has longed to hear since I was a little girl.

Our sweet Penelope has come home.

We love you.

We have missed our girl.

They kiss my head, my cheeks. My mom pulls away and looks into my eyes. "Come, Penelope, let us go be a family."

My father embraces me and I soak it in. I turn to Jesse. "See, I told you, Jess. They love me."

They pull me toward the front door of the tavern.

I look up to my mother whose face has changed. Her words distort into a moan. Their faces contort, the flesh turning and twisting before evaporating into the empty, lifeless forms of a morterro. And then I smell their stench.

What is going on? What is happening to my mother and father? "Please? Come back. Don't take them away!" I cry in a deep panic. "Not again!" I yell as someone pulls me away. "No! Don't take me from them!" I scream until my voice grows hoarse.

Anguish and abandonment push on that fragile piece of spider-webbed glass that is my innermost being, finally shattering it into a million tiny pieces, leaving an empty frame.

Stained.

Infected.

And broken.

I feel Jesse at my back. "Let me go!" I yell. I try to hit him, his head, his hands and arms. He yanks me forcefully toward the back of the bar. "Stop!" I shriek. My hands flailing like a crazy person. All rationality now gone, replaced with blind desire.

Jesse opens the door to some sort of closet and pushes me into another set of arms.

"Get off me!" I scream in a rage.

"Take her, Church. Keep her well." He runs his hands through his hair nervously.

"Of course, Jesse. Please, just come with us."

With a look of regret, Jesse says, "You know I cannot." He looks me in the eyes. "Penn, I—"

A pipe crashes down on his head. He drops to the floor without form as if all the bones of his body suddenly shatter like the spider-webbed glass of my being.

The door slams.

Kendra screams.

"Close the portal!" I hear someone yell.

Everything goes black.

EPILOGUE

Death

My body rests in the meadow behind Mason Cemetery as the morning sun pours through the giant redwood trees. The scent of earth and fresh rainfall fills my nostrils. I am calm. Nothing hurts. Every bone and every muscle in my body is free of tension. My fingers intertwine and lie across my stomach as I rests on a bed of redwood needles. I didn't know dying could be so peaceful.

Three familiar figures stand above me: Carmine, Kendra, and Church.

Yet, it is Jesse who comes to mind at this moment. The memory of him allows my heart to ache for the loss once again.

Concern and worry blanket their faces. My heart hurts for them. I want to tell them I'm going to be okay and they shouldn't worry, but I can't because it would be a lie. Kendra sits on my right and strokes my hair. Her lips are moving, but I cannot hear the words. In the distance, Carmine leans against a tree, hands in his pockets and head down. Church, beautiful Church, is beside me, staring up into the trees as I am, our heads touching. I want so badly to reach out and touch his ashen face but I cannot.

I lie there with my thoughts, unable to speak or move, waiting to die. Waiting for Evernotte.

ACKNOWLEDGEMENTS

Black Five started as a tiny little idea that meandered in the back of my brain. Then it became this annoying itch that needed to be scratched. Finally, in the spring of 2012, I began writing the book.

It took me three years to write. *Yes, three years.* Many times I wanted to quit. I wanted to scrap the entire book and just say, 'to heck with it!'

I didn't. I have people around me who just kept pushing me. So, here is where I get all mushy and talk about these phenomenal people in my life.

Dave Holper, you read Black Five in its infancy. Sometimes, I look back and think 'I can't believe I let him read that garbage!' You pushed me in ways that made me want to cry. You made me push the limits and challenge myself. You were kind with your words and gave me the best advice a novice writer can ever receive: *write for you.* Your countless hours spent proofing and typing up feedback can never be repaid but I promised you a final draft. Here it is. Thank you for shaping me into the writer I am today, Dave.

Joelle Fraser, my first editor, I love your beautiful heart. You gave Black Five focus, clear direction. You gave it the wings it needed to fly. You will always have a special place in my heart.

Marianna De Marchi, thank you for the Italian translations. You, my friend, are a gem.

Huge thank you to Lisa Falzon and Heather UpChurch for the amazing book cover and design. You made images in my head come alive. Much appreciation to both of you.

My thirteen-year-old beta readers: Haley Alves and Mackenzie Renner. You changed the ending to Black Five. You said it wasn't enough (in the kindest way possible), you said you wanted more. The ending of Black Five is dedicated to both of you. Thank you for taking time to read the book and providing me authentic feedback. I look forward to our work together with The Black Blood Chronicles.

To my four adult beta readers: THANK YOU! This book would not have come to fruition if it weren't for your candid feedback.

Dana Barrote and Julie Hagemann, your messages while reading Black Five gave me confidence in myself but, more importantly, belief in my dreams. I'll chase this dream forever.

Cassie Graham, you gave me the motivation to finish writing the book. You walked me through a lesson in grace. Your hours spent mentoring me will not be forgotten.

Fisher Van Duzen, honestly, I don't know where to start with you. Your belief in me keeps me in awe. I don't know where I would be without you in this, sometimes maddening, process. You gave me hope. You gave me encouragement when I needed it most; when I wanted to quit, you told me NO! You gave me guidance. You walked me through some *challenging* feedback and put the pieces of my heart back together. I am very lucky to have you as a mentor, but most importantly, a friend.

To my writing group, TABS: Crystal Morse and Trina Pockett. There is a reason we were brought together; we know who had a hand in that. *Wink, wink.*

I treasure our friendship, our candid conversations and the love we have of storytelling. You two never cease to amaze me and I am so lucky to be part of such a special bond.

Johanna Hurwitz, thank you for making me fall in love with reading. Your kind spirit and graciousness, I will always carry with me.

Thank you to all of the men and women, who have served, and are, currently serving, our great nation. From the deepest spot in my heart, thank you.

To my husband Brandon and my children, Teyler and Kate. *You are the pieces that make my heart whole.* Some scenes in Black Five were pretty tough to write because of the love I have for each of you. You've taught me lessons in simplicity and how beautiful life can be. You give me my truth. Only with you, I am whole.

And to God: thanks for everything. *Everything.*

Last but certainly not least, I use the relationship with Amy to demonstrate that life is precious. Amy is someone's daughter, someone's sister, and someone's friend. *Childhood cancer is real.* It's absolutely one of the most atrocious diseases to take the lives of our children. If we are lucky enough, our little ones pull through. There are two childhood cancer organizations that are near and dear to my heart: St. Baldrick's Foundation and St. Jude Children's Research Hospital. Donate and make a difference in the lives of all the *Amys* in the world.

To the readers! Thank you for taking a chance on me. I hope you will begin the next journey with me into a deeper, darker story, the second book in The Black Blood Chronicles, *Crimson Lace.*

Always love,

J.